PRAISE FOR A ... L
DEAD BITCH ARMY

"What a fun, incredible ride. I love it, man."

> **- Brian Keene, *Bram Stoker Award Winning Author of The Rising and City of the Dead***

"One of the best written, in your face horror stories in recent memory."

> **- *Creature Corner***

"You've got it all here folks: zombies, gangs, conspiracies, violence, great characters, pre and post-apocalyptic chills, and get this: parts of this one are actually SCARY! *Dead Bitch Army* is a must, and one heck of a fun read. Andre Duza is off his rocker… and that's a good thing!"

> **- *Horror Fiction Review***

"ANDRE DUZA is a sick fuck. And I mean that in the most endearing way possible. God bless him and his twisted soul."

- *Insidious Reflections*

"*Dead Bitch Army* by Andre Duza is more than a captivating, musically violent, bizarro horror (as if you needed more than that). Submerged within its sinisterly addictive pages, and explosive storyline, is a subtle-as-a-brick social commentary on everything from racism and middle-class-pseudo-liberalism to the subtle fascism rampant within our so-called democracies. Perhaps more of a danse macabre than a novel, Duza's *Dead Bitch Army* is waiting to seduce every fan of horror and innovation alike... Pick her up... Or you'll be sorry..."

- *Pretty-Scary.net*

JESUS FREAKS

(jē'zəs frēks), *n.* see ZOMBIE

Andre Duza

DEADITE PRESS
Tempe, Arizona

DEADITE PRESS

AN ERASERHEAD PRESS COMPANY
WWW.ERASERHEADPRESS.COM

Deadite Press
5929 S. Juniper St.
Tempe, AZ 85283

ISBN: 0-9762498-7-1

Dedicated to:

Brenda, Kaden, Cypress, and Raven

Thanks to:

Carlton Mellick III, Rose O'Keefe, Brian Keene,

Tom Monteleone, Travis Adkins, Keith Murphey,

Neill Brengettsey, Dennis Kroesen, Daemon Oats, Tjie Tsang, Silverfish

Geoff Baker, Lili Duda, Darin Basile,

My Girard College family

In memory of:

George "Uncle Jay" Wilkinson

Jesus vs. Jesus

Reaching his left arm up over his head, Jesus summoned the reddened clouds above to rumble and stir with activity and roll into the shape of a huge face that looked down angrily at Yeshua. Its mouth, falling open in slow-motion, spilled over with lavish swells of crackling electricity that bounced around the inside of it and into a crooked tongue of lightning that leapt out.

Zigzagging down from the sky, the furious lightning tongue smacked Jesus' raised palm, crawled down his left arm, across his shoulders, up his right, and out at Yeshua through his index finger, which was held stiff in a point. Up in the clouds, a gust of wind warped the cloud-face and ultimately broke it into many separate wisps of precipitation.

The impact from the lightning bolt blew Yeshua's hair back and danced up and down his entire frame, in and out of his clothing, and up under his crotch until he was literally covered with kinetic slivers of living light.

Jesus celebrated with a wily grin, but his triumph was quickly snatched away as the surge began to dim and fizzle out. All that was left was Yeshua, who, through it all, hadn't missed a step.

Introduction

I think it was Bernie Casey who once said that every good hero needs his own theme music. I couldn't agree more. But why restrict it to heroes? Why not expand the parameters to include the cast of characters that we all come across on any given day? In fact, I would go as far as to say that everyone already *has* his or her own theme music. It might not be a specific song, but a type of music: a distorted blues riff for the red-eyed drunk brown-baggin' it with a rotten-toothed smile and an inappropriate comment for any half-decent looking woman who happens by; a big band number for the well-kept old man cruising down the street in a Buick or a Caddy the kind of ride that takes up two parking spaces; bubblegum licks with an undertone of repressed sexuality for the Catholic School girls bouncing down the street on their way home from school; speed metal for the haggard single mother bogged down by a crying infant strapped to her chest and two unruly kids in tow; a military drum-rattle for the homeless guy who barks commands into the payphones on 16th and Chestnut Street.

All it takes is an open mind and a bit of concentration to hear it. You should try it sometime.

So what's the point of all this, right? I thought this was a book about zombies. Let's get to the flesh-eating, Duza.

Don't worry: the zombies are on the way. But I wanted to give you, the reader, a kick, something to help you understand that specific feeling that they inspire in me. For most writers, the ideas come as more than just words. For me, they come as fully fleshed-out images, like movies played out in my mind, complete with sound effects and music. They haunt me for days, months, sometimes even years, until I finally exorcise them by committing them to paper.

That's part of the reason why I like to include artwork in my books. If I had my way, I'd release a soundtrack with each book, too.

Because I don't have the means to do that (yet), I figured the next best thing would be to give you a few ideas regarding the kinds of music that set the mood for *Jesus Freaks*.

For my first book, *Dead Bitch Army*, it was Led Zeppelin's "Immigrant Song." There were a few others, but that opening wail is what I hear when I see the cover. It has the same energy.

Jesus Freaks began to affect me about eight years ago, when I worked as a subpoena server. After receiving a list of names and addresses from the office, I would spend the entire day on foot, walking from company to company (I served mostly corporations) with my headphones cranked to 10.

Oh… and I was usually high.

I noticed that with the right music, the crowds of 9-to-5 office jockeys that packed the Center City streets began to look like zombies. They all had that same lifeless expression, walked at the same pace, often greeted each other with grunts and groans.

Over time, the images began to fester and mutate into landscapes littered with walking dead: whole cities and small towns crawling with them, one scene dissolving to the next, looking up from low angles, down from aerial views that made their collective mass look like a flesh-tone tsunami flooding neighborhoods and oozing through complicated mazes of skyscrapers. The shambling pro-death marches are guided by a haunting melody, usually something bass-ridden with an underlying melancholy. Each song nurtures a different yet related vibe, sometimes kinetic and primal not all of the zombies herein are slow and sometimes sluggish and droning.

The following list is simply a suggestion, a compilation pulled from my mental soundtrack, so take it as just that. Marry each one with creeping pipe-organ chords and you've got the idea.

If you're lucky enough to live near a good DJ store, they usually stock instrumental versions of many of these. Instrumentals are always better in my opinion. Once the music gets the images going, the words just get in the way.

Enjoy.

André Duza

Beastie Boys – "Something's Got to Give" and "So What'cha Want"
Ol' Dirty Bastard – "Rawhide" and "Brooklyn Zoo II"
Led Zeppelin – "Dazed and Confused"
Nas – "N.Y. State of Mind"
Nirvana – "Milk it"
Big Jus – "Sleepy Hollow Modulation Systems (Instrumental)"
Cypress Hill – "Scooby Doo"
Method Man – "PLO Style"
Nine Inch Nails – "Eraser"
Wu Tang – "Duck Seazon"
The Diamonds – "Stroll"
GZA – "Duel of the Iron Mic"
Screamin' Jay Hawkins – "I Put a Spell on You"

Why should we die to go to heaven? The earth is already in space.

GZA

Here comes the ruckus, the motherfuckin' ruckus. Thousands of cut-throats and purse-snatchin' fucks.

Method Man

Just as there were many who were appalled at Him – His appearance was so disfigured beyond that of any man and His form marred beyond human likeness.... He had no beauty or majesty to attract us to Him, nothing in His appearance that we should desire Him. He was despised and rejected by men, a man of sorrows, and familiar with suffering. Like one from whom men hide their faces He was despised, and we esteemed Him not.

Isaiah 52:14 - 53:1-3

Chapter 1
March, 2015 – Good Friday

"What the hell do you mean restricted area?" Detective Philip 'Kane' Makane protested, shoving his way towards Special Agent Mendez, who stood 20 feet away barking orders into midair and tapping on his lobule to test the tiny, subdermal microphone's quality. He did it out of habit every time he spoke or received a message. "This is our jurisdiction."

Behind the yellow, laser-light barrier that cordoned off the smoldering wreckage of Flight 2190, flashing scrolling text that read **Federal Bureau of Investigations**, Mendez knelt down to look under yet another sheet. They were all over the place, spread out like a giant patchwork quilt constructed in honor of something macabre. Beneath most of them there was movement.

"Okay. Wrap em' up," A voice yelled.

The sheets hissed to an airtight seal around the bodies and body parts that they covered and hindered their dexterity. Yet they still twitched.

"Not any more, Detective," Mendez said while simultaneously reacting to the mangled body shrink-wrapped at his feet.

Kane backed away from the duo of FBI agents in mirror-shades who blocked his path to Mendez, sized both of them up in one quick pass, and craned his neck, head tilting to the side to see over the shorter agent's shoulder. That was where Mendez crouched over the mangled body, resting his forearms on his knees, his hands folded, and surveyed his men who were spread out across the wreckage.

At the base of the hill, approximately 30 feet behind Kane, and separated by federal officers in black riot attire standing reticent, double-fisted, liquid-light cannons held at ease, a beefy throng of police officers crowded around a single-file line of hastily parked squad cars and one, lone, unmarked Toyota that choked up the small paved road.

"Liquid-light" was the official name for the military's laser weaponry program. As of January 2011, they were standard issue for military personnel and federal agents.

The name was changed from "Laser" when the Secretary of Defense commented that the word inspired thoughts of B-movie silliness instead of strength or predatory cunning. He pointed to examples like "Stinger," "Stealth," "Talon" and "Interceptor." The scientists insisted that light wasn't a liquid, but the secretary didn't care, and he had the president, the National Security Council, and the Chairman of the Joint Chiefs of Staff on his side.

Liquid-light guns made a unique sound when fired, like a bass-heavy thump layered over a baritone hum and accompanied by a deep buzzing, like a swarm of angry, mechanical bees. The larger guns, like the double-fisted cannon, which looked like a cross between a shotgun and a long, bulky space ship, had a sonic kick that could make you nauseous if you weren't used to it.

Watching from afar, the police officers grumbled in response to the feds' big-dick waving and occasionally yelled out in support of Kane.

"So what've we got, terrorists?" Kane inquired. "And what's under the sheets, certainly not survivors?"

"Not quite," Mendez replied from the background.

"Then *what*? What is so goddamn important that you feel the need to exclude us from the case?"

Cheers from the boys in blue.

"I'm afraid that information is classified, Detective."

Wiping his palms against each other as he rose to a stand, Mendez was annoyed by Kane's persistence. But he wasn't the type to let it show. With a nod, he instructed the two agents to let Kane approach.

Kane half-turned toward his disgruntled colleagues and rolled his eyes mocking Mendez's stock reply and subconsciously gaining strength from their surly indignation.

"You *federal boys* like hiding behind your 'classified' status." Kane said, walking up to the barrier to meet Mendez, who did the same.

"Think what you want, Detective. I would think you'd be thankful that we're taking over. You don't want to deal with this mess. Trust me."

"Don't do us any favors. Most of these men here, including myself, have been on the force for a number of years. Surely we've seen worse in...."

Kane looked around at the field of twitching shapes, some large, some small. On the other side of the wreckage, men in Haz-Mat suits branded with the same federal lettering guided more shrink-wrapped bodybags on hovering stretchers into the back of a huge, armored semi as fast as they could. Whatever it was that had happened here, it was bad, really bad. Maybe he hadn't, in fact, seen worse.

To his far right, five or six feds surrounded a naked grey husk of a man with a jutting ribcage and sections of exposed bone all over his body. His face and hands were painted dark red. One of the agents held onto a nylon rope that extended about two feet from his hand to where it looped around and dug into the grey man's throat.

Leading with his mouth wide open, the grey man lunged at the agent directly in front of him, his teeth snapping shut inches short of his face when the rope pulled tight.

Kane's intuition told him that this guy was dead as a doornail, a fucking corpse.

But that's impossible, he thought.

The agent holding the rope called out to an Agent Curtis.

With his eyes, Kane directed Mendez over to the grey man, eyebrows raised, questioning: "What... the hell... is that?"

Mendez was diverted by the weird lust for vengeance that twisted Agent Charles Curtis' face into a painful mask of festering lunacy. He had just stepped out of the intact section of the passenger area and slid his hand beneath his jacket.

"Oh shit!" Mendez said, and turned to face Kane. "Get your men outta here, now!"

"Hey!" Kane groaned as Mendez shoved him backwards and hurried over to Curtis who took large, angry steps over to the grey man. "Not until you tell me what the hell is going on..."

Curtis wrapped his hand around the handle of his liquid-light handgun, and snatched his arm from inside his jacket.

The other agents who stood close by dove away to safety as Curtis capped off 16 shots that went clean through the grey man and sent sizzling chunks flying. Small dust-clouds of singed and pulverized flesh and bone settled in the air around him. Though his body staggered and twisted in tribute to physics, the grey man's only real reaction (a dry, indifferent moan) pushed Curtis over the edge.

It was all over by the time Mendez was able to grab hold of Curtis and wrestle the gun from his hands. During the struggle, he caught a glimpse of Kane and the police officers who had jogged closer to the scene, some with their guns drawn.

The police, including Kane, were packin' standard-issue Glock 61s with heat-seeker bullets.

"I said get your men outta here," Mendez grunted as he fought against Curtis' bulk. Curtis outweighed him by at least 20 pounds.

"No! Lemme go!" Curtis growled passionately. "That bastard took my Lucia from me!"

Kane raised a hand to his colleagues who stirred with pent-up aggression and long-standing emasculatory issues with the FBI, and nodded. When they calmed to an organized grumble, Kane turned back to Mendez.

"Look. Any minute now this place is going to be crawling with fire trucks and EMS units from all over the city, not to mention nosey reporters. So, unless you want to deal with all that by yourself, I suggest you let us in on what exactly is going on here," Kane said.

Mendez began to retort, until he saw the grey man sit straight up, eyes burning with insatiable hunger, and turn to face the nearest living thing, an anonymous agent who crawled backward away from him and sprung quickly to his feet.

"Goddammit Charlie," the anonymous agent yelled, "are you out of your fucking mind?"

"Well, what' didjuspect?" Mendez replied.

"Lemme go, I said. You have to let me finish it... for Lucia," Curtis begged.

He waited for the first sign of ease in Mendez' grasp to break free and run over to the grey man who had already turned his attention to him and started crawling forward to meet him halfway, expectant jaws stretched wide and salivating blackened death.

"Charlie, wait!" Mendez yelled, but it was too late.

The grey man rose to his knees when Curtis came within a few feet from him and reached out grasping delicately at the air between them. Curtis stopped to cock his leg back and kicked the grey man in the chin with enough force that it tore his head from its base and sent it flying into the thicket 25 feet away.

A chorus of "holy shit!" filled the air behind Kane.

The grey man's headless body collapsed to the ground, convulsing and grasping at air.

Mendez volleyed between disappointment, anger, and shame, as he perused a mental list of pros and cons, attempting to decide whom to yell at first. To his left, the two anonymous agents had their hands full trying to hold back Kane and his band of unruly uniformed officers. To his right, five agents stood, horrified over the grey man, who still reached blindly, and tried, clumsily, to stand. The sixth one had jogged over to the bushes where the grey man's head had landed and parted them with his hands.

"You guys are not gonna believe this," he said, "but it looks like he... it's still alive."

Mendez closed his eyes and seethed.

"Well then seal it and put it on the truck with the others," he bawled. "The rest of you take care of the body."

Shaking his head at their questionable ethics, Mendez turned to his left and headed over to the boisterous crowd of officers. He focused specifically on Kane, who stood front and center arguing with the anonymous two agents.

"I'm going to have to ask you to control your men, Detective," Mendez warned.

Kane stood defiant for a few excruciatingly awkward moments, eyes locked in a silent duel of egos. At the last minute he turned and spread his arms to corral the rising voices behind him.

"Guys! Please! Let's hear what Agent Mendez has to say."

"That's Special Agent Mendez," remarked one of the anonymous two.

"You know, technically they're not *my* men." Kane said looking past the anonymous agent without acknowledging his remark. "These men here answer to Sergeant Brooks."

"Okay… well, since you seem to be in charge at the moment, I'll address you," Mendez said. "Now, what you've seen here today can never leave this site. This is a classified matter and, frankly, your men shouldn't even be here."

"Hmmm, that's funny. I was under the impression that we were on the same side."

"Absolutely, Detective."

"So then why all the secrecy? Let me guess. Might this crash have somehow been deliberately caused? Maybe to hide, say, some kind of weapon, something that might explain why that gentleman over there seems to be quite alive despite the fact that he looks like a corpse?" Kane said, pointing at the grey man.

Mendez held his response on deck as he decided just how forthcoming he should be. He too was a cop once, so he sympathized with their anger.

"The crash was in no way deliberate, Detective, so get that

thought right out of your head. What I am at liberty to tell you is that, yes, the man who was just shot…"

"Just shot…? That's an understatement," blurted a faceless voice within the crowd of police officers.

"In short, yes, he was dead as were about 30 other ah… people who attacked us when we arrived. We think they came from the Fernrock Cemetery about 3 miles east of here. We currently have a team investigating that site as well."

From the crowd, comments launched sporadically.

"Get the fuck outta here."

"Aw, c'mon."

"What do you take us for?"

"Shhh!" Kane scolded. "I know how it sounds, guys, but we all saw what just happened. Let's just hear him out."

"Thank you, Detective," Mendez nodded, letting loose a brief look of annoyance that he tossed underhanded at no one person in particular. "The dead-man you saw was Theodore DeLong… or what was left of him anyway."

"DeLong… DeLong… Now why does that sound familiar??? You mean the serial killer?" Kane asked.

"That's the one. He murdered Agent Curtis' wife, Lucia, three years ago. Agent Curtis was the one who brought DeLong down."

A long silent pause…

"Well, you'll be sure to give Agent Curtis our condolences," Kane said.

Heads turned as the din of screeching tires fell upon their ears, and soon everyone was focused on the paved road at the bottom of the hill. Flashing lights preceded the squad car that slid to a slanted stop next to the others. The front doors on both sides swung open before it came to a complete rest. From inside, Sergeant Brooks and Detective Allison Ryan, an attractive albeit manly-looking woman, jumped out and hurried up the hill.

Lifting his hand to signify "hold on," Kane turned from Mendez and jogged down to meet them.

"You're not going to believe wha…" he started to say to Brooks, whom he approached first, but Allison yanked him aside, cutting him off mid-sentence.

Brooks, who seemed to already know something, continued up the hill to his men.

Laying her arm around his shoulder, Allison pulled Kane close and started to whisper.

"We know about the corpses… er, zombies, or whatever you want to call them." The hunter… he told us everything after we nearly creamed him when he ran out into the road."

"Hunter? What hunter?"

Allison pinched a digital notepad from the breast pocket of her coat and tapped the rectangular screen with her fingertips. A name followed by biographical text scrolled down from the top.

"Gus Rollins is his name… been coming out here for years to hunt deer with his buddies. There are five of them altogether. According to Mr. Rollins, they were crossing through the cemetery a few miles back like they always do to get to their favorite spot when they saw a naked woman wandering around aimlessly, 'like she was drunk.' When one of the hunters tried to help her, she ripped his throat out with her teeth. That's gratitude for you, huh. That's when, quote, 'bodies started climbing out of graves left and right and all hell broke loose.'"

Allison eased the notepad back into her pocket and tapped it down. She turned toward the distant wail of sirens, gave them a moment's attention, and then turned back to Kane.

"As crazy as it sounds, I believe him. If you would've seen the look on his face…"

"Don't need to," Kane replied. "We've seen it all first-hand right up the hill. To tell you the truth, I'm not sure what we saw up there."

Kane bobbed and weaved his head, looking past Allison at Sergeant Brooks's car.

"So where is he, this hunter?"

"We had Loomis take him back to station. He refused to come anywhere near the scene, threw a fit until we stopped the car, in fact. And, wait 'til you hear this: He says the feds shot his buddies on the spot when they arrived at the scene. He was still hiding from the bodies coming out of the ground when it happened so they didn't see him."

"Sonofabitch," Kane scoffed. "I knew those fuckers were up to something."

Kane subconsciously inspected the dirt beneath him as he processed Allison's information. At the top of the hill, Sergeant Brooks stood face-to-face with Special Agent Mendez, each flanked by their respective subordinates like old-fashioned street gangs facing off. For some reason, Kane imagined them growling at each other like dogs. Something about Mendez's stoic arrogance made Kane determined to get to the bottom of this.

"You said Loomis was taking him back to the station?"

"Yep."

"Well then, let's go." Kane said, directing Allison toward his car, a blue Toyota, with his palm against the small of her back. "I'll drive."

Easter Sunday

Despite the fact that his routine was the same so far (woke up to the voices on the TV [set for 12:00 pm], yelled out "snooze," scratched his balls, and fell back to sleep), Kane couldn't help feeling that something was amiss. Technically, he didn't have to work, so he automatically scratched that off, as it was known to drastically affect his mood, and continued on down the list of possible killjoys, eliminating them as he went along. His working theory had the military at fault for what happened at the crash site, some kind of testing gone wrong. It was happening all the time. Or maybe he was thinking of a movie he'd seen. Either way, it was the only reasonable explanation he could think of for what he'd witnessed.

The wake up, snooze, itchy-balls, sleep process usually repeated itself three to four times before Kane officially rose for the day, but this morning he was up on one and rubbing away the stiffness in the back of his neck. The pain generally radiated from his neck down throughout his back, especially the lower back. Every time he woke up with it, he reminded himself how he never felt this way in his 20s, which then segued into his inability to stay up all night without paying the price anymore, if he could manage to stay up at all. Lately, it was becoming harder and harder.

Kane was never one to get ready for bed. He was good for nodding off fully dressed, just as long as he took his socks off. By morning he'd either be shirtless, or pantless, but never fully unclothed. He was down with the 'that's how we're born' mindset, but something about sleeping naked just felt too vulnerable. Sometimes he used shit like that to gauge people, sneaking it into mundane conversations.

Something just wasn't right. Where was the feeling of blunted serenity that came after the dreamscape morphed painfully into waking life, dragging distorted voices and laughter and ringing with it through the ethereal muck? It only lasted a second or two before memory kicked in and brought with it all the stress that sleep tricked him into forgetting. He never remembered feeling that way at all in his twenties, back when he was high on his own bullshit and cheating on Layla, his ex-wife.

Layla was a performance artist with a penchant for the bizarre.

It was what became of her English degree, her formal dance background, and her dreams of a career on Broadway and/or Hollywood. As usual, the downward slide started with stripping. That was when Kane met her.

"Look Ma… I'm lingering on the fringe of cult acceptance," She'd say as sarcastic commentary on where her years of training had gotten her.

Layla was eventually diagnosed with depression. Then she was diagnosed with depression, with mild schizophrenia. At first, Kane told himself that they would get past it together, that love could conquer all. At first…

Back then Kane would've already squeezed in a day's worth of activity by… *what time was it?* 1:25 pm. Forty-five minutes of boxing drills and bag work, 45 minutes of cardio and free weights and a 10- to 15-minute quickie in the shower with Layla to bring him down was what a typical morning entailed.

In his twenties, Kane was an obsessive son of a bitch, consumed with fitness and physicality. And pussy. Maybe it was all to escape the dream of being boxed in that chased him awake, crying, throughout his childhood. The shrinks said the same thing, that it was a manifestation of his feelings about the Calhoun Foster Home, where he spent the most time before he was adopted. They all assured him that he would outgrow it.

Kane was pushing 38, and the last time he had that dream was two nights ago. The only difference now was that he didn't wake up crying.

Moving from foster home to foster home had certainly left him with some issues that for a time manifested in his fists and his lightning-quick temper. *Ahhh, the good old days.*

It was boxing that finally straightened him out and enlightened him to controlled aggression. His ninth-grade gym teacher recommended it one day as he walked by Kane and another boy sitting at opposite ends of the bench outside the Principal's office. The other boy was nursing a black eye and busted lip while Kane tried not to look too proud.

Kane liked to hark back to the days when he was just coming into his stride as a beat cop. The year was 2004. It was before the Jesus Freaks had any real power over the government, before things like abortion, and homosexuality, and interracial marriage (depending on the state), and using the Lord's name in vain were illegal.

Kane was 27 at the time. His head was crammed with busts, gone right and wrong, replayed from different angles, then dissected into grids, diagrams, and floating equations that broke each movement down with the intent of learning from his mistakes. Just before a big bust, he'd find a wall where no one could see him and pepper it with combinations to psych himself up and calcify his knuckles. He was a fucking machine, but he wore it with subtlety. All the gung-ho shit stayed inside his head. Most people thought of him as a natural athlete. He was not.

Dark, moody, and mysterious were the words most often used to describe Kane. Had he been easier to peg racially, his rather mundane facial features would have been just that. He was better-than-average-looking with great bed-head, but there were plenty of guys sporting that look. He would've been just another face in the crowd.

In recent years, Kane had become a "media darling" thanks to his tenacity, his proficiency with his fists and feet, and his racially ambiguous look not too black (dangerous/intimidating), not too white (homogenized/safe). It was a moniker that he refused to take seriously even if he did draw from it to lift himself out of the humdrums.

Kane's shade had its own unique stain to it. Because he never knew his real parents, his best guess put himself somewhere between blue-black and lily-white. That way, he covered all the bases. It was so silly to even speculate anymore.... Well, that's what he used to think. Now, he almost had to, depending on where in the country he was and who he was with. People seemed more than willing to ask these days. Lately he'd been telling them he was Italian. Yeah, it was only perpetuating a bigger problem, but he had too many troubles of his own and too many puzzles to mull over in his head to play crusader. Besides, it could have been true.

Sheila-Bell Makane disapproved of his curiosity and did what she could to cock-block his attempts to find out more details. When he'd inquire about his racial identity, she'd respond with some stock saying like "love has no color," which, coming from her, an uneducated white woman, meant nothing.

Sheila-Bell was stingy with her love, but when she gave it, she demanded full reciprocation. This applied to her men as well. It was probably why they all eventually left her.

That feeling...

It stayed with Kane through his entire routine: piss, shower, shave, coffee. Along the way, there were a few things that seemed strange to him.

The traffic... where was it? Where were the blaring horns, the sirens, the engines roaring, the angry pedestrians speaking their minds, the speakers struggling to accommodate as car stereos shouted profanities and conveyed pent-up frustration beneath too much bass, riding on an ominous rhythm that crept up and spoke of anger, aggression, and unresolved conflict. Where was the music of dawn that echoed like dubious animal calls throughout the forest canopy and haunted the environment from two or three layers within the dense asphalt flora and fauna? It always reminded him of just how much he loved living in the city.

Even on Easter Sunday, he expected to hear some activity in the streets. Instead, there was the occasional car driving erratically by as if some tumult was going on inside.

The talking billboards and holographic ads for the day's paper that floated above the newspaper bins could be heard loud and clear from his third-floor apartment. Any other time he could hardly hear them over the hustle and bustle.

And where were the birds that chirped away outside his bedroom window every morning? Some mornings it seemed like they were fucking with him, they were so loud.

Maurice, the homeless flautist, was sleeping outside the all-night coffee shop across the street like he always did, but gone were the endless feet stepping over him as faceless trendy-folk exited with their overpriced lattes, locked in obligatory discussions about the horrors of big business, or oil, or animal rights, or religion, as if there was a list of topics in which to plug their angst. On the weekdays, they were replaced by the corporate slaves, who they both envied and ridiculed. Instead of the fancy shit, they preferred a simple cup-a-Joe, usually 20 ounces, to help suppress feelings of failure and regret that haunted low-level and managerial types alike. It birthed all kinds of unnecessary stress that, in the end, sped them along toward an early grave.

For as long as he could remember, Kane craved action. The idea of sitting behind a desk from nine to five drove him mad. Watching the cycle in various stages from his car when he'd park in the crowded business district to eat his lunch, exasperated him. He couldn't understand how people could be so accepting, so complacent in a life so short.

Fifteen years of action had aged Kane more than he liked to admit. So really, what was the difference? Even if he didn't have to sit on his ass all day, he was still just as much a victim, risking his life day in and day out for people who always managed to find fault with something he and his colleagues did. It was enough to drive a person like Kane to want to brutalize the thankless community. But that would hurt his image.

Besides the prospect of action, the appeal of authority attracted him to the force. Being a true alpha-male, he had a problem taking orders, but giving them was good therapy. He knew it was probably the wrong reason for joining, but he was a levelheaded guy with no prejudices, except maybe for fat people who used their weight as a crutch or an excuse. That was more than most of the guys he'd gone through the academy with could say.

Doesn't it figure?

The one day Kane set aside to veg-out, and just about every friggin' channel was running a special report. Initially, it tricked him into getting all cozy for the big lie. He tried to guess what they might say, what kind of bullshit the feds might come up with to explain what he saw Friday. But the anchorman kept talking about a strange storm front that was approaching rapidly, and a rash of overnight violence: people attacking each other unprovoked, several reports of people being bitten by strangers. They also kept flashing an image of Reverend Jesse James Dallas, the televangelist. Apparently he had some major announcement planned for later this afternoon. It had something to do with the homeless man who supposedly walked on water to save a drowning boy earlier this morning. Kane wasn't really listening when they brought it up on the news. Stories like that always set off his bullshit alarm, especially when they were mentioned in the same breath as Reverend Dallas, who irked the hell out of him.

Kane felt bad enough sitting on his ass for more than 15 minutes at a time, and now there was nothing by which to escape from reality on an exceptionally quiet Sunday afternoon while he waited for some news about the crash. He sat through the special reports until they began to repeat themselves, then, out of curiosity, he flipped over to the channels up in the 500s, where Reverend Dallas reigned. His empire spanned five stations altogether. Strange that he'd run a repeat on Easter Sunday of all days.

Had he known it would be like this (nothing to watch but the kind of news he lived every day), Kane probably would have slept at the station last night. Fuck the department shrink and his mandatory day off. He warned Kane that he was a likely candidate for a heart attack if he didn't slow down and "experience life in the present." It was a nice gesture and all, but there was still so much work to be done.

He didn't leave the station until 2:00 am this morning, and didn't get home until sometime after 3:00. He only lived about 20 minutes away, but he took the scenic route just to collect his thoughts.

He had spent a good part of his evening interviewing Gus Rollins and making phone calls. He was trying to reach Special Agent Mendez, whom the FBI receptionist claimed didn't work for them. He called the Maryland airport where Flight 2190 originated, but they claimed to have no knowledge of a Flight 2190. He put out a called to his many informants to see if what the feds were up to had trickled down to them yet.

Between calls, Kane tried to figure out the identity of his "secret admirer." That's what his partner, Allison Ryan, called the man with the Danish accent who, for the past six months, had been leaving cryptic messages on Kane's video-phone. They went something like this:

"This message is for Philip Makane… Detective Philip Makane from the 13th Precinct. I don't know how exactly to explain this without coming off like some kind of nut-job, but I had a dream about you… a terrible dream… You see, I'm psychic…"

That was usually when Kane pressed erase and moved on. The video signal was always scrambled, so Kane never saw the man's face. Crank calls and death threats were commonplace to him; still, he liked to check them out whenever he could, even if only to find out the number and give the caller a taste of his own medicine.

Kane crossed his legs and held the steaming cup of coffee to his lips, waiting for it to cool as he channel-surfed with his mind. It always turned out to be much more of a pain in the ass than the commercial suggested.

Kane preferred the stereo for his entertainment. Oldies like Zeppelin and Gang Starr rocked his ass, but he didn't want to miss the report.

Fucking brainwave chips, he thought, focusing his half-eyed glare just enough to switch the TV to manual and retrieve the old-fashion remote control from the coffee-table drawer. The big electronics manufacturers included brainwave chips in all their models as of 2010. They were supposed to make it easier to channel-surf, but all they really did was hand out migraines.

Sirens… out of the blue it seemed, all of a sudden sounding near and far. They had sneaked up on him, a distinctive variety, different from the cry of squad cars.

Kane started over to the window, fingered the mini-blinds apart, and immediately leaned away from the bone-rattling hum of the sleek, dinner-plate-sized security cam-bot that whizzed by too close for comfort, broke hard left, and disappeared down the side street.

Then the phone rang.

As he turned, four more cam-bots darted into view outside his window and followed the first one's beacon call down the side street. Whatever it was, it was big.

Kane grabbed his gun stared suspiciously before walking over and lifting the phone from the cradle. Of course it had something to do with the sirens and the attacks on the news.

Kane to the fucking rescue again.

Max Hedberg's Journal

Entry #1

I just watched my 3-year-old son turn into a zombie. There, I said it. I couldn't bring myself to... let's just say that I locked him in the storage room across the hall. His name ~~was~~... is Eric.

It all came to a head when I returned home from work to find my wife, Maria, naked, straddling the UPS guy (whom my son aptly named the Big Fat

28   **ANDRE DUZA**

Man). My first inclination, after I puked all over the front steps, was to bash both their heads in. I've never considered myself a violent man; however, given the situation, I was willing to explore my "dark side," so to speak. I paced outside the front door for the next 15 minutes, struggling to keep myself from lashing out. As I tried to calm myself, I began to notice a few things that just didn't sit right with me.

1. The Big Fat Man, who was fully clothed, I might add, didn't even flinch when I walked in the door. Neither did Maria for that matter. And I wasn't trying to be quiet.

2. Maria was covered in suds and I could clearly hear the shower running in the background. Even though she had a body to die for (thanks to Pilates), Maria had never been the type to walk around the house nude. In fact, after 8 years of marriage, we still make love in the dark. Pitiful, I know.

3. What I could see of her arms and thighs were rubbed raw and blistered. I later found out that she had tried, in vain, to scrub away the infection with scalding water and her favorite loofah during a moment of semi-clarity.

4. If anyone was going to stray in our marriage, I was sure it would've been me. Call me naive, but Maria just didn't have it in her. No pun intended. She'd developed a "thing" "call it a crush" on good-looking black and Latino men over the years, but I just chalked that up to harmless fantasizing. It was always my belief that healthy fantasies are one of the things that make a marriage last. Whatever the case, she certainly wouldn't be attracted to a 250-pound UPS delivery guy with blubber-face (also known as meat-face).

When I went back inside (I was prepared for the worst), Maria, whom I must have caught in the middle of a clear moment, sprung to her feet and spun around. It took every ounce of my being to keep from passing out at the sight of the Big Fat Man's throat dangling from her flared teeth, and the blood. It ran from her chin down to her pubic hair. Between violent lurches, she looked me in the eyes and said "Oh God, honey. Wh⬚what did I just do?"

Entry #2

Seeing the Big Fat Man up close and personal the way I did when I had to dispose of his body, I couldn't help thinking that he was so unappealing looking that maybe Maria did him a favor by putting him out of his misery.

I saw from his schedule that we were the last stop on his daily route, marked in for 5:00 pm on the dot, so you have to consider the day's worth of sweat and B.O. that festered in his cracks and crevices. Now, add that to the load of shit in his pants, and you've got a funk to contend with. The smell was so bad that I had to do it in brief spurts, taking a prolonged break between each to suck in some fresh air. In the end, I couldn't bear to dismember him like I originally planned, so I wrapped him in the throw rug from the study and put him in the upstairs closet where we keep the off-season clothing.

I should tell you that he eventually woke up, too.

If you're wondering about Maria, I put her in the freezer. Besides the lights, it's the only thing in this damn panic shelter that works anymore.

I'm starting to worry about what I'm going to do

about food. My stomach is already turning. It doesn't look good for me.

I'm sorry, I can't do this right now...

Talk to you later.

Chapter 2

Four things happened on Easter Sunday, 2015:

1. The dead walked.
2. The sky rained blood.
3. In Philadelphia, a WTXN Traffic Chopper recorded video of a homeless man with long blonde hair who jumped off a pier into the Delaware River and walked 150 feet on water to save a teenage boy who tried to commit suicide by leaping off the Walt Whitman Bridge. When asked his name, the homeless man responded, "I am the Christ, Jesus."
4. In Mandali, Iraq, a little brown man who called himself Yeshua walked out of a crowd of international volunteers and, before the eyes of 15 members of Mandali Hospital staff and a National Geographic crew there to film a documentary on postwar Iraq, miraculously healed an entire ward-full of men, women, and children who had been quarantined and left to die from exposure to the various chemical and biological agents deployed during the last act of the war.

One week later...
Vatican City, Rome

They had come from far and wide to witness, first-hand, the pope's address concerning the red rain, the walking dead, and the two men who claimed to be Christ. The news was predicting that the Vatican was going to officially endorse the white one, Jesus, as the true Son of God.

The pope asked Jesus, personally, to appear alongside him during his announcement. He and Reverend Jesse James Dallas had been guests of the Vatican all week. Reverend Dallas had trumped the Vatican by offering his live broadcast to Jesus on Easter Sunday, only hours after he revealed himself and long before the Vatican was ready to accept him as genuine. Their relationship took on an almost symbiotic quality ever since.

Never had St. Peter's Square seen such a diverse crowd. Thousands of moderate believers, full-fledged devotees, fanatics, and even recently reformed atheists hid beneath a flickering laser-light canopy projected from hastily erected posts that did little to shield them from the heavy downpour of bleeding rain.

Representatives from as many religions as there were people boasted of their self-righteousness and, in the case of the Muslims, Buddhists, and Hindus, their disdain and opposition to what was being touted by the media as the 'the End Times as prophesied by the bible' via automated banners sprouting up from shoulder-mounted PHPs (personal holo-projectors) flashing wildly imaginative fonts in mid-air and, from the lower echelon, scrawled, handwritten signs taped to yardsticks and detached broom-handles.

Heated arguments erupted from various points within the unruly crowd, further polarizing small factions and causing the holographic riot-cops, who patrolled the crowd (literally walking through it), in sets of two, to alert their physical counterparts. The real riot-cops were watching from a few hundred feet away behind laser-light blockades set up at all but one corner of St. Peters Square.

Though they were in the minority in terms of numbers, the group there to protest the Catholic Church's handling of the numerous clergyman accused of inappropriate acts with young boys seemed to be causing the most trouble. In the week since Jesus and Yeshua made themselves known, hundreds more came forward, fearing judgment for their sins, and seeking repentance from Jesus himself.

From one of the portable bleachers, a well-organized Baptist choir passionately sang familiar hymns with little concern for the rain that coated their robes in a layer of dark red and weighed them down.

An army of journalists, like worker bees for the global mass media machine, each housed in a tight community of raised booths flashing four-digit call signs that together resembled some intellectual red-light district, angled for the big scoop in hopes that it might kick-start their dream of a movie career.

Melting from person to person within the crowd, reporters from each outlet searched, like scouts in a war of popularity, for the most colorful, or the most vocal, in an environment wrought with mer-etricious interpretations of proper church attire and ceremonial garb.

Melanie Hargrove, a 30-something female reporter sporting a vintage black umbrella, used her forearms as bumpers as she jogged hastily through the crowd and up the metal stairs to the booth marked WTXN. She shook hands with the middle-aged man who stood in the doorway waiting for her.

"Felix… Felix Mac." He said as he handed her a tablet-monitor containing the loose script that she was to use.

Reaching over to the counter on his left, Felix slid the wireless keyboard closer to him and typed in a series of commands that activated a smooth metallic disc that lay beside it.

Melanie perused the script and cursed aloud, ignoring the soothing hum of the disc, which was now hovering between them. A small compartment crept open to reveal a quarter-sized lens that clicked and buzzed as it focused.

Melanie never liked working from a script. She had a reputation for speaking her mind and coloring her left-wing views with off-kilter humor, which was why her superiors didn't trust her.

"What????????? You've gotta be kidding me! They want me to say this?"

When she looked up from the tiny screen, Felix directed her attention to the hovering camera, its lens adjusting its iris and locking on her. He had already begun counting down.

"Five… four… three… two… one…"

Without missing a beat, Melanie turned on her game-face.

"This is Melanie Hargrove reporting from Vatican City, Rome, where I'm standing shoulder to shoulder with thousands of people who've all come here today to hear the pope's address. In his speech, which is slated to begin within the hour, the pope will try to shed light on the two mysterious figures who claim to be Jesus Christ himself, as well as the phenomenon of bleeding rain that has many people looking to religious leaders for answers. According to a recent, worldwide poll, 82% see the rain, which has been tested by experts around the world and verified as human blood, as a sign of a biblical apocalypse. With diseases like AIDS and Ebola on the rise, there is also a growing concern about possible unsanitary conditions caused by the blood, which has resulted in gas masks and other protective clothing flying off the racks at record rates. We at Channel 7 News are also waiting on verification of reports coming in from all over concerning… the dead…" Melanie scrutinized the sheet of paper and let out a pompous snicker that she meant for everyone to see. "That is to say, corpses of those thought to be deceased somehow returning from their graves…"

Melanie's shrinking posture and rolling eyes illustrated her reluctance to totally commit to the words that fell awkwardly from her mouth. It forced her to pause as if to distance herself from her last statement while all around her, giant flat-screen monitors mounted on scaffolding flashed disjointed images of varying quality that quickly satiated her skepticism. As she stood, mouth agape, trying to fathom what unfolded on the screen directly in front of her, Melanie shook her head at her timing. Usually she was the first to know. Now some local Italian news outlet was scooping her. At least it wasn't Fox News, her old employer. She never got over the way they treated her.

It had only been about an hour since Melanie got off the laser-prop transport. She'd spent the past month at her ex-husband James's cabin deep in the Appalachians, away from civilization, to cashing in her fuck-buddy chips.

Granted that the bleeding rain perplexed her, Melanie actually laughed at the text message that her assistant left on her bracelet-phone (that she promised not to bring) when she finally broke down and checked it behind James's back. *Dead people attacking the living...End Times...Second Coming...* was how it hit her.

"Melanie??? Melanie, we're live. Melanie?" The director's hollow voice nagged at her from the communicator implanted in her ear canal, but she was too preoccupied with the events up on the screen. She wanted so bad to have the thing removed, but it was required of all WTXN mobile staff.

Felix Mac was just about to nudge her until he followed her eyes up and fell immediately under the screens' glowing spell. Without looking, he typed in a command instructing the hovering camera to give the audience at home a peek as well.

On the screens...

The heavy downpour infected each vignette with a morose red glow.

From Tokyo: *About 10 feet offshore, anonymous brows sporting hairlines of bone and patchwork flesh break the surface like rounded dorsal fins on some flesh-toned, bipedal sea serpent, as waterlogged corpses stumble up from the depths of the blood-red Sea of Okhotsk and make their way inland.*

From Paris: *Bodies everywhere. People running to and fro, screaming en Français. Outdoor cafés and tourist hot spots over-*

run with zombies; tables overturned, broken glass; everyday essentials (jackets, purses, etc.) left behind. In the background, the Eiffel Tower in flames, leaflets and various unidentifiable objects litter the air all around it. Police roaming the streets, calling out to survivors of the initial onslaught through megaphones mounted to the roofs of their cars. A swarm of zombies marching out of the Père-Lachaise Cemetery. Among them, a skeletal fellow in sagging leather pants who staggers, drunkenly from a graffiti-swathed grave marked Morrison.

From New York: *Factions of armed citizens in gas masks, Haz-Mat suits, and improvised protective clothing take to the streets. Chaos at a grand level. Zombies being picked off at close range, from rooftops, and passing vehicles packed with vigilante types. Others taking the opportunity to loot and act out against a society that has all but neglected them. Police doing their best to maintain calm.*

From Washington: *Military vehicles form an impenetrable barrier around the White House, fending off zombies and the living desperate to escape it all.*

From Ohio: *Rural flatland pounded by aggressive snowfall punching downward and stained pinkish-red by the rain that falls with it. The rain washes away the surface layers of strawberry water-ice covering, creating a fatty layer of slush, and repeating the same cycle as more snow accumulates. Three tiers deep into the stained curtain of snowfall, a vast graveyard drools corpses up through the ground. Human shapes walk with herky-jerky strides, approaching a massive traffic jam as poor visibility and black ice claim its quota of victims on the crowded roads.*

From Mississippi: *Mass prayer vigils in the streets. Churches* *filled to capacity. Improvised regiments of good-ol' boys in slick rain coats and gas masks lean out from the back of retro pick-ups with monster-truck tires and take out their frustrations on the darker-skinned walkers and zombies alike.*

Somewhere on the fringes of the crowd, a drastic parting of bodies introduced an elderly woman shuffling hand-in-hand with what looked like the long-dead corpse of an even older man.

"Dammit, Mel. Get with the program," the director interrupted again. "I say, WE ARE LIVE!!!! Do you hear me? Can she hear me…?"

Melanie zeroed in on the old woman like a famished predator locked on some weaker species. Her head whipped around to the competition and saw that she wasn't the only one eager to snag the first interview with a corpse. Felix was still glued to the screen when Melanie snapped her fingers repeatedly and pointed. She waited for him to readjust the hovering camera's aim before she grabbed her umbrella from the floor, jumped down, and made a mad dash for the old woman.

From his vantage point above the crowd, Felix watched as seven distinct lines formed within the sea of heads and moved quickly toward the woman. So far, Melanie, who was probably in the best shape of all the reporters, was in the lead.

"Who's shooting for her?" Desperation gave the director's voice a dry rasp.

Felix listened through his own implant, wondering whether or not he should respond.

"Says here Felix Mac…." An unfamiliar female voice on the other spoke for him.

"I'm right here, sir," Felix chimed in tentatively.

"You listen to me, Mr. Mac," the director replied. "You get her ass back in front of that camera or it's your job."

"Just watch that red shirt moving through the crowd," Felix

responded. "You won't be disappointed."

"What was that? A red shirt? Are you kidding me?"

"Just trust me, sir."

For a moment, Felix lost Melanie in the jumble of people closest to the old woman who struggled to get a good look at her dead partner while simultaneously scrambling backward in disgust.

The woman was suddenly yanked to the side.

Felix followed the hand that reached through a hole in the crowd, latched onto the woman's shoulder, and pulled. The hand was small and delicate, which seemed to contrast with Melanie's personality. He assumed it wasn't her until the tangle of bodies loosened and more of the arm came through. He was looking for signs, like the color red. And there it was, a red sleeve pushed up to the elbow.

Felix's chest tightened.

Melanie spotted Felix at the same time. She motioned the crowd back with one hand, held on to the old woman with the other, then gave Felix a thumbs-up.

Felix instructed the hovering camera to focus.

"May I ask you your name, ma'am?" Melanie huffed, struggling to catch her breath, while trying not to seem as though she was.

"Excuse me? Oh, my name is Patricia Kaminski. Most people just call me Pat," the old woman responded. Though a bit flustered, she seemed oblivious to the crowd's reaction to the wobbling zombie that stood beside her, staring at her exposed neck as if it were a slab of prime meat.

Melanie turned discreetly to the man and, now that she was close enough to see him in detail, winced at his appearance: the exposed bones and remnants of muscle fiber from his forehead to his nose, the rotten, baggy flesh that dangled from the lower half of his face and threatened to slide right off, his dry, blackened lips curling up to reveal a few remaining teeth that jutted out from receded gums and relaxing as if he tried in vain to snarl and will his jaw to clamp down, but apparently it was locked in place. And he smelled even worse.

"And this isss…?" Melanie said.

Pat's eyes lit up.

"This is my husband, Norman. Three years ago, congestive heart failure took him away from me after 45 years of marriage. I've spent every day since waiting for the time to come when we could be together again. I was literally at the end of my rope when I got a knock on my door last night. And when I opened it..." Caressing his face, she began to well up. To her, he was as handsome as the first day they met.

Melanie massaged Pat's upper back, then draped her arm around her shoulders and gave her a squeeze.

"I know. I know...."

The rest of the crowd continued to stare at Norman, who swayed silently, his eyes rolling lazily to those who stood closest as if trolling a hearty buffet selection.

"When I opened the door—praise God!—I saw my Norman standing there. He came back to me. My Norman came back to me!"

Pat turned and wrapped her frail arms around her dead husband who, for all his effort, couldn't bend his arms at the elbows to return her embrace. Though he was too far gone to be of any real danger, he somehow managed to finally bring his teeth together against the loose skin at the side of her throat.

Pat let out a gurgled shriek as he yanked his head from side to side and pulled away from her, taking a few elastic strands of skin with him.

EMERGENCY! EMERGENCY! EMERGENCY!

This is not a test.

This message is a service of the Emergency Broadcast System in cooperation with your federal, state, and local authorities. In light of the recent influx of critically wounded men, women, and children arriving by the minute at emergency rooms nationwide; as of midnight, April 6th, all Pennsylvania-area hospitals will be closed to further admissions. If you have the means to defend yourself against the infected, state and local police ask that you do so with discretion before attempting to contact them for assistance. This, by no means, advocates vigilantism, however, considering the extreme nature of the threat posed by the infected, authorities are asking for your help, as they are currently overwhelmed with calls. A list of alternative medical and police contact numbers will be posted shortly.

When dealing with the infected:

● Total destruction of the body is the only means of stopping them. Although disabling the legs will slow them down, they still pose a considerable threat in this state.

● Once bitten by the infected, the victim (whether it be family, friend, spouse, etc.) should immediately be placed under quarantine. Although preliminary tests show a gestation period of 18- to 24-hours before full-blown, or "active," infection sets in, scientists are still vague about the communicable nature of the infection in this gestation period.

● Although the infected may at times seem to function normally during the 18- to 24-hour gestation period, they are prone to sudden acts of violence and should be considered extremely unstable.

● Studies have shown that death by any means (even natural causes) will ultimately result in reanimation. In these cases, the 18- to 24-hour gestation period does not apply. Subjects have been known to reanimate anywhere from five minutes to an hour after clinical death.

● As of yet, the etiology of the virus that causes infection is not known, nor is there any known cure.

● Unless absolutely necessary, travel is prohibited. If you do need to venture outdoors, always travel in groups (preferably with an armed chaperon), and avoid high-risk areas.

● Until scientists determine whether or not the "virus" that causes infection is airborne, safety equipment (gas masks, Haz-Mat suits, layered clothing, etc.) should be worn at all times when venturing outdoors.

Symptoms of early infection include the following: fever, nausea/vomiting, migraines, cold sweats, dementia (fits of rage), euphoria, forgetfulness, dizziness, insomnia, muscle aches, muscle spasms, stiffening/weakening of joints, abdominal pain, bloody stool/urine/vomitus, seizure/convulsions.

EMERGENCY! EMERGENCY! EMERGENCY!

Max Hedberg's Journal

Entry #3

So, I guess I should start from the beginning because, if you're reading this journal, you probably
pried it out of my cold dead hands. Isn't that
what the bumper sticker says? "You can have my
gun when you pry it out of my cold dead hands." Or
something like that.

My name is Max Hedberg, by the way.

What I failed to mention in my last entry is that I'm
stuck down here in the panic shelter. We all are:
me, my wife Maria, and my 3-year-old son, Eric. I'm
in the main room, a small windowless box with a
control panel, a high-backed, leather desk-chair,
and security monitors that don't work. And when I
do communicate with Maria and Eric, it's muffled
by two thick walls, which only adds to the frustration.

For the past few days (my best guesstimate, as the
clocks aren't working), I've listened to them
unravel. On top of being deader than Eric, Maria is
claustrophobic as all get-out, and the freezer is
no bigger than a walk-in closet. In retrospect, I

should've seen it coming. It happened just like in the movies, for Christ's sake. She got bit, she turned; she bit Eric, he turned. And I call myself prepared.

Because she wasn't fully turned when it happened, I thought, I hoped that maybe there was a chance that Eric would pull through. I waited until the very last minute before I locked him up. It was an experience that I wouldn't wish on any parent, the way he kicked and screamed and begged me not to leave him alone in that precocious tone that he used when he knew he was on my bad side. I literally thought I was going to die.

You'd think I would've been ready for it, because Maria did the same thing, but with more vigor, when I made her come down here and get into the freezer at gunpoint. I know how it sounds, but she wouldn't go any other way. Believe me, I tried everything.

It broke my heart to know that after witnessing that, Eric probably held me responsible for what was happening to his mother. I know that he was too young to completely understand what was going on, but... well, I'm sure those of you with children understand.

Eric seems more scared than anything else. He screams for his mommy, but she simply growls back. She's too far gone to even answer him anymore. I try my best to console him, but I feel so guilty for lying to him over and over, telling him that every-thing is going to be alright, that I am going to find a way to make him and mommy better, that I will take him to the store and buy him any toy he wants if he would only stop crying. We were never close, but there was a definite bond. It took awhile for it to set in between us, but when it did, I finally understood why my wife fawned over him so.

Why weren't we close, you ask? Well, mainly because I'm a workaholic. I had to be to keep a woman like Maria happy. She's what they call high maintenance.

Hold on.... I think I hear Eric calling me.

Entry #4

"Why does mommy want to eat me?" Eric asked me. I didn't know what to say so I covered my ears and pretended not to hear him.

Did I tell you that I found some food? Yep. It was

only a few candy bars. Three actually. They were taped to the bottom of the console. I was so hungry that I didn't even want to start speculating why someone would do that, especially knowing what I know about this house's former owner. Remind me to tell you about him later.

I ate the first candy bar right away, wolfed it down like some kind of beast. You're thinking that I'm going to regret that in the long run. Maybe, but Goddammit, I was so hungry that that candy bar went down tasting like steak.

Who knew we would ever need to use the panic shelter. It came with the house, and I had planned to turn it into a basement hideaway where I could get my work done without listening to Eric tear up the house with his toys. His idea of playing with them is to hold one (action figure or car, let's say) in each hand and smash them together as hard as he could. He's a good kid really, but he's at that age where he likes to fire off questions like a fucking machine gun and fixate on particular sounds (usually high-pitched ones), repeating them over and over until either my wife or I yell for him to stop. Maria is a lot more tolerant of it than I ever was. I guess it's that whole mother/son bond thingy that I used to think was bullshit. In retrospect, it makes me feel like I let him down as a father. Maybe I could've been more patient with him, but I was always so busy. I work from home you see. Sorry, I'm getting off track here...

The realtor warned us that there were a few things that needed to be fixed before the panic shelter was usable; namely, the main generator, which controlled the TV, phones, surveillance system, and the computer. There were separate generators for the freezer, the ventilation system, and the lights. Then there was the door. The police had to call the panic-shelter manufacturer to get it open after repeated shotgun blasts did little more than mangle the handle and locking mechanism. I guess I should tell you, although I never like to admit this, but the previous owner was a serial rapist who used to bring his victims down here and keep them captive. One of them was smart enough to play dead and escape once he moved her upstairs to dismember and bury her in his backyard. That was where he kept the bodies.

As a result of the police raid, the door is impossible to open from the inside once it's closed, making this place more like a tomb than a shelter.

So here I am, trapped in this tomb with no food, no connection to the outside world, and a pocket-sized holographic photo album that makes me cry every time I scroll through it. The last thing I remember from the news was that some guy had walked on water somewhere in Philly. Your guess is as good as mine on that one. I'm thinking it's probably some kind of publicity stunt.

Pardon me for sounding like a baby, but I feel so alone. It's that feeling that frightens me most. I'm sure if you ask me in a couple hours, my answer will be different. We'll see.

Chapter 3

In the news today: Police were required to use deadly force to stop a gunman who took a hostage and opened fire in a crowded mall last night, killing five people and wounding dozens more. The gunman, who police have identified as 42-year-old Gus Rollins, of Bucks County, Pennsylvania, was shot and killed when the hostage managed to get away and Rollins, as a result, opened fire on police. The hostage, 17-year-old Meleeza Duncan, was treated and released from Pennsylvania Hospital.

Witnesses at the scene say that Rollins seemed to be in a trance, 'like a killing frenzy' according to one young witness, and was heard referring to himself as Mr. Boring.

Church-Black/Wholly Shit

Judging from the immense sculpture of Jesus on the cross splayed above the altar in audacious dimensions (someone had draped a sheet over it after some of the old bats complained that it was sneering and making faces at them during the sermon) and the stained-glass ceiling that spanned the entire length of the church, this was a congregation more concerned with outward appearances than anything approaching gratitude, or even faith.

The spirit of revolution passed down by the civil rights generation had become homogenized, tainted by greed and ignorance, following the doctrine handed down by "black" media outlets that catered to their own shortcomings. Shame on the occasional forward thinker who called them on their failures and for dropping the ball that their parents, grandparents, and even some of the 'white folks,' who many of them called enemy, fought and died to set in motion. They had become so reliant on material things and status that they viewed such statements as threats to their comfortable lifestyles.

They had evolved quick responses to discredit those who sought to uplift the community by holding a mirror to its flaws. As a means of defending their lifestyle of immediate gratification, they vomited out colorfully amusing reprieves that totally missed the point when ignorance left them without anything else to say.

The Dziko Nation (DN) was their latest foe. Once respected in the community as the saviors of Pan-Africanism, these concerned fathers, educators, and businessmen, who touted Yoruba, Akon, Shona, and Ndelela over Jesus-n-'em, had since become the scourges of church-black America once the nullified masses discovered that these "jungle religions" expected more of them than a sideways kofi or bastardized kente clothing. And worse yet, the DN had come out against Reverend Dallas' Jesus, whose airbrushed likeness smiled lovingly from every corner of St. Salacious Episcopal.

When the pope proclaimed the alabaster man the true Christ their ilk was the first to replace the paintings of a dark-skinned, dreadlocked Jesus that they had so proudly hung in testament to their cultural awakening back in the '80s with the ones that they had originally taken down.

The women swooned when they heard the soft, yet commanding voice that flowed from Jesus' mouth with a lagging gait, his words marinated in the thickening and thinning accent of a weird, bastardized archaic dialect.

The congregation of mostly older women wailed in unison, face after painted face threatening to crack under the constant stretching of aged flesh that lost its elasticity decades ago. Thin, sphincter-like lips curled up and under long teeth, as if trying to keep their faces from snapping off the tops of their heads. Those with spouses kept them close, watching them with carefully timed glances to the side. Most of the men were there against their will, prisoners of long-dead marriages. By now it was more like a friendship built on envy and resentment. The American way.

They were singing the same fucking song they'd sing at 11:42 am on any given Sunday. As decadent as it appeared, in terms of functionality, the place hadn't changed in 30 years. It was as if technology, like self-esteem, had passed them over completely.

Their slouched postures stunk of scoliosis and sedentary living, their often over-the-top, poly-cotton church costumes spoke to some underhanded pseudosexual desire to catch God's eye. These were the same slaves to envy who turned their wrinkled noses down at younger women who did the same thing to seduce common men. And this was all from a quick glance.

The song ended and silence preceded the creaking of a roomful of wood under pressure after Father Rudolph motioned for the mindlessly obedient crowd to be seated.

Rudolph was a large man in every sense of the word. It was something he'd struggled with all his life, until now. Here the women called him *big-boned*, *husky*, and *robust*. Whether it was his gender, his way with words, or his place within the church dynamic that afforded him the luxury, he milked it for every last drop.

"Praise God! Praise God! Such a joy to hear you sing his praises," Rudolph said in a practiced baritone roar. One had to be unique to be heard over the zombies' collective song. It crossed all cultural and racial barriers and reached out to every last corner of the world. "Now, I'd like to start today by addressing some of your concerns about the events that have befallen us of late. Regardless of what you might have heard on the evening news—strange weather anomalies, effects of covert military testing, global warming—our… misguided brethren in the Dziko Nation, or the talk shows with these high-and-mighty know-it-alls who make light of the pope's wonderful speech and place their scien-*tific* ideas and opinions above God's word, I assure you that what we've been experiencing is, for those of us who are saved, a blessed event. I know some of you are afraid, but I implore you to seek comfort in the word of our Lord and Savior and know that a glorious time is upon us all a time for celebration, not agitation; jubilation, not desolation."

Red rain poured in sheets down the narrow/tall stained glass windows, only to be redirected by the lurching shadows that congregated outside, pounding on the windows and tugging on the reinforced bars that covered them. As if to challenge the church choir, their semi-synchronized moans and growls overwhelmed even the blaring church organ at times. Some of them even tried to mimic the chords. Muffled gunshots from the guards posted at each entrance, and colorful expletives whispered loud enough to be heard during the quiet moments, seemed not to faze them, as this was a crowd that excelled at denial.

"Now, in keeping with the tone of celebration, I want to talk about Ruth Gordon and her wonderful youth program. As you all know, she has done great things in the past three years since she took over for Darlene Parks—God rest her soul."

A groan from the envious old crones.

Father Rudolph paused as if to scold the entire crowd. Various heads half-turned toward the suspected few who simply looked away.

"In light of current events, it is most befitting that today we present her latest success story. Many of you have known Jeanne Duncan's pride and joy, Meleeza, since she was knee-high to a grasshopper. Some of you have even guided her on her Christian journey during her years in our Sunday School Program. I like to call Meleeza our miracle child after having survived what must have been a terrifying experience at the hands of the man who was shot dead by police after taking her hostage in the mall last week, and for triumphing over the vile, insidious narcotic known as U4, that has unfortunately ravaged so many of her peers. It reminds me of the story of..."

Eyes rolled as if to say "Here we go again" before Rudolph

could finish his sentence. He was known for his awkward segues and never-ending tangents.

Back in the rectory, round bodies in their Sunday best raced back and forth, preparing Meleeza Duncan for her performance. One look at her and it was obvious that the virginal-white, full-length gown was a false representation of who this 17-year-old girl really was. Her gaunt, U4-chic malaise shined right through the good girl act that her mother made her practice to pitch-perfection. It showed mostly in her eyes, which were recessed and surrounded by dark rings.

Meleeza was growing restless by the moment as her mother applied a few finishing touches to her hair and make-up.

Jeanne Duncan was one of those lucky women who, despite her best efforts, managed to actually look about a decade older than her 42 years. "Call it a gift," she'd say whenever someone would remark about how good she looked. Their blatant sarcasm usually went right over her head. Like most of her peers, she only heard what she wanted to hear.

Jeanne was the epitome of a stage mother, a controlling and manipulative woman who sometimes referred to herself as *Queen Bitch*. With her abrasive, ghetto-fabulous dialect and her pushy nature, she was a great big thorn in the side of many of her contemporaries in the church. Alcoholism, obesity, and general bad judgment had stolen her own dream of a singing career, and she wasn't about to let her daughter make the same mistake. Not on your fucking life.

Meleeza squirmed in her chair.

"C'mon mom! I had it just the way I like it," she cried, yanking her head away from Jeanne's heavy hands.

"If you think I'm gonna let you go out there looking like some lady-of-the-evening, then you've got another thing coming," Jeanne barked with enough malice to bring down a wayward club-kid rolling on some good shit. "Now you just be still and let me finish."

"This ain't the eighties, mom. You remember what my manager said? Image is important no matter what kind of music you sing."

Meleeza couldn't stand the starched, ghetto prom queen dress that she felt smothered her from the shoulders way down to the floor. It had a way of looking both conservative and sleazy at the same time. She thought it made her look like a transvestite or, even worse, like someone from the bottom of the bottom of society trying too hard to escape that very image. Someone like her mother.

Meleeza wanted to believe that it was because of *her* that her mother tried to clean up her act, but she knew it was because of the private investigator that her father hired to follow them around.

Meleeza snaked her dress down her shoulders a few inches, then a few more.

Jeanne's eyes were already on her. If they could speak, they'd have said enough to cut deep into Meleeza's already fractured pride.

"Nobody's gonna think I'm a slut just cause my neck is showing."

Jeanne clutched the lower half of Meleeza's face and pulled her close.

"You listen to me, *girlfriend*." Her tone was wrought with malevolence. "After all I've put up with from you for the last two years, you *are* going to do WHAT I say, WHEN I say, and HOW I say to do it. You understand me?"

Meleeza fought momentarily against her mother's grasp, her welling eyes searching for an ally.

"I said, DO YOU UNDERSTAND ME??"

Meleeza shook her head yes.

Ruth Gordon was especially concerned for Meleeza as she locked eyes with her from the other side of the crowded room. She never liked Jeanne or her abrasive style of parenting. The general consensus was that Jeanne had driven Meleeza to drugs.

Ruth was one of those busybodies whose nose eventually found its way into everyone's business.

Jeanne continued applying pressure to Meleeza's jaw until

she finally turned to face her again. This time she shot back a stare that rivaled her mother's. After all, she'd learned from the best.

"All I have to do is make one phone call and your narrow ass will be sitting right back in the Burke's Rehab Center. And this time, I'm gonna tell them to keep you for good." Jeanne paused to allow it time to marinate. "Like it or not, until you turn eighteen, I call the shots... and right now, I'm telling you that you're gonna pull that pretty dress up, go out there, and make your mother proud."

Jeanne hoisted Meleeza's dress up until it covered her shoulders, then manipulated the corners of her mouth into a smile with her fingers.

Meleeza reluctantly conceded.

Leaning away to drink her in in typical matronly fashion, Jeanne actually beamed with pride.

"Now you look like my angel."

How quickly she changes faces, Ruth mused to herself.

A knock at the door gave pause to the roomful of weak tickers.

Ruth was the first one to the door. It was an especially noisy door, and only she knew how to open it without making a sound. It was as simple telling them to grab the knob and lift, but she craved control. They all did, but Ruth was the oldest.

Jason Williamson (Meleeza's boyfriend) peeked in through the cracked door. Looking over Ruth's shoulder, he quickly found Meleeza.

"There's someone here to see Leeza," Ruth called out.

Jeanne's smile mutated into a frown so fluidly that it was as if the frown had been there, unseen, the entire time, and only now did it choose to reveal itself. She didn't approve of their relationship.

Sometimes Meleeza was too observant for her own good. It was from her mother's reaction that she knew it was Jason. Aside from her father, who else would inspire that grimace?

Meleeza turned and smiled. Once their eyes met, they gazed

passionately at each other, if only for a moment.

Jason smiled back.

"H... hi Ms. Duncan. Hi Leeza." Jason spoke in the meekest tone he could muster. He loathed bowing to Jeanne, but he knew how volatile she could be. "'Zit all right if I come in?"

Jeanne turned away before he could finish his sentence.

Even if the other women didn't care much for Jason's earthy hip-hop style, and his rebellious nature, they empathized with him for what he had to go through just to see his girlfriend.

"I don't think so," Jeanne groaned without bothering to look at him.

"Oh, for Christ's sake, mom!" Meleeza yelled loud enough for the people out in the pews to hear.

There was a collective gasp from the old women.

Jeanne slapped Meleeza across the left side of her face. In this case, the other women stood behind her actions.

"Girl, don't you dare use the Lord's name in vain," she scolded. "If Jason wants to see you, then he's going to have to watch from outside like everybody else."

"But mom...."

"THAT'SSSS the way it's gonna be, Leeza."

Ruth turned to Jason, whose anger fought desperately to break the surface. She placed a calming hand on his shoulder.

"I'm sorry, Jason," Ruth said with a reassuring smile.

Jason took a deep breath and decided that it served them best to give in. He mouthed 'I love you' to Meleeza and began to walk away.

Ruth leaned her head out the door.

"She's only got one song to do. Maybe you can talk to her afterward."

"Thanks Mrs. Gordon."

"Over my dead body," Jeanne mumbled from the other side of the room.

Meleeza snatched her purse from the table next to her and, in a tear-filled huff, stormed into the bathroom and slammed the door shut behind her. The sound bounced out into the church once again, teasing the old battle-axes whose sole purpose in life was to pry and pass swift judgment on things that they knew little to nothing about.

An uncomfortable silence spanned the room until Father Rudolph, who had stopped to frown at the rectory door beyond which one of the old women peeked out, picked up where he left off, and in a matter of seconds, he was knee-deep in his own bullshit again.

Jeanne glared at the bathroom door and shook her head.

"I should've known," she said as she stomped over to the bathroom door and leaned into it.

"Leeza, you come out here right now!"

There was no reply.

Jeanne pressed her ear against the old, splintered wood and listened. She could hear movement. It sounded like something metallic....

"Don't you force me to make that phone call." Jeanne raised her voice while remaining aware of the nosey (pronounced noozey in old-school Ebonics) congregation, who were probably listening over Rudolph's tired sermon.

Considering how ancient everything looked, the bathroom was impeccably clean. The way Meleeza's distorted image slithered along the polished tile walls intrigued her... until she reached the mirror.

Meleeza sobbed in stuttered breaths as she stared at her own reflection. She looked worn, sullen, and about 10 years older, but beneath it all she was pretty enough to make it work as a look.

Wiping the tears from her eyes, she dug deep into her purse.

"You'd be done with the bitch if you had listened to me last night."

That voice.

The ER doctor told her mother it was a symptom of post-traumatic stress disorder and that given the circumstance (witnessing Gus Rollins, who had held her hostage, shot in the head by police), it was probably nothing to worry about. Meleeza hadn't told anyone that it was one specific voice, both masculine and feminine in its tone, and what kinds of things it said to her. She only said that she'd been hearing things, voices.

Meleeza was afraid that her mother wouldn't believe her, or worse yet, that she'd say it was her own subconscious thoughts sneaking to the surface… that that was really how she felt about her *own mother*. And you know what? She would've been partly right. At times Meleeza *had* fantasized about killing her mother, but they were only fantasies, the kind every kid her age harbored.

Last night she woke up standing over her *own mother's* bed watching her as she slept. In her right hand, she held a large cleaver, the one from the set of kitchen knives she bought her last Christmas. She hadn't told anyone about that either.

In the mirror, her reflection stood much more relaxed than she did, hips jutting to the right and hands tracing her breasts.

"You're body… so young and tight…. It inspires the most wicked thoughts, my dear."

"Shut up," Meleeza growled under her breath. "Just shut up and leave me alone."

Maybe it was the drugs, what with the hallucinations and all. If her mother found out she was still using, then it was right back to rehab, and Meleeza wasn't ready to give up the high. She worried that she might never be ready. It was her only escape from her mother's wrath outside of seeing Jason, which she almost never got to do.

A muffled voice seemed to emanate from the door.

"Leeza! Who are you talking to in there?" Jeanne yelled. "You'd better not have that damn bracelet-phone after I told you not to bring it."

The sound of Jeanne's voice was enough to work Meleeza into a fit. She stood, contemplating, grinding her teeth to stave off her anger.

"Don't you dare ignore me, girl. This is no time to be a prima donna. Now get your butt out here now. You're embarrassing me."

"FUCK YOU!" She couldn't hold it in any longer. "I hate you! You're nothing but a jealous old never-was trying to live through me, and I can't stand it! You hear me? I refuse to live for you any longer! NO MORE!"

Jeanne was at a loss. If she was embarrassed before, now she was absolutely mortified. The congregation had surely heard Meleeza's outburst.

"Please honey... I know we have our problems, but I thought we were making some progress lately."

And when that bullshit didn't fly...

"Dammit Leeza, can't you ever think of anyone but yourself? For goodness sake, do you have to be such a fuckin' drama queen? If you want to see Jason so bad, you can talk to him afterwards. Okay? All right? You win, Leeza. You hear me? You can talk to him all you want.... Hell, you can have his blue-black-ass children for all I care. Now would you please just come out here? Please! Think of all the time I... *we*... put into this."

Father Rudolph did his best to get his congregation's attention back (their eyes were glued to the side door that separated them from the rectory), but he never really had it in the first place. Most of these people were here in body alone, and their participation even on that level was more a result of sheer routine than any kind of loyalty to some invisible man in the sky. A good 75 percent of them didn't even buy it. It was fear that kept them from venturing any further than occasional doubt.

Meleeza relished in Jeanne's meltdown. Now everyone would know her mother for what she was. With her luck, it was bound to backfire somehow.

Meleeza inched the shoulders of her dress down with attitude. She gave her reflection one last inspection; hair, face, and... she just couldn't bring herself to appreciate the dress on any level. The thing was UGLY, plain and simple. If only her father were here to bolster her confidence. She could hear him as clearly as if he were standing right next to her.

"Well, I guess you'll be the best looking ghetto prom queen that there ever was, then." He'd find a way to make it sound like the biggest compliment a father could give his daughter.

If it were up to her, she'd have gone with him, but her mother had a way with men. Sometimes it bordered on supernatural the way she'd manipulate them. She did it to the judge during the custody hearing. Somehow she convinced him that her father had done all the terrible things she claimed without ever offering up any proof.

It took a moment for the single stream of blood to catch Meleeza's eye as it peeked out from beneath her sleeve before making its break down toward her upturned hand.

"Oh shit!" Meleeza cried out. Realizing how loud she had been, she covered her mouth.

Meleeza grabbed a paper towel, dampened it, but when she went to wipe it away, the stream changed direction, zigzagging right, then left as she chased it with her hand.

From her reflection, giddy laughter.

"That's a nasty little habit you've got there. I can help you kick it… for a price."

When she looked up at the mirror, her reflection had just let her dress fall to a swing from where it had hiked it up to her crotch, stuck its finger in its mouth, and fellated it.

It didn't take a rocket scientist to figure out where that finger had just been, or what that "price" entailed.

On the other side of the bathroom door, Ruth Gordon had joined a broken-down Jeanne. She was on her knees, leaning against the door, her ear pressed to it to listen in despite the fact that she was sobbing quite noisily. Her thick mascara had smeared in such a way that along with the layers of caked-on makeup, the form-fitting silver dress, and the knee-high boots, it called to mind some disgraced super villain wallowing in defeat.

Jeanne turned to Ruth for support, but Ruth's eyes offered only disgust.

"Did you remember to check her purse like I asked earlier?" Jeanne said, wiping her eyes, which smeared her mascara even more.

"Checked and double checked." Ruth replied trying to hide the revulsion in her voice beneath layers of congenial charm.

The other women in the room traded looks of disbelief with one another, some grinning, or trying not to, or shaking their heads in disgust, pity, etc.

"Oh God, why is she doing this to me?" Jeanne whimpered.

Ruth's lips tightened as if she held back a mouthful.

"Do you really need to ask?" she said rather bluntly.

The bathroom door swung open and Meleeza stepped out smiling as if nothing had happened.

Man, was Jeanne livid, but if she had learned anything in the past 20 minutes, it was to pick her battles more wisely.

Reaching out with both arms, she pulled Meleeza into her embrace. She really wanted to slap the living shit out of her, just as Ruth wanted to do to Jeanne for thinking that the rest of them were stupid enough to fall for her fake concern.

Refusing to reciprocate the embrace, Meleeza rolled her eyes at Ruth, who smiled and nodded as if to acknowledge some unspoken allegiance.

Out on the altar, Father Rudolph stalled as best he could until, finally, a signal. Ruth Gordon, who stuck her head out from behind the door and gave a nod, let him know that it was time for a segue from his 'Fathers, the forgotten mentors' rhetoric.

Rudolph cleared his throat, which the regulars knew as a sign that he was about to say something poignant (or something embarrassingly self-congratulatory).

"Like many parents, I used to watch the music videos with my daughter, Ayana, and I often found myself being reminded of the story of Sodom and Gomorrah. I remember feeling a deep sense of shame that we, as a society, have allowed ourselves to devolve to such a level. In these End Times, I think it's of the utmost importance that we show our children the way, lest they suffer the fate that awaits those who peddle such filth. In honor of the events that have awakened the entire planet to the very real presence of the Lord our Savior, I'd like to introduce Meleeza Duncan who is going to sing a song for us today." Rudolph turned and locked eyes with Ruth and Meleeza, who were peering out through the half-opened rectory door. "If you're ready?"

Meleeza took a deep breath and squeezed Ruth's hand.

Ruth squeezed back.

In the background, Jeanne cursed out loud as she rifled through her daughter's purse.

Ruth leaned forward and whispered in Meleeza's ear.

"Don't you dare worry yourself about your mother," she whispered. "We've all had her number since before you were even born. You just go out there and knock 'em dead."

Ruth thumbed away Meleeza's tears and gave her a gentle shove forward and out onto the altar.

Jesus Rides ~~With~~ Me

There was something about a roomful of judging eyes that stole Meleeza Duncan's enthusiasm until she was able to take a long breath and put everything into perspective.

First of all, these people were old as dirt, most of them dealing with deteriorating eyesight, so they probably couldn't even see her clearly.

Second, they were most likely too preoccupied with the rain and all its implications to even notice what she was doing, and even if the pope, the president, and all the televangelists were wrong about the 'End Times' being upon us, most of the congregation were at the end of their lives anyway and vying, harder than a death-row inmate, to get into heaven. So, as long as she kept it religious, they'd be putty in her hands. Deep down she wanted to dance and rap.

Meleeza grabbed the microphone from Father Rudolph, who winked as he walked off the altar, and mustered a shy grin at the crowd before finally settling into her game face.

"Today I'm going to sing for you a song that... that my mother helped me to write." Meleeza's eyes read momentary disgust. She hated giving her mother credit since she was usually too drunk to do anything other than yell at her. "The song is called 'Jesus Rides With Me.'"

After an extended pause, Meleeza closed her eyes, and began.

In the dark of night when I'm lon-leee...
Jesus rides with meee....

In the back of the room, Jason Williamson sat trying to somehow inflate himself so that Meleeza could see him as he mouthed the words to the song. He had heard it many times. He didn't expect her to find him as quickly as she did, though.

Meleeza winked at him and flashed a large smile.

Jason smiled back.

As if triggered by their exchange, Meleeza's eyes began to flutter. She swayed right, then left, as if succumbing to a dizzy spell. Seeping to the surface, a moist sheen of sweat accentuated her features until it began to flow profusely about her face, neck, and shoulders and on its way to staining her dress from the inside. Her eyes briefly rolled up, then fell back in place beneath heavy, lethargic eyelids.

"Waitaminute... wait...." She huffed out between heavy breaths. "I gotta... gotta get it together here...."

Jeanne, Ruth, and the other women were squeezed tightly in the small doorway, watching.

Goddammit! She's using again! Jeanne thought. She turned and glared at Meleeza's purse as it lay open on the make-up table. *But I checked it myself.*

Sporting an intoxicated grin, Meleeza started to pick up the song where she left off.

All alone I cry in ecstasy.
As Jeee-sus riii-iiides meeee...

As she sang, Meleeza sauntered across the altar to horrified gasps and cries for mercy, her hips loosening, and her eyes, once nervous and unsure, now conveying animal lust. She licked her lips and caressed her own nubile curves.

Some of the old crones got up and headed for the door with their spouses reluctantly in tow. They had seen enough.

Father Rudolph burst from his chair at the other side of the altar, his arm angling for Meleeza's shoulder as he hurried toward her. At 250 pounds plus some, Rudolph was a force to be reckoned with at full charge, yet it took little effort to stop him cold.

Extending her arm to the side, Meleeza snatched Rudolph by the throat and squeezed a strange pitch from deep within him. His hands instantly found her wrists and strained to pry them from his neck, but she was too strong, so strong that he felt his feet leave the ground.

Meleeza pulled Rudolph's face to hers. His eyes fluttered under the nauseating stank of moist heat that crawled up from her belly and smacked him in the face. It stunk of her last meal given time to fester: creamed, chipped beef, he guessed, and something fishy, with a touch of Jersey-style sulfur.

Meleeza stuck out her tongue, licked Rudolph from chin to forehead, and tossed him into the congregation. His fall was broken by two of the more annoying old women who slammed into the pew along with him, their combined weight causing it to topple over and crush the ankles and feet of whoever was left in the row behind it.

The old ladies were beside themselves with crusty, battle-axe dismay, the kind that made them feel relevant as it roused an intensity that they left by the wayside somewhere in their thirties. Rehashing their usual shtick (screaming, calling out to God, tracing a cross with their fingertips, succumbing to 'the vapors' and fainting), they directed their rancor at Meleeza. In its 150 years, nothing like this had ever happened here at St. Salacious Episcopal Church. There was the thing with Father Ramsey and the 13-year-old acolyte, but the church elders had managed to keep that one under the rug for the most part.

At center stage, Meleeza drunkenly swayed, trying to find the rhythm of skank sexuality and, despite the insults and threats thrust upon her, she mumbled the lyrics under her breath searching for her place in the song.

Flying shoes and purses and ostentatious Sunday hats whizzed by her. She didn't even try to dodge them. Some of the women shoved their reluctant husbands forward when most of them would rather kick back with a cold one and watch Meleeza's sweet young ass come apart.

Meleeza spun, as if guided by a sixth sense that allowed her to see behind her without looking, and startled the two grandfatherly gentlemen who were gradually making their way up the stairs at the side of the altar.

At the rectory door, Ruth prayed out loud for Meleeza. Behind her, the other women struggled to hold Jeanne back. She was threatening to run out there and 'kill that little bitch!'

The organist, who had played on longer than many thought he

should have, finally stopped and looked down from the balcony to see what all the commotion was about. He was nearly deaf from a lifetime on the pipe organ. He liked to lose himself in the soul-shattering vibrations and the pitch-dance of thick, layered pipes. Today was no exception.

Though intoxicated by something salient and strong that turned her limbs to jello, Meleeza's moves spoke of a confidence that her 17 years on the planet couldn't possibly have instilled in her as she wriggled out of her dress to an imaginary rhythm and slurred out a few more lyrics. She posed clumsily in the black bra and thong that Jason had bought her for Christmas, then peeled them off as well and tossed them at the two grandfatherly gentlemen who she allowed to creep closer.

Jason watched in disbelief from the back, his mother holding him firmly in her grasp to keep him from anywhere near Meleeza. Jason had a promising future and to his mother, Meleeza was nothing but trouble.

The first grandfatherly gentleman took off his blazer and held it open in front of him as he approached Meleeza's personal space.

"YOU STAY THE HELL AWAY FROM ME!" Meleeza roared. "BOTH OF YOU!"

"It's me, Meleeza. It's Mr. Wallace," the first grandfatherly gentleman pleaded. "You've been friends with my grandson Sha-Ron since you were six."

"Tell him Sha-Ron is a faggot. Tell him!"

"I don't care who you are. Sha-Ron's a FAGGOT!

"That's my girl."

I FUCKED him in the ASS with your DEAD MOTHER'S DICK!"

"Look at you, handin' out the zingers. I like it."

"Fuck you! You made me say that!" Meleeza cried, and for a moment or two, she seemed completely lucid. Grasping the sides of her head, she doubled over and yelled, "LEAVE ME ALONE!!!"

The remark clearly stunned Mr. Wallace, who nervously scanned the reactions of those who'd heard it.

"Please, Meleeza. You're not well."

"Tell him to go fuck himself."

"No! YOU'RE NOT WELL!!!! YOU'RE ALL NOT WELL!!! EVERY LAST ONE OF YOU FUCKING HYPOCRITES!"

"Behind you…."

From behind, a distinctly external voice lunged at her.

"Now calm down, Leeza. We're only trying to help you."

Meleeza whipped around to see another man, this one younger and much more intimidating than Mr. Wallace. The younger man walked with a hunch, partly to conceal the erection that threatened to burst through his dress slacks, his arms outstretched to keep her from trying to run past him.

"DON'T YOU FUCKING TOUCH ME!" She screamed and backed right into Mr. Wallace's arms. He immediately wrapped her in the jacket and muscled her into the rectory kicking and screaming all the way to catatonia.

"They're-coming-toget-youuu, Meleeza…."

Meleeza woke up propped against the bathroom sink. If she had to guess, she had been out for about 15 minutes. She immediately lashed out at the blurred hand that approached her face as if to smother her with the cloth that dangled from four fingers.

Ruth Gordon fell to her ass and glared. She turned and motioned to Mr. Wallace, who had already run up and crouched beside her, to hold Meleeza down.

"What the fuck are you doing?" Meleeza addressed them both as they pounced with geriatric dynamism. "Let go of me!"

The other women stood back and watched, threatened by the boom of their kinetic threesome and mortified to tears by the stark ugliness of the situation itself.

Meleeza yanked her left arm away from Mr. Wallace, grabbed him by the hair (he didn't have much), and sent him flying upside-down into the wall across the room.

He crumpled head first to the floor, unconscious.

Ruth Gordon took that as her cue to back away. As much as she wanted to help her, there wasn't much she could do with Meleeza raging like she was.

"Leeza… baby-girl…."

Ruth and Meleeza turned toward the door.

Standing with her hand behind her back and up under her shirt before a wall of wrinkled faces that were careful to keep their distance as they peeked in the doorway, Jeanne stood smiling from ear to ear, her thick mascara badly smeared from crying.

Draped only in Mr. Wallace's blazer, Meleeza climbed clumsily to her feet as if to initiate a challenge.

"What's-the-matter *MOTHER*? Did I embarrass you?" Meleeza was gleefully defiant. This was her moment. "Are you embarrassed that your sweet little *angel* didn't live up to your expectations? Well… ARE YOU!!!?"

Without moving, Jeanne's eyes responded, bearing down on her daughter as if she was a mere acquaintance whom Jeanne despised for some personal indiscretion left unresolved for years upon years.

"Or are you just mad because you couldn't find the needle? Hunh? Well, you want it so bad?" Meleeza reached between her legs and pulled a syringe from her vagina. "Then take it!"

Meleeza hurled the damp syringe at Jeanne, missing her completely.

Jeanne responded with a small, silver handgun that she brandished in her right hand the one that was hidden behind her back. She aimed it at Meleeza.

The old women in the doorway gasped so loudly that a few of them struggled to catch their breath afterward.

"I don't know who you are, but you are NOT my little angel," Jeanne mumbled, entranced. She had seen this day coming. "As of this moment, my daughter is dead."

"GODDAMMIT MOTHER! Don't you know that it's *your* fault I'm like this? Face it, MOTHER.... Everyone else knows you made me this way. YOU MADE ME THIS WAY!!!!"

Ruth Gordon swallowed her apprehension and placed herself between Jeanne and Meleeza. She crossed her arms at her chest and tried to appear unfazed.

"Now you listen to me, Jeanne. This is the Lord's house...."

Jeanne pulled the trigger without a moment's hesitation. The bullet caught Ruth right between the eyes and dropped her instantly.

Jeanne watched Ruth fall to the floor and begin to convulse, then calmly raised the gun and trained it on Meleeza.

Meleeza suddenly wretched and was overcome by a coughing fit. Clutching her stomach in her arms, she doubled over as it quickly escalated to full-on gagging.

Jason Williamson bolted into the bathroom (out of thin air, it seemed), and tackled Jeanne just as she pulled the trigger. The bullet smacked into the tile wall behind Meleeza and garnished her hair with a thin layer of dust.

Jeanne lay unconscious beneath Jason. The other women ran hysterically from the room.

Meleeza fell to her knees and lurched repeatedly before vomiting blood all over the floor.

Jason crab-walked away on his hands, feet, and ass as Meleeza belched whole organs onto the floor, caught in the rush of blackish blood that speckled the room: heart, lungs, liver, intestines she had to pull some of them out with her hands.

When it was all over, Meleeza reached out to Jason.

"Please don't leave me, baby. I'm scared. I don't know what's happening."

Jason was forced to rethink a great many things. Among them was the fact that he loved this girl in front of him and would've done anything for her. Now he wasn't so sure he even wanted her near him.

"Why are you looking at me like that, baby?" She whimpered, trying to direct his eyes away from the messy pile of internal organs at her feet. "Please help me. I don't know what to do!"

Jason jumped to his feet and continued to retreat backward. He eventually stumbled over Jeanne, who had just come to and was trying to sit up. On the way down, he watched as Jeanne raised her gun and let off a shot directly at Meleeza.

Meleeza's head snapped back violently, her hair whipping up to follow, and bounced down, chin to her chest.

A direct hit. But she did not fall.

Meleeza fingered the small, circular wound just above her twitching right eye and screamed.

Climbing to her feet, Jeanne fired again, and again, and struck Meleeza in the neck and abdomen, respectively.

Still, she did not fall.

Lurching backward under the influence of blunt lead biting deep, Meleeza continued to scream. When Jeanne was out of bullets, Meleeza ran out the door completely nude.

The street out front was teeming with cantankerous old men and women huddled beneath large umbrellas as they argued with a heavily armed, six-man S.W.A.T. team over the zombies who ambled about behind the fenced-in area along the right side of the building. The entire building was surrounded by the electrified security fencing (15 feet high and topped with whirling razor-wire) that they had recently pooled their money to purchase, but this separate area had been erected back in the mid-nineties to keep vandals from breaking in through the ground-level windows. It was essentially a five- by 25-foot external hallway enclosed by wrought-iron security bars and covered with canvas to keep the red rain out. It was just enough space to hold, say, 30 to 50 people. Thus, it doubled as a holding pen on Sundays to keep their loved ones, who teetered between the first and third stages of infection, from perpetual roam-and-stalk while they prayed inside.

"I know that you-all are just trying to do your jobs, but down here, we do things a little differently," an old man said to Lieutenant Barry, a barrel-chested, alpha-male stereotype and the leader of the S.W.A.T team that poured out of the old ice-cream truck that had been repainted and marked "Collection/Disposal."

The old man was unaware that his action had elected him spokesman for the parishioners by default. He was alluding to the zombies in the "holding pen" and, more specifically, the improvised muzzles and ball-gags that kept them from using their mouths should they feel the urge to bite down on something living.

"Are you out of your fucking minds?" a young S.W.A.T officer blurted out, his voice muffled by the helmet and visor that fogged up when he spoke. "Those puss-bags are no more your loved ones than I am. You think they won't take a nice, healthy chunk out of your asses if they had the chance?"

"Maybe so, but…"

"But nothing."

"Hold on, Stevenson," Lieutenant Barry ordered.

"But…"

"I said enough! Now… there's really no need to be belligerent, officer. We are simply here to do a job." Lieutenant Barry made sure to involve the entire crowd in his optic sweep, handing out eyes of inclusion to most if not all of them and even smiling to loosen up the more tight-mugged fuddy-duddies. "I'm sure these people understand that."

It was hard to hear any of what they were saying through those damn visors, but Lieutenant Barry's voice seemed to be the easiest to understand, and his eyes, which were equally hard to see through the smudges and smears of blood, looked the most sincere of the bunch.

"These people???????????" cried a tobacco-stained voice from the crowd behind the old man.

The old man half-expected a riot, but Lieutenant Barry was black, so there was a chance his remark might just blow over.

"I'm sorry, ma'am," Lieutenant Barry said with a gentlemanly nod, "that was a bad choice of words."

"Nice save," the old man squeezed out the side of his mouth and underneath the crowd's geriatrically hampered radar.

Lieutenant Barry smiled. "What's your name, sir? I'm Lieutenant Barry, but you can call me Gabe." He extended his hand.

A few of the old fuddy-duddies in the back had something to say about how quickly the old man reciprocated the gesture. Trust was harder than ever to come by these days.

"Charles... Charles Donner," the old man said.

"Well Mr. Donner," Lieutenant Barry started.

"Charles...."

"Excuse me?"

"I was saying to call me Charles," Charles reiterated in his typically disarming cadence. "Well, actually, everyone here just calls me Old Charlie. That's fine too."

"Okay. Well, Charles... Officer Stevenson here is only worried, as are the rest of us, that you won't be able to control them for long."

"I know. But it would seem that we all don't have much longer. To many of the parishioners here those... 'puss-bags'...are the only family they have. And who's to say that Uncle Sam won't come out with some kind of treatment, or cure in the near future. Certainly we owe them the chance."

"They'll probably want an arm and a leg for it too," one of the women shouted.

"Oh, and in the meantime they get to walk around craving flesh like it was crack? Thanks, but I'll take death any day," Stevenson remarked.

"You got that right," another muffled voice added.

Lt. Barry watched the zombies meander about in the holding pen, bumping into and tripping over one another. He had grown up in an area much like this one, so even though he disagreed with the Old Charlie Donner and the church-black folk, he understood their strong sense of familial loyalty.

Turning to his men, Lieutenant Barry waved them on.

"Let's go."

"What, are you kidding?" Stevenson whined. "You give me one good reason why we shouldn't vaporize every last one of those things!"

Lieutenant Barry pulled Stevenson aside and leaned in close enough to speak softly.

"Respect is hard enough to come by down here without people like us making things harder, especially with all that's going on. I don't think it's going to do much to affect the grand scheme of things if we let these people honor their dead the way they see fit. And if things get out of hand, well, then that's on them. I'm pretty sure they're aware of that."

A pair of large, firm breasts were the first things that most of the men saw when the double doors swung open and Meleeza ran, naked and screaming, out into the street. Within seconds, she was covered in blood. It appeared to jump down from the sky with more enthusiasm now that she was a potential target.

Inside, Jason attempted to rationalize what he saw, his mind divided equally between that and watching Jeanne closely. She was slumped against the far wall, hair down over her face as she cried and giggled at the same time. She was still holding her gun… and she was never shy about her dislike for him. He wasn't light-skinned enough for her daughter.

Jason wondered whether or not he should run.

Jeanne's brown eyes were locked on Jason from the moment she lifted her head and spotted him. The intensity with which they scrutinized him caused Jason to shift and reestablish himself. They rolled to the side and down at Ruth, who lay dead in a pool of her own blood.

"Never did like that bitch," Jeanne muttered, lifting the gun to her chin.

Jason considered trying to stop her.

BLAM!

Even though she was clearly dead, or damn close to it, after the first shot, Jason still expected Jeanne to point the gun at him. As he watched her hand fall, his mind gave it a cinematic grace that slowed the downward motion of her arm to a crawl and amplified the sound of contact when the gun finally hit the floor. The heat from the barrel birthed a thin wisp of smoke that rose from where the tip kissed the sheer drapes that hung from the window and eventually conjured up a tiny flame that grew before his eyes. He was about to run when Ruth sat up and looked around as if she didn't know where she was, a thick stream of blood draining from the circular wound between her eyes, and even more from the matted exit wound at the back left side of her head.

To most of the church, Ruth was 'part of the family,' and Jason's view was no different, having known her since he was a child. Hence he found it difficult to look at her as a threat when she smiled at him, her eyes clouded over, lips curling back to reveal long, thin, coffee-stained teeth. She spoke his name as if the mere sound of it ignited her libido, or her appetite.

Pushing off with his hands, Jason jumped up and sprinted out the door. From his peripheral vision he saw Ruth crawl over to Jeanne's corpse, but when she sat up as well, Ruth paused, confused. He looked back to see both of them gawking at him curiously as if they weren't sure whether to ask him for help or try to eat him.

Outside, cars screeched to avoid hitting Meleeza, who ran in and out of traffic and finally down an adjacent residential neighborhood with a crowd of well-dressed men and S.W.A.T officers thirsting for action hot on her trail.

In Meleeza's eyes, *the crowd was out for blood. Their faces had warped into demonic caricatures of themselves: exaggerated frowns, mouths stretched a little too wide, eyes completely white. They snarled and cackled as they chased her.*

Searching frantically as she ran, Meleeza found a wall of shoulder-high shrubs that separated one rundown property from another. She crouched behind the bushes and covered her mouth to muffle her loud sobbing.

An older gentleman crept along the sidewalk on the other side of the bushes, his rickety, old umbrella telegraphing his arrival as it bobbed above the tops of the shrubs.

Something made him stop and turn in her direction.

"That you in there, Leeza???"

The nice old gentleman looks demonic in Meleeza's eyes. He smiled and lunged at her. "Girlie, you look good enough to eat," he said, his voice waterlogged, his lips moving out of sync with it.

Meleeza burst screaming from the bushes. The old gentleman tried rather sheepishly to hold onto her, but she yanked her arm free and ran between two parked cars and right out into the path of an SUV going close to 40 in a 25 mph zone.

Inside the SUV, Debra Keirny had her arms folded across her chest, her chin turned up and to the right, the way she usually did when she was mad at her husband, Cliff. This time, they were discussing their stagnant sex life.

"And what a time to be bringin' this up." That was her answer no matter when he broached the subject; only now, it actually seemed justified. Still, Cliff was determined to make her face up to her aversion to discussing anything halfway titillating.

Vague as Cliff was about wanting her to be more open-minded, they both knew what he really meant. He was just too repressed himself to come out and say it.

Debra saw the way his eyes darted to her and back whenever the topic of a threesome crept up from behind the normal malaise of the tired sitcoms they liked to watch together, or the way he always asked her opinion of this girl and that, masked as an insult that usually started with, "Now why would she think a guy would go for that look?"

Debra wasn't totally against the idea. She wasn't above the occasional thought of what it would be like with another woman. Her reluctance had more to do with the fact that after six years, she fucking hated it when Cliff touched her. She gave him every signal in the world that she was unhappy, but as long as he got his weekly piece-a-ass, he couldn't give a shit about her problems. He was more concerned with having enough beer and watching TV news updates instead of looking her in the eyes while he fucked her like he held a grudge. And for some reason, she still felt obligated to spread her legs for him. Something about his money. Cliff Keirny was the founder of the Strange Fruit Smoothie and Juice Bar chain. They were popping up all over the East Coast before the shit hit the fan. Cliff was able to parlay it into a steady gig feeding the collection/disposal groups in the aftermath.

Debra only saw his shortcomings.

In the distance, the sound of tires screeching served as background fodder for Debra's busy thoughts until the bite of tiny glass shards stung her into the present. The next thing she knew, she was damn-near performing cunnilingus on Meleeza Duncan, who had flown through the windshield and landed upside-down on top of her. The impact forced Debra's mouth open as her lungs cried out with a definitive "OOMPH!" Although she was quick to ball her lips and turn away, she had unfortunately been given a taste of Meleeza's unshaven pubic region along with a large helping of her own dislodged teeth and blood from her newly shattered lower jaw moving freely beneath her skin.

Cliff stomped on the brakes. Up until then, he'd only been pumping the pedal like his father taught him. He would've done it sooner, but he was coping with irony manifested in the seat beside him. Even with the shock, the sudden jolt of adrenaline, and the ramifications of what he'd just witnessed, Cliff found himself with a hard-on.

If it weren't for her seat belt, Debra would've been launched through what remained of the windshield along with Meleeza's flopping corpse when the SUV came to a dead stop. Instead, her face met the dash with a CRACK!

Meleeza landed in a folded mess and slid until friction's makeover left her looking nothing like her former self. She lay facing up, legs spread, eyes burned away, facial features rubbed to a loose, lumpy texture. In her wake, a moist red trail extended back 36 feet. To the people watching from their second-floor windows, it looked like jet-wash bursting from the exhaust of some flesh-covered rocket ship.

"LEEZA! NO!" Jason yelled, pushing against the wall of tentative spectators who were wandering closer and closer.

Lieutenant Barry was right behind him, followed closely by Stevenson and the rest of the team.

Meleeza was barely alive and drowning in her own blood. She choked and spit as she tried to catch her breath. Jason stood over her for a full 30 seconds without so much as a thought to propel him forward, punch-drunk by her appearance and by the awful sounds she made. Bleeding rain soaked him from head to toe and caused him to shiver.

It hurt Jason physically to see her like this reached right into his chest and fist-fucked his heart. It left him feeling like he wanted to make the journey along with her, or in her place.

With horrified eyes, Jason knelt down beside his high-school sweetheart, searching along the way for an undamaged spot to place his arm and lift her to a reclined position.

"I'm so sorry, baby," he whimpered, sliding his arm around her neck, where the flesh had been burned away. He had pulled his sleeve down and stretched it over his hand, thumb clamping down to hold it there. Yet the moist, lumpy texture still seeped through. He was more concerned that cotton might feel better against her wound.

Jason could tell by the swell of her chest that Meleeza recognized his voice. Her mouth was no more than a hole surrounded by loose skin so she couldn't speak beyond a few slurps and grunts and desperate shrieking that moved him to tears.

Jason began to rock as he held her in his arms. He pulled her close to him and laid his head on top of hers as she faded away.

A sudden rise in body temperature, a peaking of adrenaline that rose tiny bumps up and down his arms, swept across the fleshy landscape of Jason's body and ultimately submerged to investigate the depths of him just before Meleeza went limp. With it came the feeling that he was being watched. If it was true that life never really ended, only changed planes of existence, and this feeling belonged to Meleeza's passing, then why did it leave him with an erection, a massive headache, and the gestating urge to hurt someone just for the hell of it?

A few blocks away, badly aged voices rose to a crescendo. It was coming from the church, but that didn't matter to Jason, who tightened his embrace as he rocked, his mind lost in the fleshy oneness of their bodies pressed together, her aura growing cold by the second and siphoning his elevated body heat.

As the crowd dispersed, Jason timed their trip back to St. Salacious and waited with his eyes squeezed shut for some kind of reaction. What he got was more screams, born of pain instead of fear or shock. Soon after that he heard gunshots.

Probably zombies, he thought, rather nonchalantly. The commotion must have brought them out of hiding, or wherever it was they went when there was nothing to eat around.

In fact, 21st and Parish was alive with zombies, most of them in the later stages, from deep second-degree to full-blown. They oozed out of narrow alleyways, stumbled from abandoned houses and store-fronts, and crawled up from under mounds of garbage left to collect in the neighborhoods where abandoned buildings outnumbered the occupied ones. Those who weren't ready to lower themselves to cannibalism just yet wandered in circles of perpetual stupor, trying to fathom a clear thought through the rapid degradation, and staring at one another like infants made to see their reflection for the first time.

A disorganized huddle of old, black church-ladies begged anyone within earshot to open the gates to the holding area. It and their loved ones were completely engulfed in flames that hissed and cackled over their pitiful moaning and their attempts to cry out names that they couldn't remember, or even pronounce if they had.

Awash in angry flames, rotting arms reached out through the diamond-shaped links of the fence.

A ripe ol' head exploded just as the zombie to whom it belonged threw its blackened jaws open and lunged at the old woman who did nothing but stand there with her arm over her face. Instead of thanking the S.W.A.T. officer who pulled the trigger, she collapsed to the ground and expired, her heart startled to sleep by the experience… and the blood. It was all over her.

"Alright. Listen up!" Lieutenant Barry commanded. "On my mark, I want a path cut through these bastards, right down the middle, heading east."

"Yes sir!" His squad responded in unison.

Taking out the kneecaps, or the base of the spine, then burning them was the preferred method. Some people swore by their flamethrowers, but they were hard to come by and didn't provide the immediate stopping power of the good-ol' Berserker, with a flame-grenade chaser.

With his arm extended to the side and bent at a 45-degree angle, Lieutenant Barry counted down with his fingers: three… two…

Spotting two old women standing too close to the holding area, Lieutenant Barry pivoted toward them.

"Step away from the fence!" He blared and tapped the trigger gently, just enough to shred that arm that reached for the first woman right from its socket.

"Why????? Why????????" the woman lamented. "My poor Eduardo! Poor, sweet, Eddie-bear…."

Lieutenant Barry tried yelling to her to look what "poor Eddie-bear" had done to her friend who lay behind her, covered in her own blood. Apparently, he yanked her arm clean off at mid-bicep trying to pull himself out of the fire.

As the remaining parishioners struggled to stand and take cover (those of them who were still able to do so), they each felt almost obligated to stop and marvel at what had become of their church. The place was completely overcome by fire. The flames roared with such zeal that they drowned out the wailing of broken old women and philandering hypocrites disguised as good, upstanding men of God.

Back at the scene of the accident, Jason continued to rock Meleeza in his arms. All around him, slow, shuffling footsteps drew closer, raspy voices played at familiar sounds, but Jason Williamson refused to open his eyes and look. Better to use his imagination and travel to someplace peaceful.

*　　*　　*

Jason Williamson, who had been waiting for at least an hour, painted invisible murals upon the flat-gray wall in his mind. Being from the 'hood, he had an almost inborn mistrust of the police that was evident in the look of anxiety he returned when Kane entered Interro-

gation Room B and nodded hello as walked over to the table, slid out a folding chair, and sat down at the opposite end.

"Sorry to keep you waiting, Mr. Wilkinson," Kane began.

"Williamson," Jason responded. "I was starting to think you guys had forgotten about me in here." His uneasiness shined through in his unwillingness to totally commit to the joke.

"You never know in this place."

Silence.

"That was a joke, son."

"Sorry for not laughing. From where I'm sitting, nothing seems all that funny."

"Fair enough. I assure you though that I'm only here to ask you a few questions about your relationship with Meleeza."

"Okay. Whatever you want to know…."

"Good. Glad to see that you have the right attitude. It'll make this a lot easier."

"For *you,* maybe."

Panting out an off-handed chuckle, Kane perused Jason's file longer than necessary, just because he could. It was a little trick he liked to use to shake up a potential suspect; however, in Jason's case, it was just out of habit.

"So, in the statement you gave at the crime scene last week, you mentioned that as far as you knew, Meleeza hadn't been using."

"That's right. It ain't like she wasn't fiendin' every once and awhile, but I never would've thought.… "

Jason's throat, full of mucus, worked in accord with muscles constricting the rhythm of sorrow to shut him up.

"And is it correct that you had done drugs, including U4, with her in the past?"

Jason's trepidation was catalyst for Kane to gaze beyond his large liquid irises centered with whirlpools of brown glass, beyond a stare that had an intensity that Jason had yet to master, beyond an archetypal angry-black-male expression that was intriguing in a way that was all his own. Down here hid someone much deeper than just some run-of-the-mill street thug-in-the-making.

Jason slouched in his chair fumbling with the edges of his button-down shirt and directed a pointed stare at the ceiling.

"Don't sweat it, son. I was a teenager once myself. At this point, I really don't care what you've done in the past."

"It's not that I'm afraid of... well, I don't want to go to jail or anything, but more than that, I can't help feeling sort of responsible for what happened to her. I think about it every day."

"If that's the case, then why haven't you tried to see her?"

Troubled by what seemed like a lack of humanity on his part, Jason's eyes began to water.

"It's just that... I mean, she's dead. We've known each other since we were kids, and to see her like that, and to know that she's walking around like one of those things...."

"I can assure you that the one thing she's not doing is walking around."

Not only did the SUV shatter her spine, leaving her paralyzed from the neck down, but also her brain was fried from whatever had happened to her. Officially, they were calling it an OD; however, Kane had his doubts. Though she was conscious, in the living-dead sense, she was little more than an angry vegetable.

"Look, there's so much going on right now that I don't know if I can handle seeing her like that."

"Actually, you seem a lot more mature and intelligent than I thought."

Jason's mind automatically jumped to race as a factor in that judgment, and the thought of it ignited a twinge of anger. Even he was guilty of passing race-based judgment on some of his peers, but he was trained to view it differently when it came from someone who wasn't black. It was a cycle that he'd been trying to break.

"Okay, well, why don't you tell me a little about your relationship with Meleeza?"

"We had been fighting a lot lately because I got accepted to college in Ohio, and she was moving to New York to focus on her career. She was really upset about that. Leeza didn't have too many friends. I'm mean, don't get me wrong, she knew everybody and everybody knew her, but because of her crazy-ass mom, she never really had time for friends. Neither of us did, really."

"So, you each had each other."

"Exactly…. It's not like I was some kind of introvert or something. Me and my brother Mikel… we used to run the streets like the rest of these knuckleheads, but… well, when I was like nine or 10, I got jumped for my lunch money. They really handed me my ass that day, broke my nose, my jaw, cracked a few ribs. And the embarrassing part was that they held me up with a fucking butter knife. These were kids we knew from the neighborhood, too. It really changed me for a while there. I was lashing out at teachers and shit. Man, it was awful. Mikel wanted to get some of his boys and go kick their asses, but my mom, she begged him not to. After that she got crazy-overprotective. All we did from then on was watch TV. After awhile, Mikel got into sports, and she eventually eased up on him. But me… she ain't let my ass go anywhere. That's how I got all geeked-out into filmmaking."

"I'm sorry to hear that. You seem to have dealt with it in a positive way, though."

"Yeah, like I said, I was a kid. Not much I could've done about it at the time so why dwell on it. It definitely wasn't easy though. Remember what I said about denial? Well, we were raised by three sheltered women, two of whom were religious, one to the point of fanaticism. They lost their mother at a young age and were raised by their alcoholic father, my grandfather, whose house we all lived in."

"Yet you and your brother persevered…."

"I guess. I was so pissed off after that that most of my friends thought I'd eventually become some kind of serial killer, and for a while, I probably was headed in that direction. I went through this phase where I was obsessed with horror flicks. I mean really obsessed. If it hadn't been for Mikel, then I might have turned out wrong."

With each revelation, Kane found himself warming to Jason's intangible charm.

"Ever consider becoming a cop?"

"No offense, but you guys play by too many rules. These muthafuckas out here, they don't give a fuck about my rights, or your rights, but you damn sure better not violate theirs. That's bullshit. The world would be a better place without some of the niggas we grew up with."

"You know... you remind me of myself at your age." Kane understood completely where Jason's head was: young, and full of vigor. It was a place that Kane often longed to revisit. "It sounds like you've come a long way. You should be proud."

"And I did most of it on my own. My brother Mikel was doing his own thing, and I kind of think he felt like it was his fault, the beat-down and all."

"So, tell me, how exactly did you and Meleeza meet?"

Leaning back as if to literally sink into the memory, a smile, unfettered by pride, leaked wider as the slant of Jason's torso increased.

"It was at church camp of all places. I think we were about 10 or 11. But we didn't really look at each other like that until the arts workshop when we were 15. Well, she was 15; I'm actually a year older... er, nine months older. The workshop was like... an after-school/weekend thing for inner-city kids. I was there for filmmaking and Leeza for song and dance. I have to say, the one thing my mom did do was believe in my dream."

"Was Meleeza using then?"

For a moment, Jason forgot that he was talking to a cop.

"Hey man, she wasn't just some fuckin' junkie. It was her mom who drove her to that shit. Everybody knew it."

"Some people seem to think that you were the one who turned

her on to drugs."

"Me! Oh, I see how it is… you loosen me up with all that fake-ass interest, then you go in for the kill."

"To be honest, yes, that's usually how I do it. Look… I know that you didn't have anything to do with her death, but in order for me to find out who *did,* I've got to explore every possible avenue."

Kane turned his forearm over and glanced at his watch.

"I promise I'll have you out of here in five minutes, okay?"

Jason nodded.

Max Hedberg's Journal

Entry #5

Christ, if only I could go back a month, or two, or five. It scares me that I no longer have a grasp on time.

I was going to ask Maria to take a sick day with me so that we could catch up on that quality time that she was always going on and on about. I got the impression that she was trying to tell me something, something that I knew I probably didn't want to hear. She had been bitching a lot lately about this and that (no quality time, feeling trapped, or bored, taken for granted). Part of me feels like it was her way of saying that I repulsed her, but then I think of the Big Fat Man.

I guess I already knew what her answer would be, that it was tax season and that she couldn't possibly even consider taking a day until April 15th. Maria was an accountant in case you haven't figured it out yet.

If I had it to do over again, I'd find some way to make her stay home. Hell, if I could take a day, as much as I worked, then she definitely could. If she had stayed home, the homeless man whom she passed every day on her way to the lot on 2nd and Chestnut wouldn't have bitten her. Apparently she was riding high from her promotion to partner when instead of ignoring him, she decided that today she did indeed have spare change, "for something to eat."

Something to eat... Yeah, right.

I was so preoccupied with planning a special dinner to celebrate that I didn't even pay attention to the warning signs. For the record, she went right to bed that night. I was so pissed that I didn't even consider that she might be telling the truth when she said she wasn't feeling well. Dinner⬜. What I wouldn't do for something to eat. These candy bars just aren't cutting it alone; one bite-size per meal, or sometimes two.

The next morning, Maria complained of nausea, dizziness, and cold chills, but I blew it off. I thought she might be trying to cover her ass for last night's excuse. For the first time in eight years, I began to entertain the thought that she might be having an affair. Up until then, I had only suspected that she wanted out of the marriage. Whew ... you wouldn't believe how hard it was to write that...

Entry #6

I'm starving, down to my last candy bar. The cramping in my gut is becoming impossible to bear now. I could literally eat a horse.

I was holding out hope that I would somehow get this fucking door open when we last spoke, so... well, fuck it. I was in denial. If you saw this fucking door....

The thing is top of the line, two feet of rein-forced steel with a double-bolted locking system. The last time I came down, I had to call Maria to come and punch in the code from the outside just to get me out.
I'm starting to think that this place might be my coffin. I'm guessing I'll eventually die of hunger, as I never stocked the freezer. Like I said, who knew...

who fucking knew...?

Try not to laugh too hard when you find me. I doubt you'd have done it any differently. Okay, so maybe you would've gotten the damn door fixed in the first place. I'll give you that, but assuming you didn't....

I'm trying to imagine how I must look to you. Hopefully it's been long enough that we've all had time to rot down to our pearly whites. A skeleton seems more dignified than a rotting corpse, don't you think? Maybe they still walk around at that stage. The movies haven't really addressed that one have they? Maybe I'll be walking around ~~when they~~... when you find me. Christ, I hope not.

In any case, you probably can't tell now, but I was a pretty good-looking guy. From my childhood through my teens, I was the biggest doofus you've ever seen. Then, somewhere between 19 and 23, I just changed. It literally happened overnight. I guess you'd call me a very late bloomer.

I was so into my books at the time that I didn't even notice. It took a few awkward missteps before I learned to use it to my advantage with the ladies, but once I did, I spent the next year and a half catching up. I almost fucked my chances of getting into the University of Pennsylvania but buckled down at the last minute and slid in by the skin of my teeth.

Skin of my teeth??? That's a funny saying, don't you think?

Anyway, it's these looks that got me a babe like Maria, 5'6", black and Polynesian mixed, athletic, long jet-black hair. She was still bouncing back from giving birth to Eric, but I had come to enjoy the baby weight. She only had about 10 pounds to go before she was back to her normal weight of 123. Most of it was in her hips and ass, but she wore it well. Maria had the kind of slender, hourglass figure that a little extra meat comple-mented in a way that made me understand what the black guys saw in thick legs and plump asses.

Oh wait, I hear Eric saying something. Gotta go.

Chapter 4

Press Conference, June 6, 2015

Christian Media Broadcasting Corporate Headquarters

Houston, Texas

Even if you liked the guy, you had to admit that Reverend Jesse James Dallas looked like a 5'11" toddler made of porcelain, from his spit-polished shoes to his bulletproof lid, like a helmet of hair fused and hardened and buffed to a glossy sheen. He had this way of lunging forward with big movements when he spoke, especially when he knew he was the center of attention. He liked grand displays to punctuate his gloom-and-doom rhetoric, delivered with comic-book-narrator cadence. At his state-of-the-art Christian Cathedral in Houston, he was never shy about his lavish taste. He was known to end his sermons with exploding pyrotechnics and/or dancing laser-light.

Draped in an expensive-looking suit, a blonde fellow (Jesus) with delicate features and beguiling eyes that beckoned to everyone and everything they fell upon to submit to their anesthetizing spell, sat a few feet from Reverend Dallas. Pouring like a golden waterfall down from the top of his head on either side, Jesus' hair teased the alabaster cliff-face with its wire-wisped touch. The brilliant yellow hues reflected off his fair skin and made it glow. Flowing way past narrow shoulders, it moved (whenever he moved) with estrogenic panache that didn't go unnoticed, like the effeminate inflections in his speech. Neither was ever questioned.

The long wooden table that they sat behind was overflowing with tangled wire that led up to a tight jumble of phallic microphones tilted at a slant to zero in on open mouths like some multiheaded cephalopod floating before a dark crevice.

"Could I be so bold as to ask where you've been for the past..." The weak-jawed reporter perused his notepad, "...2000 years?"

"C'mon, people." Steve Sommerville, from the BBC, was always causing trouble, but usually in a way that inspired deep thought. "Are we so naïve as to accept this man's claims without a thorough investigation into his background?"

Discordant grumbling swirled out like shockwaves from where he stood and traveled out to infect the whole room—auditorium, actually. Moving rigidly, with awkward pauses, like a thinking man forced to emote, Steve Sommerville rubbernecked to meet the impassioned verbal wallops that leapt out of rage-wrought grimaces, attempting in false-start fashion to defend his question while simultaneously searching for support in the eyes of his more logical colleagues. There were a few. Even if they didn't have the balls to stand publicly defiant by his side, he could see it in their eyes. He considered outing them but left that as a last option.

"Sit down!"

"Have some respect!"

"Why don't you go join your cronies out in the lobby?"

The voice was referring to two groups mainly: the Secular Soldiers, which was made up of scientists, doctors, intellectuals, and atheists, and the Coalition for Spiritual Diversity, which claimed a vast membership of left-wing politicians, activists within the entertainment industry, and leaders from various religions, both mainstream and alternative, each with their own group of devoted followers. The Jews and the liberal Christians were the most predominant.

To Jesus, the Coalition was the more dangerous of the two. It was easy to dismiss the Secular Soldiers with carefully worded summations on faith, and its power: something that science could never wrap its logical fingers around. "Pulling out the faith-card," one scientist called it.

The Coalition was different. They had money, power, influence, and, most of all, faith, plenty of it, only not in this incarnation of Christ. Constant infighting hampered their development, however, and left them somewhat disorganized.

"Like the blacks these days, they art thine own worst enemy," Jesus told Reverend Dallas when he expressed concern over their efforts to discredit him.

Both groups were barred from entering the press conference, along with a motley crew of individual atheists, goofy self-proclaimed prophets, and plain-old angry folks who placed their families' well being over their beliefs. Sometimes it was hard to hear inside the auditorium due to the general ruckus outside in the lobby as the unruly crowd argued with security.

On the stage, Reverend Dallas cupped his hand over the microphone closest to him and whispered something to Jesus, who reacted with a nod.

"Look. I was raised a Catholic just like many of you in this room." Steve Sommerville's voice swelled and settled to an even tone, and swelled again as the insults continued to fly, forcing him to speak over their raised voices. "But despite our personal beliefs, we, as purveyors of unbiased information, have a duty to approach this from a logical perspective, devoid of emotional commitment."

"The man has proven his case. What more do you want?"

"Faith…. Faith, ladies and gentlemen," Reverend Dallas bellowed into the mic. "I'm not hearing a lot of faith in here tonight. Let this man have his say. Ain't no chinks in this here armor."

"Having said that…." Steve began.

Someone yelled. "Let's hear *your* explanation about how he walked on water, or made the rain stop, then. Hidden cables? Holograms?"

As an "Act of Mercy," the headlines read, Jesus had made the bleeding rain subside with a wave of his hand two days ago.

Picking up where he left off, Steve tried again, "HAVING SAID THAT... my question to you, sir, is one of race, and geography."

"Oh please!"

"You're embarrassing yourself, Steven."

Steve flinched at the sudden iron grip that clamped down on his wrist. Tensing his arm straight, he turned to see a muscle-bound security guard glaring down at him.

"Why don't we all just hear the man out?" said the young brunette with the wide mouth and the sinful shape. She looked like someone who spent a lot of time at the gym.

Silence....

"What's your name, young lady?" Reverend Dallas inquired with his usual larger-than-life charm.

"Melanie Hargrove," she replied. "I'm with WTXN in Philadelphia."

"I've heard of you, Ms. Hargrove," he said. "You've got spunk. That kind of energy, if channeled correctly, will take you farther than any degree. Remember that."

Steve had heard of her too. She was the ballsy young ingénue with ambition written all over her self-assured mug. His inner chauvinist led him to believe she would be more bookish, like Tina Fey, the Saturday Night Live alumna who had run for governor of New York a few years back. He had a thing for that type. Though he and his logical approach were still vastly in the minority, Steve found comfort in Melanie Hargrove's bravery.

Melanie came off as slightly insulted from where Steve stood, watching her every move along with everyone else in the room.

"Thank you," she said.

Though she smiled, she snatched her face stoic before her ass hit the chair and rolled her eyes when she thought no one was looking.

Huh... Steve had forgotten about the security guard.

He yanked his arm away from the husky man and glared spitefully as he rubbed it. Steve wasn't much of a fighter, but he'd sue your ass if you touched him.

"Don't make me have to…." The security guard lunged.

"No!" Jesus called down from the stage. "Let the misguided one speak."

"Thank you," Steve said, glaring around the room until every last sidebar trailed off into the atmosphere and danced a toxic waltz with the garish fragrances that welcomed them into the fold.

As a means of fighting the prevalent stench of dead things, people were known to overdose on cologne, perfume, and body sprays. Together, the scents created an aromatic nightmare that rivaled the zombie-funk.

"My question is one that you've been asked before but never managed to answer… to my satisfaction at least. And that is, how do you explain that a man born in Bethlehem, Israel looks… well, like you?"

For the first time since Jesus entered the room, he seemed slightly annoyed.

"I have many guises, my child," Jesus said, "What thou doth witness before thee is the one that the majority of people find most appealing."

"So, then, what do you really look like?"

"Art thou certain that thou wants to know, Mr. Sommerville?"

"I think I've got a good idea what you'd really look like, and his name is Yeshua," yelled Steve Sommerville.

"Aw, for Pete's sake."

"Please, Steven, give it a rest."

"Where is he, then?" Jesus leaned closer to the jumble of microphones and spoke with a sudden intensity. "Why didst he refuse the invitation to come here and meet with ye today? Why hast he failed to provide a sample of his DNA for testing as I did?"

"That's right," Reverend Dallas added. "And, furthermore, let this be an open invitation to the man to come out of hiding and submit to the same tests. I'm only a phone call away."

Steve was ashamed that he didn't have an immediate response. He figured his hesitation would be the final nail in his figurative coffin.

"Could you at least tell us why you've chosen to align yourself with someone as… controversial as Reverend Dallas, then?" *Ah, pure gold*, Steve thought. The question came to him at the last minute. He knew everyone had wanted to ask it.

"You want quality product, you go to the top of the line, right?" Reverend Dallas blurted with a heaping dose of Texas swagger. His publicist had been nagging him about toning it down now that the whole world was watching.

"Thank you, Reverend, but I was speaking to Jesus."

Reverend Dallas smacked his palms down on the table and rose slightly, ready to   dish out his unique brand of insults disguised as constructive criticism and paused in response to the warm hand that seemed to materialize on his shoulder.

"It was the Reverend's faith that allowed him to accept me without question on the first day, when no one else would."

"You sure it wasn't his greed?" Steve blurted out.

The room erupted into cantankerous grumbling directed at Steve who batted down harsh words and wickedness eyes with a look of steadfast defiance.

From the right, he spied the security guard hurrying back over to him, arm extended, fingers separating in preparation to clamp down on his puny bicep or the surrounding area.

"It doesn't concern you that the Reverend here has twice confessed to paying for sex," Steve added, rushing his words out. "Not to mention that his views on race relations in this country border on…"

"Little man, why art thou wasting my time with this?" Jesus spoke calmly yet his words swept through the room like a tidal wave of masculine chest-pounding delivered with a curiously feminine sting that hinted at "scorned-bitch" type wickedness. "If it is undeniable proof that thy mind desires, then so be it."

Just like that, Steve Sommerville went from controlled defiance to white as a ghost. The look on his face was like something that a terminal diagnosis might induce, ever twisting in response to unfathomable things that sprinted through his head, and testing his tolerance to emotional pain.

Steve yelped out loud in a cowardly pitch and collapsed to his chair in a heap of tears and violent sobbing. To maintain what dignity he had left, he buried his head in his lap and shook the emotion out quietly, for the most part.

The entire time Jesus remained stone-faced. Most of the room had never seen this side of him. It left them speechless, imagining what kinds of unspeakable things Jesus had shown Steve Sommerville as proof.

"To answer the first man's question," Jesus said, startling them with his sudden swipe at silence, "5000 years is but a day to me. I have always been here, walking amongst ye, watching, waiting for the right time to return."

"Why a homeless man?" an anonymous reporter shouted. "Why not someone of the cloth?"

"Over the centuries, I've found that people are more honest when dealing with those whom they consider beneath them," Jesus replied. "And I've always been more interested in honesty."

"What about the dead?" Melanie Hargrove brought the atmosphere 360 degrees. "I mean, no offense, but because you were in such a generous mood two days ago, why didn't you rid us of that menace as well?"

"That, young lady, is beyond my control."

"Beyond your control??????" she replied in an unconvinced tone that provoked   multiple gasps from the crowd. "Correct me if I'm mistaken, but it's always been my understanding that this whole phenomenon the bleeding rain, the dead was all related to your return as stated in the Book of Revelations."

"It was my father's wish that I stop the rain, both as an act of mercy and as a demonstration of his absolute power lest those who put their faith in science and logic manifest any further doubt. As for the dead… they, like all of ye everyone except for Mr. Sommerville and thee, it seems have come to honor the glory that is my father's holy presence in this living vessel thou witness before thee. For me to interfere without his blessing would anger him."

"For the sake of time, I would like to get to the 'meat and potatoes' of this press conference," Reverend Dallas interjected, glancing down at his watch. "So if you'll please hold any further questions until after the announcement has been made…."

With that, Reverend Dallas turned to Jesus and nodded.

"Ah… excuse me," said a meek-mannered reporter who stood when the crowd turned in unison to face him. "My name is Glen Browning, from the New England Daily Times. I'm sorry to interrupt, but I have a question that I think most of us in this room would like to know the answer to."

Reverend Dallas cupped his hand over the microphone and leaned closer to Jesus.

"What is thy question, Mr. Browning?" Jesus responded before Reverend Dallas could whine at him about the time.

"My question is… well it's about Hell… and the Devil." Even with Jesus sitting not 50 feet from him, Glen felt silly uttering that name, like he expected his colleagues to laugh at him. "Could you give us an idea of what *it*… and *he* the Devil, I mean is like?"

Jesus smiled as if he held onto a dirty little secret.

"The concepts of Heaven and Hell that ye all art familiar with are misrepresentations, mere fantasies and nightmares fabricated by mortal men with vastly creative minds. If thou art curious to know what Hell is really like, well then, Mr. Browning, I suggest thou take a walk outside."

There was a sudden rise in the undercurrent of whispered

chattering, a precise boom of gasping and proclamations of shock, surprise, and dismay.

"And the Devil?" Glen Browning added.

"His name… is Yeshua," Jesus responded.

Once again, the crowd erupted.

"Fear not, my children," Jesus said, speaking over the vocal unrest, "for this is the very reason that you all were summoned here today. Let it be known from this day forth that December 25th of this year will mark the day that ye shall all be judged. Those of ye deemed worthy will reside in a new city, safe from the walking death, safe from this culture of immorality to which many of ye have grown accustomed, a city constructed by God's love manifested in the blood, sweat, and tears of those who chose not to accept me into their hearts. Their punishment will be to serve ye in this true Heaven-on-earth where ye shall reap the rewards of your undying faith."

"No more questions!" Reverend Dallas said right on the heels of Jesus' last syllable, before the crowd could burst with curiosity and fear, yelling over each other, thrusting hands toward the ceiling like restless second graders, waving their press-badges and electronic notepads, anything to call attention to themselves.

Without another word, Jesus stood, smiled, and calmly walked backstage.

Ever the showman, Reverend Dallas made up for Jesus' perceived curtness by waving and thanking the crowd repeatedly as he followed in Jesus' footsteps and disappeared backstage.

*　*　*

Wrapped in a thick wool blanket and hunched forward in the refurbished armchair (a reader's delight, the catalog proclaimed), the ugly brown man called Yeshua stared with solemn eyes at the monitor on the wall of the windowless room.

"Do you want me change the channel?" Qazi Hamid, his tall,

thin assistant inquired, turning from the old mahogany desk where he had been juggling online interviews with CNN and a suspicious fellow from some Christian media watchdog group who he suspected, due to his line of questions, to be a spy for Reverend Dallas' organization. Qazi had taken an extended leave from his job as a freelance journalist specializing in the Arab-American community in Chicago to volunteer his services for the rebuilding of Iraq when he rescued a man who was being stoned by a frenzied crowd of Christians. That man turned out to be Yeshua.

"That is not necessary," Yeshua responded in his native Aramaic.

"I'm just afraid that someone in your condition…"

"My health is not in question. Concern yourself only with the task at hand."

As if to mock his self-diagnosis, Yeshua began to cough violently.

During the time that Yeshua had been in his care, Qazi had become familiar with his archaic vernacular. Though he was fluent in Aramaic as well, Yeshua's dialectic had its own enlightened flavor that superseded the schoolbook version he had spent years studying. It made him feel unworthy. Instead of following his first instinct and persisting about Yeshua's health, Qazi settled for a less personal but equally presumptuous question. The selfless Yeshua treated any concern for himself, as a single entity, an unnecessary waste of time.

"I don't mean to overstep my bounds, but how can you stand to watch this over and over?"

Considering that the alternatives were news reports about the living dead, talk shows about the living dead and how they pertain to religion, religious discussion panels, footage of protesting crowds burning photos of Yeshua in effigy, and Reverend Dallas' CMB Network running at full steam, Qazi scrambled for something else to offer Yeshua, but his mind was a blank. All this, and it hadn't even been a full 24 hours since Jesus' press conference.

"Does he bother you, this… man?"

"If I may be frank, I think he's an asshole."

"Your anger has no place in my presence."

Qazi knew that Yeshua could easily read his thoughts so he tried not to venture too far down the path his mind had tried to lead him.

"Gather your things," Yeshua rasped, working a nasty cough back down his throat. "They have arrived."

Qazi rose from his seat, his hands trembling with anticipation as they had been doing quite often lately.

Before he could reach it, there was a knock at the door.

"Pardon me," the muffled voice seeped through, carrying with it an accent similar to Qazi's, "but the people from the Coalition and the Dziko Nation are here to see Yeshua."

*　　*　　*

Makane's Lament

Like many other businesses situated between the corporate and residential centers, the Lucky Star Tavern was a safe haven from what lurked outside. It was the first stop on a long trip to and from work for the slowpokes who arrived in town too late to park in the Lucky Star's fenced-in lot, which also happened to be the most expensive in the area given its proximity to the fortified throng of office buildings that made up Center City. It enabled the owner, Beau Hopkins, to upgrade from the 25-year-old security-glass windows (each one had been completely boarded up) that wore their age in lightning-streak cracks and mysterious, petrified smudges, to custom-sized, flat-screen, plasma monitors that ran prerecorded footage of peaceful shit with names like mountain spring, arctic blue, swept ashore, and manmade mecca. For a business on the fringes of deadfucked jurisdiction, it was safer this way.

Except in the high-rises, windows were moving swiftly toward extinction, replaced by high-tech substitutes like these. Depending upon your price range, they came backed with layers of reinforced steel, or electrified. Cameras mounted in the upper frames recorded the immediate surroundings outside and presented them in panoramic real-time, utilizing each screen to perpetuate a second-hand rendition through angles that sensed reflexes in the cornea of someone walking from window to window and changed to accommodate perspective.

Straight-laced, upper-management folks rubbed elbows with hardened drinkers and lost souls with sad songs to sing to anyone who'd listen as they rested up a bit before braving the outdoors for another 15-minute stint, then ducking into the next loosely designated (usually by word of mouth) rest stop and repeating the same cycle all the way to the fenced-in and indoor lots where their cars were parked, or in the case of those who made the journey on foot, all the way home.

What was once a quaint little dive wrapped in a historic shell (the same building housed one of the first post offices) and transfixed among a line-up of tall buildings, had become a popular spot to meet and trade close calls with the living dead while waiting for spouses, loved ones, friends, and acquaintances with whom to make the trip home. Lately, the topic of discussion had shifted to debates about the meaning of Judgment Day and what exactly it took to get into Heaven.

The regulars, who typically came from worlds less enlightened than the newbies, sneered and laughed at their nouveau-survivalist idiosyncrasies. In defense of their intolerance, they tried to bend logic into an argument that made sense, but it always came back to envy and resentment that, along with the influx of people, brought jacked-up prices across the board.

Like some one-eyed mechanical beast searching the room for prey, the old, 19-inch analog TV set peered down from its wall-mounted perch above the broken cigarette machine and vied for attention with the background chatter.

On the screen...

Grainy stock footage of a beautiful man with long blond hair and striking blue eyes (Jesus) as he stands behind a podium speaking to a large crowd. Though we can't hear him, we gather from the dictator-like hand gestures that he is passionate about his dialogue. His resemblance to the popular Anglicanized image of Jesus Christ smacks us right in the face. The video freezes....

ANNOUNCER: *Do you know this man? He calls himself Jesus Christ. He'd like you to believe that he, a Caucasian man from Bethlehem, Israel, is the true Son of God. Reverend Jesse James Dallas refers to a DNA test using samples from the infamous Shroud of Turin conducted privately and funded by his fat-cat cronies in the religious right as proof, but when pressed to make their findings public, Reverend Dallas regularly responds with stall tactics and comments labeling his critics' demands as un-Christian, even racist.*

In these trying times, the Coalition for Spiritual Diversity asks that you employ logic and intelligence in your spiritual journey.

HURRIED VOICE: *Paid for by the Coalition for Spiritual Diversity.*

CUT TO

A well-dressed anchorwoman nestled comfortably behind a desk.

———————————

"What does he know? His people used to worship goats and chickens and shit before we came along and taught them how to think," Rusty Collins yelled from the back of the bar, his words cut short by a sudden awareness of the new multicultural atmosphere.

"Hey Russ, how's your foot taste?" chimed one of the three barflies as he intermittently skimmed the flock of newbies who congregated over by the booths against the far wall, sliding Rusty the evil eye. Some of them still wore their Haz-Mat, Second Skin jumpsuits (in case the rain came back) while the windowsill beside them housed a row of helmets placed neatly side by side.

"Don't waste your time," said Beau Hopkins, the bartender, who was busy cutting lemons. "Ol' Rusty wouldn't know a thing about tact."

"Hey, fuck off, Hopkins, ya goddamn fudge-packer."

Rusty was slurring heavily and having trouble holding his head up. It wouldn't be long now before the inevitable.

THUMP!

He was out like a light.

"I rest my case," Beau smirked.

Lesser men would've jumped over the bar and strangled Rusty for daring to reopen an old wound that had yet to heal completely and probably never would as long as Beau Hopkins tended bar at the Lucky Star.

Homosexuality was like kryptonite to these blue-collar types, and Hopkins' error in judgment was always popping up here and there in some form a video, an ad in a fourth-tier adult magazine, a still photo plucked from the Internet.

"I was young and stupid," he'd say. "Besides, the money was good, and I went in thinking I was gonna double-team some chick with another dude. How was I supposed to know he was gonna get all… well… you know…."

There was never any penetration, just a great deal of questionable contact.

The movie was called "Sweet Sweat." It was a favorite with the female patrons, who passed it around in secret. Many of them found Beau attractive in a big, oafish, teddy-bear sort of way.

Every once and awhile, someone found the nerve to bring it up or, God forbid, make light of it.

"If you ask me, these Coalition people are grasping at straws," Beau said. "What difference does it make what people think come December 25th?"

"People need to feel included. That's all it is," one of the barflies responded.

"I guess so…. How's that one ad go…the one that says, 'a picture speaks a thousand words?' Well, that picture up on the wall…" Pointing at the crappy oil print of Anglicanized Christ, Beau continued. "That right there is the only Jesus Christ I know."

"So, are you scared?" the gamy one with the permanent stubble (Barfly #1) inquired. "I mean, seriously."

"Yeah, that seems to be the question of the day," Beau replied. "You know what I say to that?"

"What's that?"

"I say, better safe than sorry."

"Fuckin' A, man," Barfly #1 said, raising his hand for a high-five, which Beau reluctantly met with his own. "Better safe than sorry."

Beau was just about to ask one of the three barflies to help him peel Rusty from his table in the back when...

"My wife goes on and on about this fucking show. The lazy bitch!" Barfly #1 groaned, pointing at the screen.

On the screen...

An announcer speaks in voice-over against a black screen

ANNOUNCER: *Get ready for heavenly laughs!*

FADE IN

A minister and a young boy (eight or nine years old) walk hand in hand down a crowded sidewalk. They pass a scantily clad hooker who is leaning into the passenger-side window of a double-parked car.

BOY: *Daddy, why is that woman dressed like that?*

The priest takes a moment to think, then responds with an exaggerated look of cunning.

MINISTER: *Well son, Hell is a very hot place. You'd dress lightly too if you were on your way there.*

Laughter builds.

FADE TO BLACK

ANNOUNCER: Get ready for first-rate family entertainment from the people who brought you the hit show 'Heaven Sent.'

FADE IN

We now find the young boy seated at a table with his family: mother, father (minister), and older sister (16). He is in the middle of saying the blessing.

BOY: *God bless mommy, daddy, Sarah... and God bless the boy I saw climbing out of Sarah's window last night. I hope he didn't get hurt when he fell from the trellis.*

Laughter builds.

The boy sports a devilish grin. Sarah's face is frozen in horror. Her parents turn angrily to face her.

FADE TO BLACK

ANNOUNCER: *And who said religion couldn't be fun. Be sure to tune in on Sunday nights at eight for 'Father and Son' on CMB Channel 5.*

Christian Media Broadcasting: Changing the face of Christianity.

"No offense pal, but your wife needs to get out more," Beau replied. "Besides, who the fuck watches TV anymore? You might want to tell her to take a look out the fucking window."

"Here, here." Barfly #2 held his mug high in testament.

"Get out more? I'm lucky if she even gets up off her ass long enough to make me a friggin' sandwich. And my Barbra, she's in denial over this zombie shit. I don't think she could handle it if she really let it sink in."

"Yeah, can you really blame her, though?" Barfly #2 inquired. "I know a lot of folks like that."

"All the more reason why you should make your own damn sandwich," Beau snickered.

Barfly #2 raised his mug again.

Barfly #1 turned to Barfly #2 and frowned. "Hey, quit ridin' his nuts, why don'tcha."

Barfly #2 began to laugh until something (a subtle, yet dramatic shift in Barfly #1's eyes) caused him to suddenly tense up. Without turning his head, Barfly #1 rolled his eyes toward Beau, wondering if he, too, had made some sort of connection from his "ridin' his nuts" remark to the infamous tape.

"Keep your shirts on, fellas." Beau smiled as he dug his hand towel into the soapy mug and twisted. "If I was that sensitive about it, I don't think I would've survived working here so long, especially with jokers like you two and Rusty to keep reminding me of it."

"Reminding you of what?" Barfly #1 shrugged. "Ohhhhh... you mean the tape? It never even crossed my mind."

"You are so full of shit," Barfly #2 chided.

"Just because *you* might've thought of it doesn't mean I had to."

"Gimme a fuckin' break, man. We both did and you know it."

"I swear I didn't. Really!"

"Then why did you stop talking all of a sudden and look over at Beau?"

"Who said I was…?"

"Would you two please give it a rest?" a voice interrupted from the end of the bar. It was Barfly #3. "Some of us are trying to watch the news."

Barfly #1 whipped around first, his body language speaking of brutish physicality... and then he got a good look at Barfly #3, who, until he leaned forward out of the shadows that haunted the back of the place, Barfly #1 thought was someone else.

He wasn't what you'd call big, just very capable looking, and he seemed to know it. More than that, there was something familiar about this guy. He wasn't even paying attention to Barfly #1 and Barfly #2, who by now were quite obviously staring at him. Instead, he was totally committed to the TV screen, as was Beau.

Eventually Barfly #1 and Barfly #2 gave in to curiosity and joined them.

On the screen...

A typical, big-city news anchorwoman. Over her right shoulder, a graphic of the Shroud of Turin

ANCHORWOMAN: *A spokesperson for Reverend Jesse James Dallas' Christian Media Broadcasting Group met with reporters on the steps of CMB headquarters in Houston yesterday to address the worldwide protests in response to Jesus' planned Judgment Day Ceremony to be held on the 25th of December.*

CMB SPOKESMAN: *Preparations for Judgment Day are in full gear, and, as such, I wanted to address some of your concerns. First, it seems that history has confused a few things. We have learned through numerous meetings with Jesus himself that what we know as Heaven and Hell has existed beneath our very feet from day one. Life as we know it will change, but gone is the idea of some otherworldly plane upon which we might eternally exist. Those of us who have accepted Jesus into our hearts need not fear. Heaven on earth will be a joyous place where you will reap the rewards of your loyalty.*

NEWSANCHOR: *The group known as the Secular Soldiers released a statement this morning in response to the CMB confer-*

ence condemning Reverend Dallas' Jesus as a fraud and Reverend Dallas himself as the broker of age-old-racism and revisionist views. The group points to Reverend Dallas' Caucasian Jesus as an abomination of historical truth.

An excerpt from the statement in white letters flashes across the screen.

EXCERPT:

Well, there's a certain percentage of the population who see a brown-skinned Christ as a threat. You have to remember, the war in Iraq is still fresh in many people's minds, and that went on for eight years. You have others... entire segments of our populace... whose points of view are based on ignorance and misinformation; this endless mention of the   Shroud of Turin as an article of undisputed fact, for example. Below I have listed just a few of the reasons why this is not and could not have been Christ's burial cloth.

1. At the time, the Jews had a specific method of burying their dead, which consisted of being wrapped in cloths, usually linen, and not one big cloth.
2. We know that Jesus suffered a severe beating at the hands of his captors, leaving his face bruised and battered as represented in this passage from Isaiah (52:14, KJV): "His visage was so marred, more than any other man." The image on the shroud clearly shows no signs of a beating.
3. The Turin image shows a man with long hair which, according to the following passage from the first book of Corinthians (11:14-16, NIV), was frowned upon at the time: "Does not the very nature of things teach you that if a man has long hair,

it is a disgrace to him, but that if a woman has long hair, it is her glory? For long hair is given to her as a covering. If anyone wants to be contentious about this, we have no other practice—nor do the churches of God."

4. The description of cloths and not one big cloth as mentioned in John (20:4-7 RSV): *"They both ran, but the other disciple outran Peter and reached the tomb first; and stooping to look in, he saw the linen cloths lying there, but he did not go in. Then Simon Peter came, following him, and went into the tomb; he saw the linen cloths lying, and the napkin, which had been on his head, not lying with the linen cloths but rolled up in a place by itself."*

Jasper Dohan, geneticist

ANCHORWOMAN: *Despite these recent allegations, the latest polls indicate that 68% of pollsters across the globe still consider Reverend Dallas' Jesus to be the actual resurrection of Christ.*

Yeshua supporters, however, point to logic and common sense as a means of determining the truth. Yeshua himself has not been seen publicly since he first appeared in Mandali, Iraq, *this past Easter Sunday. Reports of violent protests and rioting by crowds, who believe Yeshua to be the Devil, are coming in from across the globe.*

In other news...

Police believe that the fatal batch of the drug U4, which is thought to be responsible for the death of 17-year-old Meleeza Duncan two weeks ago, came from drug kingpin Vernon Boca. As of yet, no evidence linking him to the teenager has been found.

Meeleza Duncan was struck and killed by an SUV after succumbing to the ill effects of the controversial drug during a performance at the St. Salacious Church on 52nd and Parish Streets in West Philadelphia. Eyewitnesses say that Duncan was struck with such force that her body was thrown 30 feet.

Action Live's Denice McKinnely spoke to celebrated Homicide Detective Philip Makane about the case.

"Christ, what's that guy, like, the only cop left in the city?" Barfly #1 remarked through the foam that reached over the edge of his glass and into his mouth.

"Probably," Beau replied.

"What guy?" Barfly #2 queried.

"This hotshot Makane fellow... I mean, wasn't he the one who brought down that nutcase in the mall too?"

"Yeah? So?"

"Seems to me like he's a bit full of himself is all I'm sayin'. If I was him, I sure as hell wouldn't be worried about saving the world."

"You're too much."

"How do you figure?"

"With all that's going on, you're all ruffled over some cop. We should be thankful that guys like that are still willing to stay on the job through all this," Barfly #2 smirked.

As usual, Barfly #1 was left feeling somewhat insecure by the lackluster response to his statement. This didn't stop him from finding something else to bitch about.

"Kids these days... always looking for the perfect buzz," Barfly #1 said. "If you ask me, that chick got what she deserved for messing with that U4 crap."

"You're one to talk, Mr. Sobriety," Barfly #2 snapped at him in his usual half-kidding, half-serious manner. Sometimes it was difficult to tell the difference. "When was the last time you went a full day without a few stiff drinks?"

"Yeah, I get drunk. So what? There's a big difference between drinking and shoving a goddamn needle up your ass."

"I don't think you put it up your ass... at least not the last time I checked," Barfly #3 interjected from the shadows. "That is unless you know something that we don't."

Barfly #1 was the only one who didn't laugh, excluding Rusty, who was fast asleep at his table.

"Ha, ha, ha.... Very funny. We'll see how funny you are when I come over there and shove this bottle down your throat."

Suddenly, silence.... Even the newbies stopped talking and took notice. The smell of testosteronic foolishness was in the air.

Unfazed by Barfly #1's threat, Barfly #3 took another swig from his beer, and lost himself in the chattering from the TV.

Barfly #2 placed a calming hand on Barfly #1's shoulder. It bordered on patronizing. That's how Barfly #1 saw it anyway, even if he knew that Barfly #2 meant no harm.

"Relax, man. What, you can't take a joke?"

"Look, all's I'm saying is that I've never gotten so drunk that I ran out into the street with no clothes on screaming bloody murder."

"I don't know.... I can think of a couple times when you've come pretty close."

"Still, it's just not the same."

"Well... it is when you consider that there are people out there who put alcohol in the same class as heroin, or U4." Barfly #3 threw another jab.

Beau Hopkins headed toward the walk-in freezer to escape. He was sure there was something that he could do back there to kill a good 15 minutes. A cigarette maybe?

He checked his pockets. All out.

Hold on.... What's this?

Beau fished his hand out from the bottom corner of his back pocket and held it up in front of him, his index finger curled around the middle one the way he had to twist it to get at whatever it was (a half-smoked joint) lodged in there with the lint and the crumbs.

"This'll do just fine," he mumbled to himself.

Usually he'd invite one of the guys back to smoke with him whenever he had some weed, but the roach he found was only about five-good-hits long, and Beau was feeling stingy.

"What are you, a fucking liberal?" Barfly #1's posture screamed aggression, his chest swelling, hand tightening around his beer.

Without a hint of emotion, Barfly #3 rose from his stool and walked slowly into the light. He pulled his wallet from his back pocket and flipped it open.

"So what if I am?"

Though the sight of Barfly #3's face gave them pause, it hit them when they recognized the trademark outfit (faded jeans/khakis, black sweater/shirt and a cracked leather blazer-thingy), and again when they saw the badge in his wallet.

Realizing simultaneously who Barfly #3 was (Detective Philip Makane), Barfly #1 and Barfly #2 looked up at the TV to see his doppelganger speaking to the reporter. In the background, a S.W.A.T. officer aimed his gun and "knee-capped" zombies who wandered to close to them as they filmed.

Kane was the type of guy who'd found his look some time ago (probably in his early twenties) and never felt compelled to change it. There were slight variations in his crime-fighting attire, but the old leather jacket never seemed to leave his shoulders. It was an old, worn thing that he kept for himself when no one showed up to reclaim it after the Kater Street bust back in '05.

The auto body shop was a front for a Tony Palermo's fencing

operation. The bust was small potatoes compared to Tony's more personal work. He was known in the underworld as Tony 'the Butcher.'

Kane was happy to get him on something. He was confident that Tony would never again see the light of day once the prosecutors were done with him, but there was a problem with the search warrant, and just like that, Tony 'the Butcher' Palermo was back on the streets.

Kane viewed it as a failure. He had a few Tony, Lin Kwei, from the Triads, and Carlos McCann, the serial rapist/murderer. The McCann situation was more of a disappointment, but Kane still put it in the same category.

Carlos McCann was a former seminary student who had a gig writing opinion pieces on race, crime, and the woes of secular living for a Christian magazine until he was fired him for being too controversial. McCann had already claimed his first victim by then, but his experience with the magazine soured his feelings toward Christianity, and that distaste began to play a role in his crimes.

McCann liked to taunt Kane. He would leave messages that mocked religion, his victims, and the police, addressing them to Kane directly, and placing them in his victims' mouths, usually. Sometimes the messages were found in other orifices.

The crime scenes were always littered with occult markings (inverted pentagram, horned hand, satanic cross) and strangely worded poems written in blood. According to the religious studies professor that the department consulted on the case, they were demonic symbols and incantations. "If you believe in that sort of thing," the professor added.

Kane didn't. He knew that enough people were ready to believe just about anything, however, so the department decided to keep that information from the public.

An overly eager news reporter eventually found out about the markings and nicknamed McCann "the Acolyte." The story ran on the front page of the Sunday paper.

McCann used it to his advantage to instill panic throughout

the city. Kane had always meant to pay that reporter a visit when the case was over, but he never did.

Kane had promised the parents of the victims that he, personally, would see to it that McCann got what was coming to him. The pain in their eyes scared Kane and made him wonder if he would be able to restrain himself and bring McCann in the right way when he finally caught up to him.

It took almost a year. McCann had been known to disguise himself, which made things more difficult. It was no secret that he would sometimes dress as a woman to gain the trust of some of his victims. From what Kane gathered from witnesses, McCann was pretty good at acting like a chick: had the voice down and all.

When Kane finally found him, McCann was already dead. He had burned himself alive during some kind of ceremony. His charred body lay in the middle of a giant chalk pentagram surrounded by candles. Before calling headquarters, Kane took a piss on the body and gave it a few swift kicks, but it did nothing to ease his frustration.

There were reports every now and then about McCann's grave (in his hometown of Baltimore) being vandalized, which always managed to put a smile on Kane's face.

The McCann case and the Kater Street bust made Kane a staple of the local news. Since then, security cameras routinely caught him in action, wielding his gun with confidence and being a general badass. From all the various angles, the cameras captured the moves of the great crimefighter and TV hero, but they never managed to pick up the fear and doubt that he wrestled with incessantly. Barfly #1 shrunk within himself as Kane approached. He smirked to save face and shook his head as he looked down in averse reverence.

"Figures," Barfly #2 mumbled under his breath. He hadn't really said anything bad about Kane, but he felt guilty by association.

Philip Makane pulled a five from his wallet, placed it on the bar, and gave a nod to Beau Hopkins, who was lost deep in the heart of the dense cloud of marijuana smoke that surrounded him way in the back of the freezer. He knew that Kane was a cop yet he didn't seem to care that he'd been caught in the act.

Neither did Kane for that matter.

On top of Kane's being a bit of a regular, Beau had recently hired Kane and a few of his colleagues to keep the zombies and the street-level opportunists, who thrived in these haphazard times, away from his place. Beau was hoping to get one of those holographic security guards, but they were a bit expensive.

Parting the smoke with his hands, Beau stuck his head out to return Kane's nod.

Kane turned back to Barfly #1 and Barfly #2.

"Full of myself, huh? Well, we can always use the help down at the station if you think you can do a better job."

Barfly #1 never even looked up.

"Besides, what does being a liberal have to do with what I said anyway?"

Again Barfly #1 didn't respond.

"You should learn to relax, by the way. All that pent-up aggression is bad for your heart." Kane flashed a self-satisfied grin and patted Barfly #1 on the shoulder hard enough to cause an echo that lasted a few seconds after he walked out the front door.

Against a black screen, a photo of Yeshua appears to have been taken unknowingly and at a moment of duress. It has been further doctored to make him appear frightened, weak, and slightly darker-skinned. Ominous music sets an uncomfortable tone.

The announcer begins...

ANNOUNCER: *If the Coalition for Spiritual Diversity is so con-*

cerned with racial sensitivity, then why do they repeatedly focus on race as one of the main reasons to denounce Jesus? If God is love, and love has no color, then why does it matter anyway? We see a photo of Jesus, his blue eyes retouched to almost glow. Beneath it a caption appears in white lettering.

CAPTION: *There is only one true Son of God. Because a picture is worth a thousand words.*

Max Hedberg's Journal

Entry #7

Sleep. I can hear it calling me. I'm so hungry that I'm afraid I might not wake up, although when I'm awake, my memories are my only escape from the noise, the claustrophobic paranoia, and the weird conversations with myself and with Eric. Occasionally, Maria will interject with something that only half made sense, jumping from calm to aggressive, to downright savage. She is getting worse by the day, as is Eric.

I look forward to my meals, three small pieces of candy bar a day.

I've been trying to focus on happier times, but I keep coming back to the hours and days that led up to this.

The school bus had dropped Eric off early the day I brought Maria down here. She tried to run out and get him on her side as he walked up the driveway, but I managed to block the door. Eric was almost at the door by then. I had to run out back and lock Maria in the shed until later, when Eric was immersed in one of his video games.

That night, he kept waking up screaming. He wanted his mommy, but I had to tell him that she was working late, which worked until about 9:30, when he woke up for the fifth time complaining that he could hear voices. It was rare for Maria to ever get home later than that without giving us a heads' up. I went out onto the bedroom deck and tried to calm myself with a cigarette before I pulled a story out of my ass.

That's when I remembered the intercom system in the panic shelter. There were connecting speakers downstairs in the family room, one in the kitchen, one in my office, which was right next to Eric's bedroom, and one in our master bedroom. Maria had been trying to communicate with Eric through the one in my office, but she could only be so loud, or else I would hear her.

I don't know what I expected to see when I

looked over at the Maplewood Cemetery across the street. The place went back for miles, it seemed. It was most likely only about a 1/2 mile, but from our deck, the headstones and mausoleums appeared to eventually merge with the horizon, as if the world ended at that exact point.

Maybe I was looking for a distraction. Sometimes it was fun to watch other people's lives play out when their loved ones came to watch those life-story mini-movie thingamajigs. Maplewood was one of the last places to upgrade to the voice-activated systems and life-sized holograms that played out right in front of the headstones. They still had the old version too: flat screens mounted on the faces of the headstones and the sliding card readers that were always malfunctioning and playing on their own. And it was always the loudest, most audacious, sappy, lowbrow mini-movies that were going on the fritz. After watching some of those, I thought nothing would faze me, until I noticed all the dead people.

Logical or not, I've seen enough zombie movies in my day to know what I think one looks like, but Goddammit if I just couldn't wrap my head around the idea of it as a reality. Here I was standing on my deck, 50 feet from what looked like a bunch of fucking zombies staggering and twitching over the horizon and clawing their way right out of the ground. Until then, I kept reassuring myself that it was probably just some kind of disease, maybe a virulent strain of influenza that had Maria acting so sick.

I hadn't even had a chance to let it sink in when Eric screamed, "Daddy, help! The Big Fat Man is coming to get me!"

Entry #8

Those of you with children know that there's nothing like the sound of your child in distress to energize an otherwise passive soul. Like me. Well, let me correct that. I'm only passive when it comes to women. I'm what most guys would call "whipped." I could never admit that to myself before.

Sorry, I'm getting off track again.

Eric was smart enough to lock himself in the second-floor bathroom. I was so proud of him, and so relieved. I told him to run down to the shelter and punch in the code (0370, in case you were wondering) while I distracted the Big Fat Man. I remember freezing for a moment as he lumbered toward me. In death, he somehow appeared much larger, so large that he was forced to hunch over just to fit down the second-floor hall. Now that I think about it, the hallway itself seemed an awful lot smaller. This was a guy who I'd seen many times while driving around the neighborhood, running errands, an insignificant recurring character in my daily routine whom I'm sure I've taken the time to pity as if he couldn't possibly enjoy his job. In addition to blubber face, he had tiny, receded eyes.

I used to make fun of the old B-movies, zombies covered in blue make-up and cheapo prosthetics, but turns out that he looked pretty close to what most of the low-budget flicks suggested. He would open his mouth like he was about to say something, but each time he tried, a gush of blood poured from his mouth and down his chin and from the wound in his throat. His teeth were chattering, almost like he was taunting me, or maybe relearning the instinct to bite down. His jaw was broken from where Maria said she hit him with the marble sculpture I brought her back from Istanbul. It left that side of his face swollen, but he didn't seem to care.

Then it hit me, and, in an instant, my life passed before my eyes. Eric was all alone with his mother. I didn't even think of it when I told him to run down to the shelter. Everything was happening so fast...

You don't know how relieved I was to find them locked in an embrace by the time I made it down to the shelter with the Big Fat Man hot on my trail. He was slower than constipated shit, but he made up good distance with that barrel roll down the steps from the second floor after tripping when he grabbed the loose railing for balance. Maria had been harping on me to fix that thing for months. It was next on my list, right after the panic shelter door.

I didn't notice the bite until Eric mentioned that it hurt. I was so mad that I told Maria that I would never let her out. Of course I didn't mean it. In the back of my mind, I was still hoping that she would somehow recover.

A few hours later, Eric was becoming too much to handle. I didn't mean to hit him, and with a closed fist too, right in the mouth, but I had to do something to keep him from biting me. Like I said, I waited until the last minute before locking him up.

I feel like I must've lost at least 20 pounds since coming down here. I could never seem to lose the weight any other way. Sort of ironic, isn't it? I think I'm starting to hallucinate. I ate the last piece of the candy bar at the last meal. Without food, I probably don't have much time left.

Maybe none of this is even real. Yeah, that would be great. Maybe I should pinch myself and see if I wake up out of this nightmare.

Nope. Still here...

Chapter 5

Aged vinyl never smelled so good, Philip Makane mused, relaxing his perpetually sore muscles into the seat cushions. He checked the floating red digits in the upper right corner of the windshield. It was 7:51 pm.

He had tried to keep a low profile as he made his way to his car, sprinting from vehicle to vehicle and ducking behind each one until the zombies who had seen him running looked away, confused. The ones who were too far gone were easy to fool, but the few cognizant ones knew exactly where he was hiding every time. Something about their ability to figure shit out gnawed at him like a wayward tag in an otherwise comfortable pair of underwear. They were still staring at him as he sat in his car, their eyes so plump with wanting and feral lust that he could almost feel them chewing on him visually.

On the other side of the window, the dead air and the unyielding stench of rot was as dense and persistent as it was fragrant, the kind of pungent funk that lingered on clothing and in hair. Despite the Christmas-tree air fresheners (six of them overlapping each other) and the empty aerosol cans that littered the floor, Kane knew it well. He could smell it now, over the toxic/potpourri/Christmastime stank that the elite few who had enough money to keep them from ever having to face a zombie in person; or to meet eyes with the cataract stare of someone they loved wondering if the lost one will remember; or actually try to eat them; or to cut that same loved one to pieces or set them ablaze to stop them from killing and eating; or to give in to denial and keep them in some upstairs room under lock and key and slowly fade into dementia would ever understand. Someone like Reverend Dallas for instance.

Better safe than sorry.... Being a man of reason, Kane felt ashamed for the people who held doubt but couldn't totally commit to their suspicions. It had crossed his mind as well, but he refused to entertain the idea that that 'effeminate punk,' as he called him, might be the genuine article. When he did wonder, he was usually asleep and in no control of his thoughts.

Man, that smell....

Its pungent vigor could not be ignored. It was a smell that Kane was certain he'd never get used to. Not in a million years.

Kane shot a glance at the collage of decay and tattered clothing that marred the borders set by the 15-foot electrified fencing that surrounded the parking lot and the Lucky Star itself.

Dead folks from all walks of life intermingled with the kinds of people that many of them would have likely shunned in legitimate life. What irony, that it took this to happen for Martin Luther King's dream to finally come to realization. Kane was an introspective bastard. His friends called it 'sensitive.'

The fence buzzed and snapped to the touch of too many zombies to count, so many that they blocked out the dormant signs and vacant storefronts that made up the flooded strip mall across the boulevard.

At the entrance of the lot, two empty, hollowed-out trailers resting end to end served as a tunnel in and out. Kane had a bad experience once when the door at the other end, which lowered into a ramp, didn't open fast enough. On top of that, his car barely fit through the damn thing.

What was left of municipal services worked with a when-we-get-to-it mentality to drain the blood-flooded streets in the areas where money was scarce, while private contractors (most of them former municipal employees) did double the work in half the time for those who could afford it. This left the mom-and-pop businesses shit out of luck and whole inner-city neighborhoods submerged beneath a river of blood and festering death. The news said that the military and the National Guard were supposed to be helping out, but reports were coming in from around the world about soldiers deserting their posts by the thousands to be with their families when Judgment Day arrived. Everyone was down to scraps, including the 13th Precinct, which Kane called home.

The Lucky Star was situated at the top of a steep hill, so Beau Hopkins got off lucky.

Startled out of introspection by electricity's boisterous hiss and its quick-tempered glow, Kane turned to his right and watched a trio of zombies standing knee-deep in a long, asymmetrical puddle of blood dance to the surge of 800,000 volts, smoke rising from their bubbling flesh. Because it had become such a problem, the fencing company guaranteed against short-circuits with their upgraded models, but Kane had his doubts.

The rickety walkway that ran from the front door of the Lucky Star, up and over the fence, clearing it by a good five feet, and off to the next pit stop (Cho's Dry Cleaning, two blocks away), shook under the breeze, it seemed, until a momentary parting of bodies revealed a contingent of zombies pushing and pulling on its hastily erected scaffold foundation and attempting unsuccessfully to climb to the top.

A wave of relief came over Kane when a group of newbies exited the bar and ran up the walkway together. They had taken the zombies' focus off of him. There was this one, though, a cute little girl of 12 or 13 years, who kept her clouded eyes on him. She tilted her head inquisitively as if he was familiar to her. The look on her face scared him the way the statues in church used to when he was a kid.

Kane's weary eyes rolled up to the rearview, where they met their reflection and feigned sobriety. They rolled over to the lit audio icons floating beneath the red digits on the windshield, then down to the bullshit factory-speaker in the dash as it coughed out "Sussudio" by Phil Collins. Until then, he hadn't even been paying attention to the radio.

"Phil Collins??????? Are you kidding me?"

"Hey, back off. He helps me sleep."

It was almost ethereal, this slight, disembodied feminine voice emanating from the thin air behind him.

"I think he helped everybody sleep back in the '80s."

"Would you rather I listened to that racket out there?"

She was referring to that proverbial moan, like a lazy chorus, and the constant buzzing of the electric fence.

"So, what took you so long?" she said. "I thought you were just going to pick up your check. Lemme guess... you had a drink."

"Check?"

"Oh, excuse me, your cash."

"And what makes you think I had a drink? Maybe I was just bullshitting with Hopkins."

"Well, for one, you smell like alcohol, and secondly, knowing Beau Hopkins, he probably wouldn't have much to talk to you about other than some hot piece of ass that happened into his bar."

"Tavern. There's a difference."

"Right. Okay."

"I was quoting Hopkins, actually."

"Gee, now how did I know that?"

"All right, so I had a drink.... Just as long as you keep it to yourself," Kane groaned at the voice behind him. "Technically, I'm still on the clock."

"Don't worry, I think they all know you well enough by now."

"That was cold."

"Well, they don't call me the ice princess for nothing."

"That's QUEEN ice queen.... Don't sell yourself short."

Detective Allison Ryan sat up in the back seat. She was Kane's partner and his occasional fuck-buddy.

"Forgive me for forgetting my own nickname, as completely juvenile as it is."

Allison had the perfect kind of face for delivering heavy sarcasm. She had sly, somewhat slanted eyes and a mouth that always slid to the left side of her face whenever she made an underhanded comment. Otherwise she looked like one might expect a police woman to look: hardened, somewhat masculine, with a trace of femininity beneath her tough exterior, as if maybe she'd be quite a piece had she chosen a different path.

"Look, I just needed a drink after talking to Meleeza Duncan's father yesterday morning, and watching him try to cope with seeing his little girl in the shape she was in. That SUV really did a number on her. She could barely move."

Meeleza's father wept like a baby right in front of Kane. There was no shame, no concern with coming off like less of a man. Just pure agony manifested. There was something delicious about it. Kane never knew love like that, not even close, and the thought of it stimulated his beaten-back paternal instincts. In the back of his mind, he always knew he'd make a great father. He saw himself with a son, someone in whom he could instill bravery and strength. It was looking more and more like that would never happen.

"I heard they had to strap her down to the hospital bed."

"You should've seen it. It was a mess. She kept whipping her head around, trying to bite anyone who got close, even her father. That was when he broke down. Poor guy."

"Thanks, but I think I'll pass on that."

"After all that, I'm starting to regret trying to talk her boyfriend into going to visit her. This is going to sound weird coming from me, but... I don't think it was the drugs that made her flip out on the stage like that."

"Altar."

"Excuse me???"

"It's an altar. She flipped out on an altar, not a stage."

"Well what's the fuckin'..." Kane stopped himself and took a breath.

"Okay, so let's say it wasn't the drugs, then what was it?" Allison posed. "She wasn't bitten, right?"

"I can't quite put my finger on it yet, but it's there, waiting for me to figure it out."

"Face it, Phil. She was a junky."

"She was just a kid, Ally."

"What happened to the jaded realist, Mr. 'if it doesn't concern me then I don't sweat it?'"

"You wanna know what happened? Well, where the hell should I start?" Even after a few drinks, Kane was feeling tense. He felt like maybe he should've beaten the shit out of Barfly #1. Maybe that would've put him in a better mood. "First of all, I'm almost certain that the answer to Gus Rollins' meltdown lies somewhere in that plane wreckage that the federal boys kept us from investigating. I can't help feeling that we might have been able to stop him before the mall, and maybe even this whole zombie epidemic, if we were given access."

"Now, wait a minute…."

"I know. I know. The zombies are all part of the Book of Revelations, blah, blah, blah. Just leave me to my opinion, huh?"

Allison was on edge, ready for battle, but she knew that Kane was bound to say something to piss her off even more, so she held it in for now.

"Well, you saw how Rollins reacted when he described that woman he found at the scene who spit in his face when he tried to help her."

"That's gratitude for you, huh?" Kane added. He was well aware of and quite thankful for Allison's decision to hold off on her angry response.

"And that was after witnessing one of his friends getting taken down back in the cemetery. Maybe he was suffering from some form of post-traumatic stress."

"Yeah, maybe. Or maybe the feds had something to do with it. They *did* kill the rest of his hunting party after all."

"I'd be careful about repeating that."

"Don't worry. I'll just keep playing the fool until I get to the bottom of this thing. I wouldn't be surprised if they weren't behind the crash itself. That would explain all the secrecy. I'm anxious to know how they were able to keep the media from catching a whiff of it though. Those fucking leeches are usually pretty good at sniffing out a conspiracy. "

"Oh, so now we're dealing with a conspiracy?"

"Well, let's see…. First, they restrict us from the scene of the crash. Then, the woman at the FBI tells me that she's never heard of any Flight 2190, or a Special Agent Mendez, or an Agent Curtis, whose name I only remembered because of what he did to that fucking zombie. Then, they manipulate the press to keep quiet about it, the fact that the bulk of the passengers consisted of reporters and clergyman, and that they discovered corpses walking around like fucking lost, hungry tourists way before this shit we're in now. On top of that, we find out that they shot four innocent men in cold blood. Then, a few days later, Reverend Dallas, the current administration's bitch, comes forward with this idiot who we're all supposed to believe is Jesus fucking Christ."

"Aha… a conservative conspiracy. I was wondering when you were going to throw the government into the mix."

"No, it's not like that. My problem ain't with the conservatives, per se. But these hard-right fuckers have been clamping down with their weird, ultra-white morality since back when W. was in office. With all their bitching about homosexuals, you'd think they'd have something to say about Jesus' effeminate ass. And the far left, they aren't much better, just less intimidating. You used to feel the same way, until recently."

Allison had her doubts before the rain and the living dead.

"Let's just say that I've been enlightened," she said.

"Oh brother."

"So how do you explain Jesus walking on water? Let's hear your intellectual hypothesis about that."

"Oh, fuck you, Ally. I never said I had all the answers, and it's not that I can't accept that there might be *things* that exist beyond our explanation, but I'm pretty sure that the biblical story is a bunch of fiction. Nothing more."

"Still the die-hard atheist, huh?"

"Actually, I'm more of a realist."

"Whatever." Allison rolled her eyes and looked away. "You know you're in the minority these days. You might not want to be so loud."

"When I blow the lid off this thing, we'll see how real they are."

"Blow the lid offa what?" Allison said. "Look Philip, you know how I feel about this. You know that I think what you're doing is wrong. Don't you have other things you could be focusing on? What about the zombies, or the vigilantes?"

When that failed to change his expression, she went for something more personal.

"What about your crank caller?"

"My secret admirer?" he chuckled.

"Well, you never know when one of those guys is for real," she responded.

"Left another message over the weekend, actually. I'll take my chances on that one, though."

"Oh, for Pete's sake, Philip. Why can't you see this for what it is? What is it that you're trying to prove?"

"For *Pete's* sake????" Kane questioned. It was odd to hear Allison censor herself as she had been doing lately. She was known at the station as someone who could swear with the big boys. "You know, I've tried to see things from their... from *your* perspective. I used to wonder, 'what if I'm wrong? What if it really is true?' But when I hear someone like Beau Hopkins, a guy who, aside from all the pot smoking, I always thought was a semi-decent guy, quote that absolutely ree-diculous 'a picture says a thousand words' commercial, I realize just how stupid we are for being duped for so long. If there really was a God, do you really think he'd have to stoop to such lowbrow bullshit to get people to believe in him? Do you think he'd really align himself with a dumbass like Jesse James Dallas? You know that every Christian and Catholic group under the sun has been trying to get their hands on him. And what about the Vatican? That's like the Hall of Justice of religion. Why not align with them? You know why? Because he's a fraud."

"Hall of Justice?????"

"You know, from the Superfriends?"

She simply stared.

"Forget it," he said.

"I thought about that too at first… why would he align himself with Dallas, I mean. The only thing I came up with before hearing his reason during the press conference was that maybe he was angry with them because of all these priests coming forward, and the way they've been brushing all these allegations of pedophilia under the rug for so long."

"Yeah, maybe. But it seems to me that most Catholics just shrug that shit off, or ignore it outright. Tell me the truth: Knowing what you do about these priests, would you think any differently of Jesus if he would've joined with the Vatican?"

Allison didn't answer, which was answer enough for Kane, who felt ashamed for her.

"So what about this Judgment Day business?" he said. "You mean to tell me that you don't find the whole thing a bit… no, totally fucking insane? Just take a look out the goddamn window, or turn on any fucking TV for more than five minutes. The whole world has lost its goddamn mind. And you know what? I'd bet good money that most people who consider themselves devout have a good amount of doubt. I mean, it's only human to wonder, right? How many people do you know who actually follow all the rules to the letter instead of twisting them to fit their own lugheaded ideals? Probably not too many. They're just scared to make that leap. You know… just in case."

Allison had already lost herself in the activity beyond the fence to avoid the upsurge of utter discomfort that Kane's blasphemous attitude unleashed in her. She felt that listening to it somehow made her an accomplice.

Leaning back into his seat, Kane glanced back at Allison, via the rearview, and smirked at her restless apprehension to examining her beliefs from a different perspective. He found it to be a common phenomenon with religious types... and bigots.

"Engage auto-drive," he said, anticipating the tickle of the automatic seat belts that snaked taut around him.

A series of icons lit up in the middle of the windshield as the engine hummed to life and set the car in motion.

Allison waited until they were safely through the trailers.

"I don't suppose you've reconsidered taking part in the test with Bio-Tech?" Allison blurted hastily. "I still can't believe that you volunteered to do it in the first place."

"You know me, big man of action. Back when I volunteered, that's all I was thinking about. Besides, it seemed like fun going back to the old campus."

"I thought you hated that place."

"What, you mean Girard College?"

Before Bio-Tech Design Systems bought the place in 2005, it had been a boarding school for boys. Kane spent 7 years there until he was kicked out for fighting in the eleventh grade.

"Are you kidding? I might've hated the fact that I couldn't go home until the weekends, but the place itself was great. It had this weird, self-contained atmosphere that I can't really describe. I guess I kind of had a problem with the male house-parents too, now that I think about it. I couldn't figure out why a grown man would want to spend 24 hours a day around young boys for such little pay. Other than that, I had a blast. We all did. What you basically had was a bunch of mischievous little boys making the best of a bad situation. Er... way to change the subject, by the way. Besides, didn't we already discuss this?"

"I can't help it, Philip," Allison huffed. "Suppose something happens to you?"

"At least you wouldn't have to have arguments like this anymore, right?"

Allison was tired of his flippant attitude. To her, it was a sign of disrespect.

"Six failed attempts, Philip. Count em': six."

"And one of them died, even."

"Exactly…. And that doesn't concern you at all?"

"Sure it does, but no more than coming in to work in this bullshit every day."

"What good are you going to do anyone when you're dead, Philip? You keep thinking the way you do, and you're going to find out quick. Especially if you're planning on starting trouble with the Bio-Tech people."

"Who said anything about starting trouble? Like I said, I'm in it for the action."

"I know you, Philip."

"If you really knew me, then we wouldn't even be having this discussion. If you must know, I found out that Bio-Tech has heavy ties with the Republican Party. Have you any idea just how difficult it is to get close to any of the zealots in the GOP these days? I'm hoping now that taking part in this test will give me a glimpse of their twisted fucking agenda. It's no secret that Secretary of Defense Weiss isn't quite sold on this whole… *religious awakening*. Hell, I wouldn't be surprised if his paranoid ass already has some kind of contingency plan to deal with Jesus should something go awry."

"Fine, Philip. You do what you want. Just don't expect me to be a part of it. I'll still pray for you, but…"

"Don't bother. I can handle myself."

"Okay, whatever…. We'll see just how well you *handle yourself* on December 25th."

His knee-jerk instinct was to slap the shit out of her.

"I guess we will, Ally. I'm fine with that."

Other than being slightly juvenile in its rushed delivery in response to Allison's whining, Kane's comment didn't warrant her latest silent spell in his opinion. This was exactly the kind of energy-siphoning shit that made him want to be alone. Sometimes he even wondered if maybe the homosexuals were on to something, as men tended to be more direct when dealing with a problem.

"I was going to wait to bring this up," Allison began, "but I might as well just come out with it."

Kane had no idea what she was hinting at. Whatever it was, he figured it would probably be painful.

"Okay…."

"It's just that… I want us to…"

"You're not thinking of skipping out on the job are you?" Kane took a shot in the relative dark. Call it a hunch. Besides, everyone was doing it.

"What would you say if I said yes?"

"I would say that you took an oath just like the rest of us when you graduated from the academy."

"You of all people have the nerve to toss ethics in my face?"

Fuck! There's no winning with this bitch, he thought.

"What, just because I occasionally bend the rules to get to the bottom of a case? That, my dear, is called going above and beyond."

"Above and beyond for what?" Allison shrieked. "These people out here don't care that we risk our lives every day to keep them safe. They didn't care before, so why on earth would they give a shit now? We've become irrelevant, *my dear*, or haven't you noticed all the crime going on right out in the open?"

For the most part, it consisted of looters fighting for high-end appliances and racing each other through post-human obstacle courses.

"Maybe so, but I'm not going to stop doing what I can to…"

"To what? Get killed? Society is collapsing all around us. Everybody who can is running; DeLay, Ford, Percy, McClennen, Walt, Dr. Danvers, Sgt. Stern: they've all gone. We're down to the new recruits, and I'm not putting my trust in these idiots that they're rushing through training. I say we go while we can and spend what time we have left together."

"I tell you what, Ally…. You go, and you let me know when you've found this magical sanctuary that everyone seems to think exists over the horizon."

She rode his words down from the peak of momentary excitement.

"Oh my God! You're impossible!!!!"

"That's funny," Kane replied. "I was thinking the same thing about you."

"When is it going to be enough, Philip? When you're burning in hell? Because that's where you're going, you know."

"Well, it can't be any worse than walking around like that." He cricked his head toward the window and the bewildered dead folks that littered the street outside.

Challenging her position was a lost cause, and Kane knew it. If only she didn't hold her newfound faith over his head as some sort of level of enlightenment that he had yet to reach.

"When are you going to wake up and see what's going on right in front of your eyes, Philip?"

"Frankly, I don't have the time or the energy to fill all the gaps in your logic. And I'm not going to brush aside the oath that we both took just because a few guys can pull rabbits out of their hats."

"Is that what you really think of him… them?"

"Well, I certainly don't think they're… never mind…. I've got a question for you."

Allison tensed up.

"So which one of *them* do you believe?"

Once again, Allison escaped to the window and beyond.

"Hey!" she pointed, instantly star-struck. "Isn't that…?"

Walking shirtless down 3rd and Pine, a tall, thin zombie appeared reflective of his condition, his big head bobbing, prominent brow falling victim to a perpetual bitch-slap from his flopping black hair.

From the corner of Kane's eye, he looked like a million other white guys.

"Isn't that Ben Damon, the actor? I think it is…."

Kane shook his head…. He had always been too much of a workaholic and cynic to pay attention to hot young actors.

"C'mon, you know the guy…. He was dating that untalented Latina… the one with the ass…."

Kane slowed down suddenly to take a look, worn brake pads squealing. He had been meaning to fix those. It gave him away too many times.

When the tall, thin zombie lurched toward the noise, Kane recognized him. He had seen that face on posters and magazine covers. On the man's naked chest, someone had scribbled "Boytoy" and "Owned" in bright, red lipstick. In his wake, a crowd of about twenty followed as if to mock his former life, or due to a brainfart of deadened recognition and resulting awe.

Kane could tell within seconds what stage of zombie he was dealing with. This bunch looked relatively fresh, which meant they could still run.

Ben Damon was the first to charge the car, his face morphing at the point of launch through savagely aggressive tones and finally into one that read murderous hunger. Ben had been in Philly filming a movie when Jesus and Yeshua made their debuts and brought with them the rain, and the living dead.

"Holy sh…."

Allison was interrupted by inertia shoving her into the seat as Kane stepped on the gas. She watched through the side mirror as Ben and the crowd tried to keep up, reaching and flailing their arms as they ran. They were still running at the point when distance blurred, then snatched them from her sight.

Gesturing silently, Allison and Kane acknowledged the moment together. Like some road-trip scenario on acid dropped in a steaming pile of shit, it was kind of fun, in a brush-with-danger, adrenaline-rush sort of way.

As he drove, his expression lingering on levity, Kane remembered that Allison had never answered his question. That was one of her tricks. He wasn't going to let her get away with it this time.

Clearing his throat…

"C'mon… I know what common sense tells you, but I bet, just like everyone else, you just can't get past all the bullshit imagery and revisionist crap to accept that a little brown man from…"

"I'm not… I don't want to talk about this anymore," Allison said.

"Figures. All right, listen. I'll make a deal with you. If I can prove to you that this is all a load of shit, will you at least hear me out?"

"But why even…"

"Well, will you? After the test, I've got to make some calls. And I have to get in touch with Vernon Boca. He's tight with the DN. Word is that they've already met with Yeshua. I know that they sometimes use Vernon's club to hold meetings and to do recruiting. I'm willing to bet he knows something about whatever they're cooking up with the Coalition."

"Now why would he be meeting up with *them*?"

Kane noticed the way her tongue curled around the word *them*, the way her tone shifted as it fell from her mouth, like *they* were the scum of the earth.

"That's what I'm trying to find out."

"Good luck."

"So, I have your word?"

It was obvious that Allison didn't want to commit to an answer, yet Kane implored her with his eyes.

"Well, I seriously doubt that anything you find out will change my mind."

"That's fine. I just want your word that you'll listen."

"Okay. You have my word."

"Now, was that so hard?"

"Make light of it all you want, Philip. Just remember that it's only because I care for you. And I don't want to lose you."

Kane didn't say a word. If the three beers and the shot of Rumplemintz that swished around in his gut could talk, they would've told her to shut the fuck up and then asked for a blowjob.

"What do you think are my chances of getting any leads from the Meleeza Duncan case?"

"This Duncan girl... I mean, yeah, she was just a kid, but she had a rap sheet as long as my arm. And on top of that she is... was a junkie, plain and simple." Allison deliberately aimed low. "I don't understand what exactly you expect to find."

"What is your problem with this girl?"

"What is *my* problem?????" Allison's eyes bulged the way they did when Kane stuck his dick in her asshole for the very first time. "I saw what she looked like. I saw the way you were salivating while you leafed through her portfolio."

"You can't be serious, Ally."

"I'm not saying that you wanted to fuck her or anything, but had she been some ugly, fat broad, you wouldn't still be obsessing about her, would you?"

"Obsessing????"

"For that matter, I think I liked it better back when you were obsessing about Carlos McCann."

"You know what, Ally…. Just forget I even brought it up," Kane said as he switched off the auto-drive and muscled the steering wheel into submission. Clutching the wheel at 10 and 2 o'clock, he squeezed to give anger a small taste of the attention it begged for.

"Fine with me," Allison said, seasoning her tone like a well-trained smartass.

Kane stepped on the gas. Instead of turning and indulging her silent goading, he didn't take his eyes off the road for the rest of the drive. After a good 15 minutes, he forgot about her bullshit entirely.

There was so much to see.

To the far right:
A mixed group of civilian volunteers dressed in riot gear were doing their best to clean the large pools of blood left in the street and working together to push dumpsters, mailboxes and over-turned cars into a makeshift blockade as the lumbering nuisances slowly marched toward them.

To the far left:
Zombies chasing down automobiles (only to be struck down and a sucked beneath the vehicles in many cases), cornering the occasional looters who risked being eaten just to get their hands on a top-of-the-line TV or stereo. Some were nimble enough to negotiate the moving labyrinth of shuffling death. The unlucky ones, who were often the most greedy, found themselves trapped, like the thuggish teenager who begged for his life as the zombies closed on him, even going as far as trying to offer them the television he'd just stole. When that didn't work, he tried money.

Kane considered stopping and helping him, but his priorities were different now, especially when it came to criminals. And it was too late to do any good anyway.

In the distant background:
A dozen or so first-stagers hovered around insignificant reminders of their pasts, or spent their time expounding on reputations that they'd built in life. Names like Bundy, Dahmer, Voorhees, and Mezerak.... Only now, they were much more brazen and care-free. They looted alongside the living, organized in small gangs to fight off the police, and killed for the hell of it.

Max Hedberg's Journal

Entry #9

I did it. I fucked her. I just made love to a fucking zombie! I know what you're thinking, but I had to do it. All right, so maybe I even wanted to do it.

I doubt I can make you understand how someone could be so... desperate for affection, so hard up for the way things were that they could screw a corpse. I could claim temporary insanity or something like that, but then I would be lying. At least I think I would.

I had just awoke from the most vivid dream of Maria and me enthralled in passion the likes of which we hadn't experienced since we first met. It was the third time since I've been down here that my dreams were of a sexual nature, and masturbating just wasn't doing it for me since I rubbed my penis raw beating off to the holographic slideshow of our trip to the Jersey Shore when Maria wore the bikini I bought her. It was a red mesh thingy with a thong bottom. It took some convincing (like a diamond bracelet) to get her to wear it. Man, I'm getting all excited just picturing her walking away from me on her way to the water.

I knew what I was doing when I opened the freezer door. In my mind, it was just another night, and I was walking up to bed after waking up downstairs on the couch. I must've done that 1000 times.

Yesterday, I cut off one of my fingers, twisted it off actually, and ate it in small bites. Goddamn if it only made me hungrier. I'm hallucinating all the time now. I can't imagine things getting much worse.

Excuse me for a moment. I think I'm going to puke.

Entry #10

Sorry I had to cut it short last time. These hunger pains are no fucking joke. I ate my third roach today, for Christ's sake. I was going to twist off another finger, but now that I know how bad it hurts, I just couldn't go through with it again. Oh, but you can fuck a corpse, right? I hear ya.

Aside from the stench of death intertwined with urine and shit; the strange texture and icy feel of her skin; the frigid aura that gave everything within two feet of her a serious chill that was degrees colder than the freezer itself; the wound on her forearm that had spread and eaten away at her firm olive flesh all the way up to her shoulder; the milky glaze that coated her eyes and the insane, primal hunger that inhabited them; her rancid breath that made my stomach turn even with her mouth stuffed; and the fact that for all my sweet-talking (and I pulled out all the stops in a last-ditch attempt to somehow coax the old Maria to the surface), I was basically like a stranger to her, it was the wildest sex that I've ever had.

The freezer had helped to preserve her, so the smell wasn't all that bad. Not nearly as bad as I thought it would be. And it's not like she just laid there. That's what she usually did as a matter of fact. So this new, animated Maria was, in a strange way, kind of a treat.

I knew I'd have to tie her down and gag her, but guess what? That was one of my fantasies. I'm not a pervert or anything. It's just that I've always had this thing for seeing a woman bound and gagged like the girls on the covers of the old detective magazines I used to see in the grocery store as a kid.

Still doesn't answer your question, I know. Well, I don't know what else to tell you. I'm not going to stop loving my wife just because she's... well, dead. Who's to say that she can't occasionally think, or feel?

Entry #11

Bad day today. Haven't had more than an hour of sleep at a time in almost a solid week. At least I think it's been a week. Could be a month, could be two months. Who the fuck cares anymore? Right now, I think I'd rather eat than sleep. What I wouldn't do for a cheeseburger, or another roach. I haven't eaten in days.

Remember the stuff (the noise and weird conversations) that I couldn't talk about before? Well, Maria, she would say different things to persuade me to open the freezer door. Or she'd talk only to Eric, but say things about me, as if I weren't there. "You know, daddy put us in here because he's mean and he doesn't love us," she'd say. Or, "Daddy wants to hurt us, Eric. It's up to you to get us out of here."

When that didn't work, she'd start with the apologies, and empty promises not to "freak out" again if I let her out, then came the tearful confessions about how much she loved me, and how she was planning on doing something special to prove it. "Just let me out and I'll show you." Yeah, right.

She was like the old Maria then, the one I married. When she was like this, the three of us would talk for hours sometimes, reminiscing and laughing like everything was everything. Once she had me at ease, she'd turn on her seductive voice and try to lure me in with dirty talk, and she didn't hold back on the descriptions even though Eric was still listening.

These freak-outs were unpredictable, but I generally knew when Maria was near the end of her rope. Her grammar would start to degrade. Whatever we were talking about at the time, it would always come back to how hungry she was, which in turn reminded me of how hungry I was. She'd begin to slur her words, then Bam! as Emeril Lagasse would say. The next thing I know, she's kicking and screaming and banging on the door and going on and on about how much of a man I was not, and how she couldn't wait to sink her teeth into my flesh to see what real pussy must taste like. Eric would start balling in reaction to her breakdown, and of course she'd turn her attention to him, calling him names and cursing him for not helping mommy like a good boy would. "You know what Mommy does to bad little boys?" she'd say. "Mommy eats them."

Eric shrieked like a banshee the first few days. I could just picture him stomping and flailing his arms. There was a standing and a lying-down version, you know. Now he just kind of chanted in sing-song fashion, "Daaa-deee, I'm hungry," or "Daaa-dee, why you put me in here?" or "It's dark in here, Daaa-deee" or "Am I died, Daaa-deee?" or "Why Mommy not talkin' to me, Daaa-deee?" or "Is Mommy died too, Daaa-deee?"

Now neither of them have much to say outside of the occasional groan. It kills me to think that any shred of my wife and son are gone. I don't know how much longer I can hold out down here. God, I'm so fucking hungry. I feel like my own stomach is eating me from the inside out.

I think this is it for me.

Chapter 6
Like Chicken for Deadfucks

Anonymous man awoke to pinpricks of white-hot pain. Having no recollection of his surroundings, himself, or how he got to be where he was, he fell hard against the warm leather seat-cushion, his fingertips massaging his clammy brow in small circles as if it might initiate recall.

A quick survey of the area returned bits and pieces of information. It was the dead of night, he had been asleep, or unconscious in the passenger's seat of someone's car. For how long he had no idea. The car sat idle in the rear section of the 24-hour Megamart's vast parking lot, back where the dumpsters lined up to gobble up refuse next to a trio of loading docks.

Brachiosaur-necked lampposts laid bright eyes on the lot-markers (X, in this case) blinking faintly in effigy of shoddy workmanship from 19-inch screens mounted on each side, and halfway down its neck.

From now on he was going to go by X. Being a black man (somehow he just knew), it seemed strangely appropriate that he adopt the lane marker (X) as his temporary identity.

A door, facing X from 100 feet away, past a few scattered cars, and patches of dried blood, looked to have been left open by the skinny Wigger clothed in store colors who had just went back inside after his smoke break. He spent the bulk of it taunting the zombies behind the electrified fence and laughing at the ever-malfunctioning parking-lot guides.

Lot Escorts they were called, holographic companions (they came in all races, genders, and physical types) that, for $125 a month, would escort the client to his or her car should they forget where they parked, or in case it was dark and they didn't want to make the journey alone. If there was trouble, the escort reacted by speaking in a commanding tone, something along the lines of:

"Step away from the customer!"

or

"Stop, or I will be forced to alert the authorities!"

If that didn't work, they gave off a brief electric charge to stun the would-be attacker.

There was talk of a "Classic Hollywood" series coming in a year or two.

To X, the whole place looked infected with pesky apparitions hailing from all walks of life, appearing and disappearing, some lingering longer than others, some stuck in perpetual stutter, some going through their normal routine and making small-talk with the empty air next to them as they walked to an empty spot, waved, then vanished.

One had walked right up to X's window: a fat, overly accommodating woman. He didn't see her until she was right up on him. He turned and there she was. She looked right at him, past him, and waved. Something about her fake sincerity gave him chills.

Like many businesses, the Megamart's parking lot was surrounded by 15-foot electrified fencing made up of concertina wire and topped with a jagged coil of barbed wire that extended the entire length and came to life like a chainsaw smile when touched.

On the other side, hundreds of full-blown zombies stood back, perusing the live menu with slack-jawed intensity, zeroing in on the meaty parts. Thanks to the malfunctioning escorts, they were riled up, their collective moan upgraded to a deep-throated growl and seasoned with frustration. 800,000 volts reacted with lively bursts of electric blue admonishment to the touch of cold dead limbs and digits. Small fires here and there awarded those who could hold on to the fence the longest.

At the entrance, double-reinforced scaffolding erected in the shape of a 25-foot watchtower lined with giant floodlights, housed three glorified rent-a-cops who took turns picking off zombies who wandered too close to the gates and to the occasional vehicle that drove in and out.

X could see the top ten feet of the watchtower from where he sat.

Instead of jump-starting his memory, the lack of cohesive relevance sent X spiraling into phobic territory. He let his head fall forward, his brow smacking the dash with a thud. He repeated it again and again.

Suddenly, the click-clack of footsteps approaching from the rear... real footsteps. There was a distinct difference.

Through the fogged windows, X noticed a police officer who had just noticed him too and was approaching to investigate, nightstick twirling in his hand.

X also noticed that the back seat-rests had been pushed forward and were lying on top of the back seat as if someone had forced their way in through the trunk of the car. It gave him his first real clue as to how he might have made it past the guard-tower around front.

The officer was close enough now that X could see the letters on his nametag: Officer D. Mira.

X quickly deferred to the rearview, as if he just now realized that it existed and was thrown for a loop by what he saw looking back at him.

Half jumping, half falling, X sprung from the car, from whatever it was in the rear-view mirror, and in turn, sent Mira back into a defensive crouch, his service revolver now in place of his baton.

"Don't move!" Mira's tightened chords blared.

Somewhere deep inside his own mind, X was pinned down by unseen hands that taunted and teased him with prolonged periods of sight, sound, and sensation, but without the ability to respond and react on his own.

X seemed to comply to the officer's demands without hesitation; however, he was frozen in residual shockwaves of mule-kick reflex action and fleet-footed understanding of a second tenant who occupied his inner space and of the ghastly warped thing in the rear-view, pock-marked with bullet-holes (hundreds at least) and exaggerated to devilish proportions.

Like everyone else these days, the thought of becoming a zombie had crossed X's mind at some point, creeping up with icy fingers sharpened to a point, replacing the fear of death itself as the motive for nonsensical countermeasures, like fanatical commitment to religion, and the acquisition of unnecessary things to clog the wheels of logic.

He'd seen people turn after being bitten. Akin to an erosive virus, it was a slow, excruciating process that started with nausea, fever, chills, violent mood swings, and dementia, none of which he had yet experienced.

His subconscious suggested that it might be demonic possession. Before Jesus, and the zombies, he would've laughed at that.

"Who… er, what *the fuck* are you!?" Mira barked, maintaining shaky composure that started and ended with the handgun that he held out in front of him, elbows locked straight. "And how did you do… what you did?"

"I… I don't know. I don't remember anything before waking up in the car," X said, his hands upturned, arms spread, beckoning, his mangled face waxing innocent as if he expected some give in Mira's stance as a result.

X took a step forward.

"I SAID DON'T FUCKING MOVE!" Mira growled, and sunk deeper into his ready-stance. "I suppose you don't remember killing those cops back in the bus station, then?"

Watching X with experienced eyes, slightly reddened due to fatigue, but sharp as a hawk, Mira leaned his head to the side and spoke into the communicator on his lapel, "This is Mira. I'm in row X of the Megamart parking lot on Lansdowne and Garrett road. I've got our cop-killer. I repeat. I've - got - our - cop-killer. Send back-up." Eyes rolling up and down X's gruesome body. "Fuck it, send a meat-wagon too. He's in bad shape now, but that's nothing compared to what he'll look like when I'm done with him."

"Mira, this is Drake," a voice blared up at him from his lapel. "Are you out of your mind!? This mutherfucker just took out twelve of us BY HIMSELF!! Just hold tight 'til we get there."

"Yeah! No shit," Mira barked back, "two of 'em were good friends of mine … yours too, Drake."

"Don't you dare, Officer!" exclaimed an unfamiliar voice, tainted with an accent that bore some distant relation to police-speak.

His gun still pointed at X, who stood with his arms in the air, eyes reading disbelief as he surveyed himself from the feet up and back down, Mira considered doing the right thing and waiting for back-up. He played out the scenario in his head and found little satisfaction in the outcome. He wasn't dumb enough to actually believe in the system. Especially not now.

"Who the hell is this?" Mira replied speaking at his lapel.

"This is Detective Makane, Officer. Now you listen to me. I understand your anger, but this case is bigger than that. You do anything to keep me from questioning that asshole and I'll…."

"Do what you have to, Mira!" Sergeant Dell interrupted. "Just don't you take your eyes off that scum. I'm on my way."

"Stay outta this, Sergeant!" Makane demanded. "You and your men have no idea what you're dealing with."

"I'm sorry, Detective. It's not usually my style to step on someone else's toes, but this guy took down 12 of my men."

"Thirteen, actually," X teased in a voice vastly different from, yet equally genuine to, the one that resonated from his diaphragm only moments ago. With its distinctly feminine cadence, and deep Appalachian drawl, it made Mira's hands tremble and constrict around the butt of his gun when he realized that it sprung from this teenage boy who stood before him. Mira put him at 17 or 18 years at most.

"Wh… what did you say?" Mira inquired tentatively, like part of him cringed at the thought of hearing that voice crawl from those lips again.

"Goddammit officer!" Kane yelled via the lapel-receiver. "Just get out of there. Now!"

"I said that I killed 13 little piggies, you dumb cunt. You forgot to count yourself."

Mira had only begun to squeeze the trigger when he saw hundreds of what looked like bullets punch free from X's torso, legs, and face and zip to a livid hover at either side of X's head and shoulders. Pulsating with aggression and taunting with half-lunges, the living swarm restlessly awaited their cue from X, who was clearly caught in some kind of trance.

Mira fired three times. In retrospect, it seemed like a stupid move, what with the bullets (which they clearly were, bullets) hovering in a sentient mass all around this kid.

X buckled and tensed in an orgasmic flutter in reaction to Mira's attempt to bring him down. The most it did was energize him.

Turning to face Mira, X lurched, and coughed. With his tongue, he fished something small and round with a deadened glow and smeared with residual streaks of red up from his throat, rolled it between his teeth, and spit it at him.

Mira cried out when his own recycled bullet bit him in the gut and dug into his soul. It was the worst pain he had ever experienced.

He pulled his hand away from his stomach and watched the dark stain in his uniform expand before his eyes. Dying was the last thing Officer D. Mira expected to happen today when he woke up. In fact, he awoke looking forward to using his new vibro-shock baton to crack some zombie skulls.

Mira did his best to ignore the pain and react as he was trained. It was all he knew.

He lifted his gun and pointed.

X, who was still entranced, had plenty of time to react.

Mira was fading, swaying to a seductive song called creeping death. He managed to squeeze the trigger one last time, half involuntarily.

The brutish verve of hundreds of bullets pounded Mira from every angle as he spun away and danced into the dark uncertainty. His last thought, that there might be no afterlife, worked with his relaxing muscles to guide his last meal out into his underwear.

Mira's own bullet hadn't even left the barrel before he expired, on his feet, dancing to the beat of lead projectiles, and crumbled to the ground when they were done with him, nerves twitching, electrons firing Hail Marys.

On the ground, Mira's body twitched to the POP, POP, POP of gunshot sounds as the living-lead exploded out of him one by one and settled into a swarm in the air above him. Individual bullets darted and lunged before chasing each other into braided formations upon their return to their host-body (X) who accepted their heavy-handed homecoming with open arms.

Just like that, X awoke from the trance.

Now that he was himself again, and armed with selective recognizance, X was able to deduce that he was most likely responsible for whatever happened to the police officer (Mira) who lay broken at his feet. And he was instantly reminded of the bigger threat.

FUCKING ZOMBIES....

They were everywhere. Their collective moan, so pervasive that it drove a few folks to suicide, was hypnotic at times. X could see in their eyes, how bad they wanted to come through the fence and eat his ass. They seemed to look at him differently than they did the escorts, as if they knew.

Vying for the top spot in the background din, the haunting wail of police sirens bounced from building to building and out into the open where X stood searching for somewhere to hide. Around front, the rent-a-cops in the tower had their hands full with an aggressive faction of zombies that had begun to rock the tower to get at them.

Still, the front gates were locked, the fences all around him humming with current. X was trapped.

Forgetting, for the moment, his brief collection of memories, X focused on his best option (blending in with the late-night shoppers in the Megamart), and took off running toward the back of the building.

He took a moment to catch his breath. He had underestimated the distance between where he originally stood and the stockroom door and ran the entire length at close to top speed.

When he turned the knob, it gave.

The stockroom was damp and cold. The generator's unabashed rattle drowned out any noise he made, so once he realized that he was alone in the room, he didn't worry much about stepping lightly. He hurried to the door on the other side, and teased it open to a crack.

As was usually the case at this time of night, the store was fairly empty, which seemed to give the music more room to reveal the overhead speakers' poor quality and add to the surreal atmosphere.

What X could see from where he crouched at the back corner of the store gave him incentive to further explore the Megamart as a potential pit stop.

There was an obese single mother dressed in ill-fitting designer knock-offs and large gold earrings with the words 'Bad Girl' written in cursive, and mounted on the gaudy triangular frame, and her obnoxious young son who she ignored completely, except when he wandered out of her sight and she yelled out his name "DARIUS!!!!!!!" at the top of her lungs.

Zit-faced employees stocked shelves and talked smack about the store hottie, a fine, young brown-skinned thing, who sat facing a large monitor keying in irregular items up in the manager's booth that was situated high above the colorfully stocked aisles at the back like some administrative watchtower.

A group of stoned college students snickered at shit like 'butt shank portion,' 'turkey necks,' and store substitutes for popular brand name products, 'Mega-tussin,' and 'Mega-jock itch cream'.

A broken-down store security drone rested next to two older models that didn't work either in their station a few yards from X.

X had not yet seen himself since the last blackout, and what he looked like was suspiciously left out of his recent memory. Still, he maintained a crouch to avoid being seen as he made his way to the nearest empty isle (Tools and Hardware) and fell on his ass between two columns of stacked boxes marked Sure-Grip.

He tried to steady his breathing, to escape reality by losing himself in the holographic celebrity spokesman that stood before a pyramid of stacked socket-sets and a state-of-the-art riding lawn mower that could hover 6 inches off the ground and cut grass with lasers. Then there were the animated mascots that touted this product and that from their respective packages, talking over each other with repetitive sales-pitches that eventually bled into one voice that X was pretty sure instructed him to **"KILL THEM ALL!**

You can start with that fine young thing up in the manager's booth. I bet her shit even smells like roses."

Voices in his head were one thing, but these were external. Could it have been a personalized ad via retinal scan, or facial-recognition software built into the package itself? Tools and Hardware weren't usually known to use profanity and vulgar sexual references as part of their repertoire, though.

"If it's Meleeza you're worried about, she'll never know, not unless you dig her up and tell her."

The voice was clear this time, deep and gravel-pitched, yet feminine, and made all the more peculiar by the fact that it was coming from the mouth of a praying mantis in a tool belt looming from an angled-down flat-screen placed above the Mantis Tools alcove in the middle of the aisle.

With it came total recall.

He remembered the following:

His name, Jason Williamson…

He had a brother, Mikel, who was 3 years older.

The rush of heat that seemed to leap from his girlfriend Meleeza's body into his when she died in his arms.

How, in complete concert with aggression, anger, and hatred, the sentient heat made him feel for the split second before he vomited all over her...

The days that followed were wrought with drastic mood swings and bouts of violent sickness.

The confrontation with the police in the bus station was where he gained his bullet-down guise. Up to that point, he had been possessed in the classical sense.

How good it felt to break that security guard's fucking neck and toss him to the ground like he was a child when in fact he was much bigger than Jason. Sensing that something was wrong with him, Jason was trying to leave town before he lashed out at his mother or anyone else close to him like the new tenant in his body was trying to convince him to do.

Worst of all, Jason remembered how he looked and exactly how painful it was being shot repeatedly. Most of the cops were armed with Glock 61s, which, according to the manufacturer, could stop an elephant.

Listening over the choir of hucksters, Jason scrutinized every sound he heard and labored to understand the source of the voices coming from the next aisle over. In any case, he knew that he couldn't stay where he was for long without being seen.

Lifting himself enough to see over the highest box, Jason peered to the left, then right, then turned to inspect his rear. He was just about to give himself an "all clear" when...

An eye, widened to a full circle, stared back at him from the minimal confines of a woman's compact mirror. It was the brown-skinned hottie in the manager's booth. Apparently, she had been checking her make-up when she saw him.

Startled to a flushed hue by what she saw down in aisle 13,

the brown-skinned hottie dropped her compact, spun around, and backed all the way into the opposite wall.

His reaction delayed by fear, it wasn't until she picked up the phone that Jason thought to drop out of sight.

A frigid embrace began to claim him as the thought of facing the police again, who were surely out for blood now, gestated. He couldn't hear the sirens over all the jingles and holographic spokesmen. *They must be close now*, he thought.

From the ass-end of the aisle just below the manager's booth, the metallic screech of rusty wheels sliced through his concentration and finally brought Jason to the balls of his feet and off in the opposite direction.

The mouth of the isle jumped from side to side as he ran. The brighter light at the end beckoned, brilliantly illuminating the talking magazine and tabloid covers and flashing candy bar wrappers that were strategically placed to snag the dormant majority as they waited to check out. More importantly, he focused on the automatic doors that lie just beyond the checkout counters to the left of the large windows that stretched along the entire front wall.

Jason focused on the one directly in his path, the one with the empty shopping cart wedged between it and the next. He was confident that he could clear it in one dive and roll, but decided to simply plant his hands on the counter and throw his legs over the cart at the last minute. He fully expected to nip it with his foot; he didn't expect that his ankle would become momentarily lodged.

Landing awkwardly, Jason adjusted his footing and turned to run out the double doors. They were conveniently blocked by a man he hadn't noticed before, a stout serial-killer type who had bent over to retrieve the groceries that had just fallen through the bottom of his paper bag. He nearly jumped out of his shoes when he saw Jason.

Thinking quickly, Jason opted for the window. Pushing the serial-killer type aside might have been easier in theory, but Jason was afraid of what might happen to the man if he should retaliate. Besides, what were a few shards of broken glass compared to another death on his hands?

Against the backdrop of night, Jason's reflection stood out. He was about to stop when he saw it move out of synch. And there was something else… something distinctly solid moving behind his two-dimensional doppelganger, growing larger as… as it approached from the parking lot. It was a man, someone he had seen before (Kane). He was carrying a double-fisted, liquid-light cannon, and he was pointing it right at Jason.

Exploding glass chased Jason along the window-lined front of the store as Kane squeezed and held the trigger. In his wake, headstrong stalactite blades of glass refused to fall from the top of the giant window frames until they could hang on no longer. He managed to stay just ahead of projectile shards that nipped at his back, and dove to the floor at the mouth of the L-shaped vestibule.

The burly, serial-killer type sprung from his hiding spot between two vending machines when Jason slid to a stop near him and stepped right into the path of a molten bullet with Jason's name on it. He never knew what hit him.

From the parking lot came a passionate yell, faint, affected by less restricting acoustics as it had come from outside, and delivered with a certain authoritarian zeal.

"Freeze, or I'll blow your ass…!"

Jason didn't wait for Kane to finish. Had he listened to the voice that advised him **"We can take him,"** then he would have most likely had another dead cop on his hands—and his conscience.

Running as fast as he could, through the check-out lane, into the main area, and up aisle 9, which was empty, Jason just missed being struck by rippled potato-chip fragments traveling at high velocity as Kane continued to fire his double-fisted cannon.

Kane was beside himself with guilt that he didn't make it to the bus station before the boys from the 22nd Precinct. They patrolled the ass-end of the city, and they had a reputation for shooting first, which is exactly what they were going to do to Jason when they got here. On a side note, Kane saw it as some kind of cruel joke that the cops of the 22nd, who abused their authority with impunity and were rumored to be corrupt, should still have double the men, and good men in terms of skill, than were left at the 13th Precinct. Maybe they were on to something.

By all accounts, Jason Williamson was a good kid who just happened to be at the wrong place at the wrong time, and now Kane would have to kill him too. There was no other way. Kane had been smitten by Jason's quick wit, and the glow of wisdom beyond his years that swirled beneath those big brown eyes. If given the chance, this kid was going places, he remembered thinking... well, maybe not now.

Too often the bad examples seemed to make the most noise, finding empowerment and pride, or something resembling pride, but owing more to rage and insecurity, in the belligerent attitudes that victimization produced. Jason was different: intelligent, charismatic, and street-smart. And look what had become of him. Somehow, it just wasn't fair.

Deep in his subconscious, Kane looked to redirect blame, pointing the finger at Jason's poor judgment in the people he associated with. Meleeza Duncan certainly was attractive, and seemed nice enough, but for a girl of only 17 years, she came with a lot of baggage, most of all that whack-job mother of hers.

Jogging toward the shattered front window with his double-fisted cannon held at the ready, Kane filed his guilt away and concentrated on making as little noise as possible as he traversed the moat of crystalline shards, climbed in through the empty frame, and crouched behind the check-out counter.

With his back against the filthy bag-bin at the end of the check-out counter, Kane looked to his right, at the mess of red flannel that blocked the entrance, and quietly apologized to the burly man (serial-killer type) who lay bloodied on the floor, feet facing into the store, arms stretched up over his head blocking the automatic doors that repeatedly opened and closed on him.

Peeking over the check-out counter to develop a visual layout of the store, Kane waved the scattered bystanders who were jockeying for his attention back into hiding. As big as the place was, Jason could've been anywhere.

He was such a good kid. Such a good kid...

Snippets from their past conversation at the station reacquainted Kane with Jason's winning smile.

Kane thought it was a joke when he first heard Sgt. Stern mention the name Boring. His colleagues were notorious practical jokers. But how on earth would they have known? His mother and Layla, his ex, were the only people he ever told about Boring, the talking pterodactyl with large human eyes and a long, devious smile that would fly in his bedroom window every night when he was 10 and berate him for being too afraid to look out from under the covers. Kane never actually saw it so he could've looked like anything; if he had looked, he might've saved himself from the horrors that his imagination conjured up over the years. It had haunted him ever since, this imaginary friend who, despite Kane's skepticism, he knew in his gut to have been real. Could it be that they were one in the same, that *his* Boring had resurfaced 25 years later?

...or...

Maybe this was just some hyper-contagious virus. All three hosts (Gus Rollins, Meleeza Duncan, and now Jason) had come into close contact with each other. Rollins had taken Meleeza hostage before he was killed by police during his shooting spree at the Springfield Mall, and Meleeza died in Jason's arms.

But then, why the games, why the stab at poignancy with Jason, in his bullet-down guise, representing some twisted metaphor on urban violence? Maybe he was wrong, but that's how Kane saw it.

"Jason!" The voice cut into Jason's concentration with the

subtly of a dull blade slicing through gamey beef as he hid in the frozen meats and seafood area at the back near where he originally entered the store. "This is Detective Philip Makane. We spoke at the police station a while ago."

"**Don't listen to him.**" The voice inside Jason's head demanded just as he was rounding the corner to recognition.

"I know that you're a good kid, Jason, and that you're being forced to do these things."

"**He doesn't know shit. He'll say anything to get you to come out.**"

"The police will be here any minute and I'm sure you know how they feel about cop killers. To put it bluntly, I'm the only hope you've got. Now, come out with your hands up, and I'll do my best to see that you get some help."

"**Fuck him! Make that piglet work for it.**"

Jason had yelled out to Kane, whom he now remembered vividly as someone he could trust, only his voice never left his mouth, and even there it was but a mumble.

"**Don't you fight me, boy.... I'll rape your insignificant little ass from the inside out.**"

Working within the limitations of his cerebral lock down, Jason searched his mental database, digging deep for something to distract him from the present: his mother's smile, his dog Emmitt jumping up to greet him, Meleeza purring in his arms in the afterglow of sex.

"Goddammit!!!!!" Kane growled, watching with grave disappointment as four police cruisers sped into the parking lot, slid to various slants, and vomited officers left and right. Two of the officers ran back to the entrance to assist the rent-a-cops, who had lost one of their men to the zombies.

Warmth fled Jason's body as he marinated in what-ifs: what if *their* bullets, laced with tangible scorn, somehow hurt more; what if he went out looking like some run-of-the-mill thug with a supernatural upgrade. He hated being lumped into the same group with the corner jockeys, who warmed the steps outside liquor stores in his neighborhood taunting average-looking women and intimidating those whom they envied.

"Relax, boy. You ain't just in here by yourself. And I don't intend to make it easy for those pigs this time."

"Maybe you didn't hear me Jason," Kane yelled, louder this time to compensate for the sirens that blared from right outside. "Do you hear *that*, then? They're right out front. Do yourself a favor and come out now, before it's too late for me to…"

"Save your breath pig!" the voice spoke via Jason's mouth. **"You might need it to scream bloody murder when all those teeth are ripping into your flesh."**

Kane gave the threat little merit. Realizing that he *was* going to have to kill Jason, he tried to find something that might comfort the boy.

"For what it's worth, Jason, I'm sorry," he said, aiming his ear toward the back of the store to gauge Jason's position, from his voice, when he replied.

He waited and waited, but there was no response.

Where are you, you bastard? Kane whispered, his eyes rolling from left to right. He ignored, for the moment, the frightened shoppers who were starting to make tentative movements toward the front of the store hoping to greet the police.

A loud CRASH from the lot spun Kane around.

The guard tower and fencing along the front of the lot lay flat, with dead rent-a-cops entangled in the broken scaffolding, chain links bouncing beneath slipshod feet that shuffled away the weakened electric tentacles that reached up and danced around their legs before fizzling out.

Hundreds of full-blown zombies staggered into the Megamart parking lot and immediately went after the escorts, stumbling over and trampling each other along the way. Something resembling enthusiasm grew in their deadened eyes as they walked up on them and either reached or lunged right through them.

Reacting as they were programmed, the escorts each spoke one of two warnings.

"Step away from the customer!"

"Stop, or I will be forced to alert the authorities!"

But the zombies continued to attack them, falling right through the holographic people until phase two of their security system ignited an electric burst that sent the ravenous corpses flying sloppily through the air.

Most of them climbed drunkenly to their feet and tried again.

The rest of the zombies followed the general flow of undead husks toward the front of the store like a tidal wave of molasses rolling both slow and fast toward the cops who stopped, turned, and opened fire.

With all their firepower, they probably didn't expect to be overcome as quickly as they were, caught in the undertow of grasping hands and dragged down beneath the surface.

Jolts of light popped with brilliant yet brief life-spans from the officers' Glock 61s providing a "you are here"-style position marker as some of them tried, in vain, to shoot their way out of the swarm. Others punched, clawed, and scratched the anonymous hands and teeth that tugged their flesh and pinched it away from the bone.

There was a certain pitch of scream that seemed specific to being eaten alive. It was an awful sound, one that came as close as possible to translating the experience, especially the first and last bite.

Fuckers are worse than roaches, Kane thought as he turned away from the scene and cleared his throat to block out the sound.

"You were saying about the police?" The voice resonated with maniacal glee. **"The question now is… is it too late for you to help yourself, or the rest of these sheep who you've sworn to protect?"**

While the words had reached his ears, Kane was busy

breaking the parking lot down visually into feet between himself and the zombies. Most of them were on their last legs, so they were slow and easy enough to maneuver around, but it took a certain kind of person to let them get so close and still remain calm enough to workout a path through the maze of bad meat, open wounds, and funky stenches.

Kane had no idea what kinds of people he was dealing with here in the store. Nine times out of 10, they weren't the right kind. And with Jason running around to boot, their composure was most definitely stretched thin.

The lead zombies already had Kane focused in their sights. When he saw the carnal anticipation bulging from their clouded eyes, as if they knew that his flesh was somehow tastier than the norm, he looked down at his body almost expecting to see a big red bull's-eye painted on his chest.

This fucking place... flat and rectangular, with sickening hospital-white light pouring out from the large jagged-toothed opening in the front of the building as if to advertise all the edible goodies inside.

As it was close enough to present the possibility of danger, the slap of flat, heavy feet wrapped in hard-soled shoes, and traveling at a living stride from his immediately left-rear sent Kane back into action-mode.

Leading with his double-fisted cannon, Kane spun around too late to stop the obese black woman from running out the door with her son Darius in tow.

Kane's arm check-beckoned, his lips curling around the words "Stop! Wait!" in silence as he realized just how much momentum she had gained during her short sprint, and just how hard it would be to stop her without hurting her.

What is she thinking? The cops were dead, all but the one whose severed torso was being tossed around a small cluster of zombies who pulled and yanked at each other's grip and sent him sailing in different directions, their dumbstruck gazes following his trajectory back and forth.

"Sweet Jesus!" The obese woman cried out when the burly husk that blocked the doorway (serial-killer type) reached out and grabbed Darius' ankle as he attempted to step over him.

Trapped in a tug of war, Darius shrieked at the top of his lungs.

By the time Kane came within reach of the serial-killer zombie's feet, the obese woman had fallen out of the doorway onto the parking lot. Darius, who snapped like a whip out of the zombie's grip, fell on top of her, and then bounced off. The automatic doors closed behind them, rejoicing with a hiss, and trapped Kane's echoed footsteps in the L-shaped vestibule.

The serial-killer zombie whipped around on his hands and knees and flashed a dripping red snarl. Between his teeth dangled a ripped swatch of blood-soaked fabric. It looked like denim.

In the parking lot, the obese woman examined Darius' ankle as he whined at her twisting and turning. There was a large chunk missing from both his jeans and the back of his ankle at around the hemline.

The obese woman held Darius close to her enormous bosom and rocked back and forth. She appeared to whisper something in his ear, but Kane was both too far away and too distracted by his own set of circumstances to hear it.

The tidal wave of rotting flesh and rasped moaning grew deafening as the zombies approached with greater purpose than before the obese woman and Darius stumbled onto the scene.

She pulled Darius away, grasped his face in both hands, and ordered him to stand on his injured leg.

"Try dammit, try harder than you've ever tried before!" she insisted, but Darius simply cried louder and louder as he watched the zombies close on them.

Maybe you'd be able to carry him if you weren't so fucking fat. Kane had a "thing" about obese people, especially the ones who sported fake satisfaction in their size. "God gave me plenty of food to eat" was their credo. The obese woman definitely fit the description.

As he watched the zombies draw closer, eyes bulging, mouths opening wide, yellow, red, and black-stained teeth clacking in expectant glee, there was no doubt in his mind that the obese woman and Darius were as good as dead, and there wasn't much he could do about it save for dying with them, or in their place if he tried to rescue them. Maybe under different circumstances, and dare he think it, for more deserving people, or person, as Darius wasn't really to blame for his mother's lack of will power, self-respect, and independent thought. Maybe it wasn't even her fault, but the fact was that she was an adult.

Without even looking, Kane kicked the serial-killer zombie backward onto his ass, then raised his gun and, operating with robotic efficiency, blew off all of his limbs.

For a moment, the zombies outside looked up, distracted by the gunshots.

Kane looked down past the long, bulky barrel of his gun, whose length and proximity to his right eye warped his perspective, at the limbless zombie that still struggled to reach him, slamming its face into the floor and using it to inch himself closer and closer like a caterpillar. This was once a man, proud in his beer swilling, chain-smoking, white-trash malaise, but a man nonetheless.

Lifting his gun in disgust, Kane aimed down at the serial-killer zombie who, upon reaching him, pushed with his forehead against the end of the barrel. Stiffening his hold, Kane held him at a distance, then at the last minute took a few steps back and whipped towards the screams of "Lord help us!" coming from the parking lot. He could barely hear it over the zombies' collective voice, the muzak that poured from the overhead speakers, the overlapping jingles, and holographic pitchmen and pitchwomen.

Thumbing a button next to the scope, Kane zoomed in his view of the obese woman and Darius as the zombies began to encircle them and reach down. There were only seconds in which to decide who to shoot first.

Kane cringed at his options.

Darius was facing away, so at least he wouldn't have to see the look on his face should he take the mother out first, which was what Kane finally decided to do.

He just didn't know if he had it in him to shoot the kid, let alone deal with the mother's reaction should she survive the first shot and witness Darius' demise. Maybe if he was lucky he could pick them both off in one shot.

That would be ideal.

Kane pulled the trigger in mid-thought. In his haste, he forgot to close his eyes, and he didn't even look away when he lifted his foot, stomped on the limbless, serial-killer zombie's head, and pinned him to the floor.

Every nuance of the gun's devastating punch into the obese woman's face resonated with nauseating discomfort: the way her fat body seized and jiggled, fingers curling into a claw; the way her legs kicked; the sound that rushed out of her mouth along with the blood and brain matter that landed all over Darius, herself, and the first tier of zombies, some of whom recoiled due to residual flickers of instinct.

Worst of all, the obese woman was still clinging to life.

Wobbling on her knees, she made an attempt to reach Darius, who fell on his ass after she dropped him. Confused and overcome by fear, Darius crawled backwards away from his mother and right into the arms of the famished undead.

Her head turning jerkily, loose meat bobbing and spitting, the obese woman spotted Kane and, with one eye left, begged him to put Darius out of his misery. A second later, she was completely surrounded by dead folks.

Kane, who was still watching through the scope, turned the gun on Darius as hundreds of ravenous hands yanked at him. Darius was a crying heap, balling tighter as his clothes were torn from his body and his naked flesh touched first by the chill of night, then by skin hardened to edges, protruding bone ripping like talons, and finally by teeth meeting teeth.

Zeroing in on Darius' head, Kane tried to keep a steady hand. He promised himself a direct hit this time. Darius managed to escape the zombies' grasp only to be recaptured again, and again, as there was nowhere for him to run.

"MommmmMeeeeeeee!" he called out in desperation.

Once he was certain that he had Darius square in his sights, Kane closed his eyes and pulled the trigger.

CLICK!

The small window on the barrel of his gun blinked, "Recharge Battery Pack."

"No! No! No!" Kane spit out in rapid succession, inspecting the empty chamber as if he expected it to magically recharge.

Thankfully, Darius' screaming was short-lived, though memorable in its bubbly-pitched urgency. It ended in a gurgle that suggested to Kane that Darius' throat was torn out, but he had already looked away, so he couldn't be sure.

Now there were only zombies. Hundreds of them, thousands counting the lone roamers that began to arrive from deep within the neighborhoods that bordered the Megamart plaza. Fat, thin, old, young, recently deceased, and long dead, they approached with dumbed-down determination that made their primal desire seem all the more frightening. Lazy, yet eager, their feet dragged and slid as if a normal gait was foreign to them anymore, foreign as the tear the crawled down Kane's cheek as his guilt multiplied 10-fold in the afterglow of Darius' horrible death.

A curious blur exploded from the ass-end of aisle 7. Without hesitating to think, Kane lifted his gun, thrust off the balls of his feet, and pulled the trigger in mid-stride. CLICK!

"Goddammit!!!!!" Energized by the sudden activity, he forgot that the gun was out of juice.

Kane's knee-jerk decision to hunt Jason down was probably the wrong one. The zombies were more of an immediate threat to these people, who seemed to forget about Jason for the time being. However, he continued on his path, reminding himself that there was probably battery packs back in Sporting Goods.

He was headed for the manager's booth. Jason knew that much. He had a good idea why, too (to fuck the brown-skinned hottie, probably kill her too; maybe kill her, then fuck her).

Boring liked to irritate him by making him suddenly wake from his trance-stupor feeling as if he had only been dreaming. Then… BAM! It came back with a vengeance, affecting him like it did the first time he realized that someone… something else was inside him.

If there was an upside to being possessed, then this was it. The sting of lust was like nothing he'd ever felt, and he had done his share of experimenting. His dick was hard as a rock, hard as victimization complexes were to shake for some folk, and a true understanding of minority status and all that it entailed was to reach for others.

It felt good, damn good so good, in fact, that Jason greeted the zombie feeding frenzy he passed on his droning march to the manager's booth steps with the same indifference that he showed to the random acts of violence he occasionally walked up on while cruising through the 'hood high as fuck.

When their eyes met (Jason's and Kane's), Jason flashed a detached smile, looked away, and continued on, his mind tripping on carnal lust that dripped from his penis, and zeroing in on the brown-skinned hottie through the booth windows.

Kane was up to his waist in zombies, thrashing the chainsaw with the "Clearance" tag dangling from its handle from right to left, jagged teeth biting deep into and through flesh and bone and muscle. Like some badass zombie-killing machine, Kane swung with all his strength, teeth gnashed together, lips curled into a snarl. Behind him, two collegiate types with aluminum tee-ball bats took out the stragglers and the zombies smart enough to attempt a sneak attack from the rear.

As a result of his parasitic sickness, Jason's interpretation of events was beginning to filter through a haze that made things drag and skip and mold to fit some unappeased adolescent fantasy scenario.

He climbed the short, narrow stairway to the manager's booth with purpose, leaden feet lingering with each step to allow the shockwaves of impact to travel up from the floor to the fire in their loins.

Teenage Fantasy

An arm, pock-marked with day-old bullet-hits, reaches into the frame, fingers spread, opened palm easing into contact with the black door marked

Manager's Booth. Employees Only Beyond This Point.

The door swings open, the room inside falling upon his eyes gradually. Inside, a portable MP3 boombox cues up "Broken Wings" by Mister Mister.

Her back is to him. Peeking out from the valley between the bottom of her white sheer blouse knotted at her sternum, the small of her back, smooth and tight as can be, begs for attention. She is wearing tight jeans, the kind the white-trash girls liked to sport. Jason called them camel-toe jeans. They lay like a second skin against the meaty "W" shape of her hips and ass as she squats fumbling with something on the lowest shelf of a dented metal bookcase. Her legs are slightly thick, just enough to make the rebound jiggle of her apple-shaped ass linger against the scrotum after each thrust and speak its mind long-winded. She knows that she is being watched. If it wasn't evident before, it is now, as she stands with a serpentine sway, leaving her ass to jut out at the end of her hypnotic rise.

Her thick, raven locks flop and slide across her back as she pivots her head from side to side, then turns to face Jason.

The music swells!

A gust of wind lifts her hair from her shoulders, where it whips horizontally two feet behind her, snapping like a flag in the wind. Her eyes light up as if she'd been expecting him, longing for his specific touch. They creep down to his crotch, and back up with a naughty glint. Against her glistening brown hue, a white lace bra screams at him as she works loose the knot in her shirt and lets it slide from her arms, her erect nipples making a strong case for freedom from underneath. Her ample breasts spill out from the top while below, her waist and the suggestion of a finely tuned abdominal wall lures his eyes down in pursuit of her dexterous fingers as they unsnap her jeans and drag the zipper down. The V-shaped opening gives him a preview of what lies beneath.

She glides toward Jason as if on wheels. They embrace.

As they kiss, Jason too succumbs to the cinematic wind, and an overall feeling of flight, the song's pop antics, merged with easy-listening sedative qualities, lulls his brain into a cloudy bliss.

When he opens his eyes to reassure himself that this is really happening, he sees a scene of fast-moving clouds projected on the three rectangular windows set high on the right side of the room.

CUT TO:

They are naked on the floor, the brown-skinned hottie on her stomach, Jason thrusting away on top watching her plump ass bounce to the rhythm. Her face, turned sideways, enough so that she can occasionally seek out his eyes to truly understand his hang-jawed rapture, rests on her folded forearms. Looking down upon her, Jason uses her reaction to fuel his stamina while at the same time fighting to stifle the cum that crawls slowly toward the light.

CUT TO:

They are in missionary position. It seems like hours have passed, but judging from the song, which is only half-over, it has only been a few minutes. Lifting his torso off of hers, Jason arches his back to thrust deeper, and bracing himself with his right hand, reaches down and manipulates her breast with his left, circling her nipple with his fingertips, pinching and pulling it taught, before letting it snap back into place. Her perfect face is alive with ecstasy. For the tenth time at least, Jason reiterates to himself the fact that he never would've gotten a girl like this on his own. In a moment of genuine emotional connection, he caresses her face, cradling the side of it in his palm. He lets his hand slide down to her neck and around.

The music begins to distort….

*   *   *

This time it was different, waking to reality, or something close to it. Jason's fantasy girl had suddenly hulked-out on him, thrashing violently beneath him, once beautiful beyond words, now wrought with bruises about her face and upper chest, and struggling, with open-mouth gulps, for her breath as Jason tightened his grip around her throat.

Instead of the usual symbiotic sucker-punch that kept Jason disconnected, the detached haze that currently separated him from reality was from shock, then horror, then shame, each coming right on the heels of the other. Jason had no time to react, to brace himself for whatever might come next. He expected that it would be the same old shit. Boring and his fucking tricks…. However, it had been a full five minutes (the moments of clarity usually lasted a minute at most), and in that time, things had melted to extra sharpness; the abrupt wave of pain as the brown-skinned hottie wrapped her thick legs around his waist and squeezed, the volume at which her twisted, ugly expression screamed utter contempt for him, the sting of her palm as she slapped him across the face again and again, the burning sensation as she clawed him and dragged her hand down his cheek, neck, and chest, or the fact that her naked body no longer incited a sexual response. Worse yet, it made him feel sick.

On the radio, an advert for tea, distinctly AM band because of its lack of texture. The sterile whine of an old-fashioned teakettle cut through the kinetic stillness in the manager's booth. The surgical brightness intensified to a white-hot glow that sizzled.

"SOMEBODEEEEE HELP MEEEEEEE!!!!!!!!!" the brown-skinned hottie screamed, thrusting her face up at him as if she intended it to somehow stun him with the weight of her audible wrath.

Jason hadn't figured her for an around-the-way girl, but he knew that accent well. It was one that he ran from until he found himself. Based on the way she doctored her moaning to sound more innocent (or maybe that was his mind's doing), he pictured her being more soft-spoken, all breathy and sweet. It was clear now that she was running from the same thing that he used to.

She probably worked around mostly white people, probably treated it as a safe haven from the unwanted catcalls that always reached her physically, the sinsemilla-soaked words like hands tugging at her belt, fingers sliding across her ass and digging in for an ample chunk to squeeze. They called her names like "shawtee" or "thick legs" or "bitch" if she didn't respond. Sometimes they even followed her for a block or two, looming over her with their primal funk, arms spread as if they were about to wrap them around her and snatch her up at any moment. This was where she could take off the mask of bastardized masculinity that she, and other girls like her, wore as a result.

Her name was LaToya. She had been wearing her nametag the whole time, but Jason only just noticed it as she slid backward on her hands and ass reaching for her clothes along the way and trying her best to cover herself, first with her arm, then by draping the shirt with the nametag pinned to the front across her knees which she cradled close to her raw bosom.

Jason sprung to his feet and attempted to follow her, his arm extended, hand upturned to translate peaceful intentions, his flaccid penis dangling, his pubic region encrusted with blood and vaginal secretions.

He stopped to pull up his pants and underwear from around his ankles.

Falling on his ass would probably be just the sort of mistake that LaToya might capitalize on to get back at him. The Megamart had been open throughout the zombie plague so there was bound to be some kind of weapon up here in the manager's booth to deal with them just in case, something that LaToya could use to bash his brains in, or to blow them out of his head. Maybe she already had it on her, and was just waiting for an opportunity.

Shit! The zombies…

Jason hurried over to the rectangular windows that looked down into the aisles. He felt a sudden breeze blow past him.

LaToya…

By the time he turned, she was already out the door and calling out to God as she tumbled headfirst down the narrow steps just outside the booth and splashed down into the livid tide of zombies. This time her nudity frightened him.

Aside from LaToya, who was fighting to stay afloat in the dead sea, there were two people left: Kane and a younger man in his late teens or early twenties, surrounded behind the four glass bins that encased the deli area by a pulsating mass of zombies. Even the dead folk who were situated farthest away from the deli counter, or from the feast at the foot of the manager's booth, fighting over the newly dead, chowing down on their own piece, or just sitting there, mesmerized, relaxed, yet stiff as a board, acknowledged in some way, their stake of the last three warm bodies. Maybe it was a look, body language, or a grunt in the general direction of the main action.

Some of the zombies had stopped on their way to fixate on familiar things (cereal boxes with funny characters, brand names they preferred in life, flashing tabloid magazine covers, clothing, stereo equipment, jewelry), hanging onto something posing as a memory that for a millisecond sparked to life.

These were real people, these mothers, fathers, sons and daughters, brothers and sisters, and nasty little secrets reduced to chewed-upon pieces and fought over with deadfuck zeal. The lucky ones hoarded prime cuts, whole arms and legs and pulled-apart torsos, and large, unidentifiable chunks, and swatted at opportunistic hands hungry for more than just scraps. Jason had seen many of these people alive only minutes ago.

ALIVE…

ALIVE?????

The word climbed up Jason's spine and sunk its venomous fangs deep into his brain anesthetizing warmth from his core to the external personal space that his aura claimed. Beneath the layers of noise (gunshots, an authoritarian voice [Kane] yelling out profanities in the short distance, the background moaning, the electronic ads attacking from every direction, and a muzak version of the old Beastie Boys song, "So What'cha Want," that spilled out from the overhead speakers), Jason could actually hear the dead folks chewing.

Three quarters of Megamart's inventory lay smashed and

broken on the floor. Spilled food and liquids coated whole aisles both sticky and slick and stole some of the zombies' feet from under them.

Standing dumbstruck, paralyzed by the magnitude of evil that he had helped bring about, a fire ignited in Jason's arm, an unnatural warmth that he was now able to control. On top of everything else, he expected at any moment to be snatched away from this reality again.

Jason's mind charted a path, up to his shoulders, his head, and down to the rest of him until the bullets buried in his flesh began to fidget in their holes.

"This is it, kid." Spine-tingling honesty spiked Kane's tone and made the younger man, Doug Springsteen, start to out-and-out cry. "Close your eyes and turn away. I'll try to make this as painless as possible."

"No! No, wait…" Doug pleaded as Kane turned the double-fisted cannon on him and motioned with a matter-of-fact jerk of the barrel for him to turn. "B…bbbut, there must be an…"

"What? Another way? Sure there is."

Kane looked to his right at…

…hundreds of dead-ass humans looking back at them, no, thousands… thousands of vastly different interpretations of living death, but all with the same "I'm gonna eat your ass" expression.

"I'm gonna do myself right after if it makes you feel any better," Kane said as he pivoted with the gun ready to pick off anything that attempted to climb over.

The window on the barrel of his gun blinked, "Low Charge." He probably had around 10 shots left. The used battery pack that he found in Sporting Goods was nearly empty when he got it. Kane knew it wouldn't be long before the THUMP and the buzz-hum of the gun, which still seemed to half-startle them momentarily, was too old a memory to keep them at bay.

"Whatever you decide, you'd better make it quick."

The zombies were starting to climb over the counter. Kane followed the first one up with his gun and blew it back into the four or five who intended to follow.

"Fuck! They're everywhere!" Kane yelled and backed toward the absolute middle of the deli and right into Doug, who was whimpering noisily. "This is pointless, kid. What's your answer?"

The pressure squeezed a warm stream of piss from Doug's bladder. Lying thick, too thick and moist inside his lower jaw, his tongue wouldn't let him commit to answer.

Kane slid Doug one last glance, as four, five, six zombies made their way over the counter, shook his head, and placed the barrel beneath his own chin. He closed his eyes and curled his finger around the trigger.

"Suit yourself, kid."

"Wait... look..."

Up on the stairs, a mess of a man (Jason) invoked a Jesus Christ pose and shook violently, flesh undulating, eyes on their way up and back. So far, Kane had only seen the aftermath of the bullet-swarm, and he'd heard the officers who survived the bus station trying to figure out just how Jason took so many bullets without falling. Experienced cop-eyes told them that Jason wasn't a zombie. Zombies had their own specific hue. They figured him more for an addict.

"Must be some good shit," one of them quipped as Jason wobbled on his feet after they unloaded full clips into him.

"Good shit indeed," replied another. "Where can I get my hands on..."

His last word stolen by the bullet that ripped through his throat, he fell back. On his way down, he saw what looked like a circle of blue men dancing around another, who stood with his arms extended, recycled bullets jumping from his body like an organic turret.

Based on what he knew, the look on Jason's face told Kane to...

"Getthafuckdown!!!!!" Kane started to say. "Everybody getthafuckdown!!!" Less than an hour ago, he was addressing a group of people, and his mind had yet to fully acclimate to the drastic reduction.

Doug blacked out when his head hit the floor, bounced, and smacked again under Kane's weight. He opened his eyes and almost lost it at the sight of Kane's face, larger than life, and so close to his; then the extra pressure on his lungs and stomach indicated that someone was on top of him. A man. He could smell old coffee on his breath, and feel stubble when their faces touched. Oh God, what had they talked him into? He must not have locked the door to his dorm. But wait, he didn't remember drinking last night....

"Snap out of it, kid!" Doug heard the man say, as if he knew him.

Did he know him????

Doug remembered seeing Kane's thick arm coming at him and the feeling of hurried descent, but not the actual impact.

Had he been shot?

He reached up and felt the back of his head. Nothing.

SMACK! Kane's hand lagged in the baby-fat when it struck Doug's cheek, turning his head to the side and finally knocking some sense back into him. He looked into Kane's eyes. It was a look that expressed many thoughts, most of all, "Please don't kill me!"

"Just stay down and don't move!" Kane yelled over the din that had escaped Doug's ears thus far, squeezed his eyes shut and pressed himself into Doug.

As he listened, Doug broke the noise down; open hands slapping raw meat (that's what it sounded like anyway), bone cracking and splintering into calcium-flecks, electric pops and buzzes, and that familiar moan, its continuity robbed by repeated impact and challenged by the overbearing roar of a large-caliber machine gun, or some organic variant spitting perpetually.

Doug felt the tap-tapping of fragmented "things" hitting his arms and legs, and something damp that was seeping through his clothes and bespeckling his naked forearm.

"You still with me, kid?" Kane glared down at Doug, squinting at the debris.

Doug shook his head, "yes." To his left and right, everything under the sun bounced to the floor and rolled close enough to him to cause his eyes to flutter. Feet, both naked and clothed, followed haphazard patterns, knees buckled and gave out or exploded into pieces.

Kane was mumbling something about Jason, or to Jason, something along the lines of "That's right.... Make those fuckers pay." His head was positioned in a way that finally allowed Doug a good look at what was going on above them.

It reminded him of a nightclub: lights flashing, bodies intoxicated by music trying their best to translate their own personal sonic euphoria into movement, but instead looking like a roomful of sardonic comedians going for the easy laugh by pulling out their best rhythm-less white-guy impressions, and literally coming apart at the seams. All around them sparks flew, and glass, paper, and plastic fell to the ground. The air was littered with glowing lines of heat like scratches on film that marked criss-crossed paths of too many bullets to count, ripping in and out of zombified trunks and sending appendages sailing through the air where many of them were cut down to mere fibers before they even hit the ground, as were the bodies from which they escaped.

Without raising his head, Doug traced the glowing bullet-wash that chirped by. Eventually, they led him to Jason, who stood at the top of the steps stuck in organic turret mode.

Okay, first Jesus…then Yeshua, then the rain, the zombies and now this? Doug wondered what else such a short life thus far could possibly have in store for him.

*　　*　　*

The atmosphere inside the S11 Bulldog (a van-sized, military quadruped-vehicle with a short, bulky reinforced shell and loaded with state-of-the-art weaponry), was somber, and somewhat disorganized, yet the commentary always seemed to turn to playful insults. The men half-jokingly referred to themselves as the last battalion since they, and a few others like them (men without families and such), were what was left of the nation's military. They had been on their own for over a month now, doing what they could to help out here and there.

Triumphant gestures accompanied by calls of "yee-ha!" and derogatory phrases leveled at the zombies, laced the distinctly masculine conversations. One joked that they (the zombies) had become the new niggers. With no source of ventilation, their voices had nowhere to go, ramrodding into Kane's quiet dementia like radio-friendly hip-hop bogarting quaint suburban ecosystems from pimped-out lemons, bass threatening to shake them to pieces.

Bandaged up and reclined on the built-in gurney in the back, Kane felt like a zombie himself, nullified from feeling both emotional and physical by what had happened tonight inside the Megamart. Though he sat back away from the small, reinforced window in the back door of the armored vehicle, Kane could still see the Megamart aglow with ravenous flames and shrinking in the distance.

Was it over? Had he finally put a stop to Boring?

His gut told him no. However, hope was the only method of satiating the ugly images that were already haunting him: blood everywhere, trumped only by barely recognizable remnants of former people; Jason, on his knees, completely spent from maintaining the bullet-swarm for so long; the way he looked up at Kane, his eyes filled with remorse, and fear, and semi-satisfaction before Kane blew his head apart; the guilt he felt for not feeling guilty enough anymore; the immediate anxiety that chewed him up and spit him out when he realized that to be sure that Boring hadn't jumped again, he'd have to kill Doug too, probably even himself.

At least Doug went out on a high note. He was in the middle

of celebrating the fact that he made it. Kane waited until he turned his back. He used the last of his gun's juice killing Jason, so he was forced to do it the old-fashioned way, with an aluminum tee-ball bat. Strange that it felt almost good to kill at this point.

The survivors he happened upon in the storage room as he walked out… now that was a different story. He had to chase them down, three in all. Afterward, he went back and set the entire place ablaze starting with Doug and the three in the storage room in case any of them were thinking about getting up and walking around in search of live food.

They found Kane sitting, solemn in the parking lot, lost in deep thought when they arrived. Behind him, the flaming Megamart scorched the pre-dawn horizon and scared all the zombies into temporary retreat, lot escorts blinking to life and death all around him. Heavily distorted by ripples of interference, they fizzled transparent, then totally out in mid-speech, static-shrieks coming off like screams as if they reacted to the intense heat.

"Hey, I know that chick," Dewitt, the big black one, said as he peered out the back window. "Fat bitch used to live in my old neighborhood. Always braggin' about her designer bullshit and lettin' her stank-ass kids run around to all hours of the night."

It was Darius' mother. She was one of them now, a zombie.

Kane could see her just outside the window, lumbering away from the Megamart. Her stomach was torn open, and inside, an upside-down fetus curled into classic position except for an arm that protruded and dangled from the open wound.

"Man, that's just sick," commented another man who hurried over to get a look.

"I say good riddance, man," Dewitt groaned. "We've got enough ig'nant-ass-mutherfuckas like her spoiling shit for everybody else. It's people like her who make us look bad in the eyes of people like you, Keith."

"Fuck off," Keith replied. He was still feeling salty from the verbal beat-down he took from DeWitt in response to using the "N" word a few moments ago. If DeWitt wasn't so fucking big, Keith would've slugged him when he walked up face to face and stared him down.

Kane wanted to tell DeWitt that he agreed completely, but experience taught him that guys like DeWitt often jumped sensitive when someone from outside their race pointed out a flaw.

"Y'ever wonder how we must taste to them… I mean, just fer curiosity's sake?" a voice from up front interjected.

"Probably like chicken to those deadfucks," Kane said.

Chapter 7

The new Christian Media Broadcasting logo (a cross overlapping a globe) in blazing white.

An announcer begins.

(Intercut within the voice-over, we see brief shots of a pudgy, James Brown type dressed in a white suit that appears to be a few sizes too small, doing rigid karate hand movements against a dark backdrop. As he does this he fades in, then quickly fades out while the announcer speaks.)

ANNOUNCER: *Two years ago, the world lost one of the most important and influential figures to ever walk the face of God's green earth. Sought from a young age for his unique and scientifically tested healing abilities, he went on to be a world-renowned healer to the stars and for 10 years straight produced and hosted one of the highest-rated religious shows ever in the history of television, a show that he himself started more than 20 years ago in his own backyard in Philadelphia.*

(Old black-and-white still photos of the James Brown type as a young man, preaching atop a makeshift altar flash across the screen)

You knew him as the man with the healing hands and the black belt from God.

(Old black-and-white stills of him in his twenties practicing karate with an anonymous Asian man. The scenes bleed from old stills to more recent video footage, and as they progress, his healing

*methods and attire [a variety of gaudy, satin karate gis tied with
a black belt] become more and more unorthodox, from the simple
touch or shove, to intricate posing, or hand gestures that lead
into punching combinations that routinely knock people off their
feet; to flips and jumping, spinning kicks, always ending with his
trademark prayer pose. Each time the people get right back up
and react as if they have been healed.)*

ANNOUNCER: *Christian Media Broadcasting is honored to
announce the return of a phenomenon... the return of the Reverend
Raymond Tiger Lee Show.*

*(Footage of the new, living-dead Raymond Lee striking a few
mock-karate poses. However rigid they may have looked before,
it was nothing compared to the way he moved now, like an
animatronic funhouse prop stuck on vibrate. His face, which they
tried in vain to conceal with oversized shades and B-movie
prosthetics, was no more than a few patches of randomly dispersed
grey flesh in an expanse of bone. He wore gloves to hide his skeletal
fingers. His trademark gi, which was tighter-than-shit before,
hung loose from his bony shoulders.*

*The footage ends with the title of the show in brilliant gold letters
against a black screen.)*

Premiering in October on CMB TV 6.

"I did what I could to give him a proper burial," Mikel
Williamson said, as he inspected the rim of his glass before touching it
to his lips.

"Don't worry. Aside from the occasional cockroach, this place is pretty clean," Kane muttered like a man who'd spent every waking moment reliving some past indiscretion.

For a full month after the Megamart incident, Kane didn't even get out of bed. He spent whole days there watching anything and everything on TV just to keep from falling asleep and visiting that horrible place deep inside his head. On the TV, everything was scaled down and run guerilla-style. Everything. Formats and show lineups were changing by the hour due to the high turnover at the studios. It was the same as everywhere else, staff dropping like flies, the constant threat of being invaded by the living dead, or the military arbitrarily deeming another chunk of land uninhabitable, or some half-assed group of survivalist-types calling themselves a militia doing the same, then claiming it as their own, or the occasional nut-job with a gun and a mouthful of convoluted rhetoric.

It was mostly news and talk shows that highlighted survivor stories and carted out people looking for missing or recently deceased loved ones who might be adrift in the living-dead current. They'd hold up banner-sized images of smiling faces, kitschy glamour pics, actor headshots, and modeling portfolios, and ask if anyone had seen these people wandering around.

Kane had become addicted to the callers who phoned in with sightings, harrowing tales of encounters with zombified versions of some of the people in the photos, and even the occasional prank caller who'd say something like, "Yeah, I've seen your daughter… SUCKING MY DICK!!!!!!!"

Convalescence had granted Kane time to dissect his new appreciation for freestyle violence and to examine it from every possible angle. Kane had killed men in his past, most of whom deserved it, but never had he unleashed his wrath with such passion. Never had he affected so many destinies at once. Sure, most of his victims were zombies, but their relationship, the living and the dead, was still relatively new; hence, the distinction between the two had not yet soaked into the gray matter and planted roots that thickened as thoughts and observations became gospel.

Kane had also gained an extra 12 pounds during his recuperation. He jokingly referred to the time as his mental sabbatical, but only to himself. The weight showed mostly in his face, but he didn't care.

It had also opened his eyes to the magnitude of the slow-rot epidemic. Kane had been on the front lines from day one, and it was just this constant exposure to the dead menace that desensitized him to it in a way that allowed him to focus completely on this Boring case. He salivated at the thought of somehow nailing these Jesus characters too. He suspected that there was some connection between them and Boring; however, solving the case had a lot to do with satiating his macho predilections. They were still smarting from the shit that went down with the FBI at the wreckage site.

"You can never be too careful at these places," Mikel spoke into his glass as he tilted it up from the bottom, took a tentative sip, then another. "It's probably bullshit, but I heard that the infection could be spread through saliva."

"I wouldn't know, but you're probably right to worry. It's a little too soon to be calling any warning like that bullshit. But you can rest assured that you won't find any zombies in here. The Lucky Star ain't the best place around, but it's far from the worst either."

"Yeah, but everyone seems to be hiding something these days. You never know when that something is an infected bite. I've seen it happen time and time again… and to good people. Scares the shit outta me, man."

Kane glanced up at the bar, and at the hunched-back fixtures that decorated it (Barflies #1 and #2). They almost slammed into each other as they spun away from his approaching eyes and tried to play it off like they were immersed in a deep conversation.

Beau Hopkins, who had witnessed the whole thing from the other side of the bar, shook his head as he poured himself a drink, leaned back against the rear wall, and gulped it down in one swig.

"I wouldn't put it past these jokers either," Kane said. "So, how did you find me?"

"After you didn't return my calls, I called the station and told them who I was. Some woman, I think her name was…"

"…Allison?"

"Yeah, that's it. Allison Ryan. She told me I might find you here."

Kane smirked, first out of anger, and then as he thought about it, he realized that Allison had done a good thing.

Although Kane knew of Mikel Williamson, he had never seen him. When Mikel first approached his table, Kane tensed up and started to reach for his gun, until Mikel extended his hand and spoke.

"Hi. My name is Mikel Williamson. Jason was my brother," He said.

Their resemblance was uncanny. Mikel was taller and bald, and his musculature was more mature, symmetrical and defined. Other than that, he looked just like Jason.

Kane's first thought was that he might have a fight on his hands, and judging from Mikel's size and shape, it wouldn't have been an easy one.

"Your brother Jason… he was a good kid," Kane spoke softly. "I only spoke to him briefly, but in that short time, I could tell that he had a good head on his shoulders. I hope that doesn't sound too corny."

Mikel hung on to Kane's every word, and it was clear that he was trying not to well up.

"Not at all."

"Good. I just don't want you to think… I want you to know that I did my best to resolve this without…"

"I understand," Mikel said. "I know you were just doing your job. I don't blame you for that. What I want to know is what actually happened and why. The news reports said that he was shot more than 100 times. That seems like overkill to me. My head hasn't been right ever since I heard that shit. My mom passed out when she heard it. And all I kept getting from people at your station when I called was 'talk to Detective Makane.' So here I am."

It was 2:32 pm, and, except for the regulars that remained (Barflies #1 and #2), the Lucky Star was virtually empty, so there was nothing to distract Kane from the butterflies that fluttered away in his gut. The last thing he wanted to do was recount that night, but for Mikel's peace-of-mind (and on some otherworldly level, Jason's), he knew he'd have to.

"By the time I arrived at the Megamart," he said, "he… Jason had already shot up the bus station."

"But that just doesn't sound like him," Mikel interrupted. "Jason wasn't what I'd call peaceful. He'd been through a lot of shit, but he wasn't a thug or a criminal either. Do you know if he was bitten?"

"I don't. Could've been that that was the case." Kane knew it wasn't but… "Like I said, he had already shot up the bus station and taken out 12 officers in the process."

"Jesus Christ!"

Kane froze and wriggled to escape the chill that drove his fake composure into momentary submission.

"Try not to repeat that name around me. Please…."

Mikel frowned, confused.

"Sorry. I was just…"

"Don't worry about it, kid. I'm just going through some shit right now is all."

"I hear ya, man," Mikel said. "This Judgment Day nonsense is enough to drive a muthafucker crazy."

"So I take it you're not a believer? I remember Jason mentioning something about your family being religious."

"Yeah, deeply, but I was always a rebellious kind of guy. I remember our mom had this family friend…. Family friend," Mikel scoffed. "That was our mom's term for someone she was dating. Anyway, he used to take me different places: museums, football games, that kind of shit. So once we're at the Academy of Natural Sciences, and we're looking at the dinosaur bones. I remember saying something about how cool they were and he says, calm as day, 'Yeah, but how do you know they put them together, or posed them the right way? Seems like a whole lot of speculation to me.' That right there really opened my mind up. Made me start wanting to find out shit for myself. I guess being my younger brother, Jason kind of followed suit. Mom… she believed in that punk-muthafucka Jesus. She kept trying to convince us to accept him. I'm sorry, but when I look at that fool, all I see is that old actor…. What's his name? …Viggo Mortensen."

"Yeah, he does sort of resemble him." And as the visualization sunk in deeper, Kane's lips curled into a slight grin. "Yeah, he does….

After a long silent pause.

"Now, where was I?" Kane asked.

"You were talking about when you first arrived on the scene," Mikel replied.

"Oh yeah…. I tried negotiating with him… with Jason, but by that point… let's just say that, by then, there wasn't much I could do to make it end peacefully."

Mikel let his head sink forward. For the next few moments, he stared at the curly-Q whisps in the wood grain of the table and cried silently.

"I thought the least I could do was to… was to take him out as painlessly as possible before the boys from the 22nd arrived looking for payback, but before I could, the place was overrun by those deadfucks. I had my hands full trying to help the other people inside the store get out safely."

"From what I heard, there weren't any survivors," Mikel sobbed.

"Yeah, thanks to the grunts who showed up and burned the place down before I could stop them."

Mikel continued to cry. For a guy his size, it seemed inappropriate, which made Kane even more uneasy.

"I'm sorry, kid," Kane said. "You said that your head hasn't been right ever since this happened. Well, neither has mine, if that's any consolation to you. If there's anything I can do to help you and your family through this…."

"It's just me now," Mikel said. "My mom… she died in her sleep two weeks ago."

This was getting worse and worse. As he sat there, watching Mikel face down his emotional upheaval and maintain a look of noble sadness, Kane wondered what Mikel would do if he just came right out and told him the truth about what took place at the Megamart. Seeing as how he was the one who blew Jason's brains out, he held himself responsible for everything that happened as a result. He felt he owed it to Mikel and to himself as a catharsis to just spill it right here… right now….

Kane got it as far as the tip of his tongue, but that was it.

"I'm sorry for asking this, but your mother, had she been bitten?"

Mikel sobbed.

"I… I found her in the kitchen when I came home. She was eating our dog, Loomis."

"So what did you do?"

Mikel shook his head, defiant.

"I can't…" he stammered. "I don't want to say."

Kane leaned forward, agitated.

"You did make sure that she was…"

"Yes! I took care of it." Mikel raised his voice, frowning through reddened eyes. "Now I don't want to talk about this anymore. Got it?"

They had caused a scene. As if it fell upon them both simultaneously, Kane and Mikel turned in unison and caught the usual suspects' spinning retreat.

Cutting through the silence like a virgin blade, sprightly female laughter provided an escape for Barflies #1 and #2 from trying to feign interest in something that repetition had burned into their subconscious long ago. Sensing eyes on their back, Barflies #1 and #2 were happy to direct their attention to the freezer in the back where Beau Hopkins was laughing it up with some thick redhead whom Kane had never seen before. He noticed the frayed edges of a dirty bandage peeking out beneath the cuff of her pant-leg. Nine times out of 10, that meant she had been bitten and was trying to hide it.

A good woman was hard to come by these days, and he didn't have the heart to rain on Beau Hopkins' potential pussy. There was no telling how long it had been for him. Kane considered himself much better looking, and, not counting Allison, he hadn't gotten any offers or stray looks in months. He'd heard that sex was rampant in some of the enclaves of survivors as widows and single women competed for the strongest leftover men. Most of the time, they were the type of men that they wouldn't even acknowledge back when things were normal.

"I'm sorry, kid. It's just that I've seen too many good people killed by those things. Hell, I've seen good people turned into 'em, too, and doing the killing. This shit doesn't care who it infects. So, what are you doing with yourself, aside from this? Where are you staying?"

"I'm in the shelter on 69th Street. The old train station. It's probably the best one on my side of Southwest, but there's still so much infighting. Man, I've even seen that shit come to blows."

"Yeah, unfortunately you're going to find that everywhere these days. Too many alpha males confined to one place. Maybe you should think about joining the force. You look like you can handle yourself. Ever used a gun?"

"I've held one, but that's about it. And no offense, but the police aren't exactly what they used to be, and I didn't like them back then."

"Yeah, I know, but those of us who still care could use a guy like you. I could show you the ropes, get you familiar with firearms.

It's the least I can do."

Mikel took a long sip, as if adding fuel to the nascent buzz he had might help him to decide.

"Believe it or not, I've had similar offers from the Dziko Nation, and from some guy who came around trying to recruit security for the Secular Soldiers. I'll let you know after I check them out."

"You don't want to get caught up in that shit, kid. Sure, they mean well, but they come with too many rules and a whole lot of rhetoric. With us, you can be yourself. And the law ain't what it used to be. You can get away with smacking around some deserving shithead who would normally use the law to his advantage without worrying about a lawsuit, or people bitching about his rights."

Mikel smirked. It was the first time Kane had seen him smile, even if it was only a small one.

"Well, since you put it that way…" Mikel said jokingly.

October

ANCHORWOMAN: *In New York today, a session of the UN Security Council was interrupted by Reverend Jesse James Dallas, and…Jesus Christ, who easily got past heavy security and barged into the council chamber during a meeting to discuss Jesus' Judgment Day Ceremony on Christmas Day.*

Referring to the recent polls that consistently show overwhelming support for Jesus Christ, the pope's official declaration of the same man as the true son of God, and citing an end to the worldwide epidemic of…reanimated corpses attacking the living as the most important issue facing our planet, 117 of the UN's 191 members agreed to convene to consider Jesus' proposition of eternal salvation in return for public acknowledgement of his father as the one true God. This despite impassioned opposition from the Secular Soldiers, the Coalition for Spiritual Diversity, and a growing faction of survivors....

I'm sorry....

The anchorwoman pauses, looking beyond the camera for human eyes that might understand.

ANCHORWOMAN: *Please forgive me.... You would think saying these...things would get easier over time, but that simply isn't the case.*

She begins to sob....

CUT TO:

Surveillance video from the UN runs on a continuous loop, an overhead shot of Jesus walking in the front door and down a number of hallways. Soldiers crumble limp in trepidation as he passes. A few of them raise their guns at him, unsure.... For them, he makes the journey to slumber a painful one.

Moments later, Reverend Dallas peeks in the front door and follows the trail of sleeping bodies all the way to the security council chamber.

Deader Than Death

They were in the majority now, their numbers growing by the

minute. The ragtag remnants of the news media officially recognized them as zombies. They even came up with a term for the current state of the world. Post-awakening (PA) they called it. Under constant pressure from the UN and various world leaders, President Melvin Riggs, an actor/director turned politician, officially handed over power to Jesus on October 3rd and escaped with his cabinet to Mount Weather, his 61,000-square-foot mountain bunker in Virginia.

Groups like the Secular Soldiers and the Coalition for Spiritual Diversity were forced underground.

Police around the world were ordered to report to their local Catholic archdiocese for reassignment, which basically meant protecting the wealthy and the faithful while everyone else was left to fend for themselves. Most of the good cops refused to do it. But there weren't many of them left to begin with.

Kane laughed at the idea. Like they were going to come down here and do anything about it if he didn't report. Most of those people, Jesus included, probably didn't even know places like this existed real inner cities, alive with real pain and sorrow and dreams of escaping to some white utopia over the rainbow-colored El tracks.

As far as Kane was concerned, his ass was staying right here, at the 13th precinct.

Zombies crowded whole blocks, whole towns in the rural areas, decorating ramshackle land and cityscapes with upright defiance, their drive to carry on despite that which slowly pulled them downward toward an eventual end kept them in perpetual stagger-stomp. Languishing in waking death, knowing only existence and hunger, they marched along with muddled determination through barren cornfields, along lonely backcountry roads, and interstate expressways that still saw occasional traffic, through long-dead factory towns, and even waist-deep in pools of blood left over from the rain, which was most prevalent in, but not exclusive to, the inner cities.

They were passive in the presence of their undead brethren,

but let the dead catch a whiff of the living, and it was an entirely different story.

The ones who couldn't walk slid on their bellies or lay in one place, unable to effect motion in their appendages, the spark of something relearned keeping them perfectly still, like the charred bodies that polluted the terrain all around them, until something warm-blooded happened by.

Their move to dominance complete; the CLICK-CLUNK of stoplights changing colors; the distant hum of generators; the scrape of wind-blown refuse; the ring-a-ding of store-front alarms, the crackle and crunch of breakable things under flat, heavy feet replaced the wailing sirens, horns blaring in testament to gridlock, irate pedestrians, and the overall din of the former life electric as salary-slaves worked their way up the mountain of corporate and industrial servitude. But the most dominant sounds (raspy voices moaning in deadfuck glory, hundreds of thousands of feet slapping and sliding along), the ones that the resilient hangers-on who traveled stealthily in small, close-knit groups associated with approaching danger... those touched a specific place that almost always motivated immediate retreat and mechanisms of self-defense.

Bordering the jerk-step parade of dead muthafuckas (the late, late Mr. Banks, for example, whose nametag winked at the sun from the breast pocket of his UPS uniform), the larger buildings stood deceptively docile. Inside the tallest ones, groups of survivors worked to maintain some form of organization. Most of them were government employees given extra incentive to risk prolonged periods outdoors to make it in to work every day. There were weekly casualty reports posted online. A moment of silence... some jive about losing more than a coworker spoken to sad music, and it was on to the business at hand. Give it a day or two, and it was just like it never happened.

Deep in the thick of the rot, in an alley not unlike hundreds of others in the area, a similarly mundane crowd thrived, living in the extreme present, rubbing shoulders with strangers, and moving toward the vague, directionless odor of warm flesh. Slight as it was, the scent had led them here, to this place in the ass-crack of two ambitious structures, both with fire-escape spines that ran up their backs and blended in with the sky and the rolling clouds, and worked together to nauseate those who dared to climb them visually.

Something alive was here… now. Even to the deadfucks' dilapidated senses, the stench was undeniable. And the source, wherever it was, was rich with its invigorating odor. It inspired a high that only true carnivores understood, even dead ones.

Out of nowhere, a voice intruded on the day.

"That's it. They've reached the mark," the voice blared with brainiac cadence through bullhorns mounted high on lampposts and telephone poles and bounced up the walls. "It's your show, Mr. Martin."

At the southern end of the alley, a staggered wall of four mildly rotten zombies literally came to life.

Sinking, in concert, into ready-stances, they reached behind their backs and swung thick, rounded barrels into view: their weapon of choice, the XM-12 Berserker, a double-barrel, liquid-light cannon, with a 40-mm single-shot grenade launcher at the bottom. Holding them with confidence, they backed into a tight formation (back to back to back to back) and paused for the command.

"Remember to hold your positions. I want to see a controlled spread. No cowboy shit," the zombie facing southwest yelled. "Nerves of steel, people. Fire!"

Manmade mouths coughed fiery, yellow-red bursts with bombastic tonnage as the rotating nexus of liquid-light and grenade rounds retraced their steps down the alley traveling north to the other side. Bodies burst apart in testament to the weapons' power and landed in loose piles that shimmied and danced, hands curling into claws and grabbing at air, toes balling under, then flexing straight, eyes staring up from severed heads, full of hunger and intent.

They cleared the alley in two minutes.

Mikel wouldn't have believed it if he hadn't seen it flashing in the lower left corner of the screen. For the longest time, he was essentially watching footage of a bunch of zombies doing the same dumb shit that he'd seen them do a million times in person. Their creepy charm came in their bumbling naiveté. One had to be totally at peace to appreciate it, or high; otherwise, it was nearly impossible to get past the fact that they'd bite your ass if they could.

Mikel figured maybe they were trying to test his sensitivity to walking death and the brutality with which the zombies attacked their prey. He was waiting to see some innocent schmuck bite the dust royally.

Mikel had prepared himself for what he might see. They all did. There were 12 of them, seated in rows of four behind desks meant for middle-school children. Like Mikel, they had come to learn more about the Dziko Nation, and to possibly enlist. The footage was from a test conducted two weeks ago. The four zombies were actually DN soldiers made up to blend in with the real zombies.

When the footage was over, Jared Jimenez, the sleek, wavy-haired Latino man with smatterings of Asian ancestry who conducted the orientation, explained that the zombies could detect warm blood, and that the DN had been working with a Chi Kung expert to practice lowering their core temperature through meditation.

*　　*　　*

"So, I see from your appli-*cay*-tion thad-you can handle yourself," Jared said as he perused Mikel's hastily scrawled application, squinting to decipher his handwriting as they walked side by side down the smoky hallway.

"Yeah, I studied kung fu for 5 years, kali for 3," Mikel replied. "Show me a solid object, and I'll show you a weapon."

"How are you weeth firearms?"

"I can hang."

Actually, Kane had only shown him the basics in the three weeks that they had been working out together. Mikel was still working on his aim, which he always thought would be better than it was.

"So lemme äsk you thees: You genuinely een-terested in joining our organi-say-tion, or are you here out of necessity?" Jared inquired, easing it out with a sort of underhandedness that made it sound like an insult. "Is alright. I'd rather you just be hōn-est."

Jared's voice sounded different in the hall, less accessible than before due to the weird acoustics and the fact that he was no longer trying to project to an entire class. After the orientation, he had approached Mikel and asked to speak with him alone.

Mikel was in the middle of a thought about the right time to ask about Yeshua. The rumor was that he was here somewhere, in the Center City base. He saw them wheeling a sick-looking man from a van when he first arrived. The man was wearing gloves, and his head was draped in a blanket, so he couldn't see his face or the color of his skin. Judging from his hunched posture and the coughing fit that plagued him the entire time Mikel watched (it was only a matter of seconds), there was no way this guy was Yeshua, right? Why the hell would he be sick?

"The ree-son I ask is because is quite ōbvious to me thad-you have whad-it takes. I'm just wōndering why a guy like-*you* häsn't already been snätched up by the mee-litary, one of the survivalist groups, or what's left of the poleese."

The capable men and women had found their niches when the chaos was still new and had since become heroes or food. Trickling down from alpha to somewhere around gamma, this latest bunch mostly was here as a result of recently losing a spouse, or a sibling, or an entire family. Mikel was a rarity in that he was a natural-born leader and ferociously athletic to boot.

"No. I understand completely. No disrespect to all the people who came out, but they didn't look at all like what I expected to see at an orientation for something like this."

"Is thees your first time?"

"Here? Yes?"

"I mean any-wh-ere."

"Yes," Mikel said in a lowered voice, as if he was ashamed to admit it. "My mother, you see… I'm the oldest of two boys…." Mikel choked on his words. Somehow they no longer seemed appropriate. "Being the oldest, I felt it was my responsibility to make sure they were safe."

"A sense of nobility. I like-that."

Mikel was never good at accepting compliments, especially when he felt they weren't warranted. In the case of Jason and his mother, he felt that he had let them down.

"Not so sure I'd classify that as nobility."

"Whad-then, fear?"

"Excuse me?" Mikel said.

"It is quite human to be afraid, Mikel. Is what we do weeth-that fear that makes us who we are."

"I'm not afraid of death, if that's what you're getting at. Not any more. If anything, I'm afraid of walking around like one of those deadfucks."

Mikel was pleasantly surprised by the diversity of the DN membership as he walked down the hall, passing room after room full of faces that represented every continent, and disappointed in the ratio of men to women. It was something like one girl to every six guys. That was generally the case wherever he went.

"I'm ass-uming thad-your mōther and brōther are dee-ceased?"

Mikel paused. Something about Jared's tone and his line of questions seemed slightly confrontational. Was this some kind of test, or was Jared just a dick?

Slow-burning rage began its climb up on its way to igniting a volcanic eruption of withheld emotion. But what would that accomplish? Standing at 6'5", Jared Jimenez was no joke. Besides, Mikel was on *his* turf. There would be no winning this one, even if he thought he could probably take him one on one.

"Yes, they're dead," he spoke through clenched teeth.

"I'm sorry to hear that, Mikel," Jared said, turning away to hide the corner-hugging smile that tugged at the left side of his mouth. Mikel was just what they had been looking for.

"It's okay. I'm dealing with it."

Detecting a bit of anger in his words, Jared stopped and pulled Mikel aside to let the two heavily armed men who were walking behind them pass.

"Look Mikel, if you are *going* to survive out *there*, then you have to come to terms weeth your weaknesses, or they'll be your death. If the ree-son you are here is to somehow exōnerate yourself of some deep-seated guilt for something that, in the end, you häd no real cōntrol over, then you might as well walk out thäd-door ride-now, 'cause I'm telling you, I've seen a mee-llion guys… tougher guys than you, go out in the shit ready to jump off like a bad-*ass*? They were the first ones to get their asses eaten by some undead muthafucker looking for his next meal. Now, like I said, guys like-*you* don't come around too often anymore, and frōm what I can gather, I theenk you would make a great addition to our organi-say-tion. But before you deecide, you'd better be sure that you've got the nerve to deal with the fucked-up shit that I can gua-ran-tee you'll see, prōbably on a daily basis."

Mikel thought long and hard, staring past Jared's unyielding mask of fortitude at the interesting pattern of lead chips high up on the filthy wall behind him. Though he was no pussy, Mikel sensed intensity in Jared that he'd yet to reach and, being the alpha male that he was, he craved that same wicked vigor for himself.

"I'm gonna need some time to think about it," Mikel responded.

Staring down at him, Jared allowed his size to press Mikel. Finally, he shook his head.

"I'm going to be posting a leest of the new recruits for thees period. Your name will be on it. The next phase of the orient-tay-tion is in a week and a half. I expect to see you there."

*   *   *

"What is it, baby? Was it something I said?" Allison huffed out and fingered tentacle-strands of hair from her face.

More like everything you said, Kane thought. He knew better than to actually say it. Allison was a completely different person from the woman he originally envisioned fucking when they first met. That was his problem. He always put women on an unobtainable pedestal when they first woke his libido. Like fucking them would bring him some otherworldly satisfaction when it was usually just okay at best.

This new... evangelical Allison was like a powder keg. She had always been a handful, thanks to her inattentive parents and her poor education, but she went off the deep end once she started sucking God's dick. Not even a year ago, she was telling him to:

"Come on/in my tits/face/ass/mouth!"

or

"Pull my hair and call me a slut!"

or

"Fuck/spank my ass!"

or

"Hold my arms down and give it to me hard, daddy!"

Now it was all about God and love, and how, with so little time left until Judgment Day, she wanted to seal their bond in the eyes of God.

"Wha...? Are you fucking high?" was the first thing Kane said when she brought it up a week ago.

God wants us to do this. God wants us to do that, she'd say.

Kane felt his hard-on peter out with each panted statement.

By her third orgasm, he was arching his back off the mattress to keep to his next-to-flaccid penis from sliding out of her. She was especially moist, as she had been lately. She was still cumming when Kane shoved her off of him.

"Well, aren't you going to answer me?" she asked, pawing his chest so gingerly that it made him want to strangle her.

Kane's new, homicidal disposition often begged him to revisit the satisfaction of unleashing his anger. In fact, he was biting his tongue to keep from screaming for her to "LEAVE ME THE FUCK ALONE!" He'd be arguing all night if he let that one fly.

Forcing a smile, Kane turned to face Allison.

"It's nothing, really."

Kane was aware that the silent intermission, punctuated by a deliberate sigh, meant that she wasn't about to let it go any time soon. As hard as he tried to concentrate on the television, he couldn't will the channel to change. It was either news reports or Reverend Dallas' hog-shit.

Rubbing his brow with the heel of his palm, Kane gave up and reached for the old-fashioned remote. He reminded himself never to use that damn chip again, even if he was feeling especially lazy.

"Oh, so you're just going to watch TV?" Allison's tone was different now. Gone was the feminine whisper, deep-throated as it was, the words trapped in riptides of endorphin stampedes, lunging out and retreating at the beginning and end of deep, meaningful breaths.

"Ally, please.... Not now. It's not you, per se.... I've just got a lot on my mind."

Allison glowered wrathfully at the side of Kane's face as he flipped through the channels. Every little sound (the padded click of the button under his thumb, the static swish from the dead channels, which was most of them, Kane's breath traveling in and out of his parched airways) brought her closer to the peak of antagonistic fury. The hint of a smile gestating beneath Kane's deliciously full lips was the last straw.

Allison snatched the remote from Kane's hand and hurled it against the wall.

"Are you out of your fucking mind?" Kane roared, whipping around.

"You know, I'm beginning to wonder if maybe I am for thinking I could make you see the light."

"Yet you keep trying."

"Well... what would you have me do? Goddammnit, Philip, can't you see that I love you and..."

"Better be careful now. That's no way for one of God's children to be talking, is it?"

Allison felt the urge to lunge at him claws first to appropriately convey her frustration. She grabbed the closest thing she could find, a pillow.

Kane sprung from the bed and leaned away just as the edge of the pillow whizzed by his face and pulled Allison off balance at the end of its swing.

She rolled onto her knees as if preparing to launch a response, then simply pressed her face into the mattress and began to weep.

"Don't I mean anything to you?" she whimpered.

What I wouldn't do for a trap door right about now, Kane mused, analyzing every lump and fold of the sloppy husk that he used to be able to overlook before Allison became such an emotional mess.

If by 'see the light,' she meant his waking up to all of her physical flaws (her thick waist, gelatin hips, droopy ass, halitosis, and her masculine body language) then he had indeed had an epiphany.

Standing there, watching her fall apart, Kane began to question his self-esteem. He had had much better in his day. In the back of his crowded mind, he figured that he could probably still pull 9s and 10s if he lightened up a little and added a touch of variety to his wardrobe.

When Kane looked up at the flashing digital readout in the lower frame of the TV, the numbers read only a minute since the last time he checked, and, unfortunately, Allison was still sitting naked,

Indian-style, on the bed. She was staring straight ahead at the TV, but was really watching her own life flash before her glossy eyes. This was the first stage of her self-pity cycle. It was only a matter of time until she embarked on her long-winded sermon on how you're supposed to act when you love someone, talking through the tears and the melancholy. It made Kane's skin crawl to listen to her trying to stifle her emotion while she talked.

He knew it was coming soon. It had been quiet for too long.

"Fuck it!" I don't have time for this nonsense," Kane exclaimed, tripping over his own words. He had hurried to get them out before Allison's lower jaw came to a rest.

She was only preparing to clear her throat.

"So that's it? You're not even willing to discuss it?" Allison fretted, her posture snapping to aggression, legs kicking straight, frustration welling with each step Kane took toward the bathroom.

The girly stink of potpourri (lilac and eucalyptus) ambushed him when he entered the bathroom, muttered, "lights," and prepared his eyes for the sting of sudden illumination. Contrary to the soothing qualities that Allison harped about when she gave it to him as a gift, the potpourri basket only amplified his scorn for her.

"Maybe I would be if your head wasn't so far up God's ass lately."

"Well, maybe if you weren't such an ignorant SONOFABITCH!!!!" Allison started to say before she became too choked up to speak. "Uuuugh!" she growled, bounced to her feet, and stomped flat-footed toward the bathroom.

Doubling back on his way to the mirror, Kane kicked the door closed in her face and waited by it, his hand poised to stop her from turning the knob and forcing her way in.

BOOM! BOOM! BOOM!

Kane jumped back and found a defensive posture as the door rattled under the force of her spastic pounding.

"If you don't open this friggin' door, I swear to Christ I'll kick it down."

"Be my guest. I'm still not going to talk to you until you can act like a rational adult."

"Oh, if that isn't the pot calling the kettle black."

"Whatever, Ally. Look, why don't you just…"

"WHY DON'T YOU JUST FUCK OFF!" Ally interrupted, and stomped away from the door.

Closing his eyes as he listened, Kane wondered what she was up to. From the sound of it, she was gathering her clothes and getting dressed. At least that's what he hoped she was doing. That would mean that she had given up, for now. Allison was the type to argue until the bitter end, and if he was to be at the test site in North Philly by 5:00 am sharp (it was already 2:30), he needed at least an hour of sleep to feel on point.

Thanks to the media and six previous failures (two that resulted in death), the Series 7 Urban Infantry Tank, nicknamed "the Crab," was a joke in the eyes of the skeptical minority. Nowadays no one really cared, though, except for Herman Weiss, the Secretary of Defense, who initially brought the Urban Infantry Tank program to table five years ago. Now that Bio-Tech Design Systems Inc. was under Reverend Dallas' weapons development branch, Weiss hoped it failed miserably. The Reverend envisioned the tank as security for the new cities and for his own personal army.

Bio-Tech was desperate for something to make people forget about the two dead pilots when Kane called back in February of last year. His better judgment warned him against getting in bed with the government, and especially the religious right, no matter how peripheral the relationship, but now he saw it as a supreme opportunity to snoop around.

Kane was pretty sure he heard the front door slam shut. He listened a while longer....

He didn't hear anything, yet he was reluctant to open the door and see what Allison might've done to his place. Though she denied it 'til she was blue in the face, Allison had put a 17-inch scratch down the side of his car in the past. Another time she threatened to break everything important to him and toss it out on his front lawn.

First things first: He had to pee.

On his way to the toilet, Kane stopped and backtracked to the mirror. He turned and stared his reflection in the eyes.

"Closer," he said, prompting the mirror to zoom in on his reflection. "Closer... closer... perfect."

Grabbing hold of his chin, Kane twisted his face from side to side, inspecting each thoroughly. Maybe he could still get that hour of sleep if he shaved and showered right now.

Chapter 8

Bio-Tech Design Systems Inc.
(formerly Girard College School for Boys)
Philadelphia, Pennsylvania

Girard College…

It didn't matter that the sign now read, **Bio-Tech Design Systems Inc.**; it would always be the Girard College that he remembered.

Even speaking it to himself gave Kane tremors of nostalgia so vibrant that he felt as if he was 12 again, and driving up to the huge iron gates for the first time in the back of his mother's car. Bio-Tech always had friends in high places, so the neighborhoods surrounding the walled-in campus were free of zombies, which allowed Kane to roll comfortably down memory lane.

There was something about this place, like a walled-in community nestled in the thicket of technological overgrowth and bordered on three sides by mid- to low-level poverty, like refuse shat out of the ass of progress.

Thick, muscular cloud formations seemed angrier inside Girard's walls, billowing at their own speed, and frowning down on the self-contained city of regal marble structures. The single, long tree-lined street that stretched from end to end still echoed tiny footsteps and juvenile laughter and voices whispering tall tales and racial anecdotes spoken without malice. At its heart, a massive, museum-like building, formerly known as Founder's Hall, supposedly housed the body of founder, Stephen Girard in a marble coffin built up on a pedestal behind a life-sized statue of the man himself. It was also where his ghost was said to be the most dangerous. Back in Kane's day, people reported seeing him all over campus, looking for little black boys to scare.

Girard's original vision, in 1848, of a school to educate poor, fatherless (white) boys was overthrown by a court ruling in 1968. By the time Kane enrolled in '89, it was about 75% black.

Kane drifted from story to story as he crept closer to the front gate, chasing the dragon of nostalgia that had him smiling from ear to ear. Leering at him from way over the shoulders of a statue that he didn't recognize (Stephen Girard surrounded by children situated 15 feet back from the front gate), the old founder's hall hadn't changed in years. On second glance, he noticed that the doors were a different color green instead of red, like he remembered. The size of the doors, from a distance, alluded to giant things living inside.

Just as it had then, founder's hall peeked out from behind fat, Corinthian pillars standing side by side along the front that reached up some 50 feet to the roof.

"Welcome back, Detective Makane," a static-laden voice sounded from a speaker in his dash. "I expect the place has changed a great deal since you were a student here."

Nodding in accord as he crept through the slowly opening gates, Kane peered to his left, down that single, tree-lined road that he walked daily listening to Andy Wilkins' little horror tales. Now the trees (what was left of them) mingled with communications towers, company vans, curious-looking prototypes walking and rolling about and sitting idle in open-faced tents, golf-carts displaying the Bio-Tech logo and carrying important-looking men, and broad-shouldered forklifts with tank treads transporting large crates back and forth. It was the most life he'd seen in one place in a long time.

You got that right, Kane mused.

"Come on down to the old armory, Detective," the voice said. "Someone will be waiting outside to meet you."

Regardless of the drastic facelift, the place still stirred up the same warm yet anxious feeling.

There were so many stories…. The harder he tried to concentrate on one, the faster they came, like a montage of his years spent here. There was the time Terrance Alves got caught running down the halls with a homemade Freddy Krueger glove, or when J. P. Moore and Jason Widner smeared their own shit on the math teacher's door, or when Andy Wilkins lit his hunting knife on fire and chased Tony Miles down the hall, or when Andy yelled "show yourself" when a couple of them had sneaked down to the basement of their dorm in the middle of the night with a Ouija board, or when Andy sliced the gym teacher's forearms open with a broken hockey stick for calling him on his dare to "come up here and make me shut up," or when Andy came after Mr. Cypher, the auto-shop teacher, with a cleaver.

Andy was a troubled kid who balanced dark humor with violent outbursts and sociopathic inclinations. They voted him most likely to be the first black serial killer. This was before Wayne Williams.

Kane often wondered what became of him, and if one day he'd have to bust him for committing some horrible act to rival the ones he was always writing about.

SERIES 7 [CRAB] FIELD TEST
PHASE 1: HEAVY ARMS/HULL INTEGRITY

Waking up to the soothing hum of a streamlined engine, the clicks and whirls of postmodern robotica realized, and an automated female voice rattling off his vitals, Kane was still dazed from the whole experience, yet he remembered. It came in explosions of brilliant white light, only pieces at first that leapt out of the background and punched him square in the face. He remembered even that the silver-haired professor said that he wouldn't. He also said that he wouldn't feel a thing, which was a flat-out lie.

If the slices of recall were correct, then Kane had been shot at point-blank range when he first walked into the silver-haired professor's office. He was in the middle of a sentence, leading with his hand in preparation to press flesh with the old man, when BLAM! As he lay dying, he wondered why they would waste a half-day of instructions, fittings, and demonstrative videos just for this.

When Kane came to, he was facing up, at a slant, from an exaggerated low-angle perspective. A long, thin form of featureless black draped in a labcoat (the silver-haired professor) seeped along the perimeter of Kane's body, speaking in half-speed as it looked down upon him, exuding an arrogance that came through in its deep voice, its body language, and, most of all, in the twisted diatribe masked as a half-assed apology spoken to a man who, as far as the professor knew, wouldn't remember it anyway.

The next thing Kane remembered was being strapped into the tank. Rising up, disembodied, he thought it was the end of his life, and for a moment he began to fear that all the fairy tales were true, that he was in fact leaving his body. At least he was heading up.

Turned out it was only two assistants lifting him by the armpits and placing him into the tank.

Kane still hadn't found a comfortable alternative to the position he was forced to adopt to pilot the damn thing. He was basically on his knees; feet folded up like some bullshit ergonomic step-stool masquerading as a chair. High-tech as it was, it certainly wasn't made for comfort.

The outdoor test-range, spread out across 30 acres of old-world edifices of marble and stone from the old Chapel west to the Armory, provided enough combustible fodder to further soothe the flames of revenge that crackled to prominence as Kane regained his senses. Sitting atop sturdy, segmented titanium legs (four in all), the two-armed, armor-plated torso let loose on the gutted autos, military vehicles, strategically placed dummies made up to look like zombies, and fake bunkers, each branded with a large red X.

Of the multitude of weapons at his disposal, Kane's favorite was the double-barrel cannon that made up most of the tank's thick right forearm and took the place of a traditional hand. At the end of the left arm, a hand much larger than his, with a grip strength of 5,000 psi, opened and closed into a fist as Kane flexed and curled his fingers in the tight glove beneath the surface to work out a cramp. Tiny holes in the fingertips worked as multiple flamethrowers with a range of 255 feet. They also discharged water and poisonous gas.

"WEAPONS SYSTEMS DISABLED."

The automated female voice startled him, crowding him as it resonated throughout. These were official men behind the scenes, yet his gut warned him not to give them his trust. Maybe it was the bullet that the silver-haired doctor, pumped into him as... "part of the test." That was what he said right after he assured Kane that it was in no way personal.

On the right side of the 9-inch screen through which he was granted a view of his surroundings, a flashing icon marked 'UV-scope' leapt out from the crowd of symbols and scrolling text, expanding to a rectangular window revealing live footage of seven heavily armed human outlines filled with throbbing reds and yellows and oranges against solid black, as they crouched in the back of a military truck in the middle of the overgrown soccer field to the left of him.

"No need for alarm, Detective," the technician's mechanized voice reassured him, "It's all part of the test."

Throbbing colors were replaced by dull green and black fatigues as seven armed soldiers poured from the truck into daylight and opened fire as they approached in formation.

The twang of ricocheting liquid-light bursts distracted Kane. From the inside, they sounded like fingers tap-tap-tapping; however, his cop instinct encouraged him to react a certain way to gunplay. In his mind, the entire experience was amplified. Typically, Kane was great under pressure, but he had been on edge since he awoke inside the tank, sitting idle in the Armory, and began to remember.

"You disarmed the weapons systems..." Kane yelled, scouring his options, "...and the shield mode...."

Standing about five feet away, the soldiers continued to pepper the tank with ammo. At most it caused it to take a lurching step backward, although Kane's overreaction was partially to blame for that. There wasn't much he could do except raise the tank's arms in front of the smooth, no-necked dome, a vent in the center modeled after arachnoid eyes. At first glance, the thing appeared to be headless.

"That's right, Detective. We wouldn't want you accidentally shooting our boys, now would we? Please try to calm down. Your vitals are all over the place. You're going to hyperventilate if you don't relax."

"Are you fucking kidding me? I'm getting creamed out here!"

"The unit can handle light rounds, no sweat. Shield mode drains a lot of power, so we improved its overall exterior integrity, making shields a last resort."

"Well, what the fuck am I supposed to do, just stand here? You'd be hard pressed to find a cop anywhere who likes having a gun pointed at him, let alone being shot at repeatedly."

"Improvise, Detective. Isn't that what you maverick-types are good at?"

The first thing that came to mind gave Kane a sting of anticipatory satisfaction, but if he actually swung at them....

"With that in mind, I want you to try to make it to the old high school behind you on the left. Whatever you do, just don't harm the soldiers, Detective. Remember, I can override you at any time."

The technician stood back, rubbing his chin in anticipation of what a 'maverick-type' like Kane might do next. Reacting with a scrunch-faced expression, the technician hissed through clenched teeth as if to empathize with the tank's knock-kneed stumble when the antiaircraft round smacked it in the lower back and caused its joints to give out momentarily, as would a fawn's attempting to stand for the first time.

There was something about watching the tank lurch toward its destination, check-swatting at the soldiers who walked alongside it, blasting away, that appealed to the little boy in him. Smiling, the technician looked over his shoulder, then switched the large screen to black and white in homage to the old creature-features of his youth.

SERIES 7 [CRAB] FIELD TEST
PHASE 2: LIGHT ARMS/STEALTH CAPABILITIES

BOOM!

Way up in the thick of the cloud that crept downward, flecks of marble and plaster and asbestos singing dry-textured songs as they came to rest in unison upon the buffed floor of the old high-school building, a titanium sarcophagus sat, challenging the song of flecks and buffed floor with a more industrial sound. It, too was upstaged by the thunderclap of an entire wall just over its rounded right shoulder that buckled and fell and sentenced everything in sight to another infrastructure-snowfall.

"Holy mother of… Small arms only for this phase of the test, Detective."

The technician's voice poured in from the earpiece and around the helmet like a mechanized gnat begging to be swatted.

"Are you alright down there, Detective?"

"I'm fine," Kane replied. "Now if I could only get my foot outta my ass."

"Sit tight. The A.I. is just making sure the threat has subsided before disengaging the shield mode. Shouldn't be long. So, what happened down there?"

"Not sure," Kane grunted through great discomfort. "Thought I saw someone, a kid maybe, in the corner of the screen. Probably nothing though. I didn't exactly get a full night's sleep last night."

"You were chosen for this project because of your exemplary record, Detective. I'm going to have to ask that you try harder to utilize that renowned professionalism. Otherwise we'll be forced to abort the test and look for someone else. I don't think I need to mention just how much time and money that would cost us."

"Professionalism… I see…. So, shooting me in the gut without warning… what exactly would you call that?"

Guilt manifested as a stutter trailing off, an awkward gap during

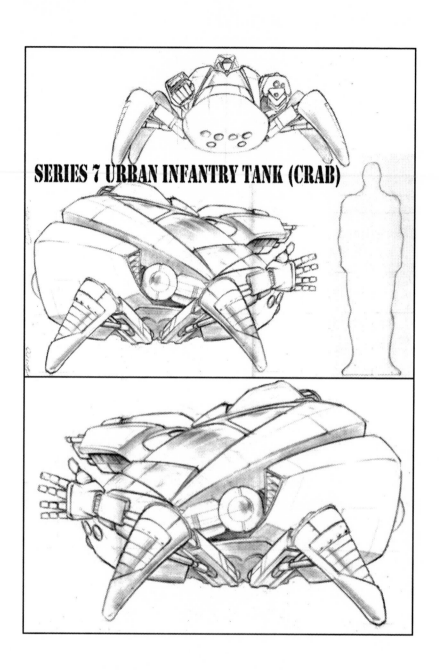

SERIES 7 URBAN INFANTRY TANK (CRAB)

which relative syllable-sounds leapt out but never took hold. A sigh beckoning to be acknowledged and understood poured from the speakers inside Kane's helmet and orbited the circumference of his head.

"You... remember that??? But Boggs assured us..."

"That's right." Kane felt empowered by the technician's alarm. "You might want to try stronger memory suppressors next time. I can put you in touch with all the best dealers. Then again, I'm sure you federal people have your own connections. Hell, I wouldn't be surprised if you guys weren't supplying the suppliers."

"I promise you, Detective, that that was *NOT* my idea." The technician's tone spoke of disappointment and genuine remorse. "The tank's self-healing system... the SHS... is the brainchild of Professor Boggs, our director."

"The silver-haired fuckhead who shot me?"

Hesitating as if his loyalties were somehow being tested... "Yeah, that's him. His methods have always been... unorthodox, to say the least. I, on the other hand, as well as most of the other scientists on this project, prefer to operate by a strict code of ethics, and I apologize for what he did to you. I assure you that had any of us known what he was planning, we would've done our best to dissuade him."

"I guess refusing to go along with his screw-brained ideas would be too much to ask."

"Well, he *is* our boss."

"You might want to tell your *boss* to rethink his methods, and not to be fooled into thinking that he, or any of the rest of you, for that matter, is above the law."

The law... Kane realized how silly it sounded nowadays.

Working to free his mind of flashes of reflection tinted red to coincide with the swell of rancorous emotion that they incited (Boggs offering his hand then, with the other, pressing the barrel of the small handgun against Kane's belly and pulling the trigger before he could react), Kane focused on the many positive memories he had collected, as a rebellious teen, in this building alone.

"Again, I apologize, Detective. How are you feeling, by the way? The SHS is showing a full recovery; however, your heart rate and blood pressure are a bit erratic."

"Oh, I see.... Now we're concerned about my well-being. Nice touch. But because you asked, that would be the hard-on I've got to give your boss a piece of my mind. Other than that, I'm fine."

"Be careful, Detective...." A second, more self-assured voice jumped into the fray. "Someone could misconstrue that as a direct threat, and threats against high-ranking officials are not something that we take lightly."

"Nice of you to join us, Dr. Goebbels," Kane said. Beneath the dry wit, rage breathed deep as it lie in wait. "I was beginning to think that you were hiding from me."

"That's *Professor Boggs*, Detective. On the contrary, I have every intention of participating in every aspect of the test."

"Well, that really eases my mind."

"I'm sorry that you had to remember that. It seems that I underestimated your tolerance to the suppressants."

"Yeah, thanks for the half-assed apology."

"SHIELD-MODE DEACTIVATED," the automated voice interrupted.

Unfolding from the smooth structure, insectoid legs met the floor with a THUMP and splintered the buffed marble where they planted, and bore down. Extra layers of reinforced armor withdrew section by section into the body of the tank as it came to a stand, check-stepping to find its balance.

"You mentioned seeing something in the corner of the screen. Could you please elaborate?"

"I don't know... looked like a bunch of kids, but you know, transparent. Listen, I know how that sounds...."

In fact, Kane recognized many of the transparent figures: the little round boy with the demented glaze, hugging the wall as he walked, for instance. Andy Wilkins was famous for roaming the halls when he should've been in class.

"Just imagine what the press could do with a statement like that."

"Excuse me? What was that supposed to mean?"

"Doesn't have to mean anything, Detective. Just want us to have an understanding."

"Oh, I understand. You can bet your ass on that."

Kane was the type who'd scratch to infection once he developed an itch. He made a mental note and filed it away, marked urgent. Trying anything now with his anger so palpable and new would be suicide. And if he was going to gain their trust he needed to at least leave on good terms, he would have to bury his feelings for now.

"Good. I'm glad," Professor Boggs replied. "Now, what you saw was the EMI sensor working as it should. You must've accidentally activated it."

Silence.

"The EMI sensor picks up electromagnetic traces, or EM fields left behind by the buildings' former occupants throughout its history," the technician added, sensing Kane's confusion. "It's basically what people used to think of as ghosts."

"You guy's come up with everything.... Now if you could only come up with a scientific explanation for Jesu..."

"You sure you want to finish that sentence, Detective?" Boggs warned. "Don't forget where you are."

"Trust me, I haven't. I'm curious, though, about the suppressant. Which one was it: Bexanol? Flovamax?

"Bexanol, if you must know."

"Sneaky bastards..." Kane commented under his breath.

"If it's any consolation to you, what I did was for the sake of getting the tank on the streets and saving lives as soon as possible."

"You can save that shit for the Jesus Freaks, doc."

"TARGET IN MOTION." The automated voice seemed to have a thing for insinuating itself into other people's conversations.

On the screen, an obtrusive pop-up displayed a bird's-eye digital blueprint of the building, angles and perspectives everchanging to appropriately translate the manmade terrain. In the northeast corner, a blinking, red human-shape crouch-walked toward what looked like a ladder mounted in the wall. Scrolling text revealed it as the roof access. It also revealed that the human-shape was well armed.

"I was going to wait to go over stealth mode, Detective, but because your little accident seems to have awakened our guest, I might as well tell you that I was able to persuade an old acquaintance of yours to join us today."

"Old acquaintance???" Kane was reluctant to acknowledge.

"That's correct, and one who I can safely say that you'll be more than happy to see."

Focusing on the red human-shape that continued to blink at him, Kane riffled through his mental gallery. It was a crowded place to say the least, full of lowlifes and thugs, many of whom were his own colleagues.

"Who is it? This better not be another one of your..."

"Why don't you try asking the A.I.?"

Of course, Kane thought, rolling his eyes.

"Computer, can you give me the identity of..."

"'COMPUTER' IS NOT A VALID COMMAND."

"Oh, give me a fucking break, would you?"

"'GIVE ME A FUCKING BREAK' IS NOT..."

"...not a valid command.... I got it, I got it."

Kane paused to evaluate his next command.

"Can you give me the identity of the target, please?"

On screen, another pop-up joined in the jumble of overlapping windows. The image, a mug shot and scrolling rap sheet, startled him. Exploding outward into a rectangular box, the face appeared to rush him and stop inches away from his own face.

"TARGET IDENTITFIED AS ANTHONY "TONY THE TIGER" PALERMO. MALE. AGE 54. HEAVY TIES TO ORGANIZED CRIME. LIST OF CHARGES INCLUDE EXTORTION, RACKETEERING, FIRST DEGREE MURDER, RAPE..."

Tony's name was all Kane needed to hear to get his blood going.

"Save it. I *know* who he is."

"...NARCOTICS TRAFFICKING, AGGRAVATED ASSAULT, MANSLAUGHTER..."

"I said save it. Stop! Please!"

"I'd like you to activate the stealth mode, Detective," Boggs said. "I'll talk you through it as we go. Remember to try and stay calm."

The last thing Tony Palermo remembered was wondering how he was going to explain that the chick who had just blown him like his dick was made of gold was really a guy. And on top of that, he was beginning to think that she'd... that he'd slipped something in his drink.

He thought he was being raided again when he awoke to an explosion coming from a few floors below. Not only did he not know where he was, or how he'd gotten there, but also he was armed with a gun he didn't own (an XM-12 Berserker) and clothed in a pair of torn silk pajama pants.

Tony banged on the hatch that opened onto the roof until his hands were numb. He didn't even want to begin to wonder who might have been behind this. He had more enemies than he could count, each worse than the next.

Dangling momentarily from the top rung of the ladder, Tony dropped to his feet as quietly as possible and stood still long enough to feel the rhythmic thump that caused the marble floor to vibrate every three to five seconds. Turning slowly, he peered down the hallway that led to the staircase. He eventually made his way to the edge of the staircase and looked down. Despite the fact that the thunderous footsteps grew closer with each thump, there was nothing to be seen, until…

A hint, a wave of light traveling right to left revealed, for a for a split second, a shiny, metallic bulk, and wire-wrapped legs ending in imposing points, like a giant, manmade insect. It was only a glimpse before it disappeared beneath the landing above which he crouched. Being the undereducated, traditional sort of fucker that he was, Tony was instantly sold on the big scary monster concept.

*   *   *

"Now, what part of 'tell me where he is' don't you understand, boy?" Reverend Dallas barked at the fat man (Martin Stringer, *Esquire*) who floated upside-down in mid-air, in the center of his lavish office. Along with the overstated religious art that hung from the walls, the room was enlivened with the spirit of a successful big game hunter. There were deer and antelope and buffalo heads mounted on wooden plaques, photos of Reverend Dallas standing triumphant over various animal carcasses, and whole, stuffed animals posed in action.

His distinctive voice caught the wind with ease and rode it around the building. Out in the church area, it provided a giggle for the guards and continued through the walls, out into the old graveyard out back that served as a holding pen for the zombies that Jesus had been using to assassinate his enemies who didn't believe in him.

"Please? I can't breathe…." Martin Stringer gurgled out through a backwash of vomitus, the bulk of which had oozed down his right arm and slapped the floor or gone up his nose and choked him. "I swear… I don't know where he is."

Using a handkerchief to wipe the moist flecks of bile and half-processed food from the lapel of his jacket, Reverend Dallas looked with disgust over at Jesus, who sat back in the shadows humming "Rock of Ages" and tapping his long fingernails against the wooden arm of the grand ol' Texas-style chair. Reverend Dallas referred to it as his throne. It was a gaudy thing with bullhorns mounted at the top of the high back. Against the stained-glass window behind him, Jesus' silhouette haunted the dark corner of the office.

"Okay.... I worked for the Dziko Nation, yes, but I was only their lawyer," Martin huffed out, his excessive weight working against him in every way. "The only time they told me anything was when they needed advice from a legal standpoint. And that was back before Easter. They let me go soon after."

"Let you go?"

"They fired me.... They said that lawyers were obsolete."

"Where have you been staying since then?" Reverend Dallas spit out quickly.

Martin paused. He had nothing but the truth, which he was determined to keep to himself.

"You've been staying with them, haven't you?"

Martin closed his eyes and tightened his face as if to aid in fighting off the dizzying effects of a stalwart buzz, or to squeeze out a stubborn shit.

"He doubts me," Jesus whispered with shades of anger. "The fool is trying to bury his thoughts."

"I'm afraid that dog won't hunt, my friend," Reverend Dallas said. "You see, what I got sittin' back there is the best damn lie detector that all the money in the world can't buy. And he says you're lying."

Martin's semi-steadfast will chased his sobbing and gasps for air into brief remission. Squeezing his eyes shut, he floated silent, feigning defiance when really he was three rungs away from dying of fright.

"Open thine eyes, Martin," Jesus said, soft embers of his androgynous tone stroking Martin's constricting nerves and seducing them to relax with its weird dragging cadence, "and cast them upon me."

Martin knew that he was as good as dead. He had learned that disbelief was the only way to fight them, and to keep them from getting in his head. From what he'd heard, it was far worse than anything physical that a person could imagine.

Martin held his eyes closed as long as he could until something like an overwhelming urge that stung like a motherfucker left him fiend'n for a look. He could feel the longing in his teeth, and in the cold, then hot, then cold sweat that poured down toward the top of his head. All he had to do was open his eyes, just a quick peek to quench his sudden, undeniable thirst.

Martin opened his eyes, and screamed at the image that played out at Jesus' feet. He had only glanced for a second before turning away, but it was already too late. The damage was done.

Reverend Dallas knew never to look, but he always wondered, and in the back of his mind, feared that one day he might be made to see. Based on the reactions he had witnessed, he was sure that it might have ill effect on his dubious heart. Just listening to Martin's scream had caused it to stutter, though he played it off like everything was everything.

Through the coughing and spitting, Martin wailed a dry-throated song of mental defeat that came out in short "ma-ma-ma" breaks due to his loose jawbones bouncing off one another as he trembled in shock. The vision at Jesus' feet was of his wife being molested by zombies.

"Certainly thou wouldst agree that a woman of such beauty, whose indiscriminate taste enables her to overlook thy irreprehensible hygiene, doesn't deserve such an unspeakable and lengthy ordeal," Jesus said.

"I'll tell you what I know," Martin mumbled, "but it really isn't much."

Suddenly, a soft female voice (Grace Holden, Reverend Dallas' secretary) poured from the intercom on his desk.

"Sorry to interrupt you gentlemen, but I have a Lin… Kwi… or Kwei, holding on line 2."

"Who?"

Confused, Reverend Dallas turned to Jesus.

"Lin Kwei, from the Triads," Jesus said. "I summoned him."

"Now, hold on a hot minute. How do you expect the public to follow us... you... when we're associating with out-and-out criminals?"

"Let me worry about that, Reverend."

Reverend Dallas curbed his disappointment before it grew to something that he couldn't control.

"All right, Grace. Tell him that I'll have to call him back. I'm in the middle of something."

"Will do."

"Thanks, Grace."

Reverend Dallas was itching to argue. He was still learning how to play second fiddle to Jesus, whom he had come to know now and at times looked upon as just another man. Having spent more than 20 years as the highest-rated televangelist, he was used to calling the shots and throwing his weight around indiscriminately.

Redirecting his anger, Reverend Dallas frowned at Martin Stringer.

"Well, we're listening," he grumbled.

"Just please... don't hurt my family. They're all I've got left."

"You ain't in the position to be making demands, boy," Reverend Dallas said. "Now quit your bellyaching and spit it out."

"All I know is that he... that Yeshua came to the Center City compound for a meeting sometime around August or September. He was supposed to be meeting with the Coalition for Spiritual Diversity after us. He stayed for two days and then left."

"You were right," Reverend Dallas remarked to Jesus.

From the background, a succinct chuckle sneaked out through Jesus' glossy lips.

"I'm always right," he replied.

"This Yeshua is going to be the end of us, and you're joking?" Reverend Dallas whined. "Can't you do something to force him out from under his rock?"

"Watch thy tongue, Reverend. Or hast thou forgotten to whom thou art speaking?"

"No. Heaven's no. Forgive my tone. I'm just a little concerned."

"Yeshua is very powerful; however, faith in him is small. As long as that is the case, then thou needn't worry. I will deal with him once and for all when the time is right."

"What about *him*?" Reverend Dallas pointed at Martin.

Whimpering like an infant coming down from a ferocious tantrum, Martin lifted his arms (they had gotten heavier since the last time he tried) and folded his hands in prayer.

"I told you everything I know," he cried. "Please let me go. I'm begging you."

"Silence!" Jesus commanded, "and take comfort in the knowledge that thy family will not be harmed."

"Okay… thank you.… Thank God.… Whatever you want me to do: Just tell me, and it's as good as done." Martin didn't really mean *anything*. It just seemed like the right thing to say.

Bursting aglow like a supernova, Martin's eyes shot open, and from the nexus of his soul, he groaned in unconditional agony, startling Reverend Dallas, who had prepared to respond facetiously to his plea.

"Lest thou hast forgotten who is in charge here, Reverend," Jesus whispered.

Martin's screams grew deafening, his lips peeling back, teeth and gums jutting out like the jaws of a hungry great white shark, provided a starting point for the unseen fingers that dug in and yanked him inside out.

Reverend Dallas attempted to turn away but the cold ghostly hand that tightened around the back of his neck forced him to watch.

Chapter 9

Once rife with activity, the 13th precinct was a shell, occupied by vacant offices and desktops abandoned in haste. In recent months, the lobby had gone from jammed to capacity with people looking for their dead relatives, recently turned zombies who could still think straight seeking justice or some kind of cure for what was done to them, volunteers for the cleanup program waiting to be deputized, bible-thumpers, and drunks, to a jumble of overturned chairs, leaflets, and half-filled applications scattered about and signed with dirty footprints.

As if to hide from what was going on, the walls, with their off-white and nicotine-smoke hue, were covered with layers of fliers and posters screaming over each other to "LOOK THIS WAY!"

The first layer was dedicated to serene settings thanks to Allison, who felt that they might uplift and raise morale among the remaining crew; the second to sign-up sheets for volunteers, lists of active shelters and businesses that provided safety and parking for a fee, grainy Xeroxed photos of missing persons, and lists describing what to and not do if confronted by a zombie; and the third to archaic slogans, popular in-jokes relayed in police jargon, silly acronyms for organizations that, in the end, did little to rid the world of whichever vice they claimed to oppose, wanted photos, and crime-scene classics.

As usual, the precinct was on lockdown. Steel shutters and doors sealed tight snatched the day away and left most of the skeleton crew of seven suffering from perpetual cabin fever.

As the highest-ranking officer, Kane was exempt, as he made sure to keep himself occupied with grunt work. It didn't start out that way. Most of the new recruits, who made up five of the seven on duty, had minimal experience with extreme violence, and what they did know came from watching a family member or friend devoured by zombies; they had joined simply to have a safe place to stay. Temporary housing within the station was one of the perks of joining the force.

Allison, who was the second in command, was down in the shooting range with two new recruits. Although they still fucked from time to time, she and Kane had drifted apart. Deep down, she still loved him, and although she feigned disinterest, she was secretly committed to persuading him to be with her by Judgment Day.

As much as he bitched about it in the past, Kane longed for the noise, the sense of doom, and the occasional wig-out as the reality of prison time sunk in with self-proclaimed bad-asses who more often than not ended up in tears.

The plusses? Well, they were bittersweet. There was definitely no shortage of action, or criminals, or zombies upon which to unleash his inner savage. Taking his stress out on them was surprisingly therapeutic, even better than boxing. His rules were basically the same: spar with the unstable motherfuckers, the ones with anger in their bones, like energy from some unresolved grudge in a past life. They brought it full steam each time. Sometimes they even took it too far, but he was always cool with that. That uncertainty… it was the only way to stay sharp in the street.

In post-awakening terms, that meant Kane sought out the rapists, murderers, freaks, thugs, bikers, and muscleheads. It was a general criterion that applied to the living and the dead. With zombies specifically, he focused on the ones with enough meat left on them or some hint of aggression, or deep, dark anger in their affected stride to give their wild attacks some real sense of danger. He felt that he was jaded.

The activists would say that he was still profiling. They were few and far between these days, and like every other group of survivors, their turnover rate was extremely high. Many of these groups outnumbered the police by double digits, so Kane made it a point to keep his extracurricular crime-fighting on the down-low, making stops in desolate areas, or parking in dark alleys and waiting for some hapless deadfuck to wander by. When he was feeling especially angry, he liked to arm himself to the hilt and go for long walks. It was the reason he seemed so disconnected lately, though he called it being in control of his emotions.

"Dammit!" Kane growled, thumbing the button, then shoving the video-phone away and knocking the framed quote that sat on his desk to the floor. **"The ends justify the means,"** it read in bold letters. "Emergency satellite is down, AGAIN!"

He was on the phone with his "secret admirer" when the connection failed. He had finally gotten around to listening to the entire message, and he convinced himself to call the recorded number. They had only been talking for a few minutes, mostly awkward small talk and mano-a-mano formalities, feeling each other out and such, so Kane hadn't learned much about him aside from the fact that he was from Denmark, that he was psychic, and that in his dream, Kane had done something bad. He never even found out the man's name and as usual, the video signal was scrambled.

With the satellite down, Kane would have to wait to call the number that the skinny technician with the ponytail slid to him, in secret, during his post-exam at Bio-Tech.

"You were lucky," the technician said. "The other pilots left here with something permanently wrong with them. You took a big risk getting into that thing."

Kane had literally become obsessed with this grand conspiracy that his intuition kept suggesting. It was how he got through the long days without flipping out at something minor. Sometimes his mood swings were so drastic that he worried he might be slipping, but as long as he kept on working… kept on digging, the roots were bound to intertwine at some point.

Speaking with the skinny technician gave him hope. He was a spy for the Secular Soldiers. He said that they knew that Kane was investigating the crash. The plane was full of reporters, he said. They were traveling from Maryland with a priest, a Father Maldonado, who, against the Church's wishes, planned to allow cameras to document an exorcism for the world to see. They still weren't sure why the plane went down, or how the exorcism fit into the rest of the puzzle. Supposedly, the victim, a nun by the name of Angelica Downy, had all the classic symptoms.

"I say she probably just needed a good cock to straighten her out," the technician joked.

He went on to tell Kane that Jesus was a fake, Yeshua too, and that they had heard word that Yeshua was planning something big before December 25th. The Coalition for Spiritual Diversity and the Dziko Nation were in on it.

"Take this," the technician said as he quickly scrawled a number on the corner of a sheet of paper, tore it off, and handed it to Kane. "Call this number and ask for Keith Barnes. He'll be able to tell you more."

With the emergency satellite down for the third… no, fourth time this week, it was looking like he'd have to wait awhile longer to speak to this Keith Barnes and to Vernon Boca, who never even called him back. That wasn't like Vernon.

For now, Kane had to rely on what he already knew/had at his disposal, which wasn't much: a few numbers and names, copies of the pre-test exam results for three of the four pilots who survived the tanks before him, and clips of old news briefs on two of the tests. The reporter mentioned that the pilots in both cases were treated and released from the hospital in a matter of hours, and there was even footage of a handful of technicians helping a dazed pilot regain his equilibrium, and then toppling over with him as he fell to the ground. They played that part up for laughs.

Kane wasn't able to find anything else about their post-test condition, or what ever became of them. He was beginning to think that they had either died during the test, or were paid to disappear, and the media were paid to look the other way.

Kane made his rounds checking the entrances and making sure the recruits were okay. People had been known to lose it at a moment's notice, though that kind of thing usually happened in the heat of a zombie bum-rush, or during some similar heightened scenario.

One of the younger recruits, David Owens (he was only 18), was nursing a case of the chills and the cold sweats, but he assured Kane that he could handle it. He said it was just a cold, and that he'd rather be doing something productive than wallowing in bed.

Fair enough.

Trying to conceal a slight limp, Kane made his way upstairs to the second floor. He refused assistance from the recruit at the top of the stairs who offered to place his hand on the palm reader and open the 2nd floor door for him.

Kane turned the knob quietly when he reached the rec room. They had been using it as sleeping quarters and, in case people were sleeping inside, he didn't want to wake them.

The sounds from the TV leapt out at him when he opened the door. The place was a mess, the kind of mess that would drive him crazy had this been his house, chairs left where the last people to use them had left them. He had this thing about pushing them back to designated places at the long table at the back of the room. Half-drunk bottles of beer and soda were scattered about; ashtrays full of cigarette butts were stacked in a sloppy pyramid; sleeping bags were left unzipped and balled into bunches next to articles of clothing and toiletries.

Ehhhh…relax why don't cha, Kane told himself. *You've got far more important things to stress about.*

Just beneath the wall-mounted flatscreen, the light bounced off a smooth, round surface (Mikel's bald head) that peeked over the top of the room's only recliner.

"Must-see TV, my ass," Kane called out.

"Wha' was that?" Mikel said, whipping around toward the voice that sneaked up on him and yanked him out of the fast-edit coma that the TV had seduced him into.

"Never mind. I'm dating myself," Kane quipped. "It was an

old saying. So, howya holding up? Did you sleep all right?"

Rubbing his bald head from back to front and back again, Mikel stood, stretched away his lethargy, and walked over to Kane.

"Can't tell you the last time I had a decent night's sleep," he said, squeezing his eyes shut to wash away the glaze. "Every time I close my eyes, I seem to have the same fucking dream."

"Lemme guess. It involves zombies?"

"How'd you know?" Mikel joked. "What makes it worse is that they all look like members of my family."

Kane caught a chill, and a flash of Jason's face, his eyes pleading for death right before Kane shot him. What would Mikel do if he knew the truth? Would he understand that he had no other choice? The questions began to pile up, but Kane was quick to wipe them from his mind, fearing that some hint of a confession might materialize on his face.

He reached out and gave Mikel a fatherly tap on the back as they walked over to the table and sat down. Internally, Kane remarked how cute it was that Mikel swung his chair around and straddled it backwards. Something about that stunk of youth.

Kane glanced up at the TV. The news…. What a surprise. Aside from the CMB stations, which ran Reverend Dallas' most popular sermons, revisionist history lessons on Jesus' life, and footage of cameras following Reverend Dallas and Jesus around, the news was all that was left; all news, all the time.

Kane nodded at the TV.

"That shit is like fingernails on a chalkboard to me. Didn't you want to watch a movie or something? They told me that there was a shitload of 'em saved up there. Hang on."

"What are you doing?"

Kane froze in squat/stand, the back of his knee just about to nudge his chair back away from his legs.

"I was going to change the channel."

"So what are you getting up for?" Mikel said, flipping

downward through the channels and stopping on a menu of movie titles without moving a finger, or even looking. At the top of the screen, a smaller box opened, containing a catalog of movies he had on deck or had already watched: *The Good, the Bad, and the Ugly, Shaw Brothers Classics, Vol. 1, Badassss, Death Wish 1-3, Airplane, Blazing Saddles, Best of The Simpsons.* "See. I watched *Blazing Saddles* this morning. I'm saving the rest for another time, though. It takes me so long to get through each one because I'll only watch them for 15 minutes at a time before I switch over to the news for a few. I always feel like I'm missing something when I don't watch the news."

"A news junkie, huh?"

"'Fraid so."

Twisting his lips to the side, Kane playfully scolded Mikel with his expression as he grabbed his chair, slid it underneath him, and sat down.

"You can have those chips. They give me the worst headaches."

"Never bothered me any."

"Great. Then I really am getting old."

They laughed.

"So whose idea of a sick joke was it to download *Night of the Living Dead?*" Mikel inquired.

Kane laughed unexpectedly.

"Is that right? Aw man, that's rich."

Mikel found it odd that Kane would laugh so hard at that.

Sensing his sudden tension, Kane brought the laughter home with a sigh earlier than he would have liked.

"You gotta learn to relax a little, Mikel," he said, using his hand in a sort of bouncing, five-fingered point as he spoke. "You go out there with your asshole squeezed tight like that, and this shit will get into your head and fuck your brain from the inside out. Trust me, I know you've been through your share, but I've seen shit out there that would…"

"…make me question my sanity? I know, I know," Mikel said.

He had heard that statement many times during their weird father-son courtship. "I believe you, man. Just give me some time to digest all this shit."

"I'm telling you... I've seen guys blow their own brains out rather than deal with so much death."

Kane had upped Mikel's training in the past few weeks, graduating from simple handguns (heat-seekers, smart-guns and liquid-lights) to the various cannons (double-fisteds, Berserkers, etc.) and taking him out on his nightly hunts. For such a tough-guy, Mikel was a bit tentative the first time Kane had him go buck-wild on a group of zombies with only a bat and a machete at his disposal. The chill in the air was especially sharp that night, slicing through his clothing and pricking his skin. Once he got into it, though, the rush of adrenaline warmed him, and he began to move like a natural.

With all that martial arts training, Mikel's strikes were much more elegant-looking and crisp than Kane's. He was a born zombie killing-machine. Now, if only Kane could get him to suppress his emotions more, to bury them deeper. There was simply no room for emotion when dealing with the dead.

"Anyway, I wanted to tell you that I've made my decision," Mikel said.

Kane's face melted solemn. He had grown close to Mikel and didn't want to see him go.

"I was going to wait until after I had a chance to meet with the Secular Soldiers, but after spending some time here, it looks like you need all the help you can get."

Kane tried not to look as elated as he was. Though he considered himself a father figure, because they weren't officially related, he couldn't help feeling that there was something gay in the corny, "Hallmark moment" sense, about his feelings for Mikel. And Kane didn't do Hallmark moments. At least he liked to think he didn't.

"Are you sure?" Kane questioned, partly to mask his excitement. "A lot of people see us as irrelevant these days. You sure

you wanna risk your ass for no reward?"

"Reward?"

"Money. Gratitude. That kind of thing. Not that there was ever much of it to begin with in this line of work."

"From what I've seen, it's not much different anywhere else. Plus, after all you've done to help me, what kind of asshole would I be if I left you to deal with all this shit with that bullshit crew you've got downstairs? I had a chance to talk to some of these guys, and no offense, but except for one or two, I'd say they're as good as dead already."

Although he agreed wholeheartedly, Kane wondered if he should take offense to Mikel's statement. After all, he and Allison had handpicked the new recruits.

"What?" Mikel asked, regarding Kane's sudden moment of quiet introspection.

"Nothing…" Kane replied, distracted. "I was just thinking that you're right."

"So, is it official then?"

Kane stalled as if to consider Mikel's request.

"I-don't-knowwww…" he said, trying to conceal a boyish grin that pushed its way through his lips, and eventually jumped out at Mikel. "You know I'd love to have you here. I just want you to understand…."

"Trust me. I understand."

"Alll-right. All right." Kane lifted his hands, surrendering. "You're in."

"Cool," Mikel said, looking around the room. "Now I just have to scope out a good spot to shack-up."

"Screw that. I wouldn't let you sleep down here. You can have the shrink's old office upstairs. Just remind me to give you the keys so you can throw your stuff in there. I think they're in my desk downstairs. It's kind of a mess right now, but I'll help you clean it out. Shouldn't take more than an hour."

"You don't have to…."

"I insist. End of subject."

Suddenly, a voice lashed out from the intercom mounted next to the door. It was Allison.

"Philip! We need you downstairs now!" She was breathing heavily, her words rushed. "We've got a problem."

In the background, they could hear a raised voice.

"I SWEAR I'LL DO IT!" were its exact words.

Kane and Mikel looked at each other for a moment before a name and a face to match the voice popped into Kane's head and initiated his launch up out of his seat. It was David Owens, the kid.

"C'mon!" he yelled to Mikel, who was already in motion a few steps behind him.

They could hear David Owens yelling even before they opened the door at the bottom of the staircase and jogged down the hall that opened out onto the main office area.

"I'M TELLING YOU, I CAN FIGHT IT! I KNOW I CAN!" David said, tears streaming down his face and mingling with snot and drool, both of which were allowed to flow freely.

David held his gun sure-fisted, gripping the handle to a white-knuckled shine, whipping his aim back and forth from Allison to Alan Roundtree as they aimed back. Knowing that either of them could pop him while he was focused on the other didn't seem to dissuade him. Instead, he maintained his stance, oscillating to cover his targets, and affected by momentary tremors of deep-bellied nausea.

He was white as a ghost, his stomach sucked in, ribs expanding and retracting like they were going to blow at any second, and he was sweating like a chain-smoker running a marathon in the peak of the August sun in Louisiana. His pronounced Adam's apple bobbed as he lurched, his convulsing gut belching up phlegm and blackened blood. Even still, he was probably clear enough to pull off one good shot before one of them could tackle him. They knew it, too.

Kane's desk was only about 10 feet to the left of where he

and Mikel stood at the opening of the hallway, an easy dive and roll. However, he didn't feel threatened enough to make the leap when David spun and fixed his trembling aim on him.

"PLEASE, JUST STAY WHERE YOU ARE!" David said. "I DON'T WANT TO HURT ANYBODY!"

Kane focused on David's right arm. The sleeve of his uniform was stained a dark color from his elbow down. It appeared to be relatively fresh.

"He's been bitten," Allison said. "This genius right here knew about it, too, and kept it from us."

"I'm sorry," Alan Roundtree whined. "He's my friend. He said he could handle it."

"I *CAN* HANDLE IT! I SWEAR I CAN. JUST GIVE ME A CHANCE TO SHOW YOU!"

"Can't do it, son," Kane said, pulling his glare away from Alan Roundtree and fixing a more sympathetic gaze, albeit an impatient one, on David. "Now, put the gun down, and we'll try to get you some help."

"NO! I DON'T NEED HELP! I JUST WANT TO BE LEFT ALONE TO DO MY JOB."

It was like a game of tag played with darting glances: David Owens to Alan Roundtree, Alan Roundtree to Allison, Allison to Kane, Kane to everyone, and Mikel watching from the sideline.

Feeling left out, Mikel stepped forward.

"When were you bitten?" Pointing to David's forearm, he asked it in a way that seemed as if he was referring to something simple, like a bee sting.

"HUH?" David check-glanced, then turned his gun on Mikel. "WHY? WHO THE FUCK ARE YOU?"

"What are you talking about, man? You know who I am."

David seemed to remember Mikel for a second before he lost the thought, and regained it, and lost it again. Then, for a moment, he seemed astutely aware of what was happening to him, and what was going to happen. He sort of smiled, then outright laughed as if he expected one of them to tell him that it was all a joke.

Judging from their expressions, he was the only one who found it funny.

In his eyes, they all saw themselves. Each of them had wondered what they'd do if… you know… if *it* happened to them. It made the moment palpable, gumming up their reaction process with emotion.

"According to Roundtree, David was bitten yesterday morning," Allison said.

Mikel rolled his eyes, disappointed.

"*Heee*-was-supposed-to-tell-me," he mouthed to Allison regarding David.

It took a moment, but Allison deciphered Mikel's message, along with the gist of his botched plan.

"It was during our food run," Roundtree added. "He thought he saw his uncle. Well… I guess it *was* his uncle, but he was a zombie. I tried to stop him but he thought he could get through to him."

"Yeah! Uncle Ray!" David jumped enthusiastic. "Where is he? I told him that he could stay here with us."

"Look son, your uncle is dead," Kane said, cutting through the mind games and the gentle stroking. "And you soon will be. That is, unless you'd rather walk around like those deadfucks. The most you can do is let us make the transition easier for you."

Allison reacted to Kane's "tough-love approach" by sucking her teeth and following it with a loud gust of breath laced with a smidgen of disapproving tone. *Yeah, that's really going to calm him down*, was what the look on her face said.

David was crying now, whimpering like a restless brat forced to sit still. The gun bounced along with his shoulders, yet he kept his arms out straight, his aim floating from person to person.

"It's not fair," David whimpered. "IT'S NOT FAIR!"

"Don't listen to him, David," Allison said. "Just put the gun down, and I promise I'll make sure…"

The phone rang. It was coming from Kane's desk.

"Why the fuck didn't somebody tell me the satellite was back up?"

"Ah… we kind of had our hands full down here," Allison replied without looking.

Kane leaned toward his desk, reaching with his eyes to glimpse the name and number flashing on the phone's video-screen, but he was too far and his eyes weren't what they used to be. Not that his vision was any worse. His eyes, they watered a lot, and the more he rubbed them (orgasmic as it could sometimes be), the more they itched and stung.

Kane took a step closer to his desk, hoping that David wouldn't notice the slight shifting of his feet.

"I SAID DON'T MOVE!" David said.

Kane begrudgingly raised his hands in the air. He turned them to demonstrate that he was unarmed and motioned for another step.

David thrust the gun and himself in Kane's direction.

"I SAID…"

…was the last thing from David's mouth before Kane's bullet burrowed deep into his brain.

Mikel was impressed with Kane's speed and accuracy under pressure. It was like genuine movie shit the way he drew his gun and fired in one, liquid motion, smooth and succinct. The bullet had only stunned David, but it gave Mikel, Alan Roundtree, and Allison enough time to rush in and subdue him before he came to, screaming and thrashing in their grasp. And that was just what he did.

Kane hurried over to the phone. He didn't even bother to check the screen this time.

Glancing up at the wrestling match, he lingered momentarily to make sure they had it under control. He shook his head at the commotion and how perfect a metaphor it was for the rest of the world, and pressed the "talk" button.

"Makane speaking…."

"Jyust like a cracka,' sendin' yer boys to do yer dirty work while you sit on yer ass and take credit for it." The deep, rich voice flowed with a distinctive Caribbean cadence.

"Wha??? Who is this, Boca?"

"Y'know goddamn well 'hoo it 'tis, mon. Next time you want to set me up, don' bother actin' like my friend first. I shoulda known never to trust…"

"First of all, I haven't the slightest idea what the fuck you're talking abo…"

"Bullshit, mon. You pigs are all alike."

"Now you listen to me, Vernon…."

"No! *You* list-*on*, pig…. Don' tink dat yer untouchable jyust because yer a cop."

"And what the fuck is that supposed to mean?"

"It means dat you'd do best to watch yer back from now on, mon…."

CLICK!!!!!

Vernon Boca launched himself to a stand. He fingered the flashing "hold" button on line 2.

"'ee says it wasn't 'im, but I ain't buyin' it," Vernon said into the speaker. "Jyust get down 'ere as fast as you can, mon. I'll try to 'old dem off as long as possible."

"It was the Triads who gave you up, Vernon, not the police," a sly voice replied from the other end.

"The Triads? Muthafucking, rice-eatin'…"

"Relax, Vernon. Plans are already underway to deal with this… situation. We've known that this was going to happen for some time."

"Well… tanks for keeping me in da loop, mon."

"I'm sorry Vernon, but you're simply not important enough for us to risk ruining what we've accomplished."

"Oh? 'Zat right? I'm important enough for you to use my

clout to recruit all dem kiddies when you want to 'old yer rallies at my club, but…"

"I fail to see what you hope to gain by arguing with us, Vernon. We've given you ample time to gather your people and deal with the situation until we arrive. Now stop wasting time and do as you're told."

CLICK!

Vernon took a moment to evaluate, his thick biceps contracting and releasing as he balled his fists in response to the dial tone's acerbic song. As if to signify the birth of a plan, he punched the top of his desk and walked over to the door.

Pausing to calm himself, he was suddenly struck by an urge to act out. He pulled his gun from the holster that was nestled against the drastic curve in the small of his well muscled back and blew the phone to pieces with the first shot. The second was just an aftershock of vengeance.

Dres and Malik were on the verge of beating Vernon's high score when Toya yelled for them to "Shut the fuck up!" as she climbed down from the ladder, coughing from having to yell over the persuasive ambient rhythm at play between borders of thundering bass. If what she though she heard was in fact a gunshot, then there might be trouble. Either that, or Vernon had lost his temper again… and probably over something trivial.

Malik considered telling Toya where she could stick her fucking attitude, but she was Vernon's girl, and Vernon was a crazy muthafucka. All the stories about him were true: that he bit out a guy's throat in prison; that he beat a 17-year-old boy to death for smacking his little sister; and that it took 10 police bullets to bring him down.

In fact, it took only four. Malik had seen most of it firsthand. All Toya had to do was say the word and no more easy pussy, or free weed, or wasted afternoons playing old video games with Dres on the giant flat-screen that looked down onto what used to be the dance floor. Even if Vernon didn't kill him, he *would* make sure that Malik remembered what he did wrong. Vernon was sick like that.

Dres was too into the game to care. Besides, he was Vernon's younger and even more violent brother (they called him Li'l B). Toya held no power over him.

It was always odd to see the place so empty. Boca's Dungeon was the most popular nightclub in Southwest Philly back in the day. Famous for its roster of top-tier DJs, and for being the place where the truce between the Triads, which made up about 20% of their clientele, and the West Side Clique, which made up about 60%, was held, it was one of the few places that still made a profit, thanks to the Dziko Nation. They held their west-side recruitment meetings here when they came to Philly, which gave Toya the idea to make the place a meeting hall for the surrounding neighborhoods.

The typical crowd had shifted from playas, ballers, shot-callers, retro-pimps who celebrated the lifestyle in fashion only, and suburban wanna-bes looking to shake their asses and score a little weed, to concerned citizens looking to reach out to those less fortunate and families looking for information on where to find food, clean water, and shelter... and a little weed. Even the stuffy old housewives were doing it these days. The most common reason was that it helped them to relax. The weed sales helped Vernon pay for the electrified fencing and the armed snipers posted at the four corners of the roof (a few of his boys who couldn't shoot any better than he could) whenever they held a function inside.

To rent out his place from time to time, the DN paid Vernon in drugs (weed mostly) that they'd confiscated from the neighborhood kingpins in their vigilante days. They had no real problem with weed, as it, and many other natural herbs, played a role in some African cultures. It was the violence and hopelessness that surrounded it that they deplored.

Vernon and Holland Priest had known each other since their days wallowing in the immigration office together. They shared common views regarding black Americans, so aside from Dres's and Vernon's violent tendencies, the DN had no problem with the way he ran his business. His customers were at least successful in the "up from the 'hood" sense. Vernon couldn't stand that flashy, playa-pimp crap. To him, it stank of insecurity, but these guys had crawled out of the shit and at least made a name for themselves. If they wanted to have a little fun, then so be it.

Even though she managed the place, Toya never liked to do any real work unless she had to. This time, Vernon had asked her to help paint the wall behind the bar.

For what, she thought. *Like people really care about some chipped paint.*

She already knew she'd be doing most of it herself.

Toya bugged her eyes at Malik, who had been glaring her way since she told him to shut up, and guided him over to Vernon, who stood in the doorway to his office. The look on his face, as if something major was about to go down, was enough to make Malik reach for his gun.

Sensing it before he actually saw anything, Dres turned sluggishly from the screen, his eyes aglow with colorful leftovers from the game that danced along the fringes of his vision. His head whipped to Vernon, who was looking out the window, when he saw Malik pull out his gun.

"What?" Dres's accent was even stronger than his older brother's, as if his youthful stubbornness had kept him from watering it down. "What tiszit, mon?"

Vernon motioned them over to the window and parted the blinds with his finger. The windows, which were covered with security bars, had all been heavily tinted to keep people from looking in, so it was next to impossible to see outside, especially at night.

"'hoodafuckiszat?" Dres said, squinting to get a good look. "Iszat 5-0?"

Just outside the fence, two unmarked cars were parked

hastily side by side, their headlights illuminating eight human silhouettes that stood before them government types with dark suits and stoic body language. They wore sleek black visors that stretched from ear to ear. On the right arm of each visor, a coiled wire connected to their temples via foam electrodes.

It was one of the many technological curiosities that the marriage of science and Jesus' power had produced. The visors worked as thought projectors. They allowed the wearer to attack an enemy simply by thinking it and projecting that thought out toward them.

"I don' know 'hoo da fuck dese boyz tink dey are," Dres replied, moving his head to take them in at various angles, "but dey sure as hell ain't no 5-0."

"Maybe it's some kind of cleanup program?" Malik offered.

Toya sucked her teeth at his suggestion.

"Dressed like that? Nigga, you need to chill on the weed."

"Bee-sides, I already paid da West Side crew last week to keep dem fuckin' walkers off dis block," Vernon added.

Dres was already walking toward the front doors when Vernon turned to face him.

"Aye! Boy, what da fuck do you tink yer doin' no?"

"I ain't tryin' to 'ide in 'ere like some fuckin' bitch wit dat peekin'-tru-da-windows shit," Dres said.

"Another car just pulled up." Toya's voice interrupted the baritone volley with its nasal pitch and its flat east-coast draw. "Looks like a limo."

Vernon half-turned without ever taking his eyes off of Dres, who was reaching out for the doorknob.

"Boy, *get* yer ass back over 'ere... right no!"

"Relax, mon.... I'm jyust goin' to see what dey want," Dres said with an all-is-well sort of grin. "I promise, mon."

Dres never was one to listen to authority. Vernon knew he would be trouble from the time his father told him that he was sending Dres to the states to get him away from his crew back home. Dres had grown into the type of guy that Vernon especially hated working with. Perpetually tense and agitated, drama seemed to follow him, and he was more than willing to settle everything the hard way.

"Wait, I'm comin' wit-you...." Vernon started to say, but Dres was already out the door.

"Jeeee-zus Christ..." Toya said in an unusually high pitch. Her face was so close to the window that it muffled her voice considerably.

"What'zat?" Vernon replied in mid-step, his torso turning to face her, but his legs still trained on the door.

Toya was rendered speechless. Her small mind was ill prepared to deal with what she saw.

"Girl, I said whatizit?"

Malik, on the other hand, didn't seem all that surprised. He turned to Vernon who was already on his way back over to them.

"The guy who just got out of the limo? It looks like... like Jesus Christ," he said.

Vernon shoved Malik to the side and leaned in for a look. From the window he could see part of the front steps, but not enough to see Dres, who the government types saw as a potential threat, as Vernon read the general vibe.

Flanked by a set of effeminate Asian triplets, each dressed in white suits that complemented their lithe, sturdy frames and narrow shoulders and added to their ambiguous mystique, Jesus slithered out from behind the government types without his feet ever touching the ground. His flowing blond hair lay like a golden waterfall frozen in time against the fabric of his double-breasted blazer.

"Sometin' I can 'elp you wit, mon?" Dres questioned with deep-throated authority.

"Tell thine brother to come out here." Jesus' voice was so soft that it was barely audible yet obtrusive enough that it reached deep into the mental slop, as if it was his way of taking a look inside the minds of his victims. Even Vernon, Toya, and Malik could hear him, and they were behind layers of safety glass and in the eye of a funky rhythm whirling down from the DJ booth. It was a sensation that left the men, in particular, feeling somewhat violated. "I need to speak with him."

"About what???" Dres challenged. "You got an appointmont???"

Jesus paused and flashed a grin that seemed to be hiding something malevolent beneath it.

"Doest thee know who I am?" he replied.

Vernon started to run outside. Before his eyes, the scenery melted away to reveal an angry black sky that coughed and spit for miles and miles. There was nothing below his feet but dark, heinous clouds that frowned upon a vast sea of molten waves even further down. They crashed against jagged stone peaks that jutted up from the depths of what at first looked like water, but was actually an ocean of naked bodies twisting and writhing independently. With each cresting, fleshy wave, a few managed to hold on to the rocks, then ultimately slid back into the wailing mass, their voices louder than the baritone thunder claps, louder even than the ambient rumble of what sounded like whales singing a song of terror through miles of thick, pasty water.

It was his mother's hell down to the letter. She used it to scare the rebellious streak out of Vernon when he was a child. In his mind, Jesus spoke directly to him. *Where is thy faith? Thou should know that a mind as riddled with insecurities as thine can't possibly expect to hide anything from me.*

Vernon struggled to move against the feeling of hundreds of cold hands holding him firm, some of them trying to probe his orifices. He squeezed his eyes shut and tried to clear his mind, but frustration managed to coax him into thinking of revenge.

When he opened his eyes, he was watching his neighbor, Mr. Stokes, rape him when he was eight. It happened in an abandoned house three blocks from his own that Mr. Stokes, a swarthy, overweight father of four, lured Vernon to under the pretense of helping him clean it up. Despite all his bullshit about being in complete control, it was a memory that still caused his heart to race, his fists to tighten, and his eyes to well up to compensate for the overflow of pure rage. *"Shhhhhhhhhhhh.... Don't make a sound and it'll be over before you know it."* Stokes's voice trembled with spastic glee.

Vernon could still hear it clearly. He could still feel Stokes's warm breath on the back of his ear. He could still smell the stench of cigarettes and whiskey. He wanted to scream, to lash out like a child, or cry like one. He wanted to tell Jesus to fight like a man, but thoughts like those would only make matters worse, so he forced his himself to think of nothing. It was the only way to break Jesus' spell, or at least weaken it.

There was a jolt, like a roller coaster bucking to life. Vernon found himself falling limp to the floor beneath where he had hovered, paralyzed by Jesus' spell.

"I know 'hoo you say you are, bitch." Dres said. "But I ain't as gullible as most pee..."

Dres lurched and cried out in pain. With his hands pressed over his eyes, he doubled over.

"My eyes!!!!! You stupid muthafucka ... what da fuck didju dootame????" Dres screamed. "Goddammit, I'm blind! I cyan't see! I cyan't fuckin' see!!!!"

"Thou hast always been blind, my child. Thou just didn't know it," Jesus said in a playful tone, his hands folded in front of him.

Even before Jesus blinded him, Dres had been trying to conceal the fact that he was slowly reaching in his jacket for his gun. Because Jesus had struck first, Dres threw all subtlety out the window, snatched the gun from his waist, and fired repeatedly in the general direction of Jesus' voice. Three of the bullets would've hit him too if he didn't pull Dres's mother, wife, and baby girl from thin air directly in the paths of each one.

Of course, Dres didn't know that yet. All he knew was that

he just unloaded his gun right at him, and now Jesus was chuckling. Even then he sounded like a woman.

"Bring his brother to me," Jesus instructed the government types forward with a wave of his hand.

As the government types walked out of the backlit shadow, Malik and Toya, who were helping Vernon to his feet while simultaneously looking out the window, could see that they (government types) were all zombies, which rendered guns, especially small ones, almost useless.

When Malik turned away, he heard Dres cry out. His voice sounded so vulnerable, so utterly afraid that Malik was scared to turn back around and take a look.

"What 'appened, mon?" Vernon demanded as he slowly came to his senses. "I 'eard screaming. Dres???? Is Dres all right?"

Now that he couldn't see them through the window, Malik wondered exactly where the zombies were in relation to the front door, and what they did to Dres who was laying face down on the steps.

Malik argued with Toya via nodding glances over who was going to answer Vernon's question. Knowing of his rep, neither of them was willing to tell him that his mother, brother, sister-in-law, and his two-month-old niece were lying dead in the street.

"C'mon V," Malik said, leading Vernon to his office. "They're coming in. We gotta get you outta here."

Toya, who was right behind them, was within arms reach of the door to Vernon's office when the front doors flew open. The lobby, bar, and dancefloor lit up with strange blue light from the transparent beam extending out from the lead zombie's visor to the blurred cloud of snarling mouths and snapping teeth that flew at her.

Chapter 10

By the time Kane reached 56th and Walnut (two and a half blocks from Boca's Dungeon), he'd hit three people with his car, all zombies who, for one reason or another, just weren't fast enough, or simply didn't care about being struck by a speeding car. The third one looked a lot like a rapist he arrested a few years back who ultimately got away on a technicality. If it was him, Kane found himself hoping that the bastard felt every pound of force of the impact.

The gas stations had been dried up for some time now, and with all the debris, there was little room for moving cars on these streets. Unless you managed to stockpile gasoline, or you were connected, fuel was next to impossible to come by.

Kane had a hell of a time weaving in and out of stationary traffic that consisted of burnt-out and overturned auto husks, looted vending machines, clothing, trash, and, worst of all, slow-moving zombies. He was in such a hurry that he forgot to make the usual mental note to add three more notches for the zombies he ran down to the 47 already scratched into the dashboard. It was a little something he had come up with during his night hunts.

The shortcut Kane had taken to Boca's Dungeon took him through the ass-end of West Philly, where the zombies were abundant. The rich, connected folks in Rittenhouse Square paid a cleanup crew to dump them down here where the stink of death and aged blood, both dry and wet, was more pungent and invasive to the senses.

The streets were so overrun here that bored survivalists (usually outsiders) made a game of driving into the 'hood and trying to hit as many zombies as they could with their fortified cars and pickups. Pinball alley, they called it.

For Kane, it was just an opportunity to vent. Vernon Boca was one of his most trustworthy sources of hard-to-get information. Losing him would be a major blow to his "unofficial" investigation.

There was the skinny technician at Bio-Tech, but he was probably dead by now.

Without something upon which to obsess, Kane was just a glorified survivor with a little authority, the future of whom was in question.

Kane slammed on the brakes when he passed the alley between Boca's Dungeon and the warehouse next door. His mind was so full of assumptions and theories about who would take down Boca and why that he almost passed the place altogether. Had he not seen the bursts of blue light from the large windows along the side of the building, he might've driven right around front and wound up face to face with Jesus and the Lin Brothers.

He could see two of their cars sitting idled. If he listened, he could hear hints of a conversation in Mandarin and English.

Kane threw his car into reverse and backed up to the alley just as an imposing figure stumbled out the back door and ran right smack into the opposite wall.

"V!!!!!!!" Kane yelled, his hand clutching the handle of the door as his eyes moved from Vernon, who was still shaking off the wall's punch, to the blue light that traveled via the windows from the middle to the rear of the building.

Kane opened his door and stepped partially out. Standing on one leg, the other kneeling on the seat, he looked over the roof at Vernon.

"V!!! Over here!!!"

It took every ounce of strength for Vernon to find cohesion through the pain and the mental noise that seemed eager to see him lie down and rest for a moment in the cool crimson puddle that extended deep into the alley. Where he stood, it came up to his ankles.

Vernon worked through his hazy vision and the echoed acid-trip chords that bounced around his head and zeroed in on the familiar voice that called his name from the street. He could barely hear it over Toya and Malik's screaming.

Kane knew that Vernon had trust issues when it came to the cops, so it came as no surprise that instead of listening to him, Vernon simply stood there, his head whipping from the car to the back door that vomited him out into the alley only moments ago. For all he knew, Kane was a part of the ambush.

"Vernon, it's me… Detective Makane."

Vernon's mind had begun to supply hints and fragmented details about the identity of the shadow that crept toward him from the double-parked car just beyond the mouth of the alley. The shadow grew taller and thinner as it approached.

Vernon lifted his arms in a futile attempt to stand his ground but Kane simply ducked beneath his flailing grasp, scooped him up by the waist, and hauled his punch-drunk ass back to the unmarked car.

Knowing what kind of man Vernon was, Kane couldn't help but congratulate himself at how easily he captured him. The hard part was backing down the street without looking.

The zombies had poured out into the alley and spotted him. As a result, he had to lie down into the passenger's seat to avoid the blue-light cloud of fists, clawing hands, snarling mouths and snapping teeth that pounded, scratched and bit into his car and the headrest above him as he drove blind away from the scene.

Those were zombies, Kane thought. *Zombies in suits with blue light coming from their eyes…. What the fuck is going on here?*

Then he remembered joking at some point that they'd make great soldiers if someone took the time to train them.

*   *   *

Vernon exploded awake in the back seat of Kane's car. His flailing arms grazed the back of Kane's head and startled him out of concentration. Until then, Kane had been sitting reclined, nearly horizontal, and patrolling the surroundings outside his car with suspicious eyes as he waited for Vernon to regain consciousness.

Kane pitched forward, turned, and wrapped his hand around the handle of his gun. It was an automatic reaction, but when his mind caught up, he kept it there just the same.

Sensing Kane's change of position, the driver's seat automatically adjusted to compensate.

In Vernon's case, reality traveled on wobbly legs that sprinted awkwardly in short bursts toward his conscious mind, battered and shaken as it was. Although he was in great shape physically, whatever Jesus had done to him left him feeling spent.

Beyond the fogged window, Vernon saw...

To the right:

Cityscape: *Buildings, weather-beaten and neglected, save for the pristine steeples peppered throughout that poke through the layers of asphalt and concrete, Gothic architecture seeming by their presence alone to claim supremacy over their residential brethren. In the distance, a tight-knit bunch of skyscrapers reach for the heavens frozen in a neverending race to claim dominance over the busy skyline.*

To the left:

Foreground: *A large building surrounded by scaffolding and various construction vehicles. On the front of the building is a huge mural depicting cultural heroes and general ethnic pride in arresting colors.*

Background: *Dormant trains and train cars, trolleys, and buses*

Straight ahead: *Kane's unflinching eyes staring back at him from the rearview*

Vernon recognized this place. They were somewhere near 69th and Market, where the city bordered the suburbs. The Catholic Church had the immediate area swept for undesirables and gated off.

Sixty-ninth and Market was where the terminal, a large depot for the city's public transportation in all its forms (bus, trolley, and train) was housed. SEPTA, the Southeastern Pennsylvania Transportation Authority, had dissolved, and now public transportation was run by independent contractors, who operated much like heavily armed taxi drivers, charging ridiculous rates that few people could afford. Recently a group of them struck a deal with the Catholic Church to transport the wealthy and connected, and, in keeping with their emphasis on denial, they were in the process of renovating the terminal and the surrounding area as though everything was "A-OK." Fanning out from the terminal, the neighborhoods went from brown trash, to white trash, to moderately successful, to stinking rich.

Kane had been all over looking for a place to park his car and lay low until Vernon awoke. He caught himself zoning out as he drove deeper into the suburbs, where small communities of wealthy survivors had developed. The scenery and the fact that the roads were clear and there were so few zombies out there had hypnotized him. The rich folks had been paying a crew to come in twice a month, gather up the zombies, and ship them to the inner city, and then paying former cops, probably even some of Kane's old colleagues, to patrol the area.

Once he realized where he was, Kane made a U-turn and headed back through the nouveau suburbanite areas that housed people who considered themselves a step above the city dwellers, even though they brought with them the same issues, to the terminal construction site. In fact, it was the first place he thought of to park, but it was just a little too close for comfort to Boca's Dungeon, on 56th and Walnut, and there was still the fence to get around. Luckily he found an opening where it looked like some of the construction workers had created a smoking/drinking alcove, as suggested by the cigarette butts and empty bottles of beer lying around.

"Dres? Toya?" Rubbing his head, Vernon rasped as if he already knew the answer.

"I don't know," Kane said, suspecting that they were all dead. "You were the only one I saw come out."

Vernon picked up on the tone of Kane's reply, rich as it was with meaning. It reached like icy fingers, deep into Vernon's chest, and yanked at the heart that even he wasn't aware he possessed. Vernon shuddered in reaction.

"If I find out dat you 'ad anyting to do wit dis…."

"I don't think you're in any position to be making threats, my friend," Kane said, half-turning to face Vernon. "But if it's any consolation, I had nothing to do with it."

Vernon deferred to Kane's judgment. He felt that Kane was probably telling the truth, but it was exactly that feeling that he questioned.

"So, what the hell happened in there?" Kane asked.

"Yer da fuckin' detective. You tell me, mon."

"Look, don't you think I would've gotten here a little sooner if I knew about it?"

"Maybe. But I wouldn't put anyting past you muthafuckas," Vernon snapped. "Dis could all be some ela-bo-rate set-tup to gain my trust. Isn't dat 'ow you boy scouts werk?"

"This ain't no cop show, Vern. We're a bit more low-brow than that here in the real world."

"I jyust lost my brotha and my girl in dere and yer crackin' jokes, mon?"

"Look, we don't have time for this shit. Just tell me what happened. Did it have anything to do with what you were going to tell me?"

"Don't 'ave time????" Vernon's eyes, though beleaguered and wrought with guilt, suddenly came alive.

He lunged forward.

"Dres... 'im was just a kid, mon."

For a moment, Vernon was face to face with Kane, who didn't even flinch when he initially lunged.

"Like I said before..." Kane replied, casual as could be, "you aren't in any condition to be making threats. Now if you want me to help you, you're going to have to sit your ass down and tell me what the hell happened in there."

Any other time and Vernon would've wiped the pavement with anyone who was stupid enough to stand up to him. This time, he leaned back into the cushion and weighed his options. Dres, his only brother, was probably dead, as was Toya, the mother of his two-year-old daughter, Magda, whom he credited with giving him a new, more sympathetic outlook. What he wanted to do was go for broke and take out Jesus and his boys, or die trying.

"I'll tell you what you wan-ta-know, mon, under one condi-tyion," Vernon said.

"And what's that?"

Vernon leaned forward to make certain that Kane understood him clearly.

"Soldiers from da Zee-koo Na-tyion are on deir way."

"Great. That's just what I need... a protest march."

"Dey ain't coming 'ere ta march," Vernon groaned. "Dey'll be bringin' someone wit dem 'hoo knows da truth about dat hippie-muthafucka. You 'ave to promise me dat you'll 'elp dem... and tell yer boyz down at da sta-tyion to back off my club and da Zee-koo Na-tyion."

"What boys? In case you haven't noticed, we're down to scraps."

"Jyust da same, mon."

"All right, you've got yourself a deal. Now tell me what happened."

"It-twas Jesus, mon. And 'im brought da Lin Brothas wit 'im."

"The Lin Brothers???" Kane paused to connect the dots,

staring out the window at the blood red sky as if it had all the answers, yet the one he searched for seemed to elude him. "Why the hell would he need help? I mean, no offense, but you ain't all *that* hard to get to."

"Hey, fuck you, mon," Vernon snarled. "Don' tink I won't…"

Kane slid Vernon a *'don't fuck with me'* glance that spoke from the corners of his eyes.

"Relax Vern…." Kane knew how much Vernon hated being called that. "I was just trying to make a point."

In such a confined space, the constant volleying of testosterone left Vernon feeling small and in need of a diversion to take his mind away from the insecure squabbles that would surely set him off if he allowed them to. Instead of responding, he let his eyes scan the scenery outside.

"This person they're bringing, you said he 'knows the truth.' Truth about what?" The slight rise in Kane's pitch gave away his enthusiasm. If his hunch was right, this could be the big break he was looking for. "Or should I say who? And if it's Jesus we're talking about, I don't wanna hear anything about how he's really Jah, or Haile Selassie, or whatever."

"Not all of us black folks bee-lieve in ghost stories, mon." Kane smirked.

"What about the Dziko Nation? They aren't exactly atheists."

"Holland Priest is a good friend of mine. But when 'im starts talkin' all dat earthy, spiritual shit, I jyust tune 'im out. At least da Zee-koo Na-tyion teaches knowledge of self. Dat's 'ard ta come by 'round 'ere."

"You never fail to reel me into your shit, Vernon. I'm trying to understand something though. Exactly how does selling drugs to your own people play into this cultural awakening?"

"Don' get it twist-tod, mon. I sell stress relief to people old enough to know what dey're doin'. I never fuck around wit da kiddies, or wit dat life-alterin' shit, mon. Not unless I don't like yer ass…. What does dis 'ave to do wit dat faggot 'hoo killed my brotha, anyway?" Vernon said. "I know one ting…. Dat muthafucka is going to regret not killin' my black ass too."

"You know, that's a good question. Why didn't he kill you back there? And correct me if I'm wrong, but those *were* zombies, right?"

"Aye. Dere 'ave been rumors floatin' round dat dey were using 'em, but dat was da first I seen it."

Kane shook his head. *What next?*

"So what's this big secret?" he said.

As if to validate the weight of his 'big secret,' Vernon paused, dense brown eyes riding the silence beyond which ghostly moaning and the sounds of clumsy activity swirled around in the distant muck of nighttime.

"Da see-cret is dat dat long-haired pretty-boy is a fraud. Both of dem are."

"Well, *I* knew that much," Kane said, disappointed. "So what… or who are they, then?"

"I don' know what you'd call dem, mon: oddit-ties, genetic freaks, psychics…. Whatever it 'tis, da main ting is dat dey are jyust men, men wit extra-ordinary abili-tees, but men jyust da same, mon. We know dat dey trive on faith. Dey can do whatever you bee-lieve dey can. Dat's 'ow deir… gift werks."

"Who's we?" Kane said.

"Me, Priest, da Coal-li-tyion, da Secular Soldiers…."

"How do you know all this?"

"B'cause Yeshua told us. 'ee wants to end all dis figh-ting over ree-li-gyion. Dat's da reason 'im come out of 'iding."

"And how exactly does he plan to do that?"

"By killin' da man 'hoo stole 'is iden-ti-ty, mon."

"You mean Jesus?"

"Dat's right, mon. Jesus' real name is Augustus and 'im was… is Pontius Pilate's son."

"So you're telling me that Yeshua…."

"I'm tellin' you dat Yeshua is da real Jesus, mon, real in da sense dat 'im was alive and walkin' around 2000 years ago."

"And you all believe this story he's told you?"

"I didn't at first, but da Secular Soldiers ran tests on 'is DNA. If dey say ee's da real deal, den dat's all I need-ta-know. Doe-san't mean 'im was da son of God or anyting."

"So what about Jezz... ah, Augustus?"

"Augustus was a sickly boy accordin' to Yeshua. 'is father, Pilate, was desperate for someting to cure 'im. 'ee never bought da son of God story, but 'ee 'ad seen Yeshua's power firsthand, so as 'im 'ung from da cross, Pilate 'ad one of 'is centurions puncture Yeshua's side wit-a-spear an drain 'is blood into a chalice, which he den fed to Augustus."

Kane sat perplexed, half ready to yell out, "Oh, c'mon now." He had prepared himself to hear something unusual, but this story tested his skepticism. Lately though he had seen enough crazy shit to open his mind to the possibility that it just might be true. Still, all he could do was shake his head at what he'd just heard.

"Dere's more, mon," Vernon said.

"Now how did I know you were going to say that?"

"Once Pontius Pilate real-lized what was 'appening to 'is son, dat by drinking Yeshua's blood, 'is health 'ad improved, an on top of dat, 'im 'ad gained dis incredible power, 'im used it to 'is advantage. 'ee 'ad Yeshua's followers killed or captured and coerced into denouncin' 'im. To spare deir lives, Yeshua went into 'iding. Pilate bee-gyan a campaign of propaganda claimin' 'is son to be da Lamb of God. When Augustus was in 'is twenties, Pilate 'ad a painting commissioned, a portrait."

"And I take it that this portrait was the basis for all the Anglecanized pictures of Jesus Christ?" Kane said.

"Dat's right, mon."

"Interesting story. If Yeshua is so powerful, then why didn't he just stop Augustus at some point?"

"Dat's da trick to da power, you see. Wit-out people to bee-lieve, dere is no power. We've all seen da polls, mon. Augustus 'as almost double da numbers. Dat's double da people 'hoo bee-lieve in 'is shit. For 2000 years, 'is 'as been da more predominant image, infectin' genera-tyion after genera-tyion while 'im uses 'is strength to keep Yeshua too sick to react. Dat's da most 'im can do wit-out knowing where 'ee is. Dat's why dey've been moving 'im around so much."

"So why now?" Kane asked.

"Progress, mon. Progress. Dey've been figh-ting for centuries, quietly, through us. Once da scientists realized all dat forensic science an DNA could tell dem, it twas only a matter of time before da idea to use da technology in da search for da truth about Christ came about. Most of dem brainiacs already knew dat he wasn't da lily-white man we all grew up bee-lieving in. It twas 'round dis time, toward da end of da 20th Century, dat Yeshua star-ted gaining strength. It was 'is idea to come for-ward first, to make tings right. Augustus knew dis and feared dat Yeshua would ruin 'is reputation."

Something outside caught Vernon's eye and coaxed him away from their conversation. Returning half-focused on the window, he spoke slowly, as if between each word he ran down a mental checklist of suspicious objects and crevices large enough to conceal a person, checking them off as he surveyed each with a squinted glare before moving on to the next one.

"Lis-ton to me…" Vernon said, distracted. "You promise me dat you'll do everyting you can to get dis muthafucka?"

Kane nodded, confused, but curious to know what had gotten into Vernon. He found himself repeatedly looking out the window.

"Whatever you do, mon, don' let Augustus get inside yer head," Vernon warned. "If 'ee knows you don' bee-lieve in 'im, he'll try to scare you, to make you weak so dat you bee-gin to ques-tyion exactly what it 'tis you bee-lieve. Jyust keep telling yerself dat 'ee's full of shit. As long as…"

There it was again, a shape, darting from darkness to light, just as Vernon blinked. Could've been nothing, could've been an animal, or an illusion caused by the inside of his eyelids as they lowered and lifted. Now his mind swirled with intense emotion manifested as screw-faced masks that told the tale of terrible things afoot somewhere on the other side of the window.

Kane whipped from 12 to 3 o'clock and back to cover the general territory claimed by whatever it was that had Vernon looking ready to fight. As he was only guessing, Kane figured that his inability to see anything was his own fault. Nevertheless, his hand snake-lunged for his gun and snatched it from his armpit holster. It was a tiny thing. In situations like this, it did little to reassure him... until he pulled the trigger. It happened every time.

"What is it? What do you see?" Kane asked. The look on Vernon's face tickled his anxiety. Part of him liked that kind of feeling. In his twenties, it used to make his dick hard.

In Vernon's eyes, he saw *Toya screaming in pain. She was strapped face-down to an elaborate torture rack that left her unable to move and arched her supple black ass high in the air at an angle that allowed maximum penetration for the large wooden baseball bat that Vernon's own mother ass-fucked her with. Judging by the larger-than-life smile on her face, the mad glint in her completely white eyes, and the tenacity with which she crouched and thrust as hard as she could, Celestine Boca seemed to enjoy what she was doing. She didn't even stop when it was clear that Toya had expired... or when she inexplicably awoke and begin to curse at Celestine the way she liked Vernon to do in the heat of passion.*

Although it made no sense that this was happening in the middle of a construction site, Vernon was fragile as a sheltered momma's boy when it came to Toya. When he was finally able to summon his voice again, he cried out a gibberished grunt that said it all.

Kane was just about to reach back and slap him out of it when...

Vernon lurched and coughed up a cry of sudden panic. His belly belched out a sound that almost got Kane's stomach going on its own journey. Vernon wrapped his forearms around his swollen abdomen and bit down with every ounce of his distinctively shaped jaw's strength. Moaning and spitting through clenched teeth, he rocked himself back and forth groaning in pain.

Knowing Vernon like Kane did, the look on his face was the last expression Kane ever expected to see coming from such a man's man. Vernon was terrified, as if he knew what was in store just as his face expanded into a surreal caricature cast in a funhouse mirror.

Kane watched as a gaunt, hairless arm reached out from Vernon's warped mouth. A second arm followed suit, jerking and yanking until both were free up to the elbows, squeezed together in an awkward embrace that resembled a position a contortionist might attempt, or a child gripped with sudden claustrophobic terror struggling to fit his/her arms through the neck-hole of a T-shirt.

Vernon, who was still alive, thrashed like a fish plucked from the water in the back seat of Kane's car, his legs flailing, feet stomping and pushing against the empty passenger's seat in front of him.

Kane started to raise his gun, then tried instead to open the door and escape, but somehow the handle was stuck on both the driver's and passenger's side. The windows resisted his attempt to break them with the butt of his gun.

Kane was always good under pressure, and, as such, he eventually managed to block out the liquefied crunching and the frenzied activity in the back seat that shook the entire car as he waited for the impetus of a decent plan to arise within him.

By the looks of it, there was no way he could still be alive, yet Vernon clawed at the air, his body trembling so fast that it began to blur. His face was horribly stretched and misshapen, his flesh ripple-distorting into an oversized, flesh-toned canvas of human-like features that washed away his strong African nose and cheekbones better than he was ever able to accomplish during his self-loathing phase.

Reaching blindly, the arm-mandibles tore the skin at the corners of Vernon's mouth as they bent spider-like and fell to their respective shoulders. Long, thin fingers dug deep into Vernon's taught flesh as delicate looking hands pressed down for leverage and pushed out the head and shoulders of a man (Jesus) whose eyes instantly rolled over to taunt Kane.

Jesus yanked Vernon's death-grip from his wrist and hair and tossed his limp arms down with malice. As Kane watched, Jesus shimmied himself out of what remained of Vernon like he was a tighter-than-usual skirt, and with his foot, casually flung the bag of flesh and bone out into the street and closed the door.

Kane didn't have time to be afraid, not if he was going to survive Jesus' game. By the looks of it, the alternative was far more painful than anything he was ready to experience. With fear out of the way, or at least temporarily distracted, his disdain for all things religious gave him a certain sense of superiority. He was as American as obesity, so he was no stranger to biblical metaphors and scripture masked as children's rhymes being sneakily shoved down his throat on a daily basis since he was a child. He made sure to keep Vernon's warning about keeping his mind clear at the forefront of his thoughts.

Unlike Vernon, Kane was resolute in his disbelief. He was, however, curious to know exactly what Vernon saw. Was it really that bad? He wondered if it would've broken him as well. His bullheadedness had already convinced him that he would have fared much better. Still he repeated to himself mentally... *I don't believe in you...I don't believe in you....*

"Didst I frighten thee, Philip Makane?" Jesus spoke in a soft, almost feminine tone, stroking his long blond hair as he checked himself in the small round compact mirror he held in front of his face.

Snapping it shut with his middle and index fingers and thumb, Jesus lowered his hand and gave his mesmerizing, aquamarine eyes a clear path to Kane's eyes.

"If you're so powerful, then why not just force me to believe?" Kane replied. "Why not just kill me like you did Vernon?"

"I'm disappointed. I would've thought that such a display would have convinced thee."

Kane held his gun-arm loose, his finger caressing the trigger just in case. He knew that he could get at least four shots off before Jesus could lift his arm, but wondered exactly what the rules were, or if Jesus even had to lift his arm. Just because he didn't believe, did that nullify the faith of millions of others? Did it only pertain to what Jesus could do to him mentally?

"Why don't thou pull the trigger and find out?"

Kane swallowed his concerns with a loud gulp. On the surface, he seemed as confident as ever, but for all his bravery and conviction, there wasn't anything he could do to Jesus short of convincing a million-plus followers that he was full of shit.

"Feeling vulnerable, art thou, my child?"

"I'm not your child. And I'm not one of these weak-minded fuckers looking to medicate my fear of death with fairy tales and sleight-of-hand bullshit. So, why don't you do us both a favor and knock off the King James affect, Augustus…."

It was evident in the way Jesus paused, closed his eyes, and cricked his neck that he hated that name, and that he wasn't used to being defied with such blatant disregard. Even the atheists (a good 90% of them) held some doubt that he was able to manipulate to his advantage.

"So, I see that thou hast spoken to Yeshua." Jesus slid his words through barely parted lips that chased them out in loathsome arcs. "Do not make the mistake of becoming overconfident in thine allegiance with him."

"No mistakes here," Kane said with confidence. "I'm all the allegiance I need."

Kane felt a sudden itch that started at the top of his head and soaked through to the gray matter where it jumped from region to region. Initially, he blew it off as a phantom sensation, until it began to swell with prickly heat and cause his head to throb.

He raised his gun. Again, the futility of his action nagged at him, but he held fast. Better to go down fighting.

"Get the fuck out of my head," Kane demanded. "Right now!"

Melting to the surface like a slow-stalking predator rising from deep beneath its prey, a smile, born of insecurity and nurtured on resentment, began to manipulate Jesus' thin lips, stretching long and taut.

"Thou shouldst behold thine judgment and put that thing away."

Kane thought about turning the gun on himself, but that would in essence be like forfeiture. Other than pointing it at Jesus, he hadn't a clue what he was going to do next.

"Thou needn't worry about me messing with thy mind," Jesus said. "It seems that someone hast beaten me to the punch, as they say."

"Wha?"

"Someone with whom thou hast already been acquainted."

Boring.... Mentally, Kane fled from the name. It was the first and only one that popped into his mind. Acknowledging it would certainly mean that he would have to kill himself at some point, lest he wind up like Gus Rollins, or Meleeza, or Jason.

Jesus whipped his head to the side, momentarily distracted. His eye darted, peering internally where a murky vision of a late-model SUV followed by a procession of long vehicles, regal in their deep, dark sheen, developed in his mind.

Jesus smirked and, without turning his head, shot Kane a wicked glance.

"You'd better pray that he kills thee first," he hissed before vanishing into thin air.

Kane felt a tightening in the pit of his stomach, bile rising in short sprints, climbing higher each time until he could no longer deny the queasy punch of a death sentence.

On either side of Lin Ho, Lin Kwei and Lin Su stepped in a practiced arc away from him and each other as they prepared to greet the approaching procession of sleek, black cars, led by the SUV.

Outside Boca's Dungeon, the bodies of Dres Boca, his mother, wife, and daughter lay in a pile at the foot of the steps. The prospect of flesh to feast upon further intoxicated two of the government-type zombies' drunken footing as they stumbled over to the pile, yanked off their visors and dug in.

Inside, two others devoured what was left of Malik and Toya.

Calling out unspoken commands with subtle gestures, Kwei (he was the oldest by two minutes; then Su, then Ho) primed his brothers for action, swift and efficient as always. He raised an eyebrow in response to the abandoned cars, a fallen lamppost, uprooted trees, scattered dumpsters, and a vintage phone booth that slid and bounced out of the path of the SUV's creeping blitzkrieg long before it reached each thing physically.

"Fear not this crude display," Jesus' disembodied voice sneaked out of mid-air somewhere between Kwei and Su. "I smell overconfidence in him."

Jesus' voice left their eyes guessing until a thunderclap guided them to a distinct spot in the night. Out of nowhere, bloody rain began to fall, localized within a three-foot circumference behind them, forming the shape of a man, head and shoulders aglow with a crimson sheen. Deep, dark (almost black) blood raced downward to reveal the rest of the man in three dimensions. Malevolent hues of red and black slowly faded to flesh-tones and dark-colored fabric.

It was Jesus.

Jesus let his head fall back, rolled it to the side, down and around, and back up to work out the kinks.

"Yeshua is with them," Jesus said to Kwei as he stared down the approaching convoy. "And he's brought his motley crew of nonbelievers with him."

You will NOT triumph today, blood of my blood, Jesus projected to Yeshua, who sat with his eyes closed inside one of the approaching cars.

Jesus walked to the exact center-point between Kwei and Su, his feet in motion but never touching the ground.

"You three take care of that detective, Philip Makane," he said. "I'll handle this."

* * *

Kane held his gun firm on the empty back seat where Jesus sat only seconds ago, stuck for an idea to steal him away from dwelling on the news of his new inner tenant. Like it or not, he was as good as dead. It made him more disappointed in himself than anything else.

Kane caught a spark of light from the corner of his eye. In the moment it took his mind to register muffled gunfire, three liquid-light bursts pierced the windshield and sizzle-smacked into the leather seat cushion next to him.

Kane dove forward and laid down across the front seats as four more liquid-light bursts tore into and gutted the back of the driver's seat.

"I was going to tell you to duck, but then I thought, why interrupt your moment of self-pity?"

Even though he knew right away that Jesus was referring to Boring when he mentioned that someone had beaten him to the punch, hearing that voice, both masculine and feminine, and coming from the inside out, was far more unsettling than he imaged it would be.

"This wasn't exactly how I planned to announce my presence, but since the cat has been let out of the bag..."

Kane balled his lips, fists following suit out of habit. There was so much emotion. It stung the space between his skin and his flesh and gave his heart an adrenaline kick that registered in his limbs as spasm.

"Tell me who you are, you cowardly piece of shit!" he yelled.

"A talking pterodactyl, maybe…"

"No way. That wasn't real."

"You're right. I *was* correct, however, in assuming that it would get your attention."

"How did you know about that?"

"I know everything about you, Detective. You *could* say that we're… old friends."

"Old friends… Just tell me who you are, dammit!"

"Oh, come now, Detective? Has the memory of our relationship become so stale that you've forgotten about me? I guess I could tell just you…but then I'd have to kill you," he/she chuckled.

In a sudden burst of tenacity, and rage and fear, Kane cried out with brutish, male aggression and rose to his knees, his gun-arm leading the way. If he was going out, it wasn't going to be in the front seat of his car with this fucking lunatic running around inside his head. Better to die in a blaze of glory, like he always suspected he would.

Peeking over the headrest and out the back window, Kane spotted a thin Asian man (Lin Su) with dark, wispy hair standing about 20 feet away. He was wearing a flawless white suit, and he was staring right back at him.

"Philip. Something big is going on." A voice… Allison's… leapt from his radio. "It looks like someone has jacked into the signal from the emergency services satellite. All the TV stations are showing some kind of special report. You seeing anything strange out there?"

Reloading his gun (a vintage UZI modified to fire liquid-light was the Lins' trademark), Lin Kwei stepped out of the dark crevice in the main entrance of the 69th Street Terminal and walked down the ramp toward the opening in the fence Kane had driven through and parked. He neck-flopped the patch of hair that hung over his left eye,

Asian pop-star style, and nodded to his younger brother, Su, who stood out in the open to allow Kane just enough time to realize who he might be before he lifted his gun from his side and casually approached Kane's car, coughing out bursts of light that bit deep into the bones of the Toyota and tested its neglected shocks.

"My uzi weigh ton, muthafuck..." Su managed in broken English, his mouth adopting a sadistic slant that looked almost like a smile as he fired the last three shots down into the car through the shattered driver's side window.

Su yanked open the door expecting to see Kane's bullet-ridden body pour out onto the street.

Empty.

Su's shoulders quickly found tension, then intimidating calm. His eyes darted suspiciously to every possible nook and cranny of the immediate surroundings. He looked up at Kwei in the immediate distance and shook his head.

Kwei tapped his index finger against the corner of his right eye and let it fall clockwise to a point that Su followed over to a used car lot half a block away on the other side of the fence. He could also see that Ho, who had just stepped out of the shadows at the mouth of the lot, was way ahead of him.

"This isn't like you, Philip, hiding on your belly like a coward."

Twenty-three minutes and... one... two... three... *four*... seconds. That's how long Kane had been hiding under the powder-blue cargo van, watching three identically clothed sets of legs move about the lot in search of him, fighting the dizziness. He was unable to do much of anything but nurse the thought of his worst fear (complete helplessness) realized as he lay there, wondering if Boring had affected Jason the same way. Somehow Kane felt connected to him now.

It had been at least 10 minutes since he last saw them. Ten whole minutes hiding from only the thought of them, hiding from their rep, and fourth-hand stories about their extraordinary skill and lightning speed. He had faced Kwei before, and lost. Together, the three of them were said to be unstoppable.

"All your hard work and look where it got you face down in the street. Was it worth it, Detective?"

Through the loopy spell that kept him subservient to its stupefying kick, Kane talked his legs into bending, his hands into pressing against the ground, and his shoulders and chest into assisting with lifting himself enough to skitter sideways out from under the van. Boring's shit-talk had actually inspired him. And there was his pride. Even now it nagged at him to save face and live up to his reputation. The Lin Brothers were living up to theirs.

"Masters of stealth" they were called, merciless killers whose use of shadows and light gave them an almost supernatural presence. No one knew why their victims always looked so shocked, as if they'd seen something terrifying before the bullet pierced their brains always from back to front.

"I don't believe in you!!!!!" Kane growled quietly but with passion.

"But I believe in *you*, Philip. I've believed in you from the beginning. That's why I chose you to be my liaison to the public back when we were playing cat and mouse. Don't you remember? Oh, and no hard feelings over what you did to my body."

Kane rose to a squat, his hands resting on his knees, and waited for the nausea from the memory that Boring's statement conjured up to pass. It struck him blind and fried his perception to sight, sound, and touch.

"McCann?????" Kane whimpered.

Kane noticed movement to his left. He lifted his gun, strafed left, crept sluggishly around to the rear of the van, and pulled open the door. His hands were shivering from Boring's revelation.

"I know that you were dying to kill me back then. Well, now's your chance. All you have to do is turn the gun on

yourself."

As much as Kane liked to believe that he was always prepared for the worst, what he saw inside the van buckled his knees. Had it been any less fucked-up, he might not have noticed it, thanks to McCann talking over his thoughts.

Kane finally understood the fear that the name Lin instilled. It was the last thing he would ever see before the bullet smacked him in the back of the head and dug in.

"Don't worry, old friend. I'm not done with you yet."

*   *   *

"For God so loved the world that he sent his only *other* begotten son," Jesus quipped to Yeshua, who walked out from behind the formation of well-armed soldiers who poured out of the line of cars and stood ready.

Surrounded on all sides by the remnants of underground-income mentality and victim-syndrome machinations manifested as dilapidated edifices scoffed at by high-rise corporate towers and financial hubs, like denizens of higher living, that looked down from a few miles away upon those who toiled and scavenged for comfort and peace of mind, the improvised battlefield reeked of grand confrontation.

Standing at only about 5'1", Yeshua, with his pockmarked complexion and heavy beard, was hard on the eyes. He was barefoot and wearing donated clothing dark-colored slacks, sort of baggy, and an oversized cable-knit sweater with a wide neck.

There was no escaping his ugliness. There was, however, strength in his eyes and in his stalwart mug that trumped the unpleasant arrangement of his features.

"The years have not been good to thee, my brother," Jesus said, tossing his golden locks to the side with a twist of his neck. "And cavorting with such misguided folk. I would have guessed that you were smarter than that."

Standing at varying distances behind Yeshua were Qazi Hamid, Holland Priest, and Senator Joseph Ornstein, leader of the Coalition. The latter two were each flanked by their own personal guards, associates, and yes-men.

"I came here in hopes of appealing to your humanity, not for a challenge," Yeshua said in Aramaic, but reaching all within earshot as English. "But I can see that time has washed you of that trait."

"What a shame that after all these years, thou hath come crawling out from beneath thy rock just to convince me to play nice. And to think, I used to admire thine ability to lead so many based on such a blatant lie."

"Then why carry on the charade if I disappoint you so?"

"Look around thee, my brother. These people have fought wars, wiped out and brainwashed entire cultures, and erected sprawling structures in honor of us, of thee... the man who started it all. And thou want to talk to me about being more human? No thanks. I signed off on that lowly existence centuries ago. This whole thing is much bigger than us now, and I, for one, plan on continuing to reap the rewards of the gift I was given. You should do the same. Imagine all that we could accomplish together."

"That power has warped your mind, Augustus. I had hoped that it would not have to come to this," Yeshua said, his composed demeanor riding waves of disdain that shined through in the slant of his mouth and the extended pause in the blink of his eyes.

Balling his fists to the crack, crack, cracking of his knuckles, Yeshua began a patient yet resolute walk toward Jesus, who stood about 100 feet away.

His eyes adopting an incensed squint, Jesus inhaled deep and, bending forward at the waist, he let out a guttural roar, followed by a steady stream of giant locusts that bellowed from his eyes and mouth, his lower jaw stretching to accommodate the rush of angry insects.

The dry click-clack of hundreds upon thousands of coarse

exoskeletons fighting for space on their way out drowned out the smack of Yeshua's bare feet against the ground as he continued to approach.

The angry locusts surrounded Yeshua and closed in, only to fall dead at his feet. Nose-diving faster than Jesus could vomit out more, the locusts rained down all around Yeshua and exploded into brief flashes of brilliant electric light.

In the background, Holland Priest smirked and nodded enthusiastically at the short, stocky soldier beside him who nodded back.

Jesus recoiled and flashed a slanted, "So you wanna play rough" type of glare.

Reaching his left arm up over his head, Jesus summoned the reddened clouds above to rumble and stir with activity and roll into the shape of a huge face that looked down angrily at Yeshua. Its mouth, falling open in slow-motion, spilled over with lavish swells of crackling electricity that bounced around the inside of it and into a crooked tongue of lightning that leapt out.

Zigzagging down from the sky, the furious lightning tongue smacked Jesus' raised palm, crawled down his left arm, across his shoulders, up his right, and out at Yeshua through his index finger, which was held stiff in a point. Up in the clouds, a gust of wind warped the cloud-face and ultimately broke it into many separate wisps of precipitation.

The impact from the lightning bolt blew Yeshua's hair back and danced up and down his entire frame, in and out of his clothing, and up under his crotch until he was literally covered with kinetic slivers of living light.

Jesus celebrated with a wily grin, but his triumph was quickly snatched away as the surge began to dim and fizzle out. All that was left was Yeshua, who, through it all, hadn't missed a step.

With less than 30 feet until they were face to face, Jesus regrouped, dropping his arms heavily to his sides in a huff. His narrowing eyes rolled from side to side, giving away his mind's hasty search for something to use against his foe.

In his arrogance, Jesus had underestimated Yeshua's power, thinking him weak simply because he favored a peaceful resolution. Still, he was fairly confident that he would prevail. An idea began to form and gestate and warm his heaving chest with a jolt of security.

"Not bad," Jesus said. "Thou art indeed a worthy opponent. However, I suspect that thine associates might not fare as well."

Jesus threw his arms out in front of him, fingers spread wide. A sudden rumble from somewhere beneath the street tested all but Yeshua's balance and sent the crowd behind him scrambling to remain on their feet.

"Stand without doubt and his tricks can not harm you," Yeshua called out, half-turning to face the crowd behind him.

Just inches in front of Yeshua, a 15- x 15-foot section of the street rose and buckled, then burst outward to reveal a tangle of massive pipes swathed in ferocious rust, twisting and writhing up into the sky like a gaggle of long-necked sea serpents racing toward some flying prey. Their strident voices filled the night with a chorus of metallic whining that shook the infrastructure of reality and caused windows and glass bottles to rupture and explode.

Yeshua paused and looked up at the pipe that separated from the intertwining mass, arched its neck, and lunged snake-like at him, its jagged mouth boasting sharp, hastily serrated edges where the pipe tore from the rest of its submerged bulk.

Leaning his head to the side as if to chastise Jesus for such a pedestrian effort, Yeshua clasped his hands behind his back and looked away from the approaching threat just as it slammed into an invisible barrier that surrounded him, split into five curling slivers, and fell dead to the street with a deafening THUD.

Snaking past Yeshua with definite purpose, the remaining pipes honed in on the soldiers, who raised their weapons and fired at the pipes in unison.

The first pipe tore its victim clean in half at the waist and suffused the other two men, whose fear shone through their attempts to conceal it, with motivation to run for cover.

Clamping down on the slower of the two soldiers' legs in mid-dive, another serpent-pipe pulled him up high above the street and slammed him down again and again until there was nothing left to hold on to.

A third man, an executive with the Coalition, found himself fighting to escape yet another pipe's embrace as it wrapped around his torso and squeezed a gurgling grunt from his lungs that climbed octaves until he burst.

The remaining crowd stood defiant as the serpent-pipes surrounded them, sniffing out their fear and threatening to strike with half-lunges, snapping their improvised mouths shut inches away from their faces.

With a flick of his wrist, Yeshua summoned back the two soldiers and the Coalition executive who doubted, and sent the serpent-pipes back, pulled by an unseen force until they finally disappeared underground. A second flick righted the street between him and Jesus.

Greeting their sudden return with surprise that quickly withered to panic, the three reanimated men fainted, vomited, and cried out in testament to the memory of being bitten in two, slammed into the ground, and squeezed into nothingness, respectively.

Without a hint of emotion, Yeshua continued on his path empowered by the sudden twinge of doubt that colored Jesus' caustic fidgeting.

As Jesus lifted his arm to summon forth another attack, he reacted with wide-eyed curiosity to the surge of weakness that traveled out from his core. Searching the night for a reason that never materialized, he ventured within himself, rewinding his mind's eye to the vision of the approaching SUV, then back a few mental reels to see the procession in its entirety.

Originally, there were more cars and motorcycles that veered off in opposite directions at a large intersection. At the next intersection, a second group turned right, leaving the vision as he originally saw it.

Jesus stayed with the vehicles that broke formation; his breath, heavy with anticipation, scored the vision as he watched disc-shaped, remote camera-drones jettison from their mounts at the rear of each bike and sputter to a glide before darting high above the tenements and trash-strewn lots to strategically marked rooftops to acquire a good view of the scene. Anonymous arms reached out from half-open windows in one of the cars and tossed out additional camera-drones that followed the same pattern as the first couple.

Jesus looked closer, submerging beneath the moist gleam of the camera-drone's lens, peering down cylindrical corridors of wire, plastic, and microchips, out into the atmosphere through satellites and space junk, and down into millions of pliable minds huddled in groups of various sizes in fortified homes, shelters, bars, anywhere that contained a radio, television, or computer…. They watched with bated breath, begging for direction that they were too lazy, too weak, or too preoccupied with the superficial amenities of life to find on their own.

It was a setup, a joint effort between the Coalition, the Secular Soldiers, and the Dziko Nation. They had jacked into the broadcast satellite and were filming live in an attempt to shift popular opinion by showing Jesus in his true light, thus weakening him and in turn giving Yeshua strength. And it was working. The camera-drones had filmed everything he had said, everything he had done.

Smiling to hide his anger, Jesus returned his sight to the present, ready to compliment Yeshua on his cunning and retaliate with a vengeance. He had a plan up his sleeve to deal with the public, but it would take some time. No matter. With them it was nothing, like taking candy from a blind, limbless baby.

But Yeshua was gone.

From 100 feet away, the crowd stared at Jesus knowingly, their guns held at ease.

Jesus whipped around nervously and caught a glimpse of

movement over his right shoulder. By the time he faded to a wraith and reconstituted himself to face the opposite direction, Yeshua was already on him.

Cocking his arm for full thrust potential, Yeshua plunged his hand deep into Jesus' chest, stopping him short in mid-reaction.

"Such power wielded with such juvenile naiveté," Yeshua's voice echoed throughout Jesus' mind, accompanied by flashes of his past conquests.

Jesus' mind's eye: *The Crusades, the Spanish Inquisition, 'civilized,' colonial thinking and its juggernaut march around the globe infecting everything in its path with the sickness called revisionist Christianity.*

"Have you any idea of the suffering you've caused?" Yeshua growled, retracting and thrusting his arm, this time with all his strength. "Have you any remorse for the things you've done, for the things that have been done in *MY NAME*... because of *YOU?!*"

His body seized in electric paralysis, Jesus could do nothing but watch and listen. He wanted to tell Yeshua that he *too* was partly to blame for the montage of violence that flashed before his mind's eye.

"Look at what we've done. Feeeeel the pain we've caused," Yeshua said.

Falling to his knees with Yeshua's right arm buried in his chest to just below the elbow, Jesus cried out in anguish, his face twisted to extreme proportions, his voice resonating with fierce passion for miles and miles, cajoling curious eyes skyward in search of what it was that could bring about such a ghastly pitched scream.

Contorting his body to cope with the worst of the pain, Jesus grabbed Yeshua's forearm with both hands and struggled to pull it out of his chest. In the meantime, he tried to make Yeshua understand that it was *his* fanatical influence over so many that motivated his father, Pontius Pilate, to use the portrait he had commissioned as the "campaign flag" for his claims that Augustus was "the true Christ." Although Pilate stood firm in his belief that Yeshua was a fraud, he had seen what he could do, and he had seen how resolute Yeshua's disciples were in their undying devotion to him. It frightened Pilate.

For one thing, it made Pilate entertain doubt, no matter how insignificant the thought. He considered that a weakness on his part.

Secondly, Yeshua's disciples weren't the least bit shy about their hatred toward Pilate. No telling what a group of them might attempt under the right circumstances.

And third… how the fuck was Yeshua able to do the things he did in the first place healing the blind and diseased, walking on water, or turning it into wine? Was it all just an elaborate trick? Was he really magic? Pilate had to know.

Jesus never really had a choice. He had been indoctrinated young into the belief that he was somehow special, God-like. In fact, he was born to Pilate and an Egyptian slave-girl whom Pilate raped on a regular basis. Jesus never even knew her name. He barely knew his own. He took offense to the sound of it. Augustus.… Before Kane, it had been so long since anyone called him by that name. He found himself dwelling on it.

"You dared to have force-fed your image to the world, keeping me too weak to do more than hope that one day you'd realize the implications of what your father stole from me."

His face finally knotted with fuming sentiment, Yeshua guided Jesus on a more specific visual jaunt backwards through time.

Jesus' mind's eye: *Familiar faces and scenes from his long life rabbit-punched into his cranium, stopping abruptly on a fair-haired pregnant woman writhing to the melody of anguish, her vocal chords chafed to a dry crackle as she lay strapped to an old wooden table, legs spread akimbo in the throes of childbirth. Nervous women (mostly slaves snatched from their normal duties in haste) tend to her as she pushes against the contractions way* *up in her pelvis with arched-back zeal. In the background, a group of sentinels threaten brutal repercussions should anything go wrong with the delivery of Pilate's offspring.*

"Let this be a lesson in the correct use of such unlimited power. Watch as I wipe your wretched memory from existence," Yeshua's directionless voice threatened.

Jesus' mind's eye: *A spray of blood from deep in her womb sends the women reeling back. One of them falls into a sentinel, who reacts by swatting her to the floor. "What is it? What's wrong with my baby?" the fair-haired woman pleads before consciousness escapes her, but the women are too frightened to respond, frightened of the abomination that they have just witnessed, and of Pilate's ruthless temper. It was obvious that none of them wanted to be there.*

The sound of infant cries fill the otherwise silent room. The lead sentinel yanks the fallen woman up from the floor and shoves her forward between the fair-haired woman's legs. There is a mouth where her vagina was only moments ago. It continues to regurgitate a healthy newborn. Even the sentinel turns white as a ghost when it sees it. "Bless not this vile seed," Yeshua's voice pours from the new mouth as it begins to devour the infant from its feet up.

Back in the real world, Jesus' lurching reaction to the experience reached a trembling apex, his cries of absolute pain climbing higher and higher as he started to vanish starting at his feet.

"Today you will know the terror that you have begotten," Yeshua said.

Jesus felt his life slipping away. He had never once considered his own mortality, so the thought of it stole what little masculinity his voice may have had as he whimpered loudly and shrunk lower to the ground, both hands tugging at Yeshua's forearm to no avail.

"Please... d... don't k... kill me...." Jesus stammered with eyes ablaze. His meek yet definitive timbre grew more and more urgent as nothingness climbed up his frail body. "I'm sorry.... I'll make it all better. I promise."

Saying nothing in response, Yeshua switched hands as Jesus' torso disappeared, removing his right and clutching Jesus' hair with his left. He waited until Jesus was nothing but a head dangling from his left hand, eyes bursting with unfathomable fear, mouth opening and closing silently, the death-march of nothingness on its way up.

Jesus flashed a clenched-teeth grimace to greet his demise. Squeezing his eyes shut, he bit down as hard as he could...

...and opened his eyes to see that it was all an elaborate ruse.

"A quick death is far too good for you, Augustus," Yeshua groaned, his hand still planted in Jesus' chest. "Perhaps if you had something upon which to dwell, something to rob you of that which you hold dear and fill your blackened heart with sorrow and resentment upon the slightest reflection...."

Jesus' mind's eye: *A different vision melts down from top to bottom: a palatial bedroom complete with marble pillars, flowing drapes, and a running fountain, an ornate smorgasbord of fruit and raw and cooked meat set on a table in the center of the room. The fair-haired woman hides, petrified from something...someone.... This time she is younger and without child. Her glazed eyes tremble, struggling to stay open against the seductive lure of alcohol forced upon her against her will. A hulking shadow (Pontius Pilate) stumbles shirtless, awkward, into the light, searching with ham-handed enthusiasm for his victim. He finds her cowering behind a curtain. She shrieks and bats his reaching arms with her own, but her efforts do little to dissuade his beefy determination as he scoops her up over his shoulder*

and tosses her hard onto the bed. Salivating with Cro-Magnon lust, he hoists his pants down and...

Stuttering ahead, a rounded shadow rises to a drastic arc, like a mountain range passed over by the moon's radiant smile, and falling hard to the slap of flesh upon flesh and repeating the same cycle indefinitely as night succumbs to day again and again. The fair-haired woman's vigorous screams fall upon the deaf ears of Pilate and all five of his best sentinels who fight each other over their turn with her night after night for weeks at a time.

A soothing warmth foreign to the sharp physical and emotional agony that Jesus had been experiencing up until now teemed through his veins and granted him the strength to flex and relax his muscles independently of Yeshua's mental hold.

Much to Yeshua's surprise, Jesus summoned his legs straight beneath him and from deep within his chest, a low, rumbling cackle crawled to the surface and out through a shit-eating grin.

"Foolish little brown man," Jesus said with corporeal scorn as Yeshua began to gasp, his throat chasing a swallow that it never caught, eyes startled to full orbs of brown. "I've had my fill of your history lesson."

Pulling with all his dwindling might, Yeshua attempted to yank his arm free from Jesus' chest, but he was stuck. He fought the forceful bend of his knees, looking to the tops of the buildings where the remote cameras were supposed to be watching. He already had an idea what had happened.

"The cameras.... He's done something with the cameras...." Yeshua spoke to everyone in the crowd through his mind.

Holland Priest sprinted over to the SUV. The sullen blue glow from the wall of TV screens jumped out at him when he opened the door and peered inside.

The live video feed had been replaced by stock footage from the eight-year war in Iraq given a right-wing spin to instill fear and mistrust of men of Yeshua's hue, the way they had done during President Mel Riggs's campaign. Scenes were shown of swarthy, Middle Eastern men chanting indecipherable slogans with fanatical zeal, scowling, sienna-toned faces gleaming with malicious intent, brandishing poles topped with the heads of white men and women, dragging alabaster corpses draped in tattered military garb through dirt roads while crowds hungry for American blood ripped them to pieces. Doctored images were presented of murder at the hands of brown men made to look like savages that, to unsophisticated minds, resembled Yeshua himself.

"Son-of-a-BITCH!" Priest blurted, his eyes rolling from screen to screen.

Reaching into his jacket, Holland Priest slid his gun from its holster and leaned out to see Yeshua falling to his knees, struggling to free his arm from the liquefied section of Jesus' chest that melted up his arm, to his shoulder, and up over his head, suffocating him as it dripped down to engulf the rest of his body.

Jesus turned and smiled at the crowd (Qazi Hamid, Holland Priest, Senator Ornstein, guards, associates, yes-men) who weren't sure how to react, as Yeshua's struggling grew to a fever pitch, his body vibrating to a blur.

"Behold your fallen messiah," Jesus spoke directly to Qazi Hamid. "His fate pales in comparison to what I'm going to do to you and your friends."

In the distance, Kwei, Su, and Ho walked out of the shadows and up to Jesus from behind. Behind them, the government-type zombies stumbled forward, their faces and hands dripping with fresh blood.

Holland Priest stepped between Qazi Hamid and Jesus and yelled, "Take em' down!"

Six years later…

Chapter 11

2021 PA.

A liquid bar of molten yellow is stretched taught and pinched off into rectangular sections with an electric sizzle. WAH sounds pressed him, forcing his breath out faster than he can replenish his lungs to capacity.

Red eyes roll open, seeking clarity. Rectangular sections of molten yellow become a single-file procession of overhead lights. Looming shapes find vague definition with the same electric sizzle, bleeding into human shapes, heads and shoulders standing on either side: two on the right, two on the left. They are moving fast, all of them. Three of them are wearing black body armor.

Whoever he is, Red Eyes senses urgency, and danger.

The fourth human shape, a youngish man, late twenties/early thirties, dressed like a surgeon down to the mask that covered his nose and mouth, leaned down face to face with the dry red orbs that question.

"Try to relax, Detective Makane. We'll have you out of here shortly." The surgeon's voice was deep and thick, too thick. The sheer density of it left him feeling spent.

Red Eyes roll up and flutter closed.

Lockdown

Even in Heaven City Northeast (formerly Philadelphia) there was shopping to be done, power-lunches to be enjoyed, and, worst of all, tourists, only here they were chaperoned like children, led around in single file by soldiers from the United Christian Conglomerate (UCC) armed forces, known as Archangels.

The UCC's main hub was Vatican City. Jesus had dismantled the Catholic hierarchy after Judgment Day and replaced it with his own, which consisted of various religious leaders, many of them well respected. Reverend Jesse James Dallas was his second in command. He toyed with various titles, King, Ruler, Führer, as a slight to the Jews, whom he never had nice things to say about, before settling on President of the UCC, which served as the governing entity in the Heaven City territories.

In the USA, now called the United States under Christ, there were UCC churches in every large city, each packed with survivors trying to gain Saved Citizenship and a place in one of the Heaven City territories. There were seven main territories in Houston, New Orleans, San Diego, Chicago, New York, Washington, and Philadelphia.

Those who hadn't accepted Jesus on Judgment Day were left to fend for themselves in the outlands beyond the Heaven City borders. Given time to experience long-term living without order, and infected by walking rot, many people changed their minds and decided that Saved Citizenship, with all its bullshit, had to be better than living in constant fear of being abducted and sold into slavery, robbed, raped, hunted for sport (there was a growing number of militia types who had taken to hunting live humans for sport), or eaten by zombies.

There were attempts to rebuild on the outside, mostly by the Left Hand, the largest rebel group, and by resilient survivors who were able to organize and form small communities, some of which had been going strong since before Judgment Day. Few of them lasted more than a year.

Saved Citizenship (SC) had its privileges: status, wealth, and protection from the outside world. The saved had come to know it as Purgatory, while Hell was reserved for the subway system, which hadn't been in official use for more than five years. The tunnels were ripe with zombies that had either ventured in from one of the entrances outside Heaven City, or had become infected after being sent down there as punishment. Hell was where Heaven City banished their criminals and those who lost their faith. The subway entrances inside the Heaven City borders had been sealed by electrified steel shutters that opened and closed like a garage door. There was a rumor going around that you could hear the dead talking if you stood close enough to one of the entrances. Many of the zombies that inhabited the tunnels were in the early stages, so the rumor was probably based in fact.

Heaven City Northeast was a vastly different place from old Philadelphia, Pennsylvania. At first glance, it hinted at its former glory, tall buildings full of even taller tales spit from mouths hungry for power. Only now there was a profound religious varnish that tainted everything in sight, like an Orwellian metropolis gone bible-belt: high-rise office buildings converted to vertical cathedrals, giant holographic advertisements that took up entire faces of buildings blaring down propaganda and smiling faces feigning satisfaction.

Down on the street, wraith-like images of clergymen from various Christian denominations sprouted up from holo-projectors buried beneath the pavement; an entire city block was lined with 10-foot crosses upon which petty criminals languished, crucified, as the crimes for which they suffered played out in reenactments on small, static-filled monitors just below their feet. The rumor was that the videos were heavily dramatized, but with no one willing to question it, it remained but a whisper spoken through careful lips whenever someone happened upon 'Sinners' Alley,' as it was called.

Then from the clouds that caressed the surface of the tallest buildings came the siren, wailing like some vintage, Cold War ghost-machine, echoing throughout the catacombs of steel and glass.

Frantic bodies scurried like well-fed roaches in corporate guise for the safety of the nearest open door, swiping their SC cards and gaining entry. The siren's hollow whine had a way of reaching deep into chests and manipulating weak hearts to pause and stutter. Those who weren't immediately coaxed into hiding by its intimidating bellow neck-craned up to the UCC Tower for the announcement to follow.

A giant screen made of laser-light that shot out from four distinct points and met in the middle, radiated heat and brilliant bursts of color before static interference cleared to reveal the head and shoulders of a congenial older woman, whose affable mannerisms stunk of underlying evil. Most of the crowd had come to know her face and the implications of her arrival. In the ensuing panic, they only caught hints of her dire warning: something about clearing the streets; precautionary measures; former official found guilty of treason, set to be banished to Hell; noncompliance met with arrest and immediate judgment or death.

Then came the countdown.

"10… 10… 10… 9… 9… 9…"

Mary Dodd waited nervously for her husband Frederick to emerge from the half-open subway entrance at 16th and Market when the siren sounded. The steel shutter had malfunctioned and left a three-foot opening between it and the ground. It happened quite frequently. Fred's curiosity had gotten the best of him as they ate lunch at an outdoor café half a block away from the entrance.

"C'mon, you dare me?" he kept saying. "Haven't you ever wondered what it's like down there?"

It had been at least 20 minutes since he crawled inside, and although the thought had crossed her mind, Mary wasn't ready to consider that he might have become a meal for some eager zombie. Usually it was the teenagers looking for a thrill who ventured into Hell. But Mary and Fred were adults, and full-fledged Saved Citizens. If caught, the authorities would no doubt use them as examples, as they should certainly know better.

"Fred, where are you?" she called out from a squat, as she peered into the dank blackness that breathed out a stench so pungent that it caused her to sway and consider taking an unscheduled nap. "Fred. Please. Can't you hear the siren?"

"8… 8… 8… 7… 7… 7…"

"Somebody help her!" a distressed female voice called out

inside the struggling bookstore across the street.

"Not my problem," the crotchety, middle-aged proprietor quipped from behind the raised counter. "Besides, what's to say she ain't some tourist from the outside trying to sneak in?"

It wasn't uncommon for tourists to slip away from their groups with thoughts of a better life amongst the saved. Fake SC IDs and barcode badges worn on the lapel were hot on the outside, but they rarely fooled the scanners and card readers. Another common practice was to lure a Citizen across the borders, kill them, and then assume their identity.

Since the mandate had passed requiring the destruction of all books not approved by the UCC, the crotchety proprietor was left with little to offer his customers, and he made his disapproval known to anyone who was willing to listen. He was taking a big risk by shooting his mouth off, and he knew it. His wife was always telling him to look on the bright side.

"Look at this," he whispered to her regarding the crowd that huddled in front, watching Mary Dodd call to her husband. Of course, they had no idea what she was doing: only that she looked too well kept to be crazy, or a tourist. "I've got a store full of people, and not one of them is buying."

He wanted to tell them all to look at the handwritten sign in the window that read **No Browsing.**

Mary wasn't the only one left outside. There were a few people scattered about, sprinting back and forth. And there were tourists, two of them. They ran from door to door, tugging on them and begging the people inside to let them in.

The crowd inside the bookstore turned a blind eye to the one that came knocking on their door. If they weren't saved, then they were lower than dirt. The propaganda machine had taught them well.

"**6... 6... 6... 5... 5... 5...**"

Mary got down on her knees and crawled closer to the subway entrance. She was breathing through her mouth and squinting to deal with the smell.

"Baby where are you?" Her voice was trembling now. "Please answer me. If you don't hurry, they're going to crucify us both."

"Hey! What are you doing?" the crotchety proprietor said to Shirley, the concerned black woman who opened the door and leaned out.

The crowd immediately reacted to the swell of sound that rushed in along with the breeze and the smell of creeping death from the open subway entrance.

"Oh, my word! Do you smell that?" someone said.

"Are you a citizen?" Shirley yelled to Mary.

"Yes," Mary replied, without looking away from the opening. "My husband... he's still down there."

"Leave him. There's no time."

"If he was stupid enough to go down there, then he deserves whatever happens to him," someone quietly commented.

"I'm not going anywhere without my husba..."

Before Mary could finish, a panic-stricken tourist, a gaunt young woman, pushed her aside and dove forward, into the subway entrance. Mary fell to her ass, reaching out to the woman, and scrambled to get to her knees and crawl right back to the opening.

"Hey! You! Do you see anyone else down there? Do you see a man: tall, brown hair, dressed in a suit? He might be hurt."

"**4... 4... 4... 3... 3... 3...**"

"Get back inside and close the door," the proprietor said to the Shirley.

"But we can't just let them die out there!" Shirley said.

It was a daily battle to will away the disappointment with her place in life, which never failed to upset Shirley's stomach whenever she got to thinking about it. Gone was the sense of security she used to find in simply being a Saved Citizen. She needed a challenge, something to make her think on her feet, like she used to do: something to revive her spirit. Fuck the ramifications of independent thought in this place. Like most of the people she knew in Heaven City, Shirley had become a slave to the rules and restrictions, droning about like healthy versions of the zombies outside.

"I said get back inside and close the door. I'm not going to tell you again."

The proprietor reached beneath the counter and retrieved his gun (a long, black thing with wires wrapped around the barrel). He used it to point to the sign on the back wall that read **Lockdown Shelter.**

As just about any building could be used as shelter when the siren sounded, their were rules posted high on the walls of most places, accompanied by a symbol an "S" superimposed over the outline of a house with a horn sending shockwaves down at it from the top corner.

Rule number 31a stated that proprietors, managers, ranking officials, or security personnel at such shelters were authorized to use force (even deadly force) to stop anyone who disrupted, or attempted to sabotage the lockdown process.

"**2... 2... 2... 1... 1... 1...**"

Oh God said the look on Mary's face when she turned toward Shirley and thrust herself up into a slanted, sprint-ready posture. Mary's feet had barely touched the ground when her head jerked forward, long black hair whipping in tow, and spit out an arterial spray of blood from the chunk that went missing from the top of her head in a flash.

The women, mostly, cried out when Mary collapsed to the ground and began to twitch. Those who knew where to look spotted the automatic turrets mounted on buildings and lampposts. Swiveling in all directions, the turret picked off three more. Two were recently inducted Citizens who thought that hiding behind a tree or under a car was good enough. The other was Shirley, who remained in the doorway, halfway in and halfway out of bookstore when the bullet struck her unexpectedly and fragmented her left shoulder. It made Shirley gasp, then cough, then struggle to catch her breath.

Shirley fell face-first to the ground outside the store.

"Hey!" the proprietor yelled to a man who had motioned for the door as if to help her. "Don't you dare open that door!"

The proprietor flipped a switch behind the counter and watched the uneasy crowd react as the heavy steel shutters jarred loose and slid down in front of the entire building, covering the door, windows, everything.

With all her remaining strength, Shirley tried to lift herself and belly-crawl up to the door before the shutters reached the ground. She tried until the very last minute when the shutter met her lower back and crushed her between it and the ground.

Inside the store, momentary darkness caused by the shutter gave way to an electric snap and a burst of feedback. Assaulting them with mind-numbing sound, a slew of UCC-approved product endorsements played out on the inner wall of the shutter.

Silenced by the sight of Shirley's head and shoulders situated at an upward "V" slant from the point at which the shutter pinned her down, the crowd expected her to wake up and thrash about like a savage. It took about 12 minutes before her right eye shot open. Instead of lashing out, Shirley cried and cried.

An immaculate kitchen. A housewife goes about her daily chores.

HOUSEWIFE: *If you're like me, then a part of you has been missing ever since the death of your spouse or loved one. Not a day goes by that I don't find myself overwhelmed by the fact that after 23 years of marriage I'm left alone to deal with, among other things, medical costs and accumulating bills that begin to pile up in his absence.*

The housewife walks from the kitchen into the living area and stops behind a recliner propped in front of a flat-screen TV that screams "look at me" from its perch on the wall.

HOUSEWIFE: *Well thanks to the CMB-sponsored REaniMate program, I no longer have to worry about that... right, honey?*

As the housewife leans over the back of the chair, the badly preserved corpse of her husband arches his rigor mortis-stricken neck to meet her pursed lips. Rot has officially claimed him, and despite the red rosy cheeks and layers of foundation that only call attention to the mess they tried in vain to conceal, he looks like the result of a mortuary-school neophyte given free reign over make-up duties. Nevertheless, he flashes a dry, crackling smile at the camera.

HOUSEWIFE: *Other programs claim to produce similar results through cloning, but who has time to wait for a clone to grow into the person you remember? REaniMate is the only service that reunites thousands of happy costumers with lost family members, friends, or spouses complete with their memories intact and at an affordable price.*

And for you animal lovers out there, REaniMate's REaniPet service can return to you that favorite dog or cat as well.

So don't take death lying down. Call REaniMate today and ask to have our colorful brochure sent to you free. Because death doesn't have to be the end.

The frame freezes on her smile as a deep-voiced announcer rattles off the small print too fast for anyone to comprehend.

ANNOUNCER: *Only eligible to card-carrying Saved Citizens. Customers must provide entire body of deceased at point of sale.*

Preceded by a rust-ridden bellow of steel against steel, the reinforced double doors of the UCC Tower ground open, and from within came a priest followed by four Archangels, two on either side of the condemned man, Samuel Glover, whom they escorted at gunpoint to the main subway entrance at 15th Street. Sam was Director of Immigration Services for Heaven City Northeast, and it was from his office that officials (seven of them) allowed countless spies for the Left Hand to pass through the screening process on account of their carelessness. Jesus himself executed all seven. No one knew exactly how they were killed, but the word on the street was that it was worse than anything a normal man could imagine.

Walking the walk of the dead, as it had become known, Sam held his head high, contemplating his fate along the way, as the priest recited something familiar from the bible that went in one ear and out the other.

High up on the face the UCC Tower, the laser-light screen displayed Sam's rotating mugshot, his name, and a description of his crime. About 15 feet to his left, Mary Dodd stood up, eyes clouded over, and slowly lifted her hands up to inspect the missing half of her head. Sliding her fingers down the wet, lumpy texture, Mary stopped when she saw that she was being watched. She reached out to Sam and the Archangel to his front and left, her lips bouncing off each other while trying to form a word.

Sam closed his eyes when the turrets found her and made her dance to pieces. The Archangel shoved him forward with the butt of his gun. Apparently, the sight had bothered him as well, and this was an attempt to replace the vulnerability that fear like that brought out with forced aggression.

Maybe it was denial, or shock, or the fact that they didn't kill him on the spot like they did the others, or maybe it was the hope that he would be exonerated at the last minute, but for some reason the magnitude of Sam's sentence didn't really sink in until they reached the mouth of the 15th Street entrance.

To ward off the present until the very last possible second, Sam kept himself distracted with minutiae the birds flying overhead; his mugshot up on the screen; Mary Dodd; the sight and sound of the steel shutter rising from the ground; the stench that jumped out from the entrance as he drew closer, which punched him in the face; the distant moaning and semi-lucid growls from deep down in the tunnel.

"Samuel Glover," the priest began, "you have been found guilty of the crime of treason and are hereby sentenced to wallow for eternity in the bowels of Hell."

Sam turned to face the Archangels on either side of him as if to appeal to their compassion, but the sight of himself, all beaten down and weary from lack of food, reflected in their visors made him wish he hadn't looked in the first place.

"Any last words, Mr. Glover?" the Priest inquired.

There was so much that Sam wanted to say in his own defense. He had what amounted to a lengthy monologue practiced and ready to deliver. He had intended to deliver it at his trial, but they wouldn't let him testify. All he needed was the perfect opening to get them interested enough to hear him out.

"Please follow the stairs down, Mr. Glover," the Priest said. "And may God have mercy on your soul."

"No, wait…. Wait…." Sam begged as the same Archangel who had shoved him earlier pressed the barrel of his gun against Sam's back, gave him a push down the first three steps, and, in concert with the other three, pointed the gun at his head when he turned and tried to climb back up. "Please, you have to listen to me."

"Please step down away from the entrance," the Priest ordered as he pressed a button on his wrist and set the shutter in motion.

"No. You don't understand," Sam cried out, his voice developing an echo as the door closed in front of him. "Goddammit, I was Director of Immigration Services. I demand to be heard.... Are you listening to me? I demand to be hear…"

The shutter hissed closed.

Five minutes later, storefront shutters crawled open as far as the eye could see. Joining the birds that hovered overhead, two disc-shaped clean-up drones zipped to each dead body that lay out in the open and spit their flaming venom down upon them. After burning the bodies from existence they retracted the phallic flame nozzles that protruded from the front of each one and sped off toward one of the mailbox-like receptacles at the corner of each block.

*　　*　　*

Like a monitor buzz-snapping to life, clear vision spread out in all directions from an invisible center-point. Red Eyes was aware that some time had passed since he had seen the surgeon and the three guards, but exactly how much (an hour, a day, a year), he had no clue.

Red Eyes lingered on the opening view, then wandered slowly to gain a sense of familiarity based on remnants of what looked like an old elementary school classroom faded historical flash cards, weird marriages of math equations and nursery rhymes, and posters of cultural icons peeked out from beneath a top layer of banners and signs. On the signs, an image of a crucifix within a thick-bordered circle and crossed out, and popular anti-UCC slogans:

Church + State = Oppression
~~*Jesus*~~ *Augustus is a liar*
God is the Antidote for Intelligence.

A photograph of a tiny brain inside a silhouette of a normal-sized human head with the caption *God's house*

Red Eyes shifted and rolled to cover the entire room: to the console, the unoccupied desk up front, the large flat-screen monitor mounted over a section of the blackboard that wrapped around the entire room. The monitor relayed a 3-D image of a human brain.

At the bottom right corner of the screen, letters and numbers that, aside from a fleeting sense of connection or familiarity akin to déjà vu, but much less cohesive a sensation, meant nothing to him:

Makane, Philip
Age: 38

There was a part of the room, over by the door, that Kane's eyes couldn't reach. From there, he heard voices.

"Oh shit...." a male voice whispered. "Is he awake?"

"Son-of-a-bitch.... I think so," another male replied.

"Mikel's gonna shit."

"I'll go tell him. You stay here and make sure he's okay."

"Why can't we just call him?"

"No way, man. You know how long he's been waiting for this. I want to be the one to tell him, face to face."

"You always were a kiss-ass."

"Maybe so, man, but we'll see who's talking when I'm running field ops, and you're still doing bullshit guard duty."

Kane heard a door open and close. The heavy breathing was less amplified than before, which told him that there was one fewer person in the room with him. He tried to shift his weight and roll onto his side.

"I know you must be uncomfortable, Detective, but I wouldn't try to get up just yet." The first male voice jumped at him from somewhere to the left, causing him to flinch. "It's going to be awhile before you're back on your feet."

Kane followed the voice to the front of the room where Dennis Kramer sat with his legs crossed atop the previously unoccupied desk, holding a pornographic magazine in both hands.

"Mikel should be here any second," Dennis smiled warmly. He snatched the magazine behind his back when Kane's red eyes fell upon it and took lingering interest. "He's going to be thrilled to see that you're finally awake."

Pushing off with his legs, Dennis rolled in his chair, turning along the way, over to the beeping console stacked within the rickety maintenance cart and looked up at the screen. The 3-D brain was glowing green, which meant that everything was okay. Reflected in a small screen within the console, a thin horizontal marionette (Kane) lurched and shifted and attempted to sit up on the steel table in the center of the room.

Dennis whipped around and watched nervously as Kane fumbled with the tubes and wires thrust into and suctioning his hypersensitive flesh. Dennis sprung from his chair when the heart monitor began to balk and hurried over to Kane's side.

"Please, Detective, for your own good, try not to move around too much," Dennis said, easing him back down to a lying position.

"Where am I? What's happening to me?" Kane rasped.

"You're in the old William J. Clinton Elementary."

"Why can I hardly move? Why does my whole body feel like… like wet cement or something?"

Dennis looked around the room to stall for time. He wasn't certain whether or not Mikel wanted Kane to know what happened just yet something about what the memory of the Lin brothers' actions would do to Kane before he was physically able to deal with its shock-inducing qualities. They had all heard the stories. However, Lin Ho was the only one left; hence, the mythology surrounding them wasn't as potent or popular as it used to be.

There was a chirping sound from the front of the room. Turning to the monitor on the blackboard, Dennis exhaled at the sight of Mikel Williamson's grease-stained face staring back at him in 3-D.

"Welcome back, old friend," Mikel said, his expression and his tone both revealing and withholding his elation, as he wiped his face with an oily cloth. "How are you feeling?"

Kane struggled to prop himself up on his elbows to peruse the tubes and wires that littered his naked torso, his mind repairing itself on the fly and coughing up memories out of sequence.

"Last thing I remember, I was…"

"Don't strain yourself, Kane," Mikel said. "You might not be ready to face the truth."

"Well, I'm alive, right?" Kane said, looking himself over. "As far as I can see, I'm not missing anything, or permanently damaged, right?"

Silence.

"Right?" Kane repeated, probing both their eyes.

"Technically, you're fine," Mikel replied, "but it's going to take major rehab before you're up and about. I'd rather wait 'til then to discuss…"

"Whoa… hold on a minute…. Major rehab? For what?"

Kane looked right into Mikel's giant, transparent irises.

"And give it to me straight. No bullshit."

Mikel hesitated, then cleared his throat.

"You were shot in the back of the head by one of the Lin brothers and left for dead six years ago. Thanks to your stubbornness, you survived the gunshot, but you've been in a coma ever since. Until this morning, that is."

"Six years???" Kane was flabbergasted. First of all, it seemed like he'd only been asleep for a few hours. He suddenly remembered the Lins, and what he had seen that night, and immediately forced the memory back, as it was too much to fathom all at once. So vivid an image, it spoke to Kane physically and made him appear stricken with violent chills.

"Are you all right?" Mikel asked, throwing a stare to Dennis, who hurried over to a closet and pulled out a neatly folded wool blanket.

Unfolding it as he walked, Dennis wrapped the blanket around Kane's narrow shoulders and gently guided him back into a lying position.

"My brain's just a little scrambled from the nap. I'll be fine," Kane said. "Just give me a minute."

"Take your time, old friend," Mikel said. "We've got a lot of catching up to do when you're feeling up to it. For now, I just want you to get some rest."

Kane laid on his right side, staring at the far wall, but seeing inward.

"Six fucking years of my life… wasted," he said to himself. "Six fucking years…."

*   *   *

Hell Is Where the Heart Is….

What seemed like days was actually only hours (two hours to be exact) that Frederick Dodd had been trekking through the deep dark sludge of urine, crusted-over shit, and progressive decay that he woke up lying face down in only moments ago. He was running from something that seemed, by the sound of it, to be stalking him when he tripped and fell. Apparently it was nothing, or something small and nonthreatening like a rat or a stray dog.

As he stood in complete darkness, attempting to retrace his steps to the 16th Street entrance, he was overcome by the sinking feeling that he might not make it out alive. Damn his stupid curiosity.

Poor Mary… Fred thought. *What she must be thinking.*

If she were smart, she would've tried to contact his cousin

Jonathan, a high-ranking Archangel, to help find him. Knowing her, she probably thought Fred was playing one of his pranks. She had most likely gone home expecting to find him there waiting for her.

The dense, livid aroma, laced with twangy scents reminiscent of ammonia and vinegar, burned Fred's eyes half-shut and made him debate inhaling each time he did so, fearing that it might somehow infect his lungs. He could literally feel the air heating them as they expanded.

As his eyes adjusted, they picked up the faintest traces of light, the metallic glint that winked from the floor, partially illuminating the portions of track that weren't submerged beneath sludge and spent corpses. Long, thin slivers of white sheen hugged vertical edges that turned out to be pillars, helping to translate the lumpy shapes on the ground into recognizable things, things like whole bodies strewn across the damp tunnel floor between the rows of tracks where he walked.

Persuaded by the omnipresent rumble of deep-throated wailing that seemed louder from his rear, Fred continued forward.

Bleak cavernous space stretched as far as the eye could see, the profane dark blanket was interrupted when his eyes caught focus of some far off light source and allowed him tantalizingly frightening hints of what lie in the murky belly beneath the Dante-inspired murals, scribbled name-calling, and the fluorescent yellow-red letters on the archway up ahead. **U R N HELL,** they read.

To his right a ghostly Drip, Drip, to his left, the metallic wail of rusty pipes slowly giving out after decades of neglect, and all around him a distant moaning.

Frederick Dodd had just last week been promoted to supervisor at work, and today was the day he and Mary picked to celebrate. They had the whole day planned: a round or two of routine marital sex (but sex nonetheless) to start of the morning, then lunch and a movie. He would've preferred something a bit more exciting to revive his inner child or to appease his lurid fantasies, but he had settled on the fact that that part of his life had ended long ago. Besides, that kind of thinking only led to trouble here in the Heaven City territories.

It wasn't long before Fred encountered his first zombie, a burly, shambling thing who stepped out of the shadows when he turned and responded to the female voice that called out for help from somewhere behind him. He could tell from the terror in her voice that she was alive as he was.

"Hello!" he yelled back. "Can you hear me?"

It surprised him how long his voice carried, each sonic round degrading slightly until the black abyss swallowed it.

Fred ran as fast as he could from the shambling zombie who replied with an inquisitive grunt to his voice, and began to chase him, clacking teeth against teeth, priming them for optimal tearing.

Lifting his knees to avoid tripping over the bodies and the assortment of limbs, Fred turned to check the growing gap between himself and the bouncing image of the shambling zombie. The man had suddenly stopped chasing him and now stood, watching him continue on, his posture translating disappointment.

Fred ran until he was completely out of breath, his lungs begging him for mercy. He turned one last time and satisfied his anxiety over the shambling zombie, whom he could no longer see, then stopped and collapsed into a hunch, his palms pressed against his knees to hold himself up.

It pained him to think of what they might have done to that poor girl, whoever she was. From the sound of her voice, he guessed that she was only in her late teens or early twenties. Maybe he had already stepped over her, or even worse, on her. Even though it sounded as if she was behind him, mixed with the darkness and the uneasiness that it created, sound had a weird way of changing direction when it bounced off these soiled walls.

Fred wanted to close his eyes and wake up to Bach or Haydn, chin-checking his chunky pillow to find the most comfortable spot and giving himself willingly to the down embrace of the Shroud of

Turin comforter that Mary gave him for Easter.

He closed his eyes and opened them.

Nothing.

The dark expanse was beginning to close in on him, pressuring a reaction, a scream at the top of his lungs, a mad dash into the heart of the void up ahead.

Then, to his immediate right, a sound... like something snapping under weight.

Fred whipped around and was confronted by an outstretched arm offering a handful of sandwich bags, each labeled to represent a specific urban affliction: poverty, crime, and addiction. His first reaction was to cover his face and shriek like a small child. Peeking out from beneath his raised forearm, Fred breathed a sigh of relief.

Unsettling as it was to look at, it was only a painting.

Fred traced the arm back to a pig's head, which had eyes that seemed to follow him no matter where he stood. It rested atop the shoulders of a police officer, its twisted smile brimming with malcontent.

He wondered exactly how many cans of spray paint it took to do something like that.

"They know you're here." A small voice materialized in a whisper from the pitch-black air around Fred's knees. "They've been stalking you. The smarter ones like to do that."

Fred stumbled backward and tripped over the first body his heels touched.

He sat up and prepared to defend himself against whomever the voice belonged to.

It was only a child, shirtless and malnourished-looking, hiding in a crawlspace behind the segmented vent at the foot of the wall. Fred could only see half of his face and his right shoulder, where the modest flame from the disposable lighter that the boy held in front of him bestowed him with a yellow-orange glow that pulsed against the darkness.

"What?????" Fred was so completely flustered that he didn't

mind the soft sticky mound that gave in spots when he pushed off of it with his palms and climbed to a squatting position. "Wh... who are you? What are you doing in there?"

"Keep your voice down," the boy responded.

"Sorry. Who are you?" This time Fred whispered.

"Doesn't matter who I am. Doesn't matter who anybody is down here. Now please go away."

The boy's reserve frightened Fred when taken in consideration with the fact that he couldn't see him too well. He found it hard to believe that a child of around 11 or 12, he guessed, could survive in this hell for more than...

"I heard a scream," Fred said.

"Wasn't me."

"Surely you must've heard it too?"

"Yeah, I heard her. But I wouldn't waste my time worrying about some girl. She's probably dead by now."

"How can you be so cold?" Fred asked. "Where are your parents anyway? Do they know where you are? They must be worried sick."

Fred maintained a panoramic view of the darkness all around him and the suggestions of light, brightest down in the vent where the kid cursed aloud and flailed his hand after burning himself with the lighter.

"My parents are dead. They're wandering around down here somewhere with the other zombies."

"So you're down here all by yourself? For how long?"

"I don't know. I stopped counting. I've been making my way east from 40th and Market, where they raided the train we were on."

"They?"

"Look where we are. Who the hell else would *they* be?"

"Your parents... were they Citizens?"

"Of course. We were on our way back from visiting my grandma. She lives on the outside."

"What, did they hire an sub-taxi?"

"Yeah, but the driver bailed when his train broke down just before 40ᵗʰ Street."

"That explains it," Fred said to himself.

"Explains what?"

Maintaining his crouched stance, Fred walked up to the vent, clutched the small square openings in its cover, and pulled his face as close as he could. *Maybe this kid was a zombie. Judging by his ability to vocalize coherent thoughts, he'd be somewhere within the first stages. Unless he was just bitten and hasn't turned yet. Maybe he had something to do with the girl's disappearance.*

Inside, Fred saw a scattered pile of candy wrappers and empty tuna, fruit, and soda cans.

"I'm a little lost myself, but if you've been heading east, then I've been going the wrong way. All we have to do keep heading east."

"We?" the boy said. "If you were smart, you'd forget about me and get the hell outta here."

"You're crazy if you think I'm just going to leave you down here."

"Please, just pretend that you never saw me."

"Like it or not, you're coming with me, kid," Fred said, committing his palms to the sludge unconditionally as he had to press them down to give his fingers all the length they could get. Reaching in through the segmented holes, two fingers to a square, Fred tugged on the vent cover. It wouldn't budge. "C'mon kid. We can help each other."

"No thanks."

"What, are you kidding me? Now get on out from there and come on."

"I said no."

"Look, kid. This is no time for you to assert your independence."

"I'm sorry, mister, but 16ᵗʰ Street is five blocks away. A lot can happen in five blocks. I'd rather take my chances alone."

"So, then we're on 21st?"

The yellow-orange glow was gone by the time Fred's eyes returned to the vent.

"Hey kid," he called out, but there was no answer.

Fred waited a few seconds, listening for the snick sound of a lighter being thumbed to life. Instead, he heard skittering limbs that thumped and slid against buckling steel followed by the echoed slap of something heavy. It was loud enough to send him to his feet and into a wide stance, braced for action. Beneath his clothes, he was shaking like a leaf.

"Hey, kid… you still there?"

Fred retraced his steps and peered inside the vent, his eyes straining to deduce shapes in the darkness. As far as he could tell, it was empty.

He continued to search, willing his eyes to look deeper until he could make out another segmented vent at the far end and the dull glint of tracks beyond it. There was another tunnel.

"Hey kid! Come back here!" he yelled. "You're going to get yourself killed."

It was more for his own peace of mind though, as the thought of being alone again crept up and tickled him in the worst way.

Somewhere off to his left, Fred heard a voice. Rasped and lethargic, it gargled out a single sentence that nearly sent him into complete shock.

"His legs are mine."

Fred's feet searched blindly for their former positioning as he crept slowly backward, extending his arms reluctantly but deliberately enough to push off of whatever his flexed digits came in contact with.

"Issat you, kid?" Fred whimpered to fill the silent gaps between seconds that felt like entire days.

His heart was poised to leap from his mouth as he lost his footing and stumbled into an erect standstill, his limbs flexed and stiff.

From the recessed wall in front of him, an old caged-lamp flickered on and shined its dull glow on more graffiti murals, emcee call-signs, modern day glyphs, shifty characters colored wicked by circumstance, and upright shadows that moved. It was then that he realized that the floor around him was clear of the bodies he had stepped over only moments ago.

Fred whipped around.

His first instinct was to run, but the crowd of zombies had him surrounded. Standing shrouded by darkness, they watched him break down mentally, his wide eyes traveling from one to the other but focusing mainly on the two who stood out in front, their shadowy figures containing fewer textured ridges and missing spots than the others.

"Please... I... I don't want any trouble," he said, fumbling with his pockets to distract himself.

Fred looked for an opening in the crowd, but there was none big enough for him to fit through without being touched.

"Fee-Fi-Fo-Fum, I smell the blood of a Saved Citi-zun," a somewhat waterlogged voice jabbed from one of the two who stood out in front.

In the distance, an approaching rumble, like a prolonged orchestral swell to punctuate drama, began to shake the floor and further unsettle Fred's jerky footing.

"Please..." Fred pleaded, backing away and eventually into a soft barrier that spun him around face to face with an old black man with a sallow, unhealthy complexion. "I can give you money."

"Nothing personal, young man," the early-staged zombie (an old black man) said with a bluesy drawl consistent with his gaunt, leather-bound look, "but the slow-rots are a bitch, and you just happened to be in the wrong place at the wrong time."

Just as he prepared to make a break, the caged lamp flickered out and left Fred in complete darkness.

"Dear God, no," Fred whimpered. His breath, like radar, bounced back immediately and gave him an idea just how close he was to something even fouler smelling than the lingering whiff of urine.

"STOP THE TRAIN!" Jessica Levy cried out as she ran from the front to the back of the single car, peering from window to window, to get as long a look as she could at the well-dressed Caucasian man (Frederick Dodd) she saw reaching out from the swarm of zombies that ambushed him. It looked like he was trying to grab the third rail and end things on his own terms.

"But you have to go back. That man… he was alive. They're going to kill him."

"And eat him," a masculine voice, heavy on dry wit, interjected from behind.

"Don't look at me, lady. Technically, you're on *his* dime," Ol' Reds, the driver, growled through cigar-stained teeth, snatching her away from the previous remark, then sending her right back with a head jerk toward the man who spoke it, a walking arsenal named Nat Bradley, who sat unaffected in the middle of the otherwise empty train car. Swarthy and thick-skinned, his experienced brown eyes were perfectly spaced and alive with off-kilter passion that in the right light could be mistaken for lunatic calm. "I shouldn't have even stopped for you, but he wanted to see if you knew anything about his bounty."

"Bounty? You mean the boy?" Jessica queried.

Nat nodded.

"How old did you say he is… was?"

"He'll be 13 in a week," Nat said.

"And he's been down here how long?"

"Three days."

"Three days?" Jessica whined. "You must be high if you think he's still alive out there."

"I was hired by his family to find him." Nat said. "Until I have proof that he isn't, I'm going to have to assume he's alive."

"Oh, and in the meantime, anyone else who could use your help, like that man back there, is just shit out of luck unless they pay you?"

"Something like that." Nat replied.

Disgusted, Jessica turned to Ol' Reds.

"Can't you just stop this thing and go back?"

"How many walkers we talking about out there?" Ol' Reds quipped out the side of his head, leaning to the right out the open door of the booth he sat in.

"Two... three dozen at least...." Nat responded for her.

Without saying a word, Ol' Reds tossed eyes to Jessica, looking her up and down before raising his bushy eyebrows and straightening himself in his seat.

"Hate to say it, but I'm afraid you're shit out of luck, lady."

Jessica ran to the back window and pressed her cheek against the filthy glass. It was difficult to see through the darkness, so she waited for the cage lamps to come back to life. They had been flickering on and off at their own leisure.

Flashing on with a heavy-handed punch, the cage lamp on the wall above Frederick Dodd brought with it... Fred from the waist up, moving tempestuously as he curled his fingers and anchored them in the gritty, textured floor of a large puddle left to marinate for decades. He braced his arms to drag his weight forward, but he was interrupted by a heavy boot smashing down with deliberate thrust against the small of his back.

As he cried out in pain, a ragged looking zombie leaned over and bit off his nose and top lip. Rubber-band strips of flesh connected their mouths until the gradual grinding caused the ragged zombie's teeth to meet and sent the excess skin snapping back to Fred's face.

Instead of reacting to the new wound, Fred's trembling hands balled into fists and swung blindly at any and everything, backing a few of the zombies away just long enough to turn and lunge for the third rail again. Though he fell short, he stretched his arm and twisted his shoulder in a way that looked as if he might dislocate it. He cried out repeatedly as they went to town on his legs, back, and left ear, but he was determined to abbreviate his own death.

Jessica whimpered loudly, her hands cupping the lower half of her face, her dirty fingertips redirecting the flow of tears and muffling her deep-throated gasps. Her green eyes widened as she laser-locked her gaze on the shrinking scene against the advice of the voice that told her to look away.

In the growing distance, an electric POP colored the outline of a man (Fred). His right hand clutched the third rail while the rest of his body hovered a clear foot off the ground and twitched into strange positions. The waylaying snap of raw wattage snatched the top two layers of repugnant zombies up out of the electric glow's reach.

Jessica spun away from the window and closed her eyes.

"I don't understand why we can't just stop and help him," she cried.

"Look lady…" Nat said. "If this guy wasn't dead a minute ago, then I can guarantee you he's dead now."

"Or as good as dead," Ol' Reds added.

"From your clothes, I'd say that you're doing pretty well for yourself up in the territories. You show me some money and I'll go back and get the poor bastard's corpse for you. How's that?"

"Ugggggh!" Jessica growled and stormed back to the front of the car. "And for your information, I don't live in the territories. I was…."

Jessica had become so used to keeping things secret that she stopped herself before she rambled right into a death sentence. Neither of these men looked like Citizens (the sub-taxi drivers hardly ever were), but she had lived so long undercover that she didn't trust anyone, especially after what happened to her earlier in the day.

"So you're an illegal, huh?" Nat grinned.

Jessica wasn't sure if she should answer honestly. The look on her face spoke for her.

"What, did they catch you and throw you down here as

punishment?"

"I came down here on my own, sort of," she replied after a long, brooding pause. "A coworker, who I thought was my friend, ratted me out. I ran as soon as I saw her in my manager's office. I made it outside when the lockdown alarm sounded. If I hadn't found that open shutter at the 15th Street entrance, I'd be Swiss cheese by now."

Jessica was on the run from a band of zombies who were feasting on Samuel Glover when she walked up on them. If the train hadn't come when it did, if she hadn't been standing directly in its path....

She was lucky that Ol' Reds was a sucker for a pretty face. Most of the drivers would've run her right over. In fact, she readily accepted that it was going to and tucked into a ball when the train, painted to look like a giant great white shark, bit through the darkness, its enormous mouth stretched wide open as if lunging for dangling chum. If Ol' Reds hadn't slammed on the brakes when he did, raising the low rumble to a metallic whine that tested her eardrums, she would've wound up beneath the car like the zombies who chased her, writhing, dissected, and pinned down by the heavy steel wheelframe.

"Yee Haw!" she heard from somewhere above the gaping jaws that loomed over her. Although his voice was raspy and damaged in its own right, the clarity with which Ol' Reds spoke dragged her eyes open and up to see his big arms and barrel-chest leaning out the side window. "You alive down there?"

"Yeah," she responded.

For the first five minutes after she got on the train, Jessica welcomed the sound of that gravelly voice. It reminded her of the rush of adrenaline that overcame her upon being rescued from what promised to be a painfully brutal demise. But the novelty was wearing thin as he went on and on about things for which she had no concern.

"You ask anyone from the city," he boasted. "Ask 'em who's

the best sub-taxi driver down in the tunnels...."

"Lemme guess," Nat mumbled out. "They'll say Ol' Reds?"

Ol' Reds paused and flashed eyes that questioned, rounding the corner to a scowl, but not fully committing. Nat never turned his head from the window he'd been staring out, or maybe he was looking at his reflection against the dark beyond.

"Yeah, that's right," Ol' Reds replied, salting his words with a smidgen of 'fuck you.'

Jessica's head, swirling with half-thoughts and shaky-cam footage of gore set to foreboding mental music, struggled to stay afloat in the turbulent waters of everything and nothing.

Jessica used her eyes to fill in the blanks as she compiled mental profiles on Ol' Reds, then Nat, who sat solemnly allowing the rocking train to shake him like a rag doll. For every rambling paragraph from Ol' Reds, he responded maybe once or twice.

Even now, he rambled on. Eventually Jessica caught on to the weird grunts and throat clearing in their conversation as references to her as she pouted in her seat.

"So, what do you think of the unh-unh, or ahem?" they would say.

Maybe she was feeling a bit catatonic at the moment, but she certainly wasn't deaf. She had Ol' Reds's face memorized just from the continuous peeking out of his booth to check on her as he spoke boisterously and indefinitely, it seemed, about everything under the sun. Somehow, it always came back to his job.

"I was the first!" he kept repeating. "Ol' Betsy here is the oldest in the fleet."

There were only four left, down from 12 when the subterranean taxi service started in 2015, back when things were a bit more official. Now it was every driver for themselves.

For a price that most couldn't afford, they'd take you anywhere along the old routes. Throwbacks to escort services in the far east and old west, the sub-taxi drivers, made up of meaty-armed, skiptracer types, reveled in their one-man-army sensibilities, decorating their cars to fit their individual personalities, like the great white shark of Ol' Reds.

Chapter 12

Mikel rounded the corner to the gymnasium and almost ran right into the two mechanics who had just burst through the double doors marked GY N UM and were running top speed away from… something.

"Get back! He's gonna kill somebody with that thing," the first mechanic, Kyle Dex, said, pointing toward the gym.

As he ran past, Mikel noticed that Kyle's naked skin was visible through the hole burned to blackened edges in the left side of his overalls around the thigh and ribs.

Snapping his gun-arm straight up from where it rested at his side, Mikel grabbed the second mechanic, Chip Davis, by the wrist as he zipped by on the other side of him.

"Who's gonna kill somebody? What's going on?"

"It's your friend, the detective. He's got the damaged tank."

"And how the hell did he manage to do that?" Mikel asked in a semi-accusatory tone.

"Me and Dex were overhauling the laser-prop. He must've snuck by us. By the time we realized what was going on, he was already strapped in. You should see what he did to Dex."

The ground shook from a muffled BOOM that caused Mikel and Chip to whip toward the gym while simultaneously stepping back away from it.

Mikel holstered his handgun and inched cautiously toward the double doors.

"This is the second time since you've been gone," Chip added.

"Great!" Mikel replied as he paused with his back to the wall catty-cornered from the right side door. For the past three weeks, he had been in Washington, meeting with leaders from the various pockets of resistance sprinkled throughout the outlands in preparation for the coup that the Left Hand was planning.

With a nod, Mikel ordered Chip, who was of no use to him in his flustered state, to a safe distance, then counted to three and yanked the door open.

Kane's legs were cramping up something fierce, as he hadn't had time to worry about finding a comfortable position when he entered the Series 11 Urban Infantry Tank. Though battle-worn, and rusted, it was a much more advanced model than the one he tested six years ago. The upgraded controls were easy enough to figure out once he had a chance to play with them a little.

He spent the first time, a week ago, turning the tank on and off, raising and lowering the arms, and lifting the torso from stationary to roaming position before Kyle and Chip managed to stop him.

This time he tried to take it on a walk around the room on three good legs. The fourth, unbeknownst to Kane, had taken a few too many hits from heavy artillery when Dylan Ross, Mikel's closest confidant, and interim director in his absence, jacked the tank from an Archangel.

Kane pulled with all his diminished strength on the steering lever to keep the tank from falling backward as the left rear leg buckled and stuck at the knee/elbow joint with every step and jerked him around violently.

His wiry arms flailed as a result, his hands landing on buttons that he hadn't intended to push the flamethrower, for instance, that singed Kyle Dex's oily clothing, and the main cannon that coughed out wild blasts into the four walls and made them crumble.

Mikel had just missed being struck by debris when he ran in and immediately dove back through the door into the hallway.

"Fuck!" he yelled, picking himself up off the floor and patting away the dust that covered his head and shoulders in a speckled layer into clouds of white powder.

Mikel turned to Chip Davis, who was still standing at the end of the hall.

"Get some heavy arms down here, now!" he said, and then ran past Chip, around the corner, and down the hall toward the rear entrance to the gym.

Luckily, Kane didn't see Mikel come in and leave. As far as he knew, Mikel was his only link to his past, and the last person on earth he'd ever want to hurt.

Kane worked at the controls, but the tank continued to buck and jerk him around.

"Kane! The green button to the right of the steering column.... Press it!"

Kane was both relieved and embarrassed to hear Mikel's voice coming from the internal speaker. He timed the wild bucking, and during a momentary lull looked through the cracked cockpit window (the newer models had done away with the solid-steel dome) at the control booth by the rear door and glimpsed Mikel standing over another panel full of complicated buttons, levers, and blinking lights.

"Tried it. The damn thing's stuck," Kane said.

Mikel fingered a button directly in front of him and leaned forward toward the microphone that jutted up and out from the panel.

"They should've told you that it was damaged. You're going to have to reach under the panel and sever the main line. It's a thick, black cable wrapped in small red wires."

"Got it," Kane replied, forcing himself into an impossible position to get at the wires by his knees. Looking down out the corner of his right eye, he found the black cable wrapped in smaller red ones and tugged at it until he felt it snap.

There was a deep whirling sound that preceded the power shutting off completely. The tank gave him one last buck and sank into dormancy with a hiss. Its arms fell hard and banged against its sides.

Kane took a deep breath.

"Just to be fair to those two mechanics, they did tell me that it was broken. I just didn't listen."

*   *   *

"Look Kane, I know you're anxious to get back on your feet and contribute, but it's going to take some time," Mikel said as they walked down the hall crowded with guards holding big guns and annoyed expressions from being asked to drop what they were doing and help out with the tank.

Kane felt bad that he put Mikel in this position. He got the feeling that the men around here saw him as a nuisance, like a sickly old relative. Kane was nearly half his former size, having lost 75 pounds and a significant portion of his memories during the coma.

"I wish I could make you understand how hard it is to go to sleep a strong, formidable guy and wake up like this," Kane said, holding his arms up to allow the loose fabric of his oversized shirt to dangle. "I see the way your men look at me. I'm like a pariah around here."

Kane had been working himself like a dog (and eating like one) to get back in shape, but the stronger he got, the louder Carlos McCann's voice became in his head, and the more difficult it was for him to ignore his taunting. Thus Kane settled into his new skin-and-bones look.

"Unfortunately, we lost a few good men trying to get you out of the old hospital in University City. A girl who used to work for us recognized you when she was looking for her sister in the ward where they kept all the John Does. She had seen your picture in my office."

"How long was I there?"

"No idea. It was only about a year ago that we found you. You actually opened your eyes as we were wheeling you out. Do you remember any of that?"

"Not really."

"Anyway, the UCC got wind of our little rescue mission and decided to raid the hospital. A lot of innocent people died that day."

Kane wanted to say something, but sorry just didn't seem

good enough, and that was all he could think of.

"UCC?"

Mikel stepped into the path of Sgt. Perez, a meaty-faced bruiser-type.

"Sergeant, see to it that Kyle Dex and Chip Davis have their training updated."

"The mechanics?"

"That's right."

"They've all had the basics, sir."

"Okay, well I'm instituting a new rule, effective immediately. All Left Hand personnel under my authority are to receive mandatory advanced field training. Suppose Detective Kane, here, was an Archangel, or a spy for the UCC?"

"Yes, sir. I understand your point, sir. I'll get somebody on it immediately."

"No, not somebody. I want *you* to do it, Sergeant."

"Yes, sir," Sgt. Perez said and walked away.

In the background, Kane had been trying not to smile the whole time. Now that it was just the two of them again, he let the corners of his mouth run until they pulled his dry lips apart and revealed his teeth. He hadn't shaved in a few days, so a scruffy beard surrounded them. He was genuinely proud, like a father.

From Kane's perspective, the missing time lent Mikel's metamorphosis from lost boy into leader a magical quality.

Mikel still looked pretty much the same, except for the look on his face. Before, it was angry, almost scowling, but now there was a sense of nobility and strength, and an overall glint of experience in his big brown eyes.

Kane searched for something to say that might convey his paternal delight in a somewhat masculine way, something that wouldn't sound too ingratiating.

"You really have grown into quite a man."

"It's only been six years, man."

"I know, but this whole thing is weird for me. Everything, everyone seems so... different."

"Yeah, a lot has happened since 2015."

"I guess so."

"Have you been outside yet?"

"Yeah."

"That's right," Mikel said. "You weren't even around for Judgment Day, huh?"

"Probably better that I missed it."

Mikel chuckled.

"You're right, there. Knowing you, you would've tried to bust Augustus during his big speech, right?"

"Big speech?"

"You should have seen it. The whole thing was like a big fucking circus with Augustus and his boys running things from the Vatican...."

"So you know?"

"Know what?"

"Who he... who Jesus really is?"

"Everybody does."

"Well, then, why is everyone still..."

"It's a long story, Kane. I'll try my best to give you the abridged version," Mikel said.

"Well, it ain't like I don't have the time on my hands," Kane replied.

"So, like I was saying, Judgment Day was nuts. People were trampling one another to get into the designated churches; there were huge riots between protesters, who did everything they could to interrupt the process, and the suckers who fell for it. There were bombings, shootings, you name it."

"So how did the whole process work? What, was it like an election?"

"Basically. First you had to register by filling out an application for Saved Citizenship, which was like a glorified job application with a section for all your financial information and a book-length essay section where you were supposed to write about your life and why you felt you were worthy. Then, those who were selected were called to the designated churches, which worked like polling centers, where they spent all day praying and watching the big ceremony broadcasted live from the Vatican."

"Hard to believe I slept through all that," Kane half-joked. He glanced at the camera up on the wall, and followed it as it pivoted to follow them down the hall.

"Like you said, you were probably better off. The next few months were spent clearing out the people who weren't saved ('heathens,' they called them) from what was to become the Heaven City territories. The ones who refused to leave were forcibly removed, or killed. The news reports sugarcoated everything to look like this grand event in history. There were celebrations and parades, and fireworks, which helped to drown out the noise while Augustus and his new UCC... ah... United Christian Conglomerate army took care of the heathens. If you were saved, then you got a card in the mail sort of like a license, see?"

Mikel held up an ID card with a small holographic photo of himself on the bottom left side. At the top, bold letters spelled out **'SAVED CITIZENSHIP IDENTIFICATION CARD,'** followed by a barcode.

"You wouldn't believe what we had to go through to get our hands on the technology to duplicate these," Mikel said. "Remind me to get you one made up."

Rather than try to wrap his head around everything at once, Kane focused on a few things at a time.

"Where were they planning on sending these people who didn't believe?"

"If you applied and weren't selected for Saved Citizenship, then you were left to fend for yourself out here, on the other side. They call it Purgatory. Believe it or not, there are plenty of small communities struggling to survive, but surviving nonetheless, out here. All you really need are weapons, a good, steady source of food, water, gas which is the hardest to come by and a bit of organization."

"What about the zombies? There seem to be fewer of them now."

"Hardly. They've just learned to stay away from the people with the big guns. You walk about two blocks in either direction from here and you'll find them. They tend to only pick on the weak and unarmed, mostly. But you still have the daring ones who'll attack anything that moves."

"I didn't think it would actually get to that... to this point. What about the Coalition, or the Secular Soldiers, or the Dziko Nation? I'm sure they had something to say about all this."

"We all knew it was a battle we couldn't win, not fighting it directly anyway, so we laid back and strategized."

"And what, after six years, you still haven't come up with a plan?"

"Well, it's not as simple as just rushing in half-cocked. There have been attempts."

"Any successful ones?"

Mikel hesitated.

"No. Not yet. Eventually, the groups that you remember fell apart. People died, or lost their marbles, or just gave up the fight and applied to live in the territories. They still accept people, but the waiting list is supposed to be miles long. What was left of them merged into what we have here, the Left Hand."

"So, how do *you* fit into all this? Whatever happened with the station, or with Allison?"

Mikel was hoping Kane wouldn't ask about her. He knew they had a history, and no matter how much Kane bitched about her back then, that he had feelings for her, even if he hid them from himself.

Mikel had known love since the last time he and Kane spent any real time together, so he knew how important it was to feel wanted, needed, to know that someone was thinking of him even when he wasn't around. Loneliness was a bitch in a world overflowing with walking death.

Her name was Ana, and she was the love of Mikel's life. They were eventually married at the old 13th Precinct, on the same day that she later disappeared. Mikel had been searching for her ever since.

Speaking of love and loss, Mikel had originally planned to bring up the truth about Jason's death at some point when Kane finally woke up, to tell him that he knew that Kane had lied to him back when he first asked about it. A psychic had told Mikel exactly what happened at the Megamart, but that was over a year ago, and he had since learned to deal with it. He would've done the same thing had he been there. Considering Jason's condition at the time, death was the best thing for him.

"Well… you might want to sit down for this one," Mikel said.

"Just give it to me straight," Kane replied.

"She's dead, Kane. She was bitten. She tried to fight it at first, but when it became too much for her, she asked me to help her end it. So I gave her a pulse grenade, and she blew herself to bits."

Kane was surprisingly calm. In his mind, Allison was better off dead than giving in to Augustus' bullshit, as he suspected she might have done.

"I'm sorry, man," Mikel said, placing his hand on Kane's bony shoulder.

Kane nodded.

"I took over at the station after that, but the few people I managed to recruit couldn't even hold a gun the right way, let alone stand still long enough to shoot the fucking zombies. When the Left Hand was looking to expand into Philly four years ago, I joined up, and the rest is history."

"You mentioned earlier about spies when you stopped that soldier. Why couldn't Augustus just snap his fingers and do away with all of you?"

"He's not as strong as he used to be. The night you were shot, he and Yeshua had it out. The plan was to jack into the broadcast satellite and film everything live. They... the Coalition, the Secular Soldiers, and the DN... knew that Augustus would show his true colors."

"And when the public saw him in his true light, their faith would crumble."

"Basically."

"So what happened?"

"It backfired. Augustus got hip to the plan and turned the tables on them, but not before enough people saw it, and him. He lost a lot of followers that night. Surprisingly... or not, considering that you're probably the biggest cynic that I know, most of them remained faithful. They called the footage a hoax. Since then, we've learned that we can use psychics to block or redirect his power, and cloud his vision. It's worked out quite well for us. We take them with us everywhere we go."

"You mean that flaky bunch I saw sitting in a circle meditating?"

"Yep, that's them. Then again, you might've seen a class in session. Some of them work as instructors here, teaching either chi kung, meditation, or yoga. But we always have a few of them on guard duty, I guess you could call it."

Kane shook his head and smirked.

"What?" Mikel said.

"What's to keep them... these psychics from picking your, or anybody else's, brain around here and using the information against you?"

"They wouldn't do that. Not the ones we have here. We have a rule that they aren't allowed to psych-scan anyone without that person's consent unless there is probable cause."

"You sound so sure," Kane said. "Don't you think you're being a bit naïve? There's one, in particular, who comes to mind: blond guy, about 5'8", green eyes, Danish accent. He's always watching me. Bugs me out."

"You mean Professor Janssen?" Mikel replied. "He and Master Pan are two of our most powerful psychics. The professor heads the program, in fact. Master Pan was my martial arts teacher from years back, believe it or not."

"Short, Chinese guy with the long hair?"

"Chinese-Vietnamese actually, but yeah, that's him."

"I'll be sure to keep my eye on him too," Kane said.

Whatever it was about Denmark that sparked a flash of memory just as quickly fizzled out before Kane could examine its significance.

"Nah… you're being too cynical, Kane. These guys have got too much on their plates to be focusing on you." Mikel was lying through his teeth.

In fact, Professor Janssen had warned Mikel not to bring Kane here when he was in the coma. He said that Kane would be the death of them, that he had known of him for years.

The professor's vision pertaining to Kane was like a broken puzzle that was missing several key pieces. What stuck with him though was the feeling of great pain and sorrow that it always left him with.

He had broken the rules and attempted to psych-scan Kane from outside his room when he was asleep, but there was something blocking him, which only fed the professor's suspicion.

But Mikel had come to learn that the future wasn't set in stone, that the psychics' visions were of a possible future, one that could be changed. He had to remind his men of that fact. They wanted Kane out when they heard.

Kane never knew any of this.

"So, what ever happened to Yeshua?" Kane asked.

"He's… like a vegetable… for now. Been that way since the fight. He's being kept under heavy guard at our Atlanta base."

"They told me that you were at some kind of meeting at the Washington headquarters."

"Yeah, that six-year plan you alluded to, remember?" Mikel smirked. "Speaking of which, how comfortable did you feel with the Series 11... I mean, aside from the malfunctions?"

"It was a little different from the model I tested, but it shouldn't be too hard to figure out."

"Good. I'll have someone work on getting that fixed in the next week or so. We've managed to snag quite a few of them I think 25 altogether among all the Left Hand branches. We originally had two here. One was destroyed along with its driver, Ray Curtis. Good man.... The other guy, Jackson, who was learning to use the damaged one, went AWOL a few weeks ago, and we haven't seen him since. So we're gonna need..."

As they passed a classroom on their left, Mikel noticed a particular zombie, who was being used in a hand-to-hand demo in front of a group of soldiers. His name was Max Hedberg. Mikel had become attached to this one ever since he started flipping through the journal that Max had been keeping up until the end of his life. They found him undead in his own panic shelter, along with his wife, who had gotten out of the freezer where she was being kept. They also found parts of a little boy his son, Eric, they guessed. Someone, probably his own mother, had eaten most of him.

Mikel would read the journal to Max, who would just stand there, leering hungrily at him through the bars of the cell where they kept the zombies to be used for training purposes. He wondered if hearing his own words would somehow reach Max through the zombie miasma. Not likely, it seemed, until Mikel mentioned Maria or Eric. It was a slight response, sort of a twitching above his right eye, but it was something.

"Hey!" Mikel yelled at Teagan Ryman, the instructor, who held Max, who was growling and snapping at air, in a headlock to demonstrate a difficult neck break. "I gave orders not to touch this one."

Mikel and Ana Sitting in a Tree, K-I-L-L-I-N-G

2017 PA.

Growing up deep in the shit of urbania had given Mikel insight that he never expected to appreciate the way he did now. He wouldn't change it for the world; not a fucking lick of it. That dead stare of his had gotten him laid more times than he could count. Those arms, thick and sinewy, had won him countless fights. Down in the shit, there were battles to be fought on a daily basis.

Despite the gore, the death, the brutal apathy with which the world seemed to operate these days, and the fucking smell, it was an exciting time for Mikel. He had just taken over as head of the 13th Precinct, which at that point operated like a glorified militia, and he was in love. He liked to think that he didn't need a woman in his life except as an occasional tool to satiate his lust, but Ana changed all that. He was so intoxicated by her scent, her caramel complexion, her flowing braids, and those eyes, like polished glass beneath which the most brilliant shade of hazel seemed to exist separate from the rest of her, sentient orbs capable of taming the most savage of hearts and making even dead men stop what they were doing to pay tribute to her unabashed magnetism. He thanked… well, he stopped short of thanking God for bringing her to him. It was an old habit, like God bless you, or Goddamn, that proved almost impossible to shake.

The 13th Precinct was where they first shared their mutual losses over bad coffee and reacted to occasional jump-scares whenever some audacious zombie somehow managed to get in the building. Ana had wandered in looking to align with a quality group after spending a year and a half on her own.

Before that, she lived with her parents, who both died when heavy rain flooded their hastily built shelter and forced them outside in search of another. Her father sacrificed himself so that she could escape the crowd of fast-moving zombies that rushed them.

Ana used to be so timid. She was just like her mother. Since the deaths of her parents, she worked hard to make herself a worthy opponent for any zombie that wanted to taste her flesh, or anyone else who tried to touch her without her permission, for that matter. Their colleagues at the 13th had come up with a song to mock their weird union of practiced aggression, a twisted cover of an old rhyme: "Mikel and Ana sitting in a tree, K-I-L-L-I-N-G!"

After only six weeks of knowing each other, Mikel and Ana were discussing marriage beneath cum-stained sheets.

One of the first things Mikel noticed in his new leadership role was that down here, people generally weren't ready to accept that their loved ones had passed, so they kept them around, usually hidden away in some cold, sparsely furnished basement or attic, dressing them up like low-end department-store mannequins and slathering their sullen flesh with excessive amounts of make-up that gave the men a skewed androgynous veneer and made the women look like whores. It was a syndrome that he was familiar with in the community, but usually with severely mentally challenged relatives.

In the end, it made them easier to spot. When they eventually became a burden, the majority were let go to wander the streets.

Although most of them had disbanded by 2020, the explosion of neighborhood posses somewhere around mid-2016 brought with it a certain sense of unity, missing from the black community since the sixties and seventies. It piggy-backed the down wind, and electrified blunted enthusiasm, planting seeds of creativity and ideas of oneness with the common man unless that man was from a different neighborhood.

Groups with colorful names like the Alpha Mob, the New World Soldiers of Freedom, DOA Squad, and the Council of Men in Action policed their respective neighborhoods from city to city. Over time (usually within six months), many regressed to loose organizations of street thugs dabbling in drugs and prostitution and ruling through intimidation.

Dealing with posses gone bad was Mikel's specialty.

Even the Archangels wouldn't dare come through here. Not after what happened to Lin Su and Lin Kwei. They were ambushed by a contingent of several posses a year ago. It was comprised mainly of members of the Alpha Mob.

Commissioner Lin (Ho), with his overplayed "I will avenge my brothers" agenda and that six-inch scar down the left side of his face, still hadn't managed to make his way back west to make good on his threat.

Mikel lost count of exactly how many times he watched the footage of their bodies being dragged down the street, strung up on lazy-leaning light posts and jeered by crowds of regressed humanity with little to lose and high on moments of extreme intensity to substitute for any real sense of living.

Wedding Day

An innocuous din exploded outward from total silence as the ragtag audience, flushed with vicarious sensations, watched Mikel and Ana seal their eternal union with a kiss.

The fractured pipe organ bellowed a rasped rendition of "Here Comes the Bride," yanking Mikel from the freefall into Ana's sturdy embrace, chasing away the vision of clouds and eternal blue sky, and the smell of springtime.

"I love you." Her tone rose and fell in such a way that made it sound so truly genuine each time.

"I... I love you more."

Ana smiled, warmed by Mikel's shyness.

Wiping away the hints of sweat from his forehead, she led him down the aisle and out the front doors.

Mikel felt small, naked amid the leaning wall of bodies with limbs reaching out, fingers touching and groping them affectionately. A gallery of smiles lunged at him like flashbulbs at some red-carpet Hollywood spectacle. He tried not to look as nervous as he was. He felt silly for letting the whole thing get to him, silly for being one of those guys who couldn't bear to show emotion.

Why don't you just fucking relax, he liked to tell himself during moments like these.

"We ready back there?" the limo driver yelled back to Mikel and Ana in response to the usher's tap, tap on the tinted window. He spoke with a thick-tongued slur that went unnoticed by Mikel and Ana in their moment of glory.

"Ready," Mikel blurted as he sunk into the seat, watching with quiet envy as Ana poked her torso through the sun-roof and fired her rifle into the air.

"Wooo Hooo! That's Mrs. Williamson, dammit!" she yelled playfully.

Mikel felt a rush of camaraderie when the crowd did the same thing in response.

Now that the car had begun its slow monorail crawl away from the front steps, Mikel could see in the gathered faces all the genuine affection that he failed to appreciate on his walk to the limo. Looking up, he noticed the strange patch of optimistic blue in the otherwise drab orange sky directly above the Precinct building; the way the sun's rays seemed to single out the archway above the front door and steps where the crowd still congregated; and something else that took him by surprise....

Cupping his face in her hand, Ana turned Mikel away from the window to face her, but she failed to snag his eyes, which rolled back to the crowd as if he feared missing something important.

"Look at you," she whispered through heavily painted lips that glistened and popped with moist smacking sounds. "This is supposed to be the happiest day of our lives, and you look like you're about to keel over. Don't tell me you're having second thoughts."

"It's nothing like that, babe." He tried, with a blithe tone, to dissuade her from pursuing this line of questioning so that he might figure out why he was almost certain that he saw Ted Hayes, the limo driver, run out from behind a parked car in his underwear.

Ana was about to call him on his half-hearted response until she read his anxious body language and felt the sudden shift in his mood.

"What is it? What's got you spooked?"

Rather than come right out and tell her to SHUT THE FUCK UP, like he wanted to do so that he could think clearly, Mikel directed Ana's eyes out the back window to the crowd. They had stopped waving them on to assist the stout man, clothed only in his underwear, who stumbled out into the middle of the street, fighting against the ropes, or maybe the duct tape that bound his hands together.

"Who is…? Is that…?"

"I think so," Mikel groaned beneath his breath as his head whipped from the crowd to the back of the driver's head up front.

Ana's gleeful enthusiasm withered before his eyes. Even with her penchant for tough-girl posturing, she still came with all the usual anxieties associated with women on their wedding day. As such, she found it difficult to direct her anger at anything specific.

Mikel felt a little of it as he grabbed her rifle from her lap, pressed the tip of the barrel into the soft leather barrier that separated them from the driver, and placed a finger to his lips to keep her from giving away his plan.

He felt stupid for failing to notice the telltale undead hue that the driver concealed beneath his raised collar. Had he been looking for it, Mikel reassured himself that he'd have seen it right away.

Women weaken knees. He remembered his uncle's words… words that he lived by until he met Ana and decided the time was right to let down his guard.

"'Scuse me… driver?" Mikel said. "You wanna tell us what

the FUCK is going on here?"

Neither of them was prepared for the jolt of sudden acceleration that tossed them against their seats and incited a knee-jerk reaction from Mikel's trigger-finger.

Ana cowered from the barrel's stuttered roar as Mikel fired into the ceiling.

"Stop the fucking car!" he demanded, readjusting his aim under duress.

Mikel fired off a short burst that smacked the driver in the back and caused him to briefly lose control of the wheel as he arched away from the spray of infected blood and dispersed foam.

Mikel pressed his weight against Ana, wedging her between himself and the door to keep her from sliding along the seat as the limo careened erratically.

The driver twisted as if working out a spasm somewhere in his back and stepped on the gas. He turned and lowered his Wayfarers to reveal eyes heavily clouded-over and flashed a corroded smile through horribly chapped lips lined with dried blood.

"Damon Campbell sends his regards," the driver slurred out.

To most people around here, Damon Campbell and his Alpha Mob represented all that was wrong with the neighborhood posses.

"Son of a BITCH!" Mikel groaned.

"I knew it!" Ana yelled. "Didn't I tell you he'd do something like this?"

"Not now, Ana."

"We wouldn't be in this mess *right now* if you'd listened to me. And on my wedding day for fuck's sake. All I asked for was one fucking day... one fucking day without..."

Mikel shoved Ana face-first into the seat cushion. Upon impact, Ana blurted out an unintentional grunt. She recoiled instantly and whipped around ready to reciprocate until she saw the long barrel swing around and pass just over her head. Through his motions alone, Ana caught wind of Mikel's plan.

Digging his foot into the carpeted floor, Mikel pulled the trigger and blew out the back window.

"Now look, baby," he said, knocking away the lingering shards of glass with the barrel. "I know how important today is to you... to us, but right now I need you to put that aside and follow my lead."

"Just gimme the gun," she snapped, reaching as if she fully expected him to comply. "I'll finish his crusty ass right now."

Mikel was halfway out the thin, rectangular window, volleying between the few wedding guests who chased their limo on foot, Ana, and the old nursing home on Walnut that approached fast on the other side of the front windshield, beyond the driver's bobbing head.

"Not an option," he yelled. "As fast as we're going, we probably wouldn't survive the crash. We have a better chance if we jump. Whatever you do, don't fight the momentum once you hit the ground. Just roll with it, and you should be okay. Now come on!"

Ana glanced down, through the side window, at the blurred street beneath them. Shaking her head, she fought back tears of frustration and climbed to her knees.

Watching them through the rearview, the driver sneered and yanked the wheel right, then left, and caused Mikel to fall to his belly and flail for the nearest object to keep him from sliding off of the trunk.

Ana, who caught herself in mid-slide, immediately leapt up and cradled Mikel's legs in a sturdy embrace as the driver continued his zigzagged course. He had turned to check on them when they slid out of the rearview's range.

"Okay! I'm okay," Mikel yelled and nodded for her to let go. "I'm gonna go on three."

Though she eventually relinquished her grip, Ana held on a while longer as if she knew that this might be the last time they touched.

Stifling the urge to stop him from jumping, she spoke softly and with obvious trepidation.

"Please be careful, babe."

Mikel saw the reservation in her eyes when they stared deeply at each other before he began to count. It troubled him that her faith in his plan was somewhat muddled, but he knew it was only due to her concern for his safety.

"I love you," she said.

"I love you more."

Turning back to the road, Mikel took a deep breath and blocked out any attempt his mind made to discern what might happen should he or Ana land incorrectly.

"One... two... three..."

There was an exact point at which time began to slow. It started with a lag, like the effect of old neglected film negotiating the twists and turns of an even older projector, then POP!

Strangely, the street below approached faster than Mikel fell. It was the only thing that moved in real time. Yellow lane markers raced by in a blur that gave them the appearance of one solid line. Wondering exactly when he should tuck and prepare to roll, he stuck his arms out, fingers spread wide, ready to grasp the blacktop and break his fall. Funny that now he wasn't nearly as confident as he had been before he jumped.

Until he tucked his chin to his chest and threw his torso down and under, Mikel hadn't even noticed that Ana was still inside the limo. The driver had slammed on the brakes just as he jumped and sent her toppling back into her seat.

Mikel zeroed in on her as she sat unconscious and slumped in the back seat facing him.

Mikel had just enough time to acknowledge the iron butterflies that weighed down his stomach and the sour hint of vomit that teased his throat before the ground came calling.

He twisted and turned at the peak of each sloppy bounce, attempting to steer himself before gravity snatched him back down.

As soon as he stopped, Mikel sprung dizzily to his feet and

ran, gasping for air, after the limo. Fatigue soon gave way to nausea as he watched Ana bounce from corner to corner of his shaky-cam point of view. The hastily framed portrait of her, bordered in jagged bits of treated glass, was shrinking by the second.

"Please, Ana. If you can hear me, please JUMP! JUMP GODDAMMIT! JUMP!" Mikel yelled in desperation as his mind began to digest the fact that he might never see the love of his life again. For all he knew, she was already dead from the impact.

Ignoring staunch opposition from his heart, lungs, and, most of all, his rubber legs, Mikel continued on, his arms reaching out as if to bring him that much closer to Ana. He promised himself that he'd never stop trying to find her, even if it killed him, even if he knew that she was most likely dead already.

Mikel knew what was coming next. He could tell from the way the cerebral static interference crept in from the corners of his view and offered catatonia as an alternative to consciousness.

Still he soldiered on, running on empty, yet managing to keep himself upright, his waning eyesight reduced to a pinpoint of activity surrounded by darkness. Within the circular frame, a vision of beauty floated just beyond his reach. From this fractured perspective, staring down his outstretched arm and over his extended fingers, Ana appeared close enough to touch, and small enough to scoop up in his palm and carry away to safety.

The next thing Mikel knew, he was lying on the ground.

To his left came the sound of metal fencing rattling and expanding under pressure. He turned and saw the old Peterson High School building. The playground out front was surrounded by old fencing and at least 100 zombies leering and growling at him from the other side. They pushed against each other to get a better view and to join in the struggle to topple the fence and devour his flesh. The aggressive ones had begun to climb to the top and quickly found themselves tangled in razor wire. Still they thrashed about, their eyes locked on Mikel, who just lay there, spent to hell and contemplating life and all the little nuances of loss.

Knowing that Ana was either dead or worse, Mikel tried to write her off like he'd done Jason and so many of his close friends. If Ana was walking, dead, then he owed it to her to put her down. They made sure to include that in their vows. Only now he was having second thoughts. He wasn't sure he could bear to see her like that.

Mikel watched a five-foot section of the fence, behind which the bulk of the zombies seemed to congregate, come falling down with a CLANG that was deadened by the pile of bodies that slapped the pavement milliseconds later and tumbled messily over each other. As if the memory of living flesh hit them all at once, they looked up simultaneously and spotted Mikel lying there.

Crawling and stepping over one another, they started toward him, hissing, snarling, and staring dumbfounded, yet determined to feed the insatiable hunger that drove them.

Mikel closed his eyes and waited. This wasn't the way he thought he'd go out. Sure, he considered the chance of being eaten alive, but in his version, he always had a gun handy to blow his own brains out.

Mikel tensed his entire body in expectation of pain beyond that which he could comprehend. The first bite would be the most memorable, as it would serve to warn him of the specific route that the sensation of the bodily insult would travel through his central nervous system. Or would there be many all at once? The image reminded him of piranha.

Then, suddenly, Mikel felt himself being lifted by the armpits and pulled backwards.

"I got 'em!" a voice that he immediately recognized as belonging to Ken Porter, his second in command, called out from behind. "Ritner! Jamison! Chavez! Cancel those fuckers NOW!"

Mikel was just about to let go and drift to sleep to the tangible thump and the soothing buzz-hum of liquid-light gunfire when the smell of lilacs brought him full circle, as they reminded him of Ana's favorite perfume.

Lois Ritner, who stood to the right of him, wore it as well.

"Don't worry, boss. We'll get her back. I promise." Ken spoke with confidence, like a man prepared to sacrifice his own life to keep his word.

Mikel began to chuckle at the futility of Ken's statement. Didn't he know that she was already dead?

The zombies danced backward as the wedding party unloaded their weapons into them. Their clouded eyes, which bore no sign of pain, fear, regret, remorse, or even humanity, maintained a steadfast lock on the small party of live meat no matter how much damage they took. Instinct, or hunger, or the devil himself (to some) continued to drive them forward against insurmountable odds. Even when the street was concealed beneath a layer of twitching limbs and mangled tissue, those left partially intact charged with unmitigated zeal, growling and lurching in expectation of a hearty meal.

"Everyone clear?" Lois Ritner yelled as she holstered her Berserker and fetched a small, metallic ball from one of the straps that criss-crossed her torso.

"Everybody clear?" she said.

"Clear."

"Clear."

Palming the ball in her hand, Lois thumbed a button at the top and tossed it at the lurching crowd.

"Fire in the hole!" she warned, seconds before the ball exploded into a ring of flames that traveled outward horizontally and adhered to everything within a 30-foot radius.

Slumped against an old gutted Lincoln where Ken had left him for a moment, Mikel wept.

* * *

2021 PA.

Before he could prepare himself for what might be waiting on the other side of the door, Marco Tomacelli vanished into thin air and reappeared inside Jesus' chamber.

Down the hall, everyone in the room (Bishop Anthony Cardone, the two Catholic priests who had informed on a group of illegals who came to them in confidence seeking forgiveness for their deception, and Marco Tomacelli, the Vatican secretary) had heard the noise.

Marco was the only one brave enough to head down the hall and investigate what could possibly make Jesus scream the way he did. It was a gut-wrenching sound akin to that of a woman giving birth, or dying violently.

The sound hit them in synchrony, resonating out from inside them, pulsing throughout their bodies and bringing their fine hairs to attention. They waited for an encore before anyone moved. Marco wasn't the first, but he was the only one whose actions weren't just for show. To them, and 2.5 billion followers, Jesus was the supreme, the ultimate, the captain of the team, the king of the prom. Most of them couldn't even fathom that there might be something that could fill his voice with such terror.

Inside Jesus' chamber there was an omnipresent sound, like the deep howl of a strong wind. It had been the pope's room before Jesus forced him out.

Marco could sense that there was movement all around him even before he fully materialized. The feeling reminded him of dropping fast in an elevator. The first thing Marco did was pat himself down to make sure everything was where it should be. Next, he lifted his hand and signed the cross over his chest.

Jesus screamed, his voice causing the entire room to shake and reality to vibrate.

Marco fell back against the door, knocked off balance by the sound. It weighed heavily on his lungs as well, as they had to struggle under the sonic spell that left him with goose bumps and a massive headache.

Between vocal outbursts, Jesus moaned and grunted from deep within his throat.

Marco's eyes crept open and up from the floor and fell upon the unimaginable.

Exquisite furniture dating back to the Roman Empire (tables and chairs, armoires, and ottomans) moved on their own, crashing into one another and anything else in their paths. The larger pieces rolled and slid; the smaller ones tumbled and flew through the air along with loose paper and stationery, antique lamps, and a papal gallery of sculpted busts and books that almost seemed to flap open and closed like creatures with wings and no body.

The grand canopy bed, which was the focal point of the room, sat between two 12-foot stained-glass windows that looked out onto St. Peter's Square. Curiosity had seduced the sun's rays to peer through them with such conviction that Jesus was but a shadow from Marco's perspective, arching, writhing, and kicking his legs straight beneath his sheets.

"Dio mio!" Marco said, dumbfounded.

Jesus reacted to the sound of his voice.

Marco reacted to Jesus' reaction and took a tentative step toward him. It was mostly for show, as he felt like he had been standing there for a long time, taking it all in, instead of hurrying over to Jesus' side.

"Where is he? Where is Dallas?" Jesus spit out between thick, elastic bands of saliva that stretched and broke into flying, twisting strings.

Marco leaned forward, timing the movement of the skittering furniture and flying debris, ready to propel himself. He was far from athletic, so everything about the way he moved looked painfully uncoordinated. Fortunately, he was quick enough to duck and avoid being whacked by the oval-shaped vanity mirror that flew at him end over end. Looking up as it passed overhead, Marco saw his reflection. It was pointing at him and cackling in a strange pitch-bending tone.

On second thought, there were too many obstacles between him and Jesus' bed, too many things that could do him serious harm or scar him mentally like his reflection already had. Hence, Marco languished in an uncomfortable crouch, hoping that Jesus would eventually find the Reverend. After all, he was Jesus Christ, the almighty son of God. He could do anything, right?

Marco felt a sudden tingling, and the next thing he knew, he was standing over Jesus at his bedside.

"You imbecile!" Jesus said in response to Marco's last thought. He reached blind, grabbed Marco by his shirt, and twisted his fist palm-up as he pulled Marco close enough to see the bulging veins that traveled up both sides of his face to about the temples, the moist white of his half-rolled-back eyes, and the savage intensity with which his pearly white teeth and gums jutted out from his lips and clenched together. "Dost thou think I would have asked if I knew where he was?"

"Perdonilo prego." Marco pleaded.

Without chambering his arm, or even pushing, Jesus released his grip and sent Marco stumbling backward onto his ass.

Marco climbed to his feet, ducking and leaning out of the way of a pair of scissors and a large snow globe that whizzed by. He waited for an opening between objects, then ran over to the desk that had just wedged itself between the wall and a marble pillar. Pressing the button on the intercom atop the desk, Marco leaned over it when…

Jesus screamed again, and again his voice shook the entire room.

Marco had to grab hold of the desk with both hands to keep from falling.

"Listen, please…. It's extremely urgent that we find Reverend Dallas," Marco's agitated voice spoke into the intercom. "Adesso!" he added, as if he knew that they had already wasted precious seconds wondering what exactly was going on and why.

Down the hall, Bishop Cardone scrambled to the wall monitor situated in the front of the room and tapped out a sequence on the screen with his fingertips until Reverend Dallas' itinerary scrolled down from the top.

Jesus screamed again, and even through the intercom, they could feel it in their bones.

Bishop Cardone paused until the free-roaming chill passed through him.

"According to this, he's at a swearing-in ceremony at the Church of Christ on Tractenberg and Elm, in Houston," the Bishop yelled over his shoulder.

Marco turned to Jesus, who had heard the message and was sitting up with his hands on either side of his head. The look on his face told Marco that he was trying with everything he had to concentrate.

At the foot of his bed, a clutter of limbs and merging flesh materialized and hovered in front of Marco at eye level. He closed his eyes and prayed that whatever this monstrosity was, it was not being summoned as punishment for his mistake, or for the fact that he betrayed the pope when he was offered the choice to leave with him or stay and work under Jesus.

Dripping down from the clutter, torsos and legs begin to take shape. There were three of them huddled closely together and moving in a way that suggested sexual activity.

"What in the Sam Hill..." Reverend Dallas said, his head whipping around the room until he realized where he was.

Sweaty and completely naked, Reverend Dallas shoved away the lingerie-clad woman who knelt before him, taking the full length of his short-wide penis into her small mouth. He looked over his shoulder at a second woman, who wriggled slowly, rubbing her bare breasts up and down his back.

Grabbing her by the arm, Dallas intended to spin around and

use her as a shield to hide his potbelly and stick legs. Before he could, a flying vase clocked her in the back of the head and knocked her unconscious.

The lingerie-clad woman screamed when she saw everything that was happening around her.

It startled everyone when Jesus screamed again, this time out of anger instead of pain or fear, both of which he hadn't felt since the fight with Yeshua six years ago. It was louder and deeper than the previous screams, coming with a background rumble that sounded a lot like a herd of buffalo running on an open range.

Marco, Reverend Dallas, and the lingerie-clad woman, who screamed and screamed at everything she laid eyes on, all covered their ears.

Caught in some form of sonic hold, the hurricane of furniture, paper, stationery, lamps, and books that flapped like creatures with wings and no bodies collapsed to the floor or simply stopped moving. Gone was the deep howling wind and the sounds of sliding, thumping, and crashing. All that was left was Jesus' heavy breath and the lingerie-clad woman's screams.

With a wave of his hand, Jesus replaced her mouth with a flap of smooth skin.

Reverend Dallas hid behind the armoire that had stopped right next to him.

"You could've at least called first," he said, perturbed and embarrassed but making sure not to sound too angry.

"Something's wrong," Jesus said, showing no concern or interest in the Reverend's state of undress or his weakness for high-priced hookers. "My head.... I can't see.... I can't see them...."

He sat up and slid his legs over the side of the bed.

"You may go," Jesus said to Marco, who vanished before he could respond.

Jesus hunched forward and buried his face in his hands. He sat like that for a good five minutes before parting his hands and sliding them back at either side, past his cheeks and ears and onto his hair, which he pulled into a tight ponytail, then let it fall to his back.

Frowning away the last of it, he glanced over at Reverend Dallas, who was peeking out from behind the armoire.

"Have you no self-control?" Jesus said, and then flicked his fingers.

In an instant, the room was neat and tidy, as if nothing had ever happened.

Realizing that he was out in the open, Reverend Dallas looked down, expecting to find himself naked. Instead, he was clothed in an ankle-length smock with the word "Glutton" scribbled diagonally across the front in black letters. He closed his eyes and vented. There wasn't much else he could do.

"They're up to something," Jesus said angrily. "I know it."

"Now hold on a minute here. Could you start by explaining to me what just happened?"

Jesus threw the sheets off his lap and thrust himself up off the bed. By the time he had come to a full stand, he was dressed in a dark-colored suit.

Although he was looking right at him the whole time, it happened too fast for Reverend Dallas to actually see or even notice until Jesus was already standing and adjusting his tie.

"I don't know exactly," Jesus said as he walked over to the window, clasped his hands behind his back, and gazed out at the midday sun. "It felt like… like I was being watched by hundreds of eyes, and I could hear voices, lots of them, talking over each other. It's the Left Hand. They're up to something."

"Could it be Yeshua?"

"Don't be silly. I doubt he could do more than drool at this point. It was their psychics. It felt like they were practicing."

Night Life

"Behind you!" Mikel yelled, his voice cutting into the melodic beatdown administered by an instrumental version of "Duck Seazon" by Wu Tang (one of his old favorites) that poured out from their earpiece communicators.

The communicators linked to alpha and beta waves of the brain for communication and entertainment purposes via custom-set frequencies and enabled the wearer to communicate telepathically with another as long as their frequencies matched. Before the US infected Iraq with chemical and biological agents in 2011, the government was rumored to have used a modified version that tapped into theta and delta waves for mind control on a select few of the Abu Ghraib prisoners who were released into the custody of the Iraq interim government after the scandal in 2004.

Mikel swung with all his strength and bit clean through the thug-zombie's neck with his machete. His severed head on its way to the damp ground, and falling upside-down, the thug-zombie kept his eyes on Mikel in a cold stare that spoke of black anger smoothed over with death and tainted by tremendous hunger. His headless body looming over Kane, caught in a twitching rhythm, stepped in a wild, disorganized pattern and fell into the thicket of bushes to the right of them.

Mikel stepped over Kane, who wrestled with a teenaged zombie decked out in a backpack full of rocks (someone's idea of a joke), and cocked his machete-arm to dispatch of it when Kane rolled on top and obstructed his view.

Kane dug his hand into the undergrowth of new leaves, snaking blind right to left, until his finger licked, then wrapped around a thick, sturdy branch. He raised it above his head, teeth clenched in testament to the primal surge, and bludgeoned the teenaged zombie's face and head into a bloody pulp. Rising and falling with a moist thud, Kane swung and swung until he couldn't lift his arms anymore.

"Let me get that for you." Mikel offered as Kane's pounding grew sluggish, his leaden arms burning with lactic acid.

Beneath him, the teenaged zombie continued to thrash. The indecipherable mass of tenderized flesh, bone fragments, and hair, all marinating in a thick red garnish where its face and head used to be, continued to pulsate as nerves fired, igniting the small factions of muscle fibers that remained intact. The gurgled sound of breath obstructed by liquid scored the quiet moment. Something about the teenaged zombie's will to live reminded Kane of a crushed insect and made him want to scratch himself all over.

This would be the second... no, third time Mikel had to help him, and it was wearing thin on Kane's pride. Gone was the cool-handed warrior, the zealot of aggression who thrived on controlled violence, the zombie-killing machine that had kicked ass and taken names throughout the community of the dead.

In his place was a tired old man, older than his years thanks to his atrophied muscles, the 75 pounds that left him while he slept, and the overall sense of defeat that haunted him at the thought of remaining this way for the rest of his life. The alternative (a lifelong symbiotic existence with McCann) was even worse. The thought always came with a vision of McCann, and of his victims.

Was it even worth living? Kane had asked himself that every day since he awoke from the coma.

It had been eight full months, and the men were beginning to wonder if something was wrong with Kane. He never ate, never slept, never socialized with the troops, and never participated in the group drills. Kane preferred to train alone in his room, which was on the third floor, with the high-ranking officers. That didn't sit well at all with the troops, nor did his specialty status.

They had heard the stories from Mikel. Kane, the super cop, the man who trained him; how he and Kane bonded in such a short time; how Kane was like a father to him, blah, blah, blah.

"This guy?" the men all seemed to say when Kane

occasionally made his way down to the cafeteria to refill the 5-gallon coffee canister that he kept in his room. Kane survived on the stuff. It was some bullshit supermarket brand that had been sitting half-open in a stockroom for weeks when they found it, but it would have to do.

Six years ago, Kane could've handled the teenaged zombie with ease, with morbid flair even. Instead, he found himself winded and deeply frustrated. There was no rush from the kill, or in the brutality of it, no feeling of superiority.

Seeing Mikel revel in the hunt, the way *he* used to, made Kane feel inadequate.

Mikel tried to hide his pity behind a veil of support, and words to inspire. "You'll be back to your old self in no time," he'd say.

Kane had seen the way Mikel was starting to look at him, his eyes heavy with disappointment that Kane hadn't bounced back like he thought he would, like he bragged to all his men that he would. He considered telling Mikel about his predicament, but he had taught him to be firm, logical, and devoid of emotional interference when making life-and-death decisions in this new world environment. As leader of the Left Hand, Mikel might view McCann's presence as a potential threat, and Kane didn't want to put him in that position; he also had to think of his own ass.

Mikel extended his hand and patted Kane on the shoulder after he grabbed hold and pulled himself to his feet.

Kane smacked his hand away and walked off. Though he claimed to understand Kane's frustration, Mikel was hurt by the gesture. He was starting to look at Kane differently.

The men wanted Kane banished from the base. It had happened before, twice. Professor Janssen wanted Kane dead, but there was no way Mikel would concur with that plan, not based on a feeling.

Kane swung the tee-ball bat angrily at the bushes across the path. Preoccupied with Kane's gesture, and his rage, Mikel almost forgot about the teenaged zombie who had just grabbed his pant leg and was attempting to pull its pulverized mouth up to his thigh for a bite, even though there was nothing left with which to do the job.

Mikel thought "*play*," and the earpiece kicked in full blast. If he was going to get through this, he needed a clear head, clear enough for his adrenaline to run its course uninterrupted.

Kane continued on in silence. Though he was a fan of working out to the sound of soul-stirring beats and dark, funky melodies, he just wasn't in the mood. It reminded him too much of what it used to be like.

Mikel waited for an opening where he might jump in and ride the beat with a head-nod before he sheathed his machete and pulled a cleaver from a small, homemade holster beneath his armpit. It was his favorite edged weapon. He used it to cut through bone, as he intended to do to the teenaged zombie's elbows and knees to render him immobile. At the last minute he changed his mind and decided to drag him by the leg over to an embankment five or so feet into the trees and kick him over the edge.

The teenaged zombie rolled down sloppily and landed in the creek below where another zombie stood knee-deep, looking down into the water for fish that she was too slow to ever catch.

The shit with Kane had stolen Mikel's enthusiasm. He knew he had to make a hard decision tonight. That was part of the reason Mikel brought Kane here, to Cobbs Creek Park, a 786-acre section of Fairmount Park, which stretched throughout the city. Standing in stark contrast to the mid- to lower-level economics manifested in concrete, metal, glass, and tar that surrounded it, most of Cobbs Creek was densely wooded.

Beyond the outer layer of trees, the place was littered with refuse and abandoned car husks, stripped and gutted and converged upon by nature. The zombies were more spread out, more likely to walk alone, unlike up in the neighborhoods, where they roamed in numbers right out in the open. You couldn't get more than 20 feet without running into one. Considering Kane's weakened state, and that the UCC drones would be heavy in the air, the woods were their safest bet.

Yesterday's drill, a unified psychic block between all the Left Hand bases, had surely gotten Augustus' attention.

The rule for tonight's hunt was no firearms unless absolutely necessary.

"You want to talk about it?" Mikel thought to Kane.

"Nothing to talk about," Kane replied.

Mikel gave Kane a few seconds to reconsider.

"Okay, then. Let's move," he thought and led Kane out onto the dirt path.

The nighttime was different in 2021 PA: quieter, as if the zombies now had a curfew after which they weren't allowed to scream and moan at nothing and everything the way they used to. There were still the occasional grunts and groans, only now they were spaced further apart, and they sounded more aware.

Down here, the darkness had fingers that reached out and chilled the warm-blooded minority, rigid yet flexible hands that slapped the nerve right out of brave men, and teeth that pinched and sunk into flesh and muscle and pulled them from bones. Somehow it seemed darker than before. It was a weird shade of black, harder on the eyes as it joined with the tall, thin trees and the shrubs that punched through with shades of green. It played tricks on the mind.

The Cobbs Creek zombies seemed to adapt to their surroundings over time, learning to use the trees to their advantage. Lunging out of dark shadows and falling from high branches like clumsy ninja, their attacks spoke of strategy.

Kane flipped the bat in his palm and choked up on it as the zombie from the shadows, a little girl, no more than nine years old, with a foot-long wooden handle sticking out the top of her head at an angle from the spot where someone had planted the claw-end of a hammer, engaged him in a face off.

Kane waved his bat in a threatening manner, which only riled the little girl. Suddenly overcome with purpose, she stood straight up, took a step toward him, and stopped to gauge his reaction.

Kane stepped back and shook his bat.

"Stay back, you little bitch," he said.

She stepped closer, stopped, and checked his reaction again, which was the same as before.

"Just take her out, man," Mikel thought. *"She's gonna rush you any sec...*

Mikel had already dealt with the zombie that fell from the tree split his head down the middle and shoved him over the same embankment and into the creek. But there was another. This one was big, really big, and built like an NFL linebacker.

Mikel dug his feet in and prepared his blade to bite deep as the huge zombie charged at him in a hunch, his big feet smacking the ground in unmistakable thumps, his enormous shadow swallowing Mikel whole.

Falling for the little girl-zombie's check-move, Kane swung too early and left his right side completely open to her actual attack, which immediately followed. She had him on his heels swinging wildly, backing toward the embankment. She took a few shots to the head and shoulders, but kept on coming, reaching, clawing, and clacking her teeth together. As he held her at arm's length, he could see that she had bitten off the tip of her own tongue. Bits and pieces of it oozed down her chin.

Using his body as a fulcrum, Kane grabbed the girl, swung her around, and threw her as far as he could. Flying backward over the barrier of shrubs that stood at the top of the embankment, the girl continued to reach, claw, and growl with more anger than seemed appropriate for a nine-year-old, as her forward motion gave way to gravity and she dropped out of sight. Seconds later, there was a splash that sounded like she landed in the shallows of the creek.

"Mikel?" Kane yelled out loud as soon as he caught his balance. He had seen the size of the linebacker-zombie in his periphery and only just now registered it in his conscious mind.

Suddenly, from his left, a huge shadow loomed over him. Stumbling out of the bushes in a fury, the linebacker-zombie swatted at the shrubs in search of Mikel.

Kane tried to stay as still as possible, but the zombie had already spotted him and sunk into an aggressive pose, showing off his teeth.

For a moment, they stood motionless (Kane and the linebacker-zombie), eyeing each other up; then, without warning, the linebacker-zombie charged. Kane was turning to run when he heard a gunshot.

Behind him there was a seismic thump followed by the linebacker-zombie crying out.

Mikel exploded from the bushes, behind where the linebacker-zombie knelt. The zombie's right leg was totally blown away below the knee. He swung around to meet the noise and wound up face to face with Mikel's sawed-off Berserker.

Mikel pulled the trigger and turned away to avoid the spray of blood and cerebral tissue.

"I thought you said no guns" Kane thought.

"I'm sorry, but that nigga was the exception. Now c'mon, let's go," Mikel thought, without stopping to take a breath.

Kane turned to follow Mikel, who had just jogged down a side path when something, a glint of white slicing through the darkness over his left shoulder, caught his attention.

He turned slowly, expecting to find a zombie staring him down, but instead there was a girl, naked as can be; from a short distance, she was beautiful. She was hanging motionless from a branch that reached out over the path running adjacent to the one Mikel just ran down. There was something about her that Kane couldn't resist. Maybe it was the fact that he hadn't had any pussy in months. He hadn't even had the energy to jerk off. And here was a naked girl, all virginal and lily-white, save for the dead hue. Was it her beauty that allowed her a peaceful death, he wondered, as there were no discernable marks to indicate how she may have died. Was she so pure that she was immune to the zombie virus?

Kane approached her cautiously. He was in her power, hypnotized by her hourglass shape, by the texture and the greyish-pink shade of her nipples, and by the pattern of her pubic hair. She swayed slightly in the breeze, delicate as she was beautiful.

He reached out to touch her, his mind fooled into expecting warm, soft flesh, but she was cold as ice. Running the tips of his fingers up her leg, Kane followed the crease between her thigh and pelvis, over to her....

He flinched when she grabbed his wrist, and looked up just as she opened her reddened eyes and glared down at him. She let out a juicy growl, spit-bubbles expanding and popping, and fought against the rope that dug into her neck and up under her jaw.

With his other hand, Kane punched her in the gut, and she finally let go. She reached over her head and tried to pull herself up the rope when Kane heard a familiar click-clack from behind.

He turned around slowly.

"Mikel????" he said, confused.

"I'm sorry, old friend," Mikel replied, genuinely upset, "but it has to be this way. I have my men to think of, you know."

At that instance, the woman in the tree, who tried in vain to free herself, ceased to exist to Kane. He almost expected something like this, but he always thought... always hoped that Mikel wouldn't have the nerve to go through with it. Then again, it was a sign that Kane had taught him well. Once he looked at it that way, it was hard for him to find fault with Mikel's decision.

"Like I said, you really have grown into quite a man."

"You had a lot to do with that, you know. If there was any other way...."

"So what now? You going to shoot me?"

Mikel didn't respond.

Unbeknownst to Mikel, Kane had worked his left hand around to the knife that rested beneath his belt at the small of his back. Being asked to leave was one thing, but he wasn't about to stand by and let anyone shoot him without a fight, not even Mikel.

"You could do that to me?" Kane asked.

Mikel lowered his gun.

"No," Mikel sobbed. "I figured maybe if I thought about Jason and how he died. I never told you that I knew."

Kane looked away. In a way, he was relieved that Mikel knew the truth, and in a way, he didn't care anymore, although Jason's death still haunted his dreams on occasion.

Kane pivoted to keep his left side out of view and wrapped his sweaty palm around the butt of the knife. Part of him didn't know if he could go through with killing Mikel.

"The professor and the rest of my men... They want you gone. They're afraid of you, Kane. You taught me so much, but they're my men. I'm their leader. I have to listen to them if I want to maintain control."

"So why bring me out here? Why not just do me in my sleep, or when my back was turned? I'm sure the men wouldn't mind."

"I... I wanted us to do this one last time. I thought that maybe there was a chance that it would wake you out of your slump."

"You know, you're never going to end this the way you're handling things."

"Maybe not, but I've got to keep trying. I had hoped that you would be the one to guide us to victory, but...."

"Well, son, I'm sorry to disappoint you."

Kane loosened his grip on the knife, but kept his hand close to it just in case.

There was a sudden burst of static from their earpieces. It was loud enough that they both winced.

"Sir," the harried male voice began, "we're getting reports of raids on Washington, Ohio, and Los Angeles."

"Shit!" Mikel said. "Any word on casualties?"

"Negative, sir. We tried to get through to Washington, but all we're getting is an evacuate beacon."

"I'll be right there. Mikel out."

For a moment, Kane got caught up in the news. He had been eager to take the Series 11 out for a combat run now that he felt comfortable with it.

"Listen, Kane," Mikel began.

"Spare me the long goodbye, kid. I understand."

"No, just hear me out. This is tough for me."

Kane hesitated. He was about to rip into Mikel about exactly how tough his entire life had been since he woke up, but instead, he nodded.

"I brought you out here, because I thought…. Look Kane… Philip… you were like a father to me. I never imagined that it would come to this. I want you to know that I fought this all the way, but now I have no choice. Please don't follow me back, or I might not be able to stop my men from… well, you've got the idea. There's about a month's worth of supplies and a few guns that I packed up for you in the truck."

"Gee, thanks."

"Would it be too much to ask for you to check in with me from time to time? I left my private number with the supplies."

"Oh, you'll be hearing from me," Kane said. If he needed a boost to lift him out of his funk, then this was definitely it. "Just listen for the shit hitting the fan."

"Whatever you do, old friend, be safe," Mikel said.

Both men hesitated, before giving in to the urge to embrace. Kane still wondered when he might feel a blade or a bullet sneak between his ribs or into his back, yet he met the moment unguarded.

Standing under the hanging girl who kicked and flailed and groaned bloody murder, Kane watched Mikel walk off and disappear into the darkness.

Chapter 13

Kane heard the explosions from way down in the funk of slumber. He woke up inside the abandoned family van, its tinted windows tricking him into thinking it was still night until he cracked the door and cringed as daylight screamed at him.

When he really got down to thinking about what had happened to him 48 hours ago, Kane couldn't help feeling betrayed to some extent. What he had given Mikel was invaluable and certainly deserved more of a fight than he felt Mikel took to his men or to the goddammed professor with his fucking visions and bad feelings. What happened to things like proof? Fucking McCann…. It was his fault that the professor kept getting bad vibes from Kane. What else could it be?

To dwell on it meant hours wasted fuming at the thin air around him, and occasionally at small appliances and bottles, and whatever else he may have found at his immediate disposal, and pitying himself like he had done ever since Mikel left him. He took short breaks here and there to deal with an errant zombie, or group of them.

Kane's mind was swimming with species upon species of possibilities, running hot and cold. It was too much for him to have even begun to flirt with big ideas and shape them into a long-term plan. Until he calmed down and got a grip, it was going to have to be day by day, life-by-the-seat-of-his-pants type shit. The old Kane… he'd have no problem living on the edge, without a net.

Until the van skidded onto Clearfield and Spruce Streets, where the old Clinton Elementary School sat amidst rows of empty houses and abandoned cars that clogged the entire area, Kane wasn't sure where he was heading in terms of direction. Living in the moment like he had been, he knew only the name (William Jefferson Clinton building), and the reason he was going there (an explosion). Mikel might be in trouble.

Stepping lightly through the rubble, his forearm shielding his mouth and nose from the dust-devils of asbestos and powdered cement that hovered over the site like a self-contained atmosphere, Kane hurried toward the William Jefferson Clinton building. The blast had unmasked it and left it open-faced to reveal the cubed infrastructure beneath. Rooms upon rooms, side by side and stacked; some were wholly intact, untouched save for a few overturned chairs and tables, and others were completely decimated and filled with rubble and Left Hand body parts that were starting to come back to life.

From where he was when the missile touched down (asleep, in the back of the family van on 62nd and Pine), the blast didn't sound as bad as this looked. He expected to walk in on a firefight, but instead it had been a massacre.

But how? Didn't the psychics see it coming?

Inside, Kane was careful not to disturb the weakened foundation, careful not to step on the wrong thing that might cause some catastrophic chain reaction to bring down the rest of the building.

There were survivors. He could hear them coughing and groaning in pain somewhere in the forced fog. Every hallway had something interesting to see and smell: bodies so twisted and mangled that they resembled something that a self-important expressionist might attempt. Some of the bodies were trying to crawl toward the faint smell of live flesh.

Though he tried not to look too long, Kane spotted a few familiar faces: Dex, the mechanic, who dangled from a pipe that impaled him through the chest, and Carl Freeman, one of the nicer men, who also doubled as the chef.

Carl was trying to put himself back together when Kane found him. He was past the point of return, so Kane just hid and watched him go through it, the tears, shock, and fear of the imminent dark that slithered toward him. Carl had always made it a point to speak to Kane, to ask him how he was doing and toss a filthy joke his way. He wished there was something he could do for him.

"Is there someone there?"

Kane disappeared behind the pillar, pressing his back against it and remaining still as the dead wind that left the dust cloud to linger. Looking down, he could barely see his feet through it. Looking to his right, he saw the sky and the hint of neighborhoods.

"The pain... I can't take it. Whoever you are, please... kill me. I'm begging you," Carl begged.

Kane thought about staying behind the pillar until Carl finally expired. It wouldn't be long at all judging by the way he looked. He was nothing more than a torso, and even that had been blown to shit. Moving jerkily the way he did, he looked like a bad-movie special effect.

Either help the man, or be on your way, he told himself. *He might be able to lead you to Mikel.*

Kane swallowed the lump in his throat. He found himself emotionally affected by the thought that Mikel might be dead.

Kane knelt beside Carl and slid his hand under Carl's head. There was no avoiding the blood. It was everywhere.

Above them, Dex, the mechanic came back to life with a vengeance. Thrashing wildly as he dangled from the pipe that impaled him, he glared and snarled at both of them.

Carl grabbed Kane's hand and squeezed, and looked longingly in his eyes as if he envied and somehow tried to connect with Kane's unsteady, albeit living energy.

"I'm dying," Carl said, trying hard not to choke on his words. As if given permission to emote by Kane's sympathetic stare, Carl's eyes began to well up. "Please... take my gun and end it. Let me have my digniteeeeee."

Carl lurched, his body flexing rigid as the pain coursed through what was left of him. He cried out in a way that made Kane want to run away and hide.

"What happened here?" Kane asked.

He wasn't sure if Carl heard him through the spasms and the

waterlogged groan that gargled in his throat as he whipped his head from side to side. Kane was about to repeat the question when…

"The UCC… they… they hhh-had a cell working undercover," Carl whispered with gravel-pitched determination.

"But how is that possible? What about the psychics?"

"The cell… he *was* a psychic." A familiar-sounding voice from behind leapt into the fray.

Kane spun around and reached for the handgun that he kept at his side.

"Careful, Detective," the shadowy figure said, walking out from the belly of the dense cloud, and into the brazen sunlight that dimed him out to Kane's eyes.

"Professor Janssen?" Kane said, attempting to read his intentions from his body language, his expression, and his voice. "Where's Mikel?"

"He's not here."

Oh, thank God… I mean… aw, fuck it! Kane thought.

"He left last night, before the blast. He went with the doctor to help out at the Maryland base. They were raided yesterday. But you probably already knew that, didn't you?"

"Listen to me, Goddammit…. I know what you think you feel and all, but I can guarantee you that I'm not…"

Carl Freeman screamed from his diaphragm, which caused the stump at his waist to bubble and spew as his severed muscles constricted to accommodate attempted movement.

Together they watched Carl go from raging, to calm, to raging, to panic manifested as maniacal laughter.

Above them, Dex watched intently as he dangled. He was reaching out to them, his fingers clawing at air.

The professor was pretty banged up, but intact. He held his arm at a 45-degree angle against his side in splint position, and although he managed to walk on it, his left leg was clearly broken.

There was a look in his eyes. When he saw it, Kane understood right away what mind state the professor was in. It was the same look that inhabited Kane's eyes back when he was about to close in on some criminal that he'd been hunting for awhile. Even now he recognized it.

"I guess it's true what they say about the killer returning to the scene to gloat," Professor Janssen said. "I knew if I waited, you'd eventually show up."

"You *really* think I had something to do with this?"

"I do. Yes."

"Didn't you hear anything that I said?"

"Like *I* said, Detective, Mikel isn't around. And your word doesn't hold any weight with me. There's really only one way to be sure."

That was all the warning Kane needed. He dropped his hand down and around the handle of the gun, and snatched it out of his belt.

Professor Janssen lifted his right hand, palm facing forward.

In an instant, Kane's gun became hot in his grasp. He threw it down and balked at the burning sensation. It was so hot that it was almost cold, like dry ice.

Kneeling quickly to retrieve it, Kane felt his feet suddenly leaving the ground. He tried to sink his weight, but it had no effect. The next thing he knew, he was being slammed into the wall and held three feet off the ground by an unseen force. Kane could feel the icy fingers of a giant, invisible hand pressing him against the wall, applying pressure, then letting up.

The professor approached from the hallway where they met, where Carl Freeman's torso had expired and was just now waking up dead. The professor held his right arm out as he walked, his hand open and aimed at Kane.

There was nothing but this... feeling, this sensation of being held in place to keep Kane from sliding down the wall and falling. Although there was enough floor beneath his feet to keep him from plummeting all the way to the ground, Kane was closer than he felt comfortable being to the front of the room, which sat one room back from the front of the building.

From three floors up, it looked out onto the day, onto the streets and neighborhoods. About five blocks down, there was activity. Kane could tell by the whirlwind of trash and the zombies, whose collective voice grew louder by the second, which usually meant that they were excited about something.

There was something large coming this way. Now that he noticed it, he swore he could hear a steady rumbling, like a procession of big trucks, most likely armored vehicles.

"Listen, do you hear that?" Kane said, jerking his head toward the daylight, and the rumbling. "They're coming to finish the job. Now let me down from here!"

Professor Janssen turned toward the rumbling and back to Kane. On the way, he shot his eyes to the corners and sent zombie-Carl flying out the front of the building. He hit the ground with a PLOP.

With his bad arm, the professor pulled a gun from its holster at the small of his back, and calmly placed the barrel up under Kane's chin. He rolled up the sleeve on his right arm, and primed his wrist with a twist.

"If they catch us here they're going to kill us both, or worse," Kane yelled down at him without actually looking.

"So be it, Detective. If what I feel about you is right, then my death will not be in vain. At least I will have brought you down with me."

"Why don't you just tell me what it is that I'm supposed to have done?"

"So *now* you're ready to listen? I guess you don't remember all the calls I made to you years ago? We might have avoided all this if you had listened, but you didn't have time for me then."

"In case you hadn't noticed, I was in a coma for the last six years," Kane said sarcastically. "There's a lot I don't remember."

"A likely excuse," Professor Janssen replied. "Whatever the

case, I'm going to settle this once and for all."

The professor was hesitant, at first, in the way he went about placing his hand on Kane's wrist. After the initial contact, he grabbed hold, and closed his eyes to see.

Janssen's Vision

Capture

Kane is led away in handcuffs and taken to a holding cell somewhere within Heaven City Northeast.

"I have some information that your superiors will be interested in hearing," he says to the guard who shoves him forward into the cell, slams the door shut, and walks off.

He has been left to languish for days, maybe even weeks, by the time the guard returns. Because he killed a high-ranking Left Hand official (the professor), they decide to hear him out.

Necessary Evil

Kane is left standing alone in a large, windowless room with no right angles. The curved walls are lined with detailed digital maps and blueprints. Directly in front of him, a three- foot wide, solid square stump projects a holographic slideshow of satellite images from cities suspected of containing Left Hand bases.

"What is your name?" a stern, experienced voice lunges from above. Kane looks up to see a group of official-looking men watching him from the old-fashioned observation loft that circled the top of the room. "Jason Williamson," Kane replies.

Kane has had awhile to think about what name he will use, as he is afraid that someone might remember him by his real name. And this way he could at least feel like he was somehow honoring Jason's memory.

"Tell us what you know, Mr. Williamson."

Kane takes a moment to study the holographic images in front of him.

"The end justifies the means," Kane whispers to himself, then lifts his hand slowly, and points to a spot.

Conquest

UCC forces conduct the first of many raids on suspected Left Hand strongholds that remain: Pittsburgh, New York, Cleveland, Chicago, Los Angeles, Atlanta. The survivors are taken into custody and tortured until they either divulge what they know, make up something just to get off the hook, or die during the process. The additional information leads to more raids: London, Paris, Berlin, Tokyo.

The outlands are ablaze; whole settlements are laid to waste; families related by blood and similar experiences are wiped out without a thought. As the violence continues, Kane's status rises from informant, to Citizen, to officer, to Archangel, to General.

Jesus begins to take notice of the man called Jason Williamson, and his triumphs, but doesn't recognize him from that night in the car many years ago. Things are going too well for the UCC, and, in his overconfidence, Jesus doesn't suspect anything.

Kane learns that Mikel has been missing for weeks, and is feared dead, and that Yeshua, along with a small group of Left Hand soldiers, managed to survive the attacks and were currently hiding deep in the Appalachians, in one of the more secluded outland communities.

During the quiet moments, Kane always remembers to tell himself...

"The end justifies the means."

Rebirth

Kane emerges a new man. He has gained back some of his weight, which comes with a price.

Weary from the constant mental battle, he suffers occasional blackouts during which he roams the streets at night, his face twisted into a marriage of his, and Carlos McCann's features, his hands covered in blood, chest heaving as he searches for victims. McCann's echoed laughter bounces around his mind. Flashes of violence plague him.

As a result, Kane races against time to set his plan, to infiltrate the UCC, into motion before McCann's lust for violence exposes him.

He uses his status to infiltrate the UCC, secretly collecting sensitive information from the executives, scientists, and military shot-callers, with whom he works. He finds the occasional ally within the fold.

Kane shares what he has learned with the prisoners from the Left Hand and the various outland communities usurped by the UCC. They are reluctant to trust him.

With Kane's help, the prisoners escape and spread the word throughout the communities. He provides them with maps and weapons, access codes to the front gate, the subway shutters and the UCC Tower, and a date, Easter Sunday, 2027.

Vengeance

President Jesse James Dallas is assassinated on March 20, 2027, two weeks before the territories' annual Easter Parade, when his convoy is ambushed while traveling through the outlands by masked gunmen, who massacre his entire party in a matter of seconds, kidnap him, and then drop him off naked and unarmed in an area notorious for its aggressive zombies.

Jesus stands in front of a large window that looks down on the Easter celebration from on high, gloating and drinking in the adulation from the crowd below. At this height, the crowd, which numbers in the thousands, easy, and fills the streets for blocks and blocks, looks like mere insects, and the giant, gaudy floats resemble toy cars. The view shifts on liquid wheels from Jesus' right side, heading left, around back, and to the other side, during which the scenery beyond the window morphs from city to city, each bursting with celebration.

Down in the thick of the merriment, an explosion blows a perfect circle in the crowd. The people who are too far away to appreciate the damage that the blast has caused wait in silence for a sign that everything is all right; closer to it, there are screams. *Is it part of the celebration? Was there an accident?*

From every corner of the territories, the subway shutters crawl open. Turning simultaneously, in different directions, depending on exactly where the subway entrances are in relation to where they are standing, the crowd watches, and waits.

The first wave of zombies clamber out curiously, momentarily blinded by the sunlight. They take big, exaggerated swipes at it, shielding their eyes with spoiled and incomplete appendages that have been worn down by decay and self-mutilation, as some of them had resorted to tasting their own and each other's flesh to satiate the hunger that kept them droning forward. The light proves a difficult obstacle for their ruined vision, which has been worsened by prolonged darkness. Once they lay eyes upon the vast menu, rich with variety, most of the zombies forget about the burning light and approach the living smorgasbord with gluttonous eyes, calling out with enthusiastic grunts to the rest of their army who lay in wait for the all-clear from the scouting parties.

The looks on the faces in the crowd range from disbelief, to disgust, to complete denial in the ones whose faith gives them confidence that Jesus won't let them die this way. They are the first to feel teeth upon their flesh as zombies begin to pour out of the subway in incalculable numbers and attack anything that resonates warmth. There are so many of them that they occasionally find themselves stuck at the subway openings, fighting to get out and join the Easter feast.

From Jesus' perspective, it looks like a flesh-colored tsunami spouting up from some subterranean ocean and spreading more quickly than the crowd can retreat.

At the same time, groups of rebels led by the surviving Left Hand soldiers storm the Heaven City borders in Maryland, Philly, Washington,

Rome, and Houston, where Jesus watches from the UCC Tower, fuming with childlike discontent.

"How is this possible?" Jesus questions to himself and sends out a telepathic call to his elite guards; however, something powerful is blocking his attempt.

Jesus turns from the window, expecting to see the inside of a different room across the world from where he started. At the conclusion of his 30-degree rotation, his arm is extended and ready to reach for the doorknob of his chamber in the Vatican, but again his attempt is blocked. "Who is responsible for this!" Jesus yells, frustrated. "I'll have you burned alive on the cross when I find you!"

Suddenly, the ding of the executive elevator, which opens onto the penthouse lobby, where Jesus is standing, gives him a new focal point, the gold-leaf designs on the face of the elevator doors.

They creep open and reveal two men, one standing (Kane), and one hunched in a wheelchair (Yeshua).

"I see," Jesus says, smiling to hide his fear as he backs away and prepares to do battle. He always knew this day would come.

Penance

Kane stands alone on the roof of a tall building somewhere in the outlands, looking out on the horizon. The wind whips his hair to the side and causes him to redistribute his weight to keep from stumbling sideways.

A few blocks to his left, fireworks launch from rooftops and decorate the sky with fingers of colorful light, while directly below them, crowds fill the streets in an improvised parade. The atmosphere is rife with celebration as people dance in the streets, laughing, and firing off weapons into the air. A contingent of armored vehicles patrol the surrounding neighborhoods for zombies, loud music blaring from each. In the distance, large fires illuminate the sky within the Heaven City Northeast borders. Explosions level smaller structures and cause them to topple over, engulfed in flames; zombies crowd the streets, flowing in and out of buildings, falling from the windows and rooftops of some of the skyscrapers. A disorganized path of lumbering bodies extends from the outlands outer rim to the gates of Heaven City and beyond. Kane steps to the very edge of the roof. He lifts his right hand to reveal a pulse grenade. He thumbs the pin out of it and watches it fall past the ledge.

"No! What are you doing?" McCann's voice echoes.

Kane holds the grenade to his chest with both hands. He closes his eyes and smiles. A tear runs down his face.

He takes a deep breath and...

Kane literally saw stars when Professor Janssen released his telepathic hold, leaving Kane to crumble to the floor. He had seen the vision as well, and although it would take some time for his brain to settle into a full understand of its meaning, somehow it all made sense. It also scared the shit out of him.

The professor danced in a dizzied pattern, his hands up at his temples to rub away the mental noise, and the tracers of premonition.

"I... I... but how could I... how could I have been so wrong?"

Said the professor.

"You up there!" a voice speaking through a megaphone demanded their attention. "Drop your weapon and surrender at once, and you will not be harmed."

Thanks to the vision, Kane and the professor had forgotten that the room they were in opened out onto the day in jagged edges of falling concrete and rising dust.

Down in the street, a squadron of UCC vehicles sat at the edge of the auto blockade, while a team of Archangels, led by a stout black man holding a megaphone to his mouth, watched them closely as the Archangels converged on the Clinton building with their guns drawn.

"They're lying. They're going to kill us both," Professor Janssen said, holding his gun down by his side but refusing to let go of it.

"But the vision?" Kane replied. "In the vision, I was alive until..." Kane felt his stomach drop.

The vision had left him shaken and flustered both by its physical affects and by what the visuals suggested.

"Nothing is set in stone, Detective, not even the future. You're going to have to shoot me. It's the only way you'll get out of *here* alive."

"This is your last chance," said the stout black man with the megaphone. "Drop the gun and surrender now, or we will be forced to open fire."

Without moving his head, Kane searched the ground for his gun.

Professor Janssen followed Kane's eyes and together they found it laying a few feet away, close enough to grab, but too far to do so without making an obvious move.

Shifting his stare to the other corner and down to where the stout black man stood with his troops, Kane searched, through his racing thoughts, for an idea.

There was a scraping sound.

Kane turned and dropped his hand to scoop up the gun that slid to him.

When I lift my gun, start shooting, the professor thought to Kane. *My death will set your destiny in motion.*

Professor Janssen took a deep breath, turned toward the daylight, and pointed his gun down at the troops.

Kane closed his eyes and pulled the trigger. He only remembered doing it once; however, his gun coughed out seven shots in smooth succession. By now he was used to that feeling of falling that psychic interference was known produce in its victims. He continued to feel it until the professor fell to his back and breathed his last breath.

My destiny???

Kane hesitated. For a moment, he thought about turning the gun on himself like McCann had suggested six years ago.

The troops below dropped to their knees and took precise aim at him.

Kane threw down the gun and raised his hands above his head.

"I'm unarmed!" he yelled down, yet the soldiers lingered in their positions until the stout, black man motioned for the two in front to head in and retrieve Kane.

Chapter 14

Field of...

Huddled beneath layers of the hooded parka's waterproof, 100% nylon outer shell, Mikel Williamson tightened his entire body and pulled his arms in close to the warmth of his core, which had evaded his limbs thanks to the heat-shield insulation, the zip-in quilted nylon lining, and that waterproof, 100% nylon outer shell that kept skin from skin.

He sat with his gloved hands in his deep, spacious pockets in the clearing he had made at the foot of his favorite tree, staring straight down the tubular tunnel created by zipping his hood all the way up and out almost a foot in front of his face. A ring of faux fur lined the tip.

Mikel's favorite tree, which stood a little more than five feet tall, was located at the top of a hill that looked down onto a snow-covered field that was crowded with similar trees.

There was something about this place that exuded a morbid beauty. It struck those whose mentalities were strong enough to appreciate it with a lagging punch.

Mikel had heard of this place from a man named Lincoln 'Link' Shales, whom he had spent 10 long hours lying next to in the back of the Humvee modified with tank treads and a mammoth gun that could be raised and lowered through a rectangular sunroof. Mikel had nearly lost his life in the battle to save the Pittsburgh base, which was the last one taken out during the UCC blitzkrieg.

Link's endless talking actually kept Mikel from dwelling on his condition, which at the time was critical: third-degree burns over a third of his body, four broken ribs, a busted jaw, a cracked eye socket, and temporary paralysis on his entire right side. Though he couldn't move, he could feel everything.

The rescue team from the small community that found Mikel lying face down in the street had initially left him for dead until he told them who he was and how he got there. Their supplies were running low, especially the meds. People were taking them to escape the madness. It meant that Mikel had to make the trip to Dr. Benjamin Polk's compound 10 minutes east of Toledo, Ohio, without any anesthetics. Dr. Polk was the only person they knew of outside the territories who could help Mikel.

It was Winter 2026, and the Midwest had been rocked by its worst blizzard in more than 30 years. It made for an incredibly long and incredibly cold trip.

"The woman you described… she sounds like someone I've seen before," Link said in response to Mikel's delirious rambling about Ana, the love of his life, with vivid descriptions of her specific beauty to back it up.

"Ever heard of the human trees?" Link said.

Mikel just shook his head.

"It's literally a field of zombies that froze where they stood, or crawled, during the big blizzard last month. It's located about five miles from the doctor's compound," Link said, his words gaining enthusiasm as he spoke. "In the back, by the old stone fountain at the top of the hill: that's where I seen her."

The temperature had been below freezing for the better part of the season, and today was no exception. Even with the parka, Mikel was freezing his balls off. Down on the paved road, at the bottom of the hill, the modified Humvee crept into view and stopped.

Mikel watched through the forest of frozen ghouls, twisted into and stuck in painfully uncomfortable positions as far back as the eye could see. It had been three weeks since Dr. Polk operated on him, and although he had months of therapy ahead of him, he could see out his left eye and walk very slowly unassisted, which meant it was time for them to leave the compound.

Dr. Polk had strict rules.

A female dressed almost identically to Mikel got out and took big, clumsy steps toward him, lifting her knees almost up to her chest just to walk through the snow. Most of the human trees were covered up to their ankles, or wrists and ankles for the ones who froze on all fours.

The woman's name was Donna Lowder. She was only 19, but she had the eyes of a woman who had experienced a life rich with adversity. She had her eye on Mikel since she helped to rescue him, and she even sat with him and held his hand in the back of the Humvee when Lincoln Shales was asleep during some of the ride to Doc Polk's place.

Despite all that this young girl had done for him in the past few weeks (the TLC, the blowjobs, etc.), Mikel knew he was going to have to break her heart now that he had found Ana.

He had been coming here to see Ana every day, sometimes walking the entire distance on crutches when a ride wasn't available. At first, all he could do was stare in her eyes and wonder what had become of her to get to this point: frozen in mid-step, her arms down by her sides and dragging behind her as if her shoulders were too weak to hold them in any kind of fixed position. She was still relatively fresh as far as zombies go, so she must've survived the kidnapping back in 2017.

Her hair was different, cut short, which gave her an elven look that he wouldn't have thought she'd like. Perhaps another man had recommended it to her, the same one who gave her the oversized clothing that she was wearing.

"Mikel, we have to get going," Donna yelled from 50 feet away. "There's another blizzard that's supposed to hit at noon. We've still got a couple hours to get a head start."

It was the last storm of the season, and Mikel had this idea about waiting for the spring thaw just to see Ana moving again. It was just a thought. He knew he'd never last that long out here, not unless he convinced Dr. Polk to let him back in. Those guards of his were a bunch of diesel motherfuckers. He'd have to take them out on the down-low.

From where Donna stood, between two human trees, it looked like Mikel didn't respond at all. She began to well up.

"Please Mikel," she said. "I thought we meant something to each other."

What was this, denial? He had already told her that he was staying with Ana.

Mikel unzipped his hood far enough to expose his mouth.

"Forget about me, Donna. You're young. If you play your cards right, you'll have a long life ahead of you. And you're bound to meet someone else."

It was all hogwash, really. Mikel figured that the folks she ran with would be dead in under a month. He was surprised they had lasted so long. Aside from her father, they were just too damn nice.

"But I don't want anyone else. I want you, Mikel," she said through deep sobs, crying like little girls do when their hearts are ripped from their chests unexpectedly. "She's dead, Mikel. You're gonna die out here too if you stay. Dr. Polk won't let you back in."

"I know all that, and my answer is still the same. I've been through too much. Right now, this is where I want to be. "

The Humvee's horn sounded twice… three times.

"Forget about him D, and get your ass in here," a male voice said from inside.

Donna tried to be tough, she really did, but the harder she balled her lips and tightened her face, the more her emotion swelled to compensate for her efforts to subjugate it.

Eventually, her shoulders fell. Her face settled like the day after a hard rain, interrupted by sobbing. She wiped the tears from her eyes and, after a few rough starts, found her "nothing affects me" mask.

Donna waved.

Mikel waved back.

"Looks like it's just me and you now," Mikel said to Ana as the Humvee crawled away in the background.

Mikel turned and looked lovingly up at Ana's frozen expression, which seemed to say...

Hungry!!!!

THE END

Express Elevator to

Potential Nothingness

(The Fate of Flight 2190)

Good Friday, 2015

"Mayday! Mayday!"

What is it about the sound of an airplane engine laboring to stay alive that brings about a specific type of fear, the kind of fear that even those with both feet planted firmly on the ground can understand way down to the bone? Even in the face of death, Daryl DeVries scrutinized every last detail.

"Pilot is dead! Instruments damaged! Not sure if I can hold her together much longer! We're going down! I repeat: We're going down!"

Everyone had heard the heavy thud from first class, followed immediately by the co-pilot's desperate pleas. Apparently he'd forgotten to shut off the intercom after his verbal tour of the scenery outside the windows. Background chatter shifted from "oooos" and "Aaaahs" to proverbial rumblings of terror and prayers for mercy spoken loud enough for everyone to hear, as if to validate their belief systems, doubt looming, piggy-backing on fear, which in itself illustrated their anemic faith. Overlapping each other quite clumsily, the voices attacked in unison.

In 5 years of traveling, today was the first time Daryl had flown…and it was looking like it would be the last. More than death itself, he feared the prospect of dying a nobody. Local celebrity wasn't enough. Maybe you've heard of his show: *Daryl DeVries and the MoVies?* It came on Saturdays at 7:30 pm. It was offered to him upon completion of his internship with WPIV-TV in Philly, and, popular as it had become, he only took the job to pay his bills and keep his foot in the door of ground-level show business while he spent what little free time he had cranking out screenplays.

His most recent one, a documentary called "A Window Into Hell: Real-Life Exorcism," was supposed to be his big break. Though he missed the documentary/reality TV boom of the '90s and early 21st century, he was determined to inject it with enough of his signature style that even the stuffiest of his peers (the trend-zombies they were) would have to take notice. And he was off to such a good start.

The plan was to film the exorcism of Sister Angelica Downy, a nun from Maryland.

Made up of well-known print journalists, on-camera personalities, their assistants and their assistants' assistants, the rest of the passengers on Flight 2190 (a Boeing 7E7 Dream Liner) had the same idea, but Daryl was determined to outshine them all. So what if his boss warned him about exploiting this for his own gain. Daryl just happened to be the only one in the newsroom when the call came over the tip-hotline. "You're there as a representative of WPIV-TV. Make sure you understand that," were his boss's exact words when he sent Daryl on his way.

Daryl knew they'd most likely fire him for doing his own thing. *I bet they'll beg me to come back when they see it, though,* he thought.

Halfway through Daryl's interview with him, Father Dante Maldonado, the priest who had been appointed by the church to conduct the exorcism when they landed in Philadelphia, was called to first class. The call came just as Daryl broached the subject of his questionable past. There were allegations of inappropriate relations with a young altar boy, and although the archdiocese had all but exonerated him of the charges, there was still money to be made in rehashing the subject. And Daryl knew none of the other reporters had the balls to bring it up.

A few moments later, a low, guttural roar and a deafening THUD preceded the plane pitching from side to side.

A moment of weightlessness sent small baggage dancing out of the overhead compartments where carry-on bags mingled with food wrappers, laptop computers, hand-held MP3 players, and various personal effects: glasses, wallets, shoes, jewelry, vomitus.

The plane descended at a near-perfect vertical slant, the engine whining. The passengers who hadn't belted down were hurled from side to side and end to end. The hull shifted and vibrated everything in sight into double and triple images and gave all sound a ferocious stutter. The lights flickered on and off with a POP.

And just as quickly, the plane was righted.

From first class came a deafening roar, like something called up from the belly of a fantastical beast. From the sound of it, Sister Angelica had become violent again. Daryl was hoping to get one of her fits on film. He only knew of them second-hand. Supposedly she was like a different person when the demon, who called itself Boring, claimed her.

Daryl had met Sister Angelica briefly when they whisked her onto the plane in a wheelchair. She was a petite woman. Though stricken with a horrible case of rosacea, she was pretty in a virginal way that turned most men off.

Suddenly the voices from first class were like many wrapped in one dominant voice that growled and cursed in a variety of tongues. It struck Daryl that the movies he'd seen on the subject seemed to get it right so far.

"Did you hear that?" Daryl commented to Margaret, his fiancée/cameraperson, who had slept through the whole thing.

There were people knocked out cold by flying bags, digging out from under articles of clothing, vomiting in tribute to the vomit that landed on them.

From the look of it, Daryl was one of the lucky ones.

Margaret refused to wake up despite a number of stiff elbows to her shoulder. A light tap was usually enough to make her balk. However, she was petrified of flying even more so that he was, and to make it through the flight without losing it, she had chased down a couple Valiums with a few stiff cocktails just before they boarded.

Once onboard, she strapped herself in and drifted away into a drug-induced slumber. If he wanted to film during the flight, then he'd have to do it himself.

If he'd known that any of this was going to happen, Daryl would have forbade her from taking anything, even if it meant testing her sanity. Margaret really did hate to fly.

Yanked violently from an anticipatory trance, eyes locked on the thick curtain separating first class from coach, a tall, thin flight attendant emerged white as a ghost.

Taking a deep breath, the flight attendant rallied the passengers into crash position, heads between knees.

Not now. Not yet, Daryl pleaded to himself.

Looking out between parted fingers, he scoffed at the other passengers. *Look at them. Talking nonsense to people who weren't even there as they rocked back and forth and squeezed their eyes shut in anticipation of impact.*

But not Daryl. He relished the fact that he was the only one still 'on the job'. He saw it as a badge of superior ethics. Now if he could only get into first class....

Glancing down and over between Margaret's legs, Daryl spotted her camera bag resting beneath the seat in front of her where it had slid during the turbulence. She was in such a deep sleep that he had to manually unlatch her seat belt and ease her head down between her knees to reach it.

Daryl snatched it up, pulled the camera out, stepped out into the aisle, and almost knocked the flight attendant on her ass as she braced herself in the doorway to keep from being tossed around like some of the passengers.

"I'm gonna need you to sit down, sir!" The flight attendant's tone was as firm as she could muster as she struggled to hold on to the doorframe.

Daryl paused. There was too much to say and not enough time to say it this was his big break, might be his only shot, if he could

only get some footage, didn't want to be remembered as a second-rate local film critic. Besides, he knew what her answer would be. Pushing her aside was his only option, but the airlines were strict about enforcing laws against people who disrupted flights. Should they survive the crash, he'd be in a heap of trouble.

Fuck it! Daryl thought as he barreled past her, his forward momentum aided by the plane's steep decline, and pushed through the curtain to first class.

"Stay back! Don't come any closer!" Father Maldonado yelled at Daryl when he stumbled in, wrestling frantically with the curtain and falling to his knees. The flight attendant was right behind him.

The stench was awful, like a stew of feces, urine, vomit, and something worse than all three combined. It stung Daryl's sinuses closed and squinted his eyes. Homing in on the source, he spied a smeared mound of runny shit directly in the center of the aisle. A distinct, skidding shoe-print parted it down the middle, where Maldonado or his assistant must have slipped. The print was too big to have been left by Sister Angelica.

Behind Daryl, the flight attendant conceded her attempt to stop him, and together they visually digested the scene in first class.

Through the heavy downpour of large cockroaches, the broken body of Maldonado's assistant lay sprawled across the damaged console in the cockpit right on top of the pilot, whom he killed on impact. Air hissed in through the cracked windshield as the co-pilot raced frantically to correct the situation.

Slumped against the wall just outside the cockpit door, Father Maldonado shook violently, batting at the cockroaches that swarmed all around him. A pasty brown substance decorated the sole of his shoe and dripped down the sides to the floor. Up against the ceiling, Sister Angelica lay spread-eagled, facing down at them, her eyes rolling up in apparent ecstasy as her elongated tongue reached down and stroked her vagina. From her stretched-open mouth, a stuttered moan grew in volume as if she was on the verge of reaching climax. The ceiling around her was covered with layers upon layers of skittering roaches that emanated from her crotch and crackled and fell to the floor. Some of them climbed up her tongue and into her mouth. Huddled upside down in the corner of the ceiling, the shape of a small boy, made up entirely of shiny black exoskeletons that glistened in the coughing light, pointed down at Father Maldonado.

"Why did you do it?" The boy-shape wailed, his high-pitched voice affected by sorrow, or pain, or both. "Why did you hurt me?"

The thump of the flight attendant's fainting body hitting the floor woke Daryl from his initial shock. Daryl was very much a realist, so instead of allowing fear to overcome him, he simply accepted what he saw. Swallowing hard, he clutched the chair-arm beside him to serve as a counterbalance, lifted his camera to eye-level, and thumbed the record button.

"Okay! I confess! I confess!" Father Maldonado screeched, his hands held over his ears, eyes straying up to the boy-shape as if to make him understand his sincerity. "Please forgive me, I couldn't help myself…"

Father Maldonado paused when he noticed the camera, fear of what his congregation might think of him pulling his eyelids further apart. On second thought, what did opinions really matter if he was dead? What concerned him most was repenting before the plane smacked into the ground and sent him to meet his God or as he secretly feared, nothingness.

Caught in a sudden roll, the plane turned on its back.

Daryl found himself shaking away a brief dizzy spell as a result of being thrown into the ceiling. He immediately rose to his knees and pointed his camera at Sister Angelica, whose body lay only a few feet from him now. Considering the opportunity to leave some kind of legacy, brief and incomplete as it may be, a few hundred roaches were nothing. Daryl had never been very squeamish anyway. Just as long as they stayed away from his mouth, which he held tightly shut, balling his lips for extra measure.

A vision of Margaret zipped through his thoughts. The right thing to do would be to comfort her in their last moments, even if she was fast asleep. Knowing her, she'd tell him not to worry, that the documentary was more important, or maybe that was just his guilt talking.

Next to him, the flight attendant jolted and screamed as an army of aggressive roaches engulfed her and sent her diving headfirst right back into catatonia.

At the other end of the ceiling, Father Maldonado crab-walked, half-conscious, away from the boy-shape, who crawled after him, cursing him along the way.

"PLEASE LORD, FORGIVE ME!" Maldonado yelled.

Caught in a fierce death roll, the plane descended like an enormous metal bird picked off by a hunter's rifle, its wings at full spread and locked in a static pose. Its gleaming silver plumage reflected the sun's busy fingers in a blinding array as it spiraled head first toward the earth.

A massive, charred clearing in the heart of dense woodland stretched back at least a quarter mile from where the plane actually came to rest. Twisting tongues of smoke billowed upward through the surrounding trees. Only a 15-foot section of the tubular passenger area remained completely intact, jagged teeth jutting out at either end. Singed chunks of metallic and organic flesh mingled with nature.

Daryl was alive… alive as the day… alive as the trees that reached up into the sky. He could see the tops of them swaying as if to celebrate his fortune in tandem with the rush that urged him to share his glee with anyone within earshot.

"Woo Hoo! I'm alive!" Daryl yelled. His voice bounced from tree-to-tree, riding the spaces in between with the wind that whipped through the maze of wooden giants and carried the toxic smell of gas and burnt plastic for miles. Then, as it dawned on him with a creepy-crawly itch, he whipped his head to every direction in search of the roaches. They were gone, as was Sister Angelica.

Father Maldonado was but a hand frozen in a claw that reached out from beneath a pile of seats. Daryl couldn't help wondering if he went to heaven or hell. Not that he believed in either.

Ten minutes passed before Daryl thought of his camera... and of Margaret. Looking back through the doorway into coach, he saw that her head was gone from her neck and lying a few feet from her body amid a pile of baggage and body parts. He must have stared at her, at them, for an hour, speculating as to whether or not she died right away or if she lived long enough to witness bodies coming apart. The optimistic sheen through which he viewed the scene only moments ago was snatched away, and before his reddened eyes, the scene, as it had always been (as much of it as he could see), revealed itself to him.

As it was, he could see straight up through the small square window in the wall on top of him, back into what was left of coach (where Margaret was), and if he pressed his chin to his chest, he could see down past his feet and into the woods just beyond the jagged mouth where the cockpit used to be. His left side was obstructed by the section of window-lined wall that remained intact and his right by the wall that pinned him down. He couldn't feel his legs, so he suspected the worst.

Outside the plane, there were bodies everywhere.

Finding his camera was Daryl's only hope for some sense of relief. He knew it was most likely trapped somewhere beneath the wall that held him fast. He prayed that it was still in one piece, denial chasing back the pessimistic voice that scolded him for his stubborn refusal to upgrade to the remote camera-bots that everyone else was using. But he *had to be* old-school, choosing to emulate a time when filmmakers still operated cameras manually.

Closing his eyes to prepare himself for the horrors that he fully expected to see, Daryl DeVries dug deep, pressed his palms against the cushioned panel on top of him, and pushed with all his might.

Rising from his tightening belly, a stalwart grunt slipped through clenched teeth and translated his muscles' dogged effort, tensing to their limit and beyond to where raw adrenaline cultivated superhuman strength to be used in emergencies such as this one.

The wall began to budge, his optimism rising along with it, rising…rising… enough to see what he feared all along, his camera broken into a dozen pieces just beyond his reach.

Daryl simply stared, eyes welling up, chin quivering. The impact of everything he'd seen thus far (the botched exorcism, Margaret, the bodies, his camera) hit him all at once. As usual, he tried to fight the flow of emotion until the finality of his situation sunk in and brought with it the feeling in his legs.

Daryl cried out in pain first due to his nerves' sudden awakening, then as a result of the wall falling right back onto his legs when he let go to rub the pain away.

Now the looming trees seemed to threaten violence as they leaned in suspiciously close to Daryl, who stared up at them, eyes fluttering. He was in a state of shock so ferocious that it made him appear perfectly calm.

Daryl's legs were going numb again, or maybe his mind was going numb. Either way, he felt nothing below his waist. Everything else was still where it had been.

There was an exact moment, punctuated by an audible SNAP, when restraint stepped aside and allowed the beast within to barrel toward the surface. In fact, Daryl welcomed it. He invited it, even.

Erupting to the surface like a freight train with a nitrous kick, it sent Daryl into a thrashing tantrum, growling with savage glee as he clawed, scratched, and pounded the wall above, and the floor below him. Though it wasn't his intention, the wall on top of him began to rock and slide until it shifted enough for gravity to take hold and tug it to the ground. Without the pressure from it bearing down on his legs, Daryl could feel everything again. It was even worse when the cool breeze hit his swollen shins.

He pounded the back of his head against the floor and screamed. Like a curtain falling from the ceiling, the sliding wall revealed more debris and body parts, and Sister Angelica's corpse, badly burnt and twisted into a painful pose, her flowing black habit melted to her skin in places, and completely burnt away in others. Half of her face and scalp were charred beyond recognition.

He didn't expect to see a naked grey husk of a man with a jutting ribcage and sections of exposed bone all over his body straddling her and sticking his hands into the large, sloppy wound in her gut as if looking for something that she owed him. Slipping and sliding through his skeletal fingers, her sausage-link intestines proved deceptive prey for the grey man's clumsy hands. Gritting his teeth in a snarl born of childlike frustration, exposed roots and blackened gums, decayed, and receded to virtual nonexistence, the grey man thrust his face down at Sister Angelica's. And from the ground, she growled and thrust right back up at him.

Daryl didn't recognize the man from the passengers on the flight. What he did recognize (skeletal fingers; discolored flesh sagging from his lower jaw, neck, and wrists; clouded eyes; rotten teeth) suggested that the grey man had to be dead. The same could be said of Sister Angelica, yet she seemed to be egging him on.

After a few awkward grabs that yielded nothing, the grey man leaned forward, shortening the distance between Sister Angelica's intestines and his mouth. To Daryl's horror, that was where he shoved a section of her small intestine, bit down hard, and whipped his head from side to side to tear it loose.

"By the way, you can't hear a thing, and haven't since before the crash," the voice in Daryl's head reminded him.

Is this some kind of joke? He shot back into the abyss.

Responding with snippets of memory to back up its argument, the voice in Daryl's head made its case.

"Have you noticed the singing birds that dart back and forth above you, settling on flexible branches that bounce to rest under their weight? Did you actually hear the plane's bulk cry out as it settled in the mud, or were you tricked by the vibrations they caused traveling up through your back and into your thoughts where they were translated as deep resonant thumps? What did you hear when pain forced your voice out in reverence to it?

"In short, you heard nothing."

As if to refute the voice in his head, Daryl yelled as loudly as he could. There was only silence, followed by his heartbeat's slow burn.

Thump-Thump, Thump-Thump

Daryl wasn't ready to accept it as truth just yet. It was probably just a temporary thing, or a trick instituted by whatever it was that possessed Sister Angelica.

Thump-Thump, Thump-Thump

Sister Angelica hailed him with an upside-down smile, her head cricked back, top resting on the ground, irises treading the border of her upper eyelid as the grey man devoured the contents of her belly like a savage beast tearing into a downed prey. A look of bewildered lust and confusion shined through his incomplete face, and strings of flesh and sinew marinated in a heavy red sauce dangled from the sides of his mouth.

Maybe she'd been doing it all along; however, Daryl just now noticed that she was saying something directly to him. But her lips were too damaged to read. Still, he gave it his best shot.

"I... hope... you... feel... every... last... bite," was the best he could do.

When he followed her eyes to her left, his front, where the cockpit used to be, it all made sense.

Beyond the tips of his feet (since the feeling below his waist had finally left him for good, they seemed alien to him), human-shaped shadows stumbled with derelict strides in and out of the trees. He counted at least 20.

What started as a jolt of relief at the idea of being rescued quickly changed as the closest shadow lumbered into light: a ballerina, her leotard and tutu riddled with mud stains and stiff with water damage, hissed through teeth brandished like a weapon. Though her face was more complete than that of the grey man, it had the same dead hue. Her eyes glazed over with a pasty white film, looked wantingly at a partially clothed arm that dangled from a nearby branch.

Daryl didn't need to see the rest of them up close to figure out what they were. They all walked with a similar variant of the ballerina's fractured gait.

Maybe it's a trick. Maybe she's fucking with you. He could barely hear his own inner voice over the lingering pause in his heart rate due to the approaching menace. Its dead rhythm added a certain atmosphere, like bass drums beating out a death march: **Thummm-Thump, Thummm-Thump, Thummm-Thump.**

How long before they reached him, he wondered? How long before he felt their teeth ripping at his flesh?

If they start at your feet, you'll bleed to death before you feel a thing.

Ominous as it sounded, his inner voice provided Daryl with a twinge of hope. But it was quickly snatched away along with the sunlight at his right side. He looked up and directly into the half-headed zombie's hungry eyes as it leaned forward (mouth opened wide, black-blood, saliva, and liquefied dirt swinging) and clamped down on Daryl's brow.

In the distant background, a group of hunters, four in all, dressed in camouflaged overalls and orange vests, cowered in as many trees. Beneath each one, a mob of zombies leered up at them, pawing at the air between them and trying to leap on brittle limbs. The lead hunter whipped his head from the base of the tree to his shotgun, which rested in the dirt a few yards away where he dropped it in haste during the climb up, to the wreckage where a naked zombie held Daryl's flailing limbs down and took liberal bites from his face as he choked on his own scream. The hunters had been trying to warn him, as well as call out to the fifth member of their hunting party who they thought they lost. He was, in fact, hiding in a hollowed tree stump a few yards away. Each time their calls were interrupted by the strange, burnt woman who mocked them as she too was being eaten alive.

THE END

ABOUT THE AUTHOR

Andre Duza is a member of the Bizarro movement, writing under the sub-style Brutality Chronic. His first novel, *Dead Bitch Army* was released in 2004. He has written stories for *Undead, Chainsaw Magazine,* and *The Bizarro Starter Kit,* as well as for his chapbook, *Dead Bitch Walking,* and his upcoming collection entitled, *Necro-Sex Machine: The Dead Bitch Chronicles Vol. 1.*

In addition to writing, Andre is an avid bodybuilder and a certified instructor of Spirit Fist Kung Fu. Andre still trains at the Seven Mountains Spirit Fist Kung Fu School in Philadelphia, where he has been a student for over 11 ½ years. Andre's martial arts background also includes boxing, Tae Kwon Do, and Chinese Kempo.

Visit Andre's Website: www.houseofduza.com

ABOUT THE ARTISTS

Keith Murphey graduated from Paier College of Art with a degree in illustration. He has done work for Blue comet press, Net Noise Design group, Hartford Holiday Light Fantasia, and is the founder and President of C.A.G. (Comic Artist's Guild.) He is currently doing graduate study in The Masters in Art Therapy program at Albertus Magnus College. Mr. Murphey lives and teaches at his studio in Moodus, Connecticut.
Website: http://groups.yahoo.com/group/Keithsartgroup

Dennis Kroesen is a web-designer with a passion for drawing cartoons and comic strips. Though heavily influenced by Jeff Jones, Kieron Dwyer, and Mike Mignola, his original inspiration was from Saturday morning cartoons he watched as a kid.
Website: http://www.surrealistiks.com

Damon Oats - This 29 year old from Edgecumbe, New Zealand, has been an artist for 4 years now and holds a diploma in illustration. He works alongside his brother, Kieran, who shares in his interest of machinery as well as the band *Meshuggah*.
Website: http://www.knotlikeyou.com

Neill Brengettsey has done freelance toy design for Hasbro; layouts and character designs for Marvel and DC comics; CD covers, menu jackets for local restaurants, graphics and maps for state offices; character designs for comic book themed websites and book illustrations. Personal Statement: "My current website is the product of intense minutes of labor."
Website: http://www.geocities.com/paime77

Tjie Tsang saw some comics and then he saw some scary movies and then he started drawing a lot of dead things. He graduated from OCAD (ontario college of art and design) in drawing and painting, but you can visit his best teachers at your local comic shops.
Website: http://cadaver.perception.net

Silverfish was born in Houston, Texas on March 10th, 1983. Currently living in Lake Jackson, Texas. Works largely in (sometimes macabre) surrealism, though available for illustration. Also does some clothing design. Materials used are primarily pencil, colored pencil, and ink.
Website: http://www.angelfire.com/scary/silverfish370

Bizarro books

CATALOGUE – SPRING 2006

Bizarro Books publishes under the following imprints:

www.rawdogscreamingpress.com

www.eraserheadpress.com

www.afterbirthbooks.com

www.swallowdownpress.com

For all your Bizarro needs visit:

www.bizarrogenre.org

BB-001 "The Kafka Effekt" D. Harlan Wilson - A collection of forty-four irreal short stories loosely written in the vein of Franz Kafka, with more than a pinch of William S. Burroughs sprinkled on top. **211 pages $14**

BB-002 "Satan Burger" Carlton Mellick III - The cult novel that put Carlton Mellick III on the map ... Six punks get jobs at a fast food restaurant owned by the devil in a city violently overpopulated by surreal alien cultures. **236 pages $14**

BB-003 "Some Things Are Better Left Unplugged" Vincent Sakwoski - Join The Man and his Nemesis, the obese tabby, for a nightmare roller coaster ride into this postmodern fantasy. **152 pages $10**

BB-004 "Shall We Gather At the Garden?" Kevin L Donihe - Donihe's Debut novel. Midgets take over the world, The Church of Lionel Richie vs. The Church of the Byrds, plant porn and more! **244 pages $14**

BB-005 "Razor Wire Pubic Hair" Carlton Mellick III - A genderless humandildo is purchased by a razor dominatrix and brought into her nightmarish world of bizarre sex and mutilation. **176 pages $11**

BB-006 "Stranger on the Loose" D. Harlan Wilson - The fiction of Wilson's 2nd collection is planted in the soil of normalcy, but what grows out of that soil is a dark, witty, otherworldly jungle... **228 pages $14**

BB-007 "The Baby Jesus Butt Plug" Carlton Mellick III - Using clones of the Baby Jesus for anal sex will be the hip sex fetish of the future. **92 pages $10**

BB-008 "Fishyfleshed" Carlton Mellick III - The world of the past is an illogical flatland lacking in dimension and color, a sick-scape of crispy squid people wandering the desert for no apparent reason. **260 pages $14**

BB-009 **"Dead Bitch Army"** Andre Duza - Step into a world filled with racist teenagers, cannibals, 100 warped Uncle Sams, automobiles with razor-sharp teeth, living graffiti, and a pissed-off zombie bitch out for revenge. **344 pages $16**

BB-010 **"The Menstruating Mall"** Carlton Mellick III *"The Breakfast Club* meets *Chopping Mall* as directed by David Lynch." - Brian Keene **212 pages $12**

BB-011 **"Angel Dust Apocalypse"** Jeremy Robert Johnson - Meth-heads, man-made monsters, and murderous Neo-Nazis. "Seriously amazing short stories..." - Chuck Palahniuk, author of *Fight Club* **184 pages $11**

BB-012 **"Ocean of Lard"** Kevin L Donihe / Carlton Mellick III - A parody of those old Choose Your Own Adventure kid's books about some very odd pirates sailing on a sea made of animal fat. **176 pages $12**

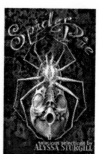

BB-013 **"Last Burn in Hell"** John Edward Lawson - From his lurid angst-affair with a lesbian music diva to his ascendance as unlikely pop icon the one constant for Kenrick Brimley, official state prison gigolo, is he's got no clue what he's doing. **172 pages $14**

BB-014 **"Tangerinephant"** Kevin Dole 2 - TV-obsessed aliens have abducted Michael Tangerinephant in this bizarre combination of science fiction, satire, and surrealism. **164 pages $11**

BB-015 **"Foop!"** Chris Genoa - Strange happenings are going on at Dactyl, Inc, the world's first and only time travel tourism company.
"A surreal pie in the face!" - Christopher Moore **300 pages $14**

BB-016 **"Spider Pie"** Alyssa Sturgill - A one-way trip down a rabbit hole inhabited by sexual deviants and friendly monsters, fairytale beginnings and hideous endings. **104 pages $11**

BB-017 "The Unauthorized Woman" Efrem Emerson - Enter the world of the inner freak, a landscape populated by the pre-dead and morticioners, by cockroaches and 300-lb robots. **104 pages $11**

BB-018 "Fugue XXIX" Forrest Aguirre - Tales from the fringe of speculative literary fiction where innovative minds dream up the future's uncharted territories while mining forgotten treasures of the past. **220 pages $16**

BB-019 "Pocket Full of Loose Razorblades" John Edward Lawson - A collection of dark bizarro stories. From a giant rectum to a foot-fungus factory to a girl with a biforked tongue. **190 pages $13**

BB-020 "Punk Land" Carlton Mellick III - In the punk version of Heaven, the anarchist utopia is threatened by corporate fascism and only Goblin, Mortician's sperm, and a blue-mohawked female assassin named Shark Girl can stop them. **284 pages $15**

BB-021 "Pseudo-City" D. Harlan Wilson - Pseudo-City exposes what waits in the bathroom stall, under the manhole cover and in the corporate boardroom, all in a way that can only be described as mind-bogglingly irreal. **220 pages $16**

BB-022 "Kafka's Uncle and Other Strange Tales" Bruce Taylor - Anslenot and his giant tarantula (tormentor? fri-end?) wander a desecrated world in this novel and collection of stories from Mr. Magic Realism Himself. **348 pages $17**

BB-023 "Sex and Death In Television Town" Carlton Mellick III - In the old west, a gang of hermaphrodite gunslingers take refuge from a demon plague in Telos: a town where its citizens have televisions instead of heads. **184 pages $12**

BB-024 "It Came From Below The Belt" Bradley Sands - What can Grover Goldstein do when his severed, sentient penis forces him to return to high school and help it win the presidential election? **204 pages $13**

BB-025 "Sick: An Anthology of Illness" John Lawson, editor - These Sick stories are horrendous and hilarious dissections of creative minds on the scalpel's edge. **296 pages $16**

BB-026 "Tempting Disaster" John Lawson, editor - A shocking and alluring anthology from the fringe that examines our culture's obsession with taboos. **260 pages $16**

BB-027 "Siren Promised" Jeremy Robert Johnson - Nominated for the Bram Stoker Award. A potent mix of bad drugs, bad dreams, brutal bad guys, and surreal/incredible art by Alan M. Clark. **190 pages $13**

BB-028 "Chemical Gardens" Gina Ranalli - Ro and punk band *Green is the Enemy* find Kreepkins, a surfer-dude warlock, a vengeful demon, and a Metal Priestess in their way as they try to escape an underground nightmare. **188 pages $13**

BB-029 "Jesus Freaks" Andre Duza For God so loved the world that he gave his only two begotten sons... and a few million zombies. **400 pages $16**

BB-030 "Grape City" Kevin L. Donihe - More Donihe-style comedic bizarro about a demon named Charles who is forced to work a minimum wage job on Earth after Hell goes out of business. **108 pages $10**

BB-031"Sea of the Patchwork Cats" Carlton Mellick III - A quiet dreamlike tale set in the ashes of the human race. For Mellick enthusiasts who also adore *The Twilight Zone*. **112 pages $10**

BB-032 "Extinction Journals" Jeremy Robert Johnson 104 pages - An uncanny voyage across a newly nuclear America where one man must confront the problems associated with loneliness, insane dieties, radiation, love, and an ever-evolving cockroach suit with a mind of its own. **104 pages $10**